About the

ROSEMARY FRIEDMAN's novels and short stories have been widely translated and broadcast. She has written commissioned screenplays and television series for the UK and the USA. A stage play awaits production. She reviews fiction and has judged many literary prizes and awards. She is currently working on a new novel and a TV drama. She lives in London.

GOLDEN BOY

Rosemary Friedman

POCKET
BOOKS

LONDON · SYDNEY · NEW YORK · TOKYO · SINGAPORE · TORONTO

First published in Great Britain by Simon & Schuster Ltd, 1994
A Paramount Communications Company

Simon & Schuster Ltd
West Garden Place
Kendal Street
London W2 2AQ

Simon & Schuster of Australia Pty Ltd
Sydney

A CIP catalogue record for this book is available from the British
Library

ISBN 0-671-85309-0

Typeset in Sabon 11/13pt by
Hewer Text Composition Services, Edinburgh
Printed in Great Britain by HarperCollins *Manufacturing*, Glasgow

For Jacqueline

'And this is the Bank of England! and do you sit here all day, and never see the green woods and the trees and the charming country? Are you contented with such a life?'

Leigh Hunt

'In opera you must make people weep, be terrified and die through singing.'

Vincenzo Bellini

Thanks are due to:

Paul Brown, Derek Cowan, Alex de Fé, Dennis Friedman, Frank Hyer, Margaret Manley, Brian Spiro, Stephanie Statton, Roy Shuttleworth, Alasdair Simpson, William Toff and Isla Yardley.

CHAPTER ONE

Certain moments. Hiroshima. The assassination of President Kennedy. The first fuzzy footfall of the first man on the moon. The photoflash of recollection. By its brief light we remember what we were doing, at the time, in the hours before. Putting the kettle on. Making love. Precedent memories quantify significant events. Cataclysm is blunted by quotidian trivia. I was listening to the Goldberg Variations/following the safety instructions/spraying the roses/walking down Whitehall . . . The icons that surround the event eclipse the event itself.

Which was why Freddie Lomax would always recall his fortieth birthday and the circumstances which preceded it. They were perpetuated on the internal cassette of things past. He played it on the VCR of his memory, fast-forwarding and rewinding it. It was accompanied by digital sound.

Days such as these begin like any other. Nothing untoward. Freddie's did. Jogging round the Outer Circle. His morning routine was important. Not only for the exercise but the structuring of his day. It was not possible to plan *and* work simultaneously. Strategy must be separated from execution. To save time, minimise effort, it must be dealt with in advance.

Circumventing the park each morning gave him the oppor-

tunity to define targets and establish deadlines. Freed him
for immediate action once he got to work. *Thump-thump.*
Thump-thump. Worry beads in one hand, telephone in the
other. A well-built man. Six foot three. Riviera tan. Soon
to be topped up at Porto Ercole. Last year it was Sardinia.
He didn't believe in owning second homes; or boats. The
economics were wrong. Freddie had his head screwed on.

Friends had villas, James and Dos – wife number two.
Wife number one, who had stuck with James when he was
struggling to build up his construction business, had been
put out to grass with what she could squeeze out of him.
'Dos'. James had had the epithet perpetuated in 18-carat
gold. Dos wore it round her neck, skinny-dipping, with her
silicone breasts, in the kidney-shaped pool. You punched a
keypad outside the iron gates to enter. The code changed
every day. A butler served bullshots. Dos was renowned
for them. By their bullshots shall ye know them. Lunch
at the villa went on all afternoon. Sometimes they ate
at the African Queen. The whole shooting match. At a
long outdoor table, over deep bowls of *moules marinières*,
overlooking the harbour. No matter where he sat amongst
the noisy gathering, Freddie Lomax was its epicentre.
Conversation was aimed in his direction, faces drawn
into the magnetic field of his charm. He turned heads.
Drawing the eyes of passing girls as bronzed as himself.
Freddie gambled with skin cancer as he did at the tables.
Never risking much. Getting out when he was ahead. He
was at his peak. Dressed to complement his physique. Had
his suits made, dark blue or grey, by Douggie Hayward in
Mount Street. Didn't begrudge the arm and the leg. The
suits were his calling card. Gave his clients confidence.
Hermès tie. Silk handkerchief. A right nerd, Rosina said.
Secretly she was proud of him.

He dropped her off at school on occasion, Queen's
College in Harley Street, before going on to the bank.

Rosina wore a bundle of rags, in decorative leather or denim. From Camden market. Freddie footed the bills for them. At fifteen, the chrysalis of puppy fat falling away, Rosina was turning into Jane as she had been when he'd first met her. Sometimes, catching sight of his daughter, Jane's freckles, her bright red hair, it startled him. Rosina was into heavy metal. Read *Rock Power*, and *Kerrang!*, when she should have been doing her homework, moshed to the thrashes of Impetigo and Recipients of Death 'singing against oppression', and had to be forcibly restrained from tattooing her arms and joining the slam pit (everyone else's parents let them) at the Hammersmith Odeon on Saturday nights.

Thump-thump. Elbows in. Freddie's shirts came from Turnbull and Asser. White only. He had his shoes made at Lobb's. The size of a man's feet was said to be directly related to that of his penis. Freddie had large feet. Charlie, at Michaeljohn, styled his fair hair — now sometimes assisted by a vegetable rinse. He had had golden curls as a baby. His mother never tired of telling him. Passers-by had stopped to admire her son as she pushed him in his pram. He watched his weight. Mineral water at lunch. No pudding. He kept in trim. Weight training at a gym in the City. Golf at weekends. Tennis in the park. Squash twice a week with James. At the Bath and Racquets. Followed by a swim. At Cambridge he had been on the water-polo team. He had shoulders like a navvy. *Thump-thump*. His vest stuck to his back. Water trickled down the inside of his thighs. *Thump-thump*. In his Nike Air. Releasing the endorphins. Every thump a pain.

Regent's Park had once been pasture land, Marylebone Park Fields: the gravel pit field, the pound field for stray cattle, sheep and horses, the bell field, the butcher's field, the field where copal varnish was manufactured. It had been used by royalty for game hunting. Ulster

Terrace: Ionic columns. York Terrace, spanning York Gate. Mr Nash in Graeco-Italian mode. Sixty-one houses designed to give the appearance of a single building. North to Cornwall Terrace. Decimus Burton, into Corinthian. Burton had wanted to elide the two terraces, Cornwall and Clarence, which had the finest views of the lake, leaving no access to the park from Upper Baker Street.

Mrs Siddons, whose house was at the top of the street, had complained to the Prince Regent about the proposed obstruction to her view. The result of the actress's petition was Clarence Gate, an entrance to the park which, as the morning progressed, would throttle itself with commuter traffic, extracted from the dreaming suburbs and heading for the West End. The half-moon of Sussex Place (Nash again) now home to the London Business School.

The Royal College of Obstetricians and Gynaecologists. Hanover Terrace. A grey squirrel darted impudently across his path. Hanover Gate. Hanover Lodge. The golden dome of the Mosque behind its picket fence, mobbed by the faithful on Fridays when it was flanked by the psychedelic stalls of Arab street vendors. *Thump-thump-thump. Thump-thump-thump. Thump-thump-thump.* A posse of bull-headed runners from the army barracks in Albany Street. Ionic Villa, Veneto Villa — a Petit Trianon in Regent's Park — receiving the finishing touches to their grotesque exteriors. Nine million pounds apiece. The rape of the park by the Crown. The iron bridge over the canal, escape route from St John's Wood, once itself steeped in history and rife with illicit love nests, home now to *arrivistes* with disabled badges, double-parked in the High Street, waging an ongoing battle with the traffic wardens.

The shuttered entrance to the Zoo. *Entrée/Eingang*. Its appalling penguin pool, brutalistic elephant house and archaic buildings recently threatened with closure, now besieged by rescue plans for walk-through aquaria and rainforest terraces, and the subject of fierce controversy. Freddie had refused to sign the petition on behalf of the families who trailed recalcitrant children clutching Zeppelin balloons round the lions and the tigers. He could not accept that it was right to immure wild animals in minimalist cages, and was reluctant to put his name to the creation of what amounted to a theme park on his own doorstep.

The Zoological Society, beneath its clock and weather vane. Gloucester Gate. Any second now the milkman should be approaching, his electric float rattling with bottles of semi-skimmed milk and cartons of orange juice for the sleeping doorsteps. He was. Everything satisfactorily to time. The roundsman did not glance in his direction. He had once tried to cheat Freddie. Unaware that Freddie could multiply the number of days by the number of pints with the speed and precision of a microchip. Now the account from the dairy accounted for no more, and no less, than had been delivered.

Gloucester Terrace. Freddie wiped the sweat from his neck, savouring the punishment he inflicted on his body, as he headed into the straight with a sideways glance at the Danish Church in St Katharine's Precinct with its echoes of Cambridge and weddings on Saturdays.

He and Jane had been married for seventeen years. They had stayed together while their contemporaries, in the throes of complex divorces or embittered battles over children or messes of contested pottage, played a marital version of musical chairs to the phrenetic music of the times. That the stability of their marriage was largely due to Jane, Freddie had little doubt. They had met in Cambridge. James, who changed his girlfriends as frequently as his socks, had brought her to the pub. Jane, on holiday from the Union Centrale des Arts Décoratifs in Paris, was his latest acquisition. They were sitting at a corner table over glasses of lager. Jane was wearing a magenta dress, a panama hat encircled with yellow ribbons pulled down over her freckles. She held a miniature wire-haired terrier on her lap and was absent-mindedly stroking its balls. The moment he saw her, Freddie made up his mind to marry her. He had no qualms about seducing her from James.

James's arm was round Jane's shoulders in a proprietorial way. Freddie brought his beer over and sat down beside them. Jane did not change her position on the window seat, did not remove James's hand from her waist where it had wandered, yet imperceptibly she distanced herself from him and moved towards Freddie as unequivocally as if she were crossing the street. They spent the night in his room. Tristan was three weeks old, and Jane and Freddie had been married for six months, before James, accepting the peace offering of being godfather to their son, forgave him.

Cumberland Terrace, its blue pediment topped with genteel ceramic figures representing the arts and sciences, was the grandest of all the terraces. As he thumped his way past its decorative arches, Freddie admitted thoughts of home and anticipated the hot needles of the shower with which he would soon reward himself.

Since his mother had taken him, first to feed the ducks, and later to play in Regent's Park as a small boy, he had been mesmerised by the blank stares of the stately façades of the terraces. It was where he would live when he grew up. As he kicked his ball in the long grass and picked daisies for her first bouquet, he had enquired if the buildings were palaces and if the Queen lived there. You have to be very rich, his mother had said, taking him later to Buckingham Palace where he had counted the windows. So he had decided to be rich; and to marry his mother who was making a chain out of the yellow-centred daisies. And make her his queen. When his father, a much-loved physician, had died from a subarachnoid haemorrhage while he was playing cricket with the 6-year-old Freddie in the garden, Freddie was convinced that he had killed him. He kept a photograph of his father beneath his pillow while he slept, and wrote letters to heaven begging him to come back. He tried hard to remember him, but had few recollections at his disposal, and after a while there was only an aching void.

Freddie's childhood had been filled with music. Its manifestation in Freddie was his passion for opera. His mother had been a professional pianist. His father, who played the violin, had belonged to an amateur string quartet, although Freddie could not remember it. He did not play an instrument. His mother, with little time to spare, had not been able to interest him in one. Her only son, born at the very end of her reproductive life, was destined to be a man who glittered as he walked. Brought up, single-handed, to be a credit to her, Freddie had conformed to her spurious vision of himself. Widely tipped to be the next chairman of his bank, he had not let her down.

Chester Terrace, with its colonnades and columns rivalling the Tuileries, was Burton's final undertaking in the park. Turning into it Freddie experienced a *frisson* of delight, the daily suspension of disbelief that this *rus in urbe* was where he lived. He had worked hard for his success. Driven by his aspirations and performing best under pressure, possessed of reserves of energy normally associated with hyperactive children and resolved at all times to excel, his work was his life. He was never happier than when he was immersed in it. A scholarship to Trinity, where he had read economics, had followed his graduation *summa cum laude* from grammar school, after which, impatiently dismissing the year off taken by many of his contemporaries, he had gone straight into commerce to master banking from the grass roots. As he gradually distanced himself physically from his mother, who was reluctant to let him go, he changed from being a happy schoolboy, to an outgoing student and now, with his extraordinary zest for life, was a popular and gregarious man, who made a point of keeping his many friendships in constant repair. Tough, but not insensitive, Freddie's name in the City was synonymous with contentious takeover bids. He was an acknowledged trailblazer, an awesome adversary, a skilled negotiator who never missed an opportunity to make serious money for his clients or to further the interests of the bank. He had been brought up to believe that good manners and self-discipline were the key to personal happiness, and he looked for the same high standards from others that he demanded from himself. A reprimand from Freddie had been known to leave the entrails of his subordinates hanging from the ceiling.

Freddie's goal, to have his own bank before he reached the age of 50, represented his deep-seated need to be in control. He coped with failure badly, was not good at forgiving himself and was incapable of forgiving others. He was hardest on those close to him, and the one closest to him was himself.

After their marriage, he and Jane had set up home in a rented, one-bedroomed flat in Earls Court where they waited for Tristan to be born. When Rosina was on the way, he had put down the first payment on a terraced house in Shepherd's Bush and his move to a more senior position in a second bank, led to a Norman Shaw semi-detached in Bedford Park. A larger Norman Shaw, this time detached, coincided with his joining Sitwell Hunt International as head of the corporate finance division. His swift promotion to vice chairman was the catalyst for their final move, to the house in Chester Terrace. Freddie had bought it in the days of the property boom upon which it had seemed that the sun would never set. By mortgaging himself to the hilt, he had realised the first of his boyhood dreams.

Outside his house, its stucco exterior painted every fourth year at the behest of the Crown, George, the postman, lopsided with the weight of his sack, was sorting letters. Running on the spot, to reduce his blood pressure slowly, Freddie waited impatiently for his mail.

'Everything okay?'

George had recently undergone coronary bypass surgery. Walking was the exercise of choice. He would always be grateful to Freddie, who never failed to stop for a morning chat, for insisting that he have a checkup for the pains in his chest which he had put down to indigestion.

'Mustn't grumble . . .' George handed Freddie a bundle secured with an elastic band. 'Not with nearly three million out of work.' He swung his bag over his shoulder. 'As long as the old ticker holds up. If I go under, the chances of getting another job . . . I'd never get past question two on the form. Question one's your name. Question two's your date of birth. If you're over forty they don't want to know. It's the kids I worry about. The kids, the mortgage, the insurance, the gas, the electric, the poll tax, the water, the TV licence . . . Everything going up every week. My wife goes shopping with a calculator. Trouble is there's no light at the end of the tunnel. To tell you the truth, Mr Lomax, and you know more about it in your line than me, I think they've bricked the ruddy tunnel up.'

Opening his front door, Freddie stopped in the narrow hall with its parquet floor and giltwood mirror, and checked his pulse rate. Picking up the newspapers from the mat, he took the mahogany balustraded stairs two at a time.

In the bedroom, Jane was still asleep. She lay on her back with the sheets round her waist. She was wearing a white T-shirt with the words 'Happy Birthday' emblazoned in scarlet across her breasts. Smiling to himself, Freddie put the mail down on the bed. As he bent to kiss her, she twined unconscious arms tightly round his neck for a moment then promptly turned over and went back to sleep. Glancing briefly at the bedside clock, he crept into his dressing-room and closed the door gently behind him.

CHAPTER TWO

While his vice chairman and head of corporate finance prepared to meet the day, Gordon Sitwell, chairman of Sitwell Hunt International – a bank founded by his grandfather to finance trade in the British Empire, America, China, and Japan – who had been knighted by Margaret Thatcher before her fall, for services to business achievement (also known as substantial donations to the party), was breakfasting in the kitchen of his mansion in Priory Drive, Stanmore, with his wife, Margaret.

'Don't forget we're going to Freddie and Jane's tonight.' Margaret, whose candlewick dressing-gown was drawn tightly over the cushion of her bosom, addressed the expanse of *Financial Times* behind which her husband might be thought to be hiding. The fact that there was no reply, that he had completely forgotten that it was Freddie's birthday and that they were expected at Chester Terrace for dinner, did not faze her.

'I'll look for something on my way to the hairdresser's. Men are always so difficult. Particularly men like Freddie . . .' Margaret pushed the marmalade jar across the wooden table into the outstretched hand which appeared from behind the newspaper. '. . . Men who have everything.' Margaret held her bone china teacup in both hands. 'A book – but then I don't know what Freddie reads – a tie perhaps, a photograph frame for the office . . .'

Gordon turned the page abruptly.

'. . . Bittermints. He probably doesn't touch chocolate. How about a bottle of something? More coffee?'

The top of Gordon's grey head, which was all she could see of her husband, moved from side to side.

'I'll have a look in that shop at the bottom of the hill – the one that used to be the fishmonger's. They sell all that in the supermarket now. Cadeaux. They've got leather things and cake plates and silver pillboxes in the window. I don't suppose a silver pillbox . . .?'

Margaret was talking to herself. It was not unusual. The *Financial Times* lay folded against the marmalade jar, Gordon's chair was empty, and he was already in his rose garden.

Growing roses was Gordon's hobby. It encompassed the world of propagating and exhibiting as well as paying regular visits to the great rose gardens of the world. The diversion occupied most of his leisure moments, enabled him to forget his disappointment in his marriage, and provided a suitable antidote to the stresses of the City. His roses, on view annually to the public in aid of the National Gardens Scheme, were at the moment faring a great deal better than his bank.

As he selected a rose for the buttonhole of his pinstriped suit, a daily decision not taken lightly, he contemplated the dismal state of the British economy. After the euphoria of the eighties with its global markets, indiscriminate asset stripping, and sky-high share indexes, which had been followed by the seismic flutters of Black Thursday and the catastrophic nose-dive of Black Monday (when £100 billion was wiped from shares and thousands of job losses were triggered in the City), the spacecraft, which had been launched so optimistically, to break through the sound barrier with the Big Bang, had finally crashed to earth.

With the collapse of the markets, the entire financial sector had suffered one of its biggest setbacks on record and was now undergoing the sharpest decline of the century. In the light of the gloomy forecasts and massive lay-offs, the party was well and truly over. There were few indications that the situation was going to improve.

In the past three months alone there had been almost 16,000 personal bankruptcies. Liquidations and receiverships were escalating, car sales were disastrous, house prices had dropped, consumer confidence had fallen, and people feared for their livelihoods. There was no area which had not been hit. The building trade had empty order books and showed the worst figures for a decade; Rolls Royce aero-engine had closed two plants, imposed a six-month pay freeze – with the warning of more cuts to come – and drastically reduced its workforce, and thousands of civil engineeering workers, highly qualified staff among them, had been paid off.

It was not only industry which was affected. There had been wholesale redundancies in publishing, insurance, advertising, television, and hospital services. Professionals, no longer able to honour their agreements with the mortgage companies, were in serious difficulties, and qualified lawyers, particularly those specialising in commercial property in London where thousands of square feet of office accommodation lay empty, were finding themselves out on the street.

Solicitors were not the only ones soliciting. Gordon excused himself the pun. Not since the time of Dickens, or the days after the First World War when amputees and gas victims rattled collecting boxes on every street corner, had London seen so many beggars. White-faced girls with shaven heads and youths with tattered trousers, had joined the winos and the bag ladies in the shadows of underground stations and shopping malls. They squatted in the doorways and declared themselves hungry. Gordon did not believe them. Many of the scavengers had been revealed to be con artists, with perfectly decent homes to go to, who belonged to begging rings and waged terror campaigns on the legitimate homeless. Be that as it may, the mendicants were a symptom of an economic climate which was as dismal as any that Gordon, at the age of 63, could remember. Although profits would be meagre and the appetite for debt, both amongst companies and personal customers, severely limited, he hoped that Sitwell Hunt International, backed as it was by so many years of family tradition and – if push came to shove – by the Bank of England, would be able to ride out the storm.

In his garden, laid out forty years ago when he had brought Margaret to Tall Trees as a young bride, Gordon Sitwell could forget the bank. Margaret, who came from Cornwall, had wanted a country garden, hollyhocks, sunflowers, fox-gloves and delphiniums, such as she had been brought up with, but Gordon was unable to tolerate such rampant chaos and had settled upon a garden devoted to roses, for which he bought the best possible stock from the most reputable growers.

There was a great deal more to roses than simply digging a hole and planting a bush. Before he even lifted a spade, Gordon evaluated his site, made blueprints of his layout and set about making the necessary improvements to the soil. Now, a formal bed, flanked by an emerald frame of grass paths, traversed the centre of the garden. His instinct had been to fill the rectangle with a single shade, a single variety of rose, but common sense had prevailed. Taking into consideration the unkempt appearance which a patchwork of different colours would create, Gordon had staggered his planting, interspersing the bushes of red Hybrid Teas with clumps of white, yellow, and pink. For added interest, and bearing in mind the fact that a bed, unlike a border, had to be viewed from all angles, he had placed a column of standard Chrysler Imperials (the full fragrant flowers of which bloomed from June to November), at intervals down the centre. He did not allow underplanting. When Margaret had tentatively suggested that they might put in a few violas, some clumps of primulas, a little ageratum or lobelia beneath the Cologne Carnivals and the Summer Sunshine, or that he consider Super Star, or Sterling Silver, as suitable for indoor decoration, he had told her that if she wanted flowers for the house he would give her money to buy them, and that the next thing that she would be asking for was gnomes.

Selecting his roses, and increasing his stock, represented only a fraction of Gordon's extra curricular activities. He protected his plants from disease and, keeping an eye out for blackspot, blind shoots, scorching, and reversion, tended them when they were sick. In the mornings, the dew soaking his slippers, he dusted the leaves against pests, and in the evenings he sprayed them. He hoed and mulched, tied and watered, dead-headed and disbudded. He waged war against the froghopper, the sawfly, and the aphids, and drew up his battle lines at the first sign of mildew, canker or rust.

Pruning was his forte. Taking care not to do it so early as to risk injury from frost, nor leave it so late that the sap had begun to flow, he carried it out at the first sign of new growth. He was a ruthless pruner, attributing the success of his roses to the efficiency with which he annually cut them back.

Now, as he contemplated a perfect bloom for his button-hole, one which would reflect his mood and set the tenor of his day, he was aware of Margaret walking towards him across the York stone terrace, between the pergolas of Golden Shower and Albertine. She was wearing a print frock, the garishly coloured flowers of which went ill with the deep, rich crimson of Madame Louise Laperrière and the orange-yellow of Beauté, and overpowered the creams and ivories of Virgo and Pascali. He disliked the frock almost as much as he disliked her candlewick dressing-gown.

Marrying Margaret, forty years ago, had been a mistake. With roses you got exactly what you paid for, bushes of good breed, purchased from a reputable grower being a guarantee of success. Margaret, a young rose from Truro, deliciously perfumed, deep-bosomed, falsely promising to flower over a long period, seemed perfect for bedding. He had been beguiled by the short-lived radiance of her bloom.

It had been a lacklustre marriage. Once the novelty of Margaret's suffused white breasts, minuscule waist, and thighs hardened by riding on the Cornish sands, which he thought would squeeze the life out of him, had palled, the children began to arrive, and she had turned her limited intellect to the romances of Mills & Boon, Gordon had found little to engage him in the girl he had married. She had been a good wife, he could not deny Margaret that. But their only meeting points, now that the children were grown up, were discussions about the grandchildren, their holiday plans, or what they were to have for dinner.

As far as sex was concerned, sleeping with Margaret was like making love to an aquiescent mound of well-risen dough, and was equally exciting. He gave her her 'jollies', which, aroused by her reading matter and lost in her own fantasies, she still expected, but for his own gratification he cruised the pavements of the London streets at night, appraising, but not handling the goods. Once, as he kerb crawled, he had found himself staring into the face of a smooth-chinned police officer through the window. Ordered out of the car, he had stood abjectly amongst the flaccid condoms and used syringes that littered the wastelands of King's Cross, while he was questioned. He had been let off with a caution, but aware of the scandal which his arrest would have precipitated in the banking world, he had restrained his nocturnal activities for some time.

'What do you think, Gordon . . .' Margaret said, holding out the shiny pleats of her skirt before him.

Gordon noticed that she had applied lipstick in much the same shade of scarlet as the poppies on her dress, and that it had leaked into small unattractive tributaries around her mouth.

'. . . for Freddie's party?'

An invitation to Chester Terrace was a high spot in Margaret's life. Although she and Gordon rattled in Tall Trees now that the children were gone, and had sufficient china and glass to feed a regiment, few people came to dinner. When they did, although Margaret was a good cook, it could in no way be compared with an evening at the Lomaxes'. No matter how hard Margaret tried, she could not turn her house into a palace and herself into a queen, not even for a night. She could not move through a room delighting the women and riveting the men, convincing each one in turn that he was the guest of honour. She could not sparkle and dazzle, giving the impression that everything that came out of her mouth was either stupendously important or devastatingly witty. She could not flirt and seduce, fascinate and entrance, captivate and charm. She was neither attractive nor animated, neither elegant nor graceful. Her eyes were not green and her hair was not red. Her skirts were not short and her legs were not long. She was not Jane Lomax.

Gordon, walking ahead of her with his pruning knife, was contemplating the orange-veined Bettina and the gilded Gail Borden for his buttonhole, with a gravitas equal to that he gave to the affairs of the bank. He would not cut a rose for Margaret and she knew better than to ask for one. Margaret did get roses. The first rose of summer, the last rose, remembrance of things past, left wordlessly by Gordon, in a tumbler on the mantelshelf at Christmas time.

She had been lucky really in her marriage to Gordon. Once they had set sail on the high seas of their life together, their ship driven by the wind of Gordon's conditioned responses, she did not have to exert herself. Once, a very long time ago, she could not now remember what it had all been about, Gordon had threatened to leave her. Had started packing his suitcase although he hadn't the first idea what to put in it. Margaret had threatened to kill herself. Notwithstanding the fact that each of them knew that the other was bluffing, they had played the game through to its predictable end. It left them, via tears on her part, and recriminations on his, back on home ground, where the daily confrontations had long ago been worked out and a lazy switch to automatic pilot was the only effort required.

Sometimes, usually inspired by a film she had watched on television, or an article she had read in the newspapers, or in her young days with the spirit of rebellion engendered by her hormones, Margaret would temporarily abandon the subordinate position she had willingly adopted and make waves. Deliberately defying Gordon, usually over some comparatively trivial issue, she would bring his wrath down on her head and a little excitement into her own bleak existence. It was not a tactic she adopted too often. It was not worth the candle. She did not expect a great deal of life and anything that was lacking was compensated for vicariously by Messrs Mills & Boon.

Gordon had decided upon the green-tinged white of Message as being an appropriate rose for the day. Standing before it, an executioner with his knife, he stopped and stared, for a long moment, at Margaret. He rarely entered into dialogue with her and *never* discussed the affairs of the bank.

Misreading his look, she let the skirt with its poppies fall. 'I suppose I could always wear my black.'

As she turned back to the house, Gordon advanced towards Message. Raising his knife, and adroitly choosing his spot, just above an outward-facing bud to avoid weakening the bush, he severed her head.

CHAPTER THREE

Lilli Lomax sat by the window of her flat in the Water Gardens, off the Edgware Road, with the mohair rug Freddie had bought her round her knees, while Mrs Williams – she insisted for some reason on being called *Mrs* Williams although sometimes Lilli could not remember her name at all – cleared away the breakfast dishes. Although Lilli appeared to be concentrating on what was going on in the street below, her vacant eyes were watching her latest carer's every move and paying particular attention to the fruit bowl which stood on a crocheted mat in the centre of the table. You could not trust these women. Certainly not as far as the fruit bowl was concerned. The last one had gone through several pounds of apples in a week. The previous one had eaten her out of house and home. It was not as if she kept them short of anything. She gave them money for the shopping – there were only the two of them except once a week when Freddie came for dinner – and insisted upon checking the receipts. They always seemed to have propensities, however, some of them quite bizarre and all of them extravagant. There was the girl from Australia who drank nothing but Diet Coke and stashed the cans beneath her bed, and the widow from Aberdeen who was allergic to yeast and refused to touch bread but filled up on cake. There was the helper who helped herself to Lilli's favourite biscuits, the divorcée who purported never to be hungry but who raided the refrigerator the moment she thought that Lilli was asleep, and the avowed teetotaller who nipped silently away at the gin. Some of them smoked – although they swore that they did not, Lilli could smell it a mile away – none of them knew how to clean a room properly, and all of them made free with her telephone. The one thing they all seemed to have in common was that they did not stay very long. Lilli had not the slightest idea why.

'It's my son's birthday today . . .' Lilli said.

'Is it now?' Mrs Williams, who had only taken up her duties the previous day, did not seem to be all that interested in Freddie's birthday.

'He's 40 years old.'

'My poor husband – may he rest in peace – always used to say that life was a two-week holiday. Forty was the start of the second week . . .'

Lilli was not listening. She was back in the maternity ward of the Elizabeth Garrett Anderson Hospital. Back forty years in time. She was still a student at the Royal College of Music when she had met Hugh, a junior hospital doctor. They had been married for six years when Adolf Hitler marched on Poland. During the nightly air raids on London, while Hugh was away in North Africa with the Royal Army Medical Corps, 'Lilliane Lomax' played the piano at the Queen's Hall, keeping the audiences entertained until the all clear. Later she joined ENSA and gave concerts with the orchestra at air bases where overhead, at the rate of one every two minutes, the bombers took off for Berlin.

When the war was over, and Hugh was repatriated, they had used his demob money to buy a villa near the canal in Maida Vale, and took in medical students to help with the bills. There was plenty of room in the house for nurseries, and a narrow garden suitable for the toddlers who did not materialise.

It was only after eighteen years of raised expectations and dashed hopes, that Lilli had succeeded, when it was almost too late, in becoming pregnant. No one could imagine the anguish she had gone through. She had been one of four children. Hugh was the eldest of six. It was an unspoken agreement between them that they would have a large family and Lilli had refused to accept the fact that she would never know morning sickness or hold a child to her breast. Her determination to have a baby had overshadowed her life.

In her heart of hearts she thought that her failure to conceive was a penalty for wrongdoing, some kind of divine retribution for she knew not what. She had no idea why she was being punished. Hugh tried to act nonchalantly, as if it did not matter to him one way or the other, as if he did not care. But she knew that he was waiting, every bit as anxiously as she was, for her to bear them a son.

She had been engaged to play in a Vaughan Williams concert, when a bout of vomiting, which she put down to something she had eaten, prevented her from accompanying the orchestra to Bath. The incredible discovery that at the age of 44 she was pregnant for the first time, put paid for the time being to her professional commitments. Eight months later, on the hottest day of the year, she went into labour.

There had been no question in those days of giving birth under water, or in the upright position supported by her partner. Hugh had not been present at her confinement. It seemed only yesterday. There was no detail that she could not remember. The obstetrician and the anaesthetist, sweating, in their shirtsleeves, discussing the test match as they waited for her cervix to dilate. Herself, an animal, writhing in distress. During all her years of trying to conceive, Lilli had not considered, not for one moment, what it would be like to give birth. It was just as well. She had been in labour for what seemed a lifetime. Hugh had brought her into the hospital in the small hours. Leaving her in competent hands, he had embraced her tenderly and enquired about the frequency and severity of the pains. She assured him that they were not too bad. She was not going to make a fuss. She had waited too long for that. As the night gave way to morning and the contractions became more frequent, the pains more severe, her resolution weakened. By lunchtime she was tired. At two o'clock in the afternoon, as she clung to the nurse's hand and swore that she was unable to go on any longer, they wheeled in the gas and air. She put the mask over her face and breathed as she was instructed, but it was little help. At three o'clock she was screaming uncontrollably. At 3.30 she knew for certain that she was going to die. They reassured her that everything was normal. Normal! And that she was doing very well. And that it would not be long. A wild thing, she wailed and thrashed, prayed, and begged for mercy. She wondered did she really want a child. Do something. Please do something. But they did nothing. Her body was being ripped apart whilst her attendants discussed the teatime scores. By five o'clock there was no break in her moaning. She had ceased to exist, consumed on some unimaginable rack. She cried, cajoled, pleaded, to be put out of her misery, out of her suffering which was beyond all human endurance. Suddenly it was quiet. Faces loomed at the foot of her bed. The test match was forgotten. There were other voices. Foetal heart. And something about distress. A trolley crashed into the room.

'We're taking you to theatre, Mrs Lomax. We have to remove the child.'

Remove.

Something was wrong. There had been no pain for some time.

The room and the faces revolved. She was on the trolley.

'No! No!'

The ghost train, carrying a white mound on a stretcher, rattled along the corridor.

'Stop!' The woman on the stretcher shrieked. The convoy did not lose speed.

'It's coming.'

Still they rattled. Approaching double doors.

'The baby's *coming*!'

The woman pushed, strained, scarlet in the face, devoid of modesty. Between her legs a baby's head threatened to cleave her in two. The walls rang with the woman's exhortations. The procession halted. The masked men gathered around. The baby's head was pushed back inside her. She's right. I want you to breathe now, Mrs Lomax. Pant. Like a dog. And push! Push! NOW!

Lilli expelled her son. *Her* son. He came, with a titanic slither, into the world. She heard his cries.

She called him Frederick after Chopin. Had it been a girl she would have been Frederica. She had had no idea of the extent to which the arrival of her child, this imprint of herself upon the sands of time, would alter her perceptions, change her view of the world.

Half sleeping, half waking, she waited for Hugh. A smile transformed her face. A sensation no man could ever know, engulfed her in peace and perfect love.

Lilli picked up the photograph of the smiling, middle-aged Freddie, golden hairs on a golden chest, legs manfully apart, taken last Christmas on the beach in Barbados, from the table beside her chair. She held it out to Mrs Thingamajig.

'This is my son.'

'I've met Mr Lomax, of course.'

Replacing the silver frame, Lilli wondered how her new carer could possibly know Freddie.

A golden boy. From the day he was born when she had put away her music and devoted herself to her son.

The harsh realities of his birth were as nothing compared with the punishing physical labour of the first two years of Freddie's life. The remorseless round of back-breaking days, followed by sleepless nights, were mitigated by the sight of his rounded limbs as he slept, the touch of his flesh against hers, his first smile, his first tooth. She fed him until he was a year old, not wanting to give up the sweet sensations as he sucked rhythmically at her breast. When the time came for him to start nursery school, she helped him hang up his coat on the peg identified by a brown egg in a blue eggcup. Abandoning him amongst the other children, amongst the plasticine and the colouring books, it was as if she'd left him on his own to drown. Freddie was always happy. She and Hugh called him their ray of sunshine. He had only to come into their bedroom in the mornings, to run towards her out of the playground when she collected him, to brighten up the day.

Lilli immersed herself in books on child care. Later, on child guidance. She steered Freddie away from unsuitable toys and games, substituting those which would promote his mental and physical growth. She supervised and shaped him, like a young tree to be espaliered, nipping out unhealthy buds and encouraging the strong ones. Dedicating herself to her son, she instructed him in creative play, supervised his reading, and taught him how to swim. Leaning over his shoulder as he pored proudly over his paint box, she amended his damp offerings in which the rivers were yellow, the trees blue, and the meadows red. She took him to museums and art galleries where she was his eyes, to concerts where she was his ears. Conscious of the fact that he was an only child, she invited school friends to the house, making sure that he was never alone.

Hugh's death, out of the blue on a summer's day, was the end of what Lilli realised had been an idyll. Numb with shock, she played weeping fragments from Fauré's

Requiem for Hugh, but did not let Freddie attend his father's funeral.

When she had pulled herself together she put an advertisement in the local paper offering piano tuition, and kept a home together for herself and Freddie. Her energy was consumed by her pupils. While Lilli was instructing them, Freddie played by himself in the kitchen. He preferred it to his nursery, notwithstanding the carefully chosen toys. He set places for the two of them for dinner, climbing up on a chair to the drawer, and putting the cutlery on the table upside down. Lilli chided him for handling the sharp knives and recited her favourite limerick about the 'Old Man of Thermopylae', who never did anything properly. When Freddie was 8 he made her a chocolate cake from the recipe corner in his comic, and by the time he was 10 he could turn out a passable meal. His school reports were poor. Could do better if he tried. Lilli drew up a timetable for his homework and declared the kitchen out of bounds.

Life as a single parent was an uphill struggle. Being the breadwinner was a Sisyphean task for which Lilli prayed daily for health and strength. She would have liked Freddie to follow his father into medicine. Freddie did not accept the assignment. As far as his musical education was concerned, Lilli tried to interest him in the piano, playing Chaminade's 'Autumn' so that he could identify the rustling of the falling leaves, and Grieg's 'Wedding Day at Troldhaugen', with its unmistakable 'clip-clop' of horses' hooves which he pretended not to hear. When she struggled with him over 'Für Elise', he was heard to mutter, 'Bloody Beethoven!' – the only occasion on which she slapped him – and stubbornly refused to practise. She gave him a quarter-size violin, a set of drums, and a recorder, with the same result. When he came home from school with a mouth-organ from which he produced cacophonous sounds, she threw it away.

Lilli's efforts were not completely wasted. From the age

of 12 to the age of 18, Freddie's pocket money was spent on records – Gerry Mulligan and Dave Brubeck – his passion was for jazz.

When Freddie left home for Cambridge, for Lilli it was like losing a limb. When, at his graduation, he had eyes only for Jane, it was a knife turning in her heart. The fact that he seemed unstoppable, that he progressed in what seemed no time from his first job in a bank to becoming vice chairman of Sitwell Hunt International, compensated a little for the fact that he had grown up. As the years went by her relationship with her son altered. Whereas she had always looked after Freddie, now it was Freddie who looked after her. She knew that she was a trial. She could not be left alone because she was inclined to put the gas on and forget to light it. Sometimes she wandered out into the corridor and found herself unable to remember the number of her flat. It was Freddie who bore the burden of keeping her supplied with carers and was responsible for their salaries. Freddie who paid the rent.

Mrs Whatsername was peering at a photograph of Lilli. She was trying to reconcile her snowy-headed charge with the young pianist, her hair flowing like a dark waterfall onto her naked shoulders, her scarlet dress brightening up the platform of the Aeolian Hall. Lilli pointed towards the other photographs.

'That's me at the Albert Hall, after the Queen's Hall was bombed . . .' She hummed a few bars from a Strauss waltz. 'Me in uniform, entertaining the troops during the war . . .'

The telephone bell wrenched Lilli from her past. She picked up the receiver. Freddie rang every morning to see how she had slept. Nine times out of ten she had not the slightest idea. She remembered that today was Freddie's birthday and wished him many happy returns, then held her hand over the mouthpiece and eyed Mrs Williams. 'My son wants to know what sort of night I had. What did you say your name was, dear?'

CHAPTER FOUR

Having decided upon *Der Rosenkavalier*, a young man's opera, as being a suitable choice for his birthday, Freddie stood naked before the full-length mirror in his dressing-room, beat time to the music with his hairbrush, and considered the significance of reaching the age of 40. He felt no different now from when he had first come down from Cambridge, although before him was irrefutable evidence that this was not entirely true. His waistline had thickened and he no longer had 20/20 vision, but if he narrowed his eyes slightly and remembered to hold in his stomach, he could, albeit with some assistance from Charlie and from Douggie Hayward, forget about his age with its implications of mid-life crisis. Physically he was in good nick, and his effect upon women confirmed the fact that he was still sexually eligible. Although in financial terms he was living at the limits of an extremely large overdraft, the balance sheet of his life was healthily in credit. He was crazy about his wife, was proud of his children, loved his work and his home (in that order), and his 84-year-old mother, although increasingly a liability, was still going strong.

Humming to the 'Walzerlied', he opened the mahogany wardrobe in which his suits hung side by side, and selected a dark grey flannel with which, in honour of the day, he would wear a pink silk handkerchief and pink tie.

Jane, relying on the opera music, as she did every morning, to bring her back from the dead – Freddie said she had a PhD in sleeping – opened her eyes and watched his brisk movements with affection through the open door of the dressing-room.

'Happy birthday, darling.'

Buttoning his shirt with one hand and reaching for his socks with the other, Freddie blew her a kiss.

'Aren't you going to open your cards?'

It was ten to eight. Freddie's life was regulated by the clock. His internal alarm was accurate, and he checked only for affirmation as he divided his day into precise instalments. He was never late for an appointment. Never kept a client waiting. Never let his meetings run over. Having just successfully defended the high-profile, hostile takeover bid for Corinthian Hotels, he was anxious to get to the bank.

'You open them for me.'

There was another matter, extremely serious, which had been brought to his notice while he had been locked in battle with Corinthian, and which now needed his most urgent attention.

'You remember Bretton Corporation . . .?'

Jane held up a scalloped-edged birthday card bearing a picture of a cottage garden. It was dedicated to 'darling Freddie' in an unsteady hand.

'From your mother.'

'. . . one of our most valuable and longstanding clients . . .'

'"For You Dad . . ."'

Freddie stopped what he was doing.

'. . . A picture of a golfer. He looks a bit like you. Love and kisses . . .'

Freddie waited.

'. . . from Rosina.'

'Bretton Corporation suddenly withdrew all their business from Sitwell Hunt and moved it to another bank . . .'

'"They say you're only as old as you feel", and inside . . .'
Jane opened the card. '. . . "It's a lie!" James and Dos.
Why?'

'My guess is an alleged leak of confidential information . . .'

'"Many Congratulations on your Fortieth Birthday". A
man fishing . . .'

'. . . to a third party . . .'

'Gordon and Margaret Sitwell.'

'. . . Which has cost the bank several *million* pounds. At
a time like this that is not good news.'

'Who would do a thing like that?'

'That's what I intend to find out.'

Silencing Baron Ochs, and erupting into the bedroom
with his two briefcases, his microcassette recorder, his
telephone and his worry beads, Freddie flung them down
on the bed while he riffled through the rest of the cards
which were scattered on the quilt. Jane knew that he was
looking for a card from Tristan.

'I expect it will come in the second post.'

'I expect he's forgotten! Too damned lazy.'

'He *is* in the middle of exams . . .'

'You don't have to make excuses.'

Employing diversionary tactics, Jane took a narrow box,
wrapped in gold metallic paper, from beneath her pillow
and handed it to Freddie. On the accompanying card which
he removed from the envelope, a young couple sat beneath
a palm tree on a desert island. 'I can go for a long time
without a lot of things but I can't last a day without you.'
Jane's signature was encircled by what he imagined – but
had no time to count – were forty kisses. Inside the box was
a chronograph engraved on the back with Freddie's name
and the date and '*La Vie en Rose*'. Jane fastened it over the
golden hairs on his wrist as she explained that the watch,
the very latest, had a perpetual calendar and moon phase

up to the year 2499; that it could stop the time to an eighth of a second and calculate how many days there were in the month for centuries to come.

The warm, animal smell of her as he held her tightly to him and slid a hand beneath the 'Happy Birthday' T-shirt, made Freddie wish that he didn't have to rush off. He released her reluctantly, touching her face still warm from sleep.

'I'll take a rain check . . .' He was already in office mode.

Freddie's credo was that if he served his clients well success would automatically follow. From the moment he arrived at the bank in the mornings, he operated hands-on throughout the day, and often, when he was engaged in an important transaction, stayed at his desk into the small hours. On call seven days a week, much of his weekend was spent either immersed in paperwork or on the telephone, which led Jane to accuse him, as he paced up and down, both of wearing out the carpet and being married to the bank. It was partly true. Much as he loved his family and derived comfort and satisfaction from the certainty that they were there when he needed them, his work was his life's blood and he was content to leave the day-to-day decisions to Jane.

This did not bother Jane in the least. She did not find it demeaning to put a meal on the table for her husband and children (she used prepared foods tasting of cardboard boxes only *in extremis*), to make sure that their clothes were clean and ironed, and that there were always fresh flowers in the house. It never occurred to her to think of herself as just a housewife, and she saw absolutely no reason to sell herself short because the full-time job she did was voluntary with no tangible end product. Running a home required managerial and financial skills, a knowledge of cooking (and in her case corporate entertaining), a modicum of first aid, nursing and teaching, some understanding of psychology and philosophy and the ability to drive a car. She had no desire whatever to improve herself at evening classes, to follow an Open University course, or to don a suit with padded shoulders and pursue a career. She accepted as no big deal that women must make allowances for the psychological needs of men – in much the same way as they accommodated their bodies and their babies – and considered such accommodation to be the natural consequence of anatomy and destiny rather than the programmed responses of a slave.

Since they had moved to Regent's Park, she had got the house to her liking, and now Tristan was away at school, Jane had turned her attentions to those in need. She was much in demand as a fund raiser by charitable organisations, to whose distinctive profiles she brought not only her personal charm but the techniques of the boardroom, and the use – with Freddie's blessing – of her beautiful home.

Jane rearranged the pink handkerchief in Freddie's top pocket as he leaned over the bed to gather up his belongings.

'Don't be late for the party – '

Freddie stopped her by covering her mouth with his own.

'As if I would!'

'Seven o'clock. Latest. Promise?'

'Cross my heart,' Freddie said.

His eyes met Jane's in mutual understanding. He would ring her during the morning. No matter how busy he was. He always did.

Even his mother had had to admit that her beloved Freddie could not have chosen a better wife. From the early days of their marriage, by making her own clothes, wild and colourful (worn with outrageous hats or scarves twisted round her forehead, and tights which she dyed to match or clash with what she was wearing), running up curtains and cushion covers from material bought in Portobello market, and concocting inventive meals out of inexpensive ingredients (which they shared with appreciative friends who always returned home from an evening with the Lomaxes with the rosy glow of conviction that the world was a better place), Jane had managed not only always to look stunning, but to turn the two rooms of their rented flat into a home.

By the time they moved to Regent's Park and there was money to complement her skills, she had got interior decoration down to a fine art.

The house in Chester Terrace behind its Nash exterior had been derelict when Freddie bought it. Under the aegis of the Crown Surveyor, Jane had devoted eighteen months to the renovation of its five floors. She had replaced the roof tiles, renewed rotted timbers, installed new electrical and plumbing services, and damp-proofed the basement. Together with her architect, keeping him up to scratch, she had ensured that the proportions of cement and sand used for the plastering were in accordance with requirements, that the joinery was accurate and the floorboards of the correct thickness. She had stood by vigilantly while the random workmen removed the original ironmongery, the keys and escutcheons, and carefully preserved them for eventual replacement. When the windows were finally refurbished, the floors relaid, and the skirtings replaced, she had set about the final embellishment.

The first-floor drawing-room overlooked the park. Given a free hand by Freddie, Jane had installed eighteenth-century panelling, and enhanced the grandeur of the room with a Louis XVI chimney-piece topped by a massive gilt mirror. Having created her shell, which she decorated in shades of deep coral, she proceeded to furnish it with the glossy patina of antique pieces, Belgian tapestries, sofas piled high with richly embroidered cushions and the silk glow of Persian rugs. Double doors, left permanently open, allowed additional light to travel into the high-ceilinged room from the hall.

The dining-room, by contrast, was dark. By the use of spotlights and mirrors, and with a certain wry humour, Jane had turned it into a *seraglio*. She employed specialist craftsmen to paint the walls *faux* tortoiseshell, and had added a lacquered dado and cornice. Moulded cupboards housed her collection of china and porcelain and cunningly concealed the dumbwaiter, while fourteen chairs with leopard-skin seats, a black marble chimney-piece, and Mexican amber glassware, completed the melodramatic setting for the Lomax dinner parties.

In the master bedroom with its king-sized bed, Jane, in a *volte face*, had used the faded tints of old prints – pastel-striped wallpaper, muted carpet, and delicate fabrics – to create an oasis of calm for herself and Freddie.

As far as Freddie was concerned his house, in addition to fulfilling his childhood dream, was an investment which was set to double in value within five years. Delivering it from its years of neglect, and restoring it to its former glory, not only made sound economic sense, but would provide a fitting setting for him in the future, when Gordon Sitwell retired and he became chairman of the bank.

In the kitchen Freddie found his daughter, in second-skin cycling shorts and a sleeveless Lycra top, the remains of the previous night's mascara still round her eyes, plugged into her Walkman and inert at the table. There were grotesque blue tattoos, one of which looked like a poor representation of the Amazon rain forest, on her forearms.

'Rosina . . .'

Without unplugging herself, Rosina spat on a finger and rubbed at the rain forest which disintegrated at her touch. She pushed a clumsily wrapped parcel towards Freddie. He assumed it was his birthday present.

Unwrapping the layers of recycled brown paper, followed by layers of newspaper, followed by layers of crumpled tissue paper, took him back to the game of pass the parcel which he had played as a small boy. Although Lilli pretended not to look as she played the piano for the circle of school friends who sat cross-legged on the floor, he knew that his mother deliberately took her hands off the keys whenever the many-layered package landed in his lap. Removing the final sheet of paper, Freddie came to a concertinaed cereal box. Inside it was a psychedelic, hand-painted glass paperweight. He assumed it had come from Camden Lock where Rosina had once sat on the kerb while a handsome Nigerian pulled the strands of her hair, one by one, through a hole in a sheet of cardboard and beaded them painstakingly. Kissing Rosina, who jumped up and down like an affectionate young puppy, and removing her clinging arms, Freddie put the pyramid into his briefcase. It would look very well on his desk.

CHAPTER FIVE

Leonard, Freddie's driver, was about to turn the Mercedes out of Chester Terrace, when he caught sight in his mirror of a frantic Rosina, her school bag over her shoulder, running to catch up with the car. Glancing at Freddie who was on the phone, and knowing that it was as much as his job was worth to ask his boss to wait, he reduced his speed as much as he dared.

Hanging up on his stockbroker, Freddie nodded to Leonard to wait for Rosina. She was well aware that if she was not ready on time and waiting for him she forfeited her lift to school for her early rehearsal, and also that her father was a soft touch. Wrenching open the door, she fell headlong into the car and collapsed on the seat beside him.

Freddie took her hand with its bitten nails but did not attempt a conversation with his daughter. Rosina would be capable of only grunts, or at the best monosyllables, for at least the next hour. He got on well with Rosina, who seemed to him to be perfectly amiable until he listened to Jane. Rosina had been an exemplary baby and a good-natured child. From the age of 12 however, when she had begun to reduce Jane to tears in communal fitting-rooms the length and breadth of the King's Road, they had been at loggerheads. Rosina was hostile to her mother and rolled her eyes to the ceiling when addressed by her. Although she had enough lotions and potions of her own to make up the entire cast of *The Phantom of the Opera*, she borrowed Jane's cosmetics and forgot to give them back. According to Jane, Rosina dropped her discarded clothes on the floor – instead of in the dirty-linen bin where there was at least a chance of them becoming clean again – and declined to do anything about her room which not only reeked of joss sticks but was a repository for boxes of Tampax, empty cassette cases, Third Eye candles, and discarded coffee mugs containing biological cultures at various stages of growth. When Jane had a migraine and was resting, Rosina would barge thoughtlessly into the darkened bedroom and demand money for the cinema or the loan of some tights. When her mother had arranged her drawing-room to her liking – Jane spent endless time moving the furniture an inch or two one way or another – Rosina would bring in her friends in their Doc Martens to watch a video, and leave 7-Up cans on the carpet, peanuts in the armchairs, and Jane's strategically placed cushions on the floor. Despite the fact that she had her own bathroom she had no hesitation, when she wanted to wash her burning bush of frizzy hair – a significant and time-consuming occupation – about monopolising Jane's and leaving long red hairs in the washbasin. Freddie, who could not really sympathise with what he saw as Jane's trivial complaints, until Rosina used his high-tech equipment to listen to rap and acid house, intervened only when called upon to do so.

Rosina played her parents off one against the other. She wheedled money out of Freddie for converse boots, or a Coach bag for her school books – she was the *only* one in the class not to have them – assuring him that Mummy had said it was all right, when Jane had said no such thing. She complained to Freddie that Jane was always 'getting at her', and swore to Jane that Daddy had said she could come in at three in the morning after a Saturday night out. Rosina was a warm and demonstrative girl, cuddling up to her father in private, and exhibiting him with pride to her friends. She was good at school, particularly at drama – the histrionics of which extended into her home life and had landed her the coveted lead in the current production of *Kiss me Kate* – and considerate to her grandmother whom she visited often and with whom she had a special relationship. Freddie could not really see what Jane made such a fuss about.

Tristan was another matter. Ever since he was born he had been able to do no wrong in his mother's eyes. At 16, thoroughly pampered by Jane, and protected by her whenever Freddie had attempted to discipline him, he constantly opposed his father whom he accused of being both a reactionary and what he contemptuously referred to as a merchant 'wanker'. At the age of 13, bright but difficult, he had brought home consistently poor reports from his academic day school where he refused to conform. He was almost as tall as Freddie, cocky and contentious, and the house could no longer contain him. Despite Jane's protests, Freddie had sent him to boarding school. At Bedales, where the staff were known by their first names and the pupils were uninhibited by authority, Tristan, wearing a black singlet, and sandals from a Dorset friary, became a useful and popular member of his year. Allowed to express himself freely, he found that he had a talent for sculpting, devoted himself to Amnesty, played tenor sax (jazz) at the parents' day concerts, and contributed esoteric poems to the school magazine. On his weekends at home he was waited on by his mother, argued with his father, and fought with Rosina, whom he constantly goaded. Sometimes Freddie could hardly wait to take him back to the station. He had willingly agreed to finance an expedition to India, which would keep Tristan out of his hair that summer, and had promised him driving lessons and a car.

As the Mercedes drew up outside Queen's College, Rosina kissed Freddie, now on the phone to Boston. Leonard opened the door for her and – with a wink at her ally – she fell into the arms of a 15-year-old Boadicea, her face almost obliterated by a curtain of plum-coloured hair, who greeted her as if she hadn't seen her for ten years, instead of two and a half days, and flashed her eyes at Freddie over Rosina's shoulder.

As the Mercedes turned into Cavendish Square, Freddie enquired about the health of his driver's wife and family who had almost been evicted from their terraced cottage in St Albans after falling behind with the mortgage repayments. The order had been served, the bailiffs had arrived to change the locks, and Leonard was already piling up their belongings on the pavement, when Freddie, who had heard about his dispossession through the bank grapevine, had stepped in with a large personal loan.

Seeing Leonard's eyes, meeting his own in the driving mirror, fill with tears of gratitude, he rapidly changed the subject to an item in the newspaper he was reading.

'I see some busybody in Birmingham is developing a "black box" for company cars.'

'Is that right, sir?'

'It can record mileage, measure the time taken for each journey, and check speeds.'

'What would be the point of that, sir?'

'Prevention of accidents. The equipment would give precise details of the vehicle's speed and braking in the two minutes before impact, and transfer the information, within seconds, through an infra-red gun, to the company's main computer.'

'We'd better watch out on the motorway then, sir!'

Leonard was referring to the fact that Freddie did not dissuade him from breaking the speed limit on the M1.

Having succeeded in diverting Leonard, Freddie dismissed from his mind such considerations as his driver's building society arrears, Rosina, his unwarranted entry into his fifth decade and the party Jane was giving to mark the occasion, and directed his attention to the business of the day.

He had every reason to congratulate himself. His successful defence of Corinthian Hotels – a personal triumph which had been announced only late on Friday afternoon after Gordon Sitwell had gone home for the weekend – had confirmed his high reputation in the City.

Working flat out over the past few months, and using all the skills at his disposal, he had managed to convince all but one of the most influential Corinthian Hotel shareholders to reject the hostile bid by Apex Holdings. Only Roger Randall, on whose vote depended the success or failure of his assignment, had remained impervious to either Freddie's blandishments or his charm.

Randall, the retired chairman of Randall's Breweries, owner of 6 per cent of the equity in Corinthian Hotels and a multimillionaire, was notoriously both an obstinate and avaricious man. Unable, even after several meetings, to persuade the old boy to oppose the Apex bid which would add a few more thousand pounds to his already overflowing coffers, Freddie backed off for a while to work out a plan of action.

Following a hunch, he flew up to Liverpool to see an old friend and one-time client, Clive Bonney. Bonney was chairman of the Galaxy Hotels chain which was, in its own small way, in competition with Corinthian. As Freddie had suspected, Clive Bonney – together with everyone else in the hotel business – had been following developments with interest.

Over a good lunch at the Adelphi Hotel, Freddie brought up the subject of Corinthian Hotels and asked Bonney what he thought of the Apex bid. Bonney's reply was exactly what he had expected.

'I'll be damned sorry to see them go to Apex,' Bonney said. '*I* know their bid's a load of rubbish. *You* know their bid's a load of rubbish.' He pointed his cigar at Freddie. 'They couldn't organise a piss-up in a brewery, never mind run a hotel. They don't know the first thing about it.'

'Why don't *you* put in a bid?' Freddie asked casually.

'Outside my league. I've had me eye on them for years.'

'It would certainly put Galaxy on the map . . .'

'It's a question of funding. Money's always been the problem as far as Corinthian's concerned.'

Freddie took a deep breath. 'I want to ask you a question.'

'Fire away.'

'Suppose I were to find the money . . .'

'You!'

'. . . With the guarantee that Sitwell Hunt will make up any shortfall.'

'Go on.'

'Would you be interested in making a bid for Corinthian sometime next year?'

'If you can put your money where your mouth is – and I've no reason, Freddie, to believe otherwise – I'd be very interested.' He ground his cigar firmly into the ashtray. 'I'd be more than interested.'

Bonney's eagerness to get his hands on the Corinthian Hotel chain was all that Freddie needed.

His next move was to do nothing at all until documents had been sent out by Apex Holdings to the Corinthian shareholders. He allowed what he gauged was sufficient time for Roger Randall to give further consideration to the offer, then called him to say there had been an interesting development which could be to his advantage. A further meeting was set up and Freddie made straight for the brewer's Achilles heel.

'I understand that the Galaxy Hotels chain, which has always had its eye on Corinthian, is considering making a bid for it sometime next year.'

'What's that got to do with me?'

'It is my considered opinion, Mr Randall, that if you were to wait a bit, you stand to make a great deal more money than you would by accepting the present Apex offer.'

The bait was taken.

'What makes you so sure, Lomax?'

'I have reliable information to that effect.'

'How reliable?'

'Extremely reliable.'

'I'd need to check that independently.'

Freddie's heart was banging like a bidder's at an auction sale. 'Would confirmation from the *chairman* of Galaxy put your mind at rest?'

The next moment was crucial. Failure to defend the Apex bid was inadmissible. As a boy he had been rewarded for good behaviour and success had been encouraged. His mother had not troubled to hide her disapproval manifested by the withdrawal of her love, if he did not perform well. He had not failed his mother, and he had no intention of failing either Sitwell Hunt or himself.

Randall's silence, in which the wheels of his brain could almost be heard revolving, was broken only by the rattle of Freddie's worry beads. He wondered if he had got the old man's number as accurately as he had thought.

When the silence became intolerable Randall narrowed his hooded eyes and said: 'I might just give Clive Bonney a bell.'

The fish was hooked.

At lunchtime on Friday – after the expiry of the final deadline – acceptances had been received from only 47.2 per cent of the Corinthian shareholders. After a long-drawn-out battle, Freddie had finally been successful. The Apex bid had failed.

CHAPTER SIX

As the Mercedes approached the bank, the sight of a bag lady wandering the city streets muttering to herself, made Freddie think of Lilli. He had taken it upon himself to care for his mother as his father would have done had he been alive, but it was not always easy. His conversation with her that morning, a circular discourse which had centred largely on the diminishing contents of her fruit bowl, had left him with the distinct impression that the days of the new carer were numbered and that Mrs Williams would last no longer than the rest. The diplomacy which stood him in good stead as head of corporate finance was as nothing compared with that which he had to employ when dealing with Lilli whose wellbeing accounted for a disproportionate amount of his time.

He visited his mother every Tuesday, often rescheduling his trips abroad in order not to disappoint her. After dinner he would force himself to sit with her for half an hour and listen to music – Lilli's arthritic fingers keeping time on some imaginary piano – until, anxious to get back to his paperwork and his unmade calls, and with a discreet glance at his watch, he would announce that it was time for him to go, a statement guaranteed to provoke the response that he had only just arrived.

When he was growing up he had assumed that there

was some stage at which you detached yourself from your parents, and that the emancipation, like graduation, would come somewhere after puberty and leaving home. He had never managed to work out why at the age of 40 he still *cared* what Lilli thought about him; why her criticism, which he was unable to accept with mature detachment as a mere statement of opinion, mattered; why, when he was capable of supporting a family, running a department, making multimillion-pound decisions, owning a home, and paying his dues to the Inland Revenue, she was still capable of making him feel like a small boy; and why, no matter how much attention he gave her, how much thought and energy he expended on her behalf, he was always left with the uncomfortable feeling that somehow he had let her down.

A silver Porsche, with the number plate H6 TAN (well known in the City as the 'undertaker's car'), drawing to a halt on the double yellow lines outside the head office of Universal Concrete, one of Britain's largest construction firms, banished all thoughts of Lilli. Telling Leonard to slow down, Freddie watched with amazement as Tarquin Chapman, senior partner in the liquidators Chapman Tansley, looking extremely pleased with himself and carrying a Louis Vuitton briefcase, got out of the car, looked quickly to right and left, and hurried into the building.

With so many businesses now either going into administrative receivership or being placed in intensive care by the banks, the sight of the undertaker, who prospered (to the tune of £350 an hour) not so much in spite of the recession but because of it, was not uncommon. When companies went bust, firms such as Tansley's were called in to salvage anything of value after the banks had recouped their secured loans, and took on the debtors to the swingeing tune of 15 per cent.

Freddie might have ignored the incident if, two weeks

ago when he had eschewed the directors' dining-room for the Italian restaurant behind St Paul's, where he went when he had no clients to impress or he wanted to be alone, he had not noticed Roland Tansley, Chapman's partner, come out of the same building. Guessing that the days of Universal Concrete (in common with 22,440 other companies according to recent figures published by the Department of Trade and Industry) were numbered, Freddie decided to take a calculated risk. In his book a risk was never justified unless it *was* calculated, and he would no more dream of taking a chance in business than of overtaking on a blind bend. Instructing Leonard to drive on, he came to the conclusion that the sight of Tarquin Chapman was fortuitous and decided to play his hunch. Calling his stockbroker for the second time that morning, he bought a put option on a large parcel of shares in Universal Concrete.

Dismissing Leonard as they drew up in front of the Sitwell Hunt building, Freddie had gathered up his brief-cases and was halfway across the pavement before the driver had time to open the car door. Acknowledging the greeting of Sam, the commissionaire, who had served the Sitwell family, with a break for military service, for over fifty years, he nodded to the waiting messengers who paced the marble floor between the pot plants, and made a beeline for the lift.

Swinging his briefcases as he hurried along the second floor corridor, his whistled rendering of 'La donna è mobile' was cut short by Conrad Verger, who, with his hands in the pockets of his Japanese designer suit, waylaid him.

Conrad, member of the Assassins club and alumnus of Harvard Business School, was married to Sir Gordon's daughter Sophie. He had recently been taken in by Gordon as an associate director of Sitwell Hunt. Despite his previous experience – including a couple of years in Hong Kong where he had picked up a smattering of Mandarin as well as some useful Chinese contacts – Conrad had a great deal to learn about banking and was heavily dependent upon Freddie who suspected that, although outwardly friendly, Conrad resented his position as head of the acquisition team, as well as his long-standing association with Gordon and his place in his father-in-law's affections.

'Morning, Freddie. Well done on the bid.' Conrad's voice sounded only slightly grudging. 'Who did you have to fuck to get Randall?'

Freddie glanced impatiently at his new chronograph. He wanted to get a few things under his belt before the morning meeting at which he planned to discuss the weekend press and the major marketing launches during the week. He explained briefly to Conrad, who seemed to be in no hurry, how, by conniving with Bonney, he had managed to persuade Roger Randall to wait for a more advantageous offer from Galaxy for Corinthian, which had produced the anticipated result.

'Jesus Christ, Freddie!' Conrad removed his hands from his pockets. 'Are you saying you committed the resources of Sitwell Hunt, on an open-ended arrangement, without any board authorisation?'

Freddie nodded.

'Without even bothering to mention it?'

'I only *intimated* to Bonney that, in the extremely unlikely event that I am unable to raise all the necessary funds in the market in a year's time, Sitwell Hunt will step in with the balance . . .'

'We're in the middle of a recession, Freddie. Who knows what's going to happen in a year's time? If you *can't* find the money in the market, Bonney's going to look to us for hundreds of millions of pounds.'

'I wouldn't lose any sleep over it if I were you. There is no likelihood whatsoever of the bank having to raise a single penny.'

'What makes you so damned sure?'

Freddie put an avuncular hand on the shoulder of the chairman's son-in-law. 'I do know my own strengths, Conrad.'

Leaving Conrad open-mouthed, he took out his key card and made for the corporate finance department, which specialised in mergers, takeovers and the raising of capital, locked away behind its Chinese wall.

Entering his domain, and without slowing his pace, he acknowledged the greetings of those of his junior colleagues who were already at work in their glass cubicles.

'Morning, Freddie.'

'Congratulations.'

'Well done on the bid.'

Grinning broadly, Freddie made his way between the goldfish bowls to his inner sanctum.

'Well done, everyone.' He looked at his chronograph. 'Twelve thirty in my office. Champagne's on me!'

On his desk were a glossy propectus, inviting him to participate in a multimillion-pound project in Brazil, half a dozen birthday cards, a wrapped bottle, and what looked like a book. Dropping his gear, he pressed the keypad on the table to suss out the market movers on the Topics Screen before zapping to the company news. A new bid for Rochelle led him to make a mental note to give the managing director of the electronics company – to whom he had marketed in the past – a ring, to see if he was thinking of changing his obviously lightweight advisors. Checking on the announcement of his own satisfactory coup, he sat down at his desk to look at his birthday mail and open his presents.

The cards (which had sexual innuendoes to do with

his age) were from colleagues, the bottle (non-vintage champagne) was from the tea-ladies, and the book, *Golf for the Middle-Aged* – which he presumed was supposed to be funny – was from one of the heads of departments. As he took Rosina's glass pyramid from his briefcase and put it in pride of place next to his leather-framed photograph of Jane, an airmail envelope, marked personal and propped up against the calendar caught his eye. Sidonie. She never forgot.

A trip to the States in search of acquisitions five years ago, when he had just joined Sitwell Hunt, had led to a liaison with Sidonie Newmark, the one and only time he had cheated on his marriage vows.

Sidonie, a New York stockbroker, had come on strong to him on Concorde. The blonde Ms Newmark, as he was to discover over the next few days spent largely in bed with her in her Manhattan apartment – where the attachments for the cooker lay unused in their bubble-pack – fucked like a small tiger, shared his passion for opera, was his intellectual match, had eyes which could freeze an opponent at twenty paces, and could, when the occasion demanded it, be as ruthless in business as he. Sidonie was ignited by power and turned on by money, the word love did not feature in her vocabulary. In every respect she was the counterpoint to Jane, who not only abhorred anything to do with opera but was also tone-deaf. For six crazy months Sidonie screwed Wall Street by day and Freddie, when he was in New York, by night. Not surprisingly he had found an excuse to visit the States frequently throughout the course of their affair, and in between times met Sidonie – who thought nothing of crossing the Atlantic to spend a night with him – in Paris, Frankfurt or Geneva. On Sidonie's sudden and unexpected betrothal to a (titled) Italian playboy, the liaison had ended as abruptly as it had begun, and a relieved and guilt-stricken Freddie had come to his senses.

Slitting open the blue envelope with his paperknife, he removed Sidonie's birthday card – 'You may be pushing 40 but you're still not over the hill' – which was signed with her name in the familiar, backwards-sloping hand. Freddie allowed himself a wry smile and a momentary remembrance of things past, before putting the card with the others, pressing the buzzer on his desk for his personal assistant, and turning his attentions to the more important business of the day.

'Morning, Freddie. Congratulations . . .' Susan, a slim brunette almost as tall as her boss, who favoured shift dresses in dark colours enhanced by a silk scarf or a brooch, came briskly into the office, with a newspaper under her arm, and put a gift-wrapped package in front of him. '. . . and Happy Birthday.'

'Morning, Susan. Is that for me? Thank you very much. Good weekend?'

'Nothing to write home about.' She put the *Independent*, its front page full of gloom and doom about dashed hopes for an economic recovery and job losses in power and petroleum, down on his desk.

'There's a photograph of you. And Wichmann has called twice. He wants to talk to you urgently. I think Frankfurt is about to burst into action.'

'Sod it! I thought I was going to have a quiet week. I need the Bretton Corporation team here. Will you sort it out? Two thirty, prompt. I want to get to the bottom of that leak. You can fix a meeting with Travers to discuss the marketing drive. Check the diaries and fix up dinner – the Savoy – for the Corinthian boys . . .'

'When?'

'ASAP . . . and chase up the weekend press cuttings on the bid, will you, Susan?'

Susan had worked for Freddie ever since he had been at Sitwell Hunt. A few years older than he, she had been passed on to him by a friend at the Foreign Office who had been posted to Lagos, and came with a glowing reference, a radical mastectomy, and a broken marriage behind her. Now, with access to both Freddie's bank account and to his diary, she was an indispensable extention of his daily life. Although their relationship had never been anything but businesslike – they simply functioned together like a pair of well-drilled ice-skaters – and Susan had not once spoken out of turn, Freddie was aware that his personal assistant was in love with him.

Opening his parcel, he knew that he would find another sweater – it was white cashmere this time – to add to his collection, and that it was, according to Rosina who had read it in a magazine, an unconscious manifestation of Susan's desire to put her arms around him. Buzzing his PA to thank her profusely for the extravagant present and to ask her to get the German broker on the line, he decided that in honour of his birthday he would take Susan out for lunch.

Hans Wichmann was acting on behalf of several companies who, with an eye on Eastern Europe, were trying to set up a chain of supermarkets in the CIS.

'Guten Morgen . . .' It was the extent of Freddie's German. 'Yes, yes, I was going to call you,' Freddie lied, having hoped for a few days to catch up with himself after Corinthian. 'Things are looking good this end, Hans.' He put his feet up on the desk. 'As far as English investment is concerned it's in the bag. You can tell your people not to worry. Sitwell Hunt International can provide all the finance you're going to need. No problem. No problem at all. But before we go any further, I think you and I need to talk . . .'

Freddie decided that it would be a good move to invite this potentially valuable client, with whom negotiations had been going on for some time, to come to London at the weekend with his wife. On Saturday night he would take them to a gala performance of *Lohengrin* at the Royal Opera House where he was in charge of the Sitwell Hunt box.

There were those who believed that corporate entertaining was an expensive and unnecessary luxury at best, and an immoral form of bribery at worst. In Freddie's book, goodwill in business was an inestimable asset. He had himself been wined and dined at some of the world's most prestigious restaurants, been taken on private tours of Venetian palaces and even – on one memorable occasion in Hockenheim – invited to shoot wild boar. His own method of establishing what he considered was a vital personal rapport with his clients, which at the same time satisfied his own predilection, was to take them to the opera.

His love affair with opera had begun during his first term at Trinity when he had accidentally tuned his radio into the second act of *Don Giovanni*, and the voice of Lisa della Casa singing 'Non mi dir' had struck him with the impact of a physical blow. This apocalypse was later reinforced when while visiting a friend on his staircase he had heard the Prisoners' Chorus from *Fidelio*, and he was hooked for life. It was not only the music which spoke to him. No matter how badly the dramatis personae treated each other, no matter how dire their acting, the ultimate revelations of the triumph of hope and tenacity over often overwhelming odds never failed to move him.

As others were capable of reflection in another language, Freddie frequently even thought in terms of opera. 'Là ci darem la mano' – Don Giovanni wooing the country lass – was the first night he spent with Jane in his Cambridge room seventeen years ago, 'Parigi, O cara' (without wishing upon Jane the fate of Violetta) was his vow to spend his life with her, while 'Pur ti miro' – Nero's double-crossing of his

Empress for love of Poppea – was his betrayal of Jane with Sidonie of which he was not the slightest bit proud.

Putting the phone down on Wichmann, who on behalf of Frau Wichmann and himself had accepted Freddie's invitation with alacrity, Freddie buzzed Susan to fix the couple up with a suite at the Connaught (plus the usual flowers and champagne), to pencil him in for the Covent Garden box on Saturday, to call Interflora and have a dozen yellow roses sent to Jane, and to bring him up to date with the correspondence.

She brought in a pile of letters and a memo.

'Your put option . . .'

Freddie glanced with satisfaction at the details of the shares he had bought. If his hunch was correct and Universal Concrete went down the tubes, he stood to gain some sixty to seventy thousand pounds before the end of the account.

'. . . confirmed. And Gordon just put his head round the door. He really wanted a quick word with you but I told him you were involved with Wichmann. He's running late – he had his knickers in a twist over the traffic on Hendon Way – and he has someone waiting upstairs. I said ten o'clock. After the morning meeting.'

CHAPTER SEVEN

When Freddie first brought Jane down from Cambridge to introduce her to his mother, Lilli took her silver pastry forks from their blue velvet nest and polished them, but the resentment which welled up within her, and which for Freddie's sake she tried hard to conceal, permeated the Victoria sandwich and cast a pall over the tea-trolley. That there was nothing personal about her feelings towards her son's red-headed girlfriend was immaterial. Freddie was *her* son and she did not want to share him with anyone.

The fact that Jane was pregnant with Freddie's child took Lilli by surprise and forced her to retrench. In an unconscious statement, she wore a white suit for the wedding, and afterwards not only rang Jane frequently to make sure that she was looking after Freddie, but called round uninvited to make sure – with a glance from her critical eye – that the home Jane had made was what Freddie had been used to and that his new wife was not going to disturb the status quo.

Gradually Lilli's fears abated, and a grudging admiration for Jane, coupled with her delight in her grandchildren whose musical education she took in hand, replaced the mistrust. As the years went by the two women grew fond of each other and Jane became the daughter Lilli had never had. Lilli invited her frequently to the house

in Maida Vale, and played Schumann's 'Träumerei', and
Kinderszenen (which were lost on Jane) on the piano while
she regaled her with stories of Freddie's childhood.

The dinner menu Jane had planned for Freddie's birthday
was a simple one. A vibrant salad of red, yellow, and green
peppers; *poulets de Bresse* roasted with rosemary, garlic
and lemon juice; a runny wheel of unpasteurised Brie;
a birthday cake made by what called itself a 'French'
pâtisserie in Charlotte Street, accompanied by a green fruit
salad for the calorie freaks.

Jane had not been brought up as Freddie had been, in
the rarified atmosphere of an only child. She did not in
fact remember actually having been brought up at all.

She was the oldest of five red-headed sisters. Her father,
Vincent Morley, was a charming but poorly paid heraldic
artist who had quietly succumbed to the complications of a
faulty heart valve when she was 13, and her mother, Odette
(*née* Bérenguier), was a distracted ballet teacher (now
remarried and living in Buenos Aires), who had taught her
daughters to *jeter* and *plier* and trained them as flower girls
and sugar-plum fairies. The 'copperknobs', as Jane and
Sylvie and Chantal and Emeraude and Julia were known
in the Barnes street where they lived – together with various
cats and tortoises and hamsters and canaries which came
and went over the years – were left mainly to their own
devices. A great deal of time, as Jane remembered, seemed
to have been devoted to standing on the derelict sofa and
looking out of the window (the only one in the street
without curtains) waiting for their mother to come home,
or dressing up in handed-down tutus, darned pointe shoes,
and fragments of stage costumes. The dressing-up box, an
oversized laundry hamper kept on the sitting-room floor,
metamorphosed, according to the game the copperknobs
were playing, into boat, raft, vaulting horse, 'home', stage,
soapbox, or throne. Sometimes, too hungry to wait for

their mother's return – when she would quite often have forgotten to go to the shops anyway – the hamper became a table for the makeshift meals which they scavenged for themselves.

When the single male copperknob made his appearance – he was delivered at home, with the aid of the midwife and very little fuss, as the other copperknobs had been – Jane was ten. When Odette had finished breast-feeding him, a process which continued long after the approved time, and had gone back to her teaching, Didier Jean-François Théodore found himself with five surrogate mothers who carried their brother around with them, fed him, and played with him as they did with their kittens.

The neighbours purported to look down on Jane's family with its ramshackle lifestyle, but it was to the Morleys' house that the children in the street came with their painted faces on Hallowe'en, and in the Morleys' wilderness of a garden that, huddled in warm clothing and stamping their feet to restore the circulation in their toes, they gathered round the bonfire on Guy Fawkes Night.

From the age of 9, Jane's school holidays had been spent in the Massif des Maures with Grandmaman and Grandpapa, who was the village baker, in the house above the *Boulangerie*. The *Boulangerie* – in those days there had been only one – was in the main street opposite the church tower, the bells of which proclaimed not only the hour (which it repeated quixotically thirty seconds later) but weddings, baptisms and funerals, and, owing to the proximity of the volatile oak forests, frequently summoned the fire brigade. The windows of Jane's bedroom looked out onto the insignia of the drying tea-towels which hung from the windows of the Bar de la Poste, below which the young men of the village assembled on their motorbikes.

Jane's memories of her grandfather were of a white-clad figure, bathed in white mist, sprinkling flour onto the turning paddles in his huge vats like a votary, before dividing the stretchy dough, with sharp cutters, into equal portions. Although each portion was flung disdainfully onto the scales, Grandpapa got it right every time. The balance, with its dented tin bowls, was merely a formality which preceded the ambidextrous rolling of two balls of dough at a time into identical shapes, and arranging them into rows on greased trays which were then slammed into the cupboard to prove. Jane was allowed no further than the door of the bakery where she stood in her nightdress watching Grandpapa. The bakery was man's work.

From the time that she could reach the till, however, Jane had helped her grandmother in the shop. The rattle of the beaded curtain as the first customers came in from the street for the stacked sticks of still-warm bread round which she would fold minuscule squares of flimsy paper, was one of her earliest recollections. It was Grandmaman who taught Jane how to use a sewing machine and to crochet, how to wash her hair in vinegar, and make a *pot au feu*.

When Jane was sixteen, Grandpapa, who had never had a day's illness in his life, had a *crise cardiaque*. He was found by Grandmaman when she came down to open the shop in the morning, lying on the stone floor of the bakery, like a loaf of his own bread, in a shroud of white flour. On Grandpapa's death it was discovered, to everyone's surprise, that he was not only the owner of a large vineyard but had money in the bank. It was Jane's legacy from Grandpapa which had taken her to Paris and the Union Centrale des Arts Décoratifs.

With Grandpapa gone, Grandmaman sold the shop to his young apprentice and took her knitting to the seat occupied by the women beneath the sycamore tree, while at the other end of the street the men, flat caps on their heads, played boules, or sat on their sacrosanct bench in tranquil immobility. She refused to leave her village, where she had lived all her life, even for Jane's wedding.

Of all the copperknobs, Jane and Didier were the only ones still in England. Of the four girls, Julia was in Australia where she was married to a TV producer; Chantal was a nurse in Malta; Emeraude, an indigent actress, shared an apartment in New York with a cavalcade of lovers, and Sylvie, the only one to follow in her mother's footsteps, lived with her soul-singing boyfriend and their twins – Quest and Journey – in Vancouver where she ran a ballet school. Didier, whom Jane saw frequently, was a partner in a successful firm of solicitors. It was Freddie, who kept a paternal eye on Jane's young brother, who had been instrumental in setting him up.

While Freddie liked nothing better than the predictable rites of a formal dinner, Jane, influenced by Grandmaman whose pragmatism had left its indelible print on her childhood, would have been equally happy to sit round a wooden table in the kitchen with a casserole of jugged hare (marinated overnight in the washing-up bowl with branches of dried thyme and savory and rough red wine) mopped up with bread, followed by goats' cheese, and washed down by a Coteaux du Layon with its bouquet of caramelised quinces.

Although Jane did her own cooking, she usually employed extra help, in the persons of her cleaning lady, who went under the unlikely appellation of Lavender, and Lavender's friend Tracey, who was a waitress at Fortnum's during the day, to dish up the dinner and to serve.

Going down to the kitchen to start her preparations for the dinner party, she was surprised to see that Lavender's 4-year-old son, Shaun, was not at school but was sitting at the table, his nose running, stertorously working his way through a bag of salt and vinegar crisps. Lavender, in black leggings and a T-shirt with the superfluous message I AM PREGNANT, followed her glance.

'I thought he might be sickening.'

Jane made no comment. Lavender lived in an unheated council flat in Hackney and was married to Tony, a laid-off bricklayer who together with thousands of others had given up looking for work. Lavender was the breadwinner. She was not a particularly good cleaner. She removed the dirt only from eye-level and left the tools of her trade in unlikely places. She was at the mercy of her children's ailments – Shaun was asthmatic and the 3-year-old Daisy had eczema – and of her unemployed husband who was not averse to giving her the odd black eye. Jane often looked enviously at the efficient and unencumbered cleaning ladies she saw arriving, punctually and reliably, up and down the terraces each morning, but fate had sent her Lavender, with her aura of stale cigarettes, who brought the children to work with her in the holidays or on the increasingly frequent occasions when the nursery was closed, and relied upon Jane, to whom she entrusted her Post Office book – she was saving up to leave Tony – for her livelihood.

Lavender, whose heart was bigger than her pocket, took two polyester ties from her shopping bag.

'Do you think Freddie'll suit them?' she said anxiously.

The house was filled with cheap china ornaments and glass pyramids encasing mauve silk orchids, furnished over the years by Lavender.

'I got them down the market. Shaun's made him a card.'

Freddie was Lavender's dream man and on the rare occasions when their paths crossed he would put his arm round her shoulders and treat her to a chorus of 'Lavender's Blue', which never failed to make her blush.

While Lavender wrapped the ties clumsily in used Christmas paper, Jane, having reassured her about their suitability, took the peppers from the fridge and found a place for them on the table amongst the wax crayons and the painting books.

'Move, Shaun!' Lavender spoke roughly to her son as she bent, with obvious difficulty, to get her cleaning equipment from the cupboard.

'Are you okay?' Jane said.

'Pain in me back.'

'Perhaps you shouldn't have come out.'

'I can't stop indoors. Not with him sat in front of the telly all day with his filthy trainers up on my coffee table. I'm glad to get out of the house.'

Tempted sometimes to bring to Lavender's notice the coating of dust which she left in her wake, or to complain about cups and saucers which had become inadvertently chipped or broken, Jane reminded herself that Lavender, for all her faults, was doing her best. Six months advanced in her third pregnancy, which entailed long waits in the antenatal clinic, and not all that much older than Rosina, she had to dress and feed the children each morning, take Shaun to school, trek from Hackney in all weathers on an erratic bus, walk half a mile to put Daisy in the nursery, queue for a second bus, make her way from Great Portland Street to Chester Terrace, do a morning's work, repeat the journey in reverse, shop, cook, and tidy her own place, and cope with the humours of a violent and indigent husband.

Delving once more into her shopping bag, Lavender produced a bunch of 'mixed' carnations.

'They were selling them off.'

Jane abandoned the peppers, which she was going to put under the grill until the skins blackened, to cut the stems and remove the lower leaves from the wilting carnations. Arranging them in an Art-Deco vase with as much attention as if they had been a beribboned bouquet delivered that morning from Pulbrook & Gould, she carried them into the dining-room. Placing them on the sideboard, she picked up the envelope on which she had scribbled the names of her dinner guests.

Piers Warburton, reformed alcoholic and close friend of Freddie's, in charge of retail banking in continental Europe at NatWest, and Alex, a feisty 25-year-old magazine editor rumoured to put herself around Fleet Street, his third wife; Lord and Lady Cottesloe – Peter and Georgina – Jane and Freddie's laid-back next-door neighbours. Georgina had her own wine business on the income from which, topped up by Peter's daily attendance allowance at the House of Lords, they lived; Jane's old school friend Babs Ingoldsby (Bingo), an ex-actress now on her fourth husband (her numerous children were said to be confused about where to send their Father's Day cards), Charles, another merchant banker; Robert Gould, a divorced executive of Sitwell Hunt whom Freddie had suggested Jane introduce to Caroline Hurst, a young widow on her committee; Gordon and Margaret Sitwell; and their oldest friends, James and Dos.

Turning over the envelope, Jane drew a facsimile of the table round which she had been mentally seating her guests for days, moving them around like chessmen. Later she would transcribe the names, in the illuminated calligraphic hand she had learned from her father, onto hand-painted place cards.

Piers Warburton, whose tongue on Perrier water would remain immobilised all through dinner, would be her responsibility. She would seat Bingo, who never *stopped* talking and was incapable of conversing at all without clutching onto the nearest limb of her companion, on Freddie's right. The bankers had to be separated and Robert had to go next to his blind date. She put Peter Cottesloe next to Bingo – who was impressed by titles – and

Gordon Sitwell, by virtue of his seniority, between herself and Georgina, who had her eye on becoming his wine merchant. Poor Margaret Sitwell, terrified in company, would be put at her ease by Freddie, with the sociable James – who hopefully would not come out with too many risqué stories at least until after the pudding – on her left flank. Alex, on his other side, could easily handle James. With Dos next to Robert and Charles on Georgina's starboard the arrangement was complete.

Returning to Shaun and the kitchen, Jane switched on the grill and turned her attention once more to the peppers. Dressed with olive oil, garnished with hard-boiled eggs and anchovies, and arranged on a silver platter, they would give a colourful start to the evening for which, although she was producer and director, Freddie, with his talent for giving the *élan vital* to any gathering, would be the star.

CHAPTER EIGHT

On the fifth floor of Sitwell Hunt International, Gordon Sitwell, Message in his buttonhole, stood by the window of his panelled office hung with commissioned portraits of his father and his grandfather, the two previous Sitwell incumbents, dictating a letter to his secretary and contemplating the dark aurioles of her nipples clearly visible beneath the thin silk of her blouse. His secretaries were hand-picked, not for their skills at the word processor but for their youth and innocence, although today not even the youngest of them was unsullied. None of them stayed long. They left to get married. Or had problems with their boyfriends. Or were bored. Or pregnant. Sometimes he got his satisfaction by directing them to the S-Z drawer of the mahogany filing cabinets so that he could get an undisturbed view of their buttocks, and sometimes, according to his mood, he made them fetch a volume from the top-most bookshelf, which necessitated their clambering onto a chair in their skirts which were no bigger than a Band-aid and which revealed, at the very least, their thighs. He did not shame the girls. He did not frighten them. They did not know.

His kerb crawling (which now often took place on foot) had become a twice-weekly habit, although since the time of his caution he took care to avoid the area of King's Cross. He could not help himself. He got a thrill from his addiction and a buzz out of his clandestine life. The risk that he might be apprehended intensified the excitement. It was not the best part. When he wasn't actually kerb crawling, he was contemplating kerb crawling; it gave him a sense of power. He never had sex with the hookers. He paid them to listen. He went with them to their rooms where he told them exactly what he would like to do to them, and what he would like them to do to him in return. Afterwards he would drive home and in the privacy of the bathroom, he would masturbate to the tune of the evening's fantasies while from outside the door, contributing to the moment, Margaret enquired politely if he were going to be long. Sometimes, on the infrequent occasions that he made love to Margaret, he would imagine that she was a prostitute he had picked up. It was the only time he despised himself.

'With some reservation . . .' The current secretary, a Madonna look-alike, had her pen poised over her notebook. She repeated Gordon's last words, prompting him, breaking into his thoughts.

He dragged his eyes from her blouse and exited his reverie.

'With some reservation. Stop. I'm prepared to consider helping you. Stop. But before doing so I shall require further information, details of which . . .'

Gordon noticed that she had her legs crossed in such a way that you could almost, almost, see the shadowy triangle that separated her thighs. He liked it when the weather was warm and the girls went bare-legged.

'. . . further information, details of which our accountants will send you this afternoon. That's it, Dorothy.'

'Deirdre.'

'Deirdre.' Gordon leaned back in his chair and fingered the rose in his buttonhole. 'Get Courtauld for me, will you, Deirdre? Tell him I want a word.'

The morning meeting had finished early and Freddie had spent the last five minutes on the telephone chatting to Jane.

'It isn't *my* birthday,' Jane said, referring to the yellow roses which had already been delivered.

'They were to thank you for my present,' Freddie looked at his wrist. 'I love it. I love you.'

'I'll put them on the dining-room table. They'll go with the peppers.'

'Before I forget, I have a surprise for you. There's a client and his wife coming from Frankfurt at the weekend. We're taking them to *Lohengrin* on Saturday night.'

'Freddie!' Jane groaned.

'I thought you'd be pleased.'

'Is that the one where Gottfried turns into a swan?'

'Hardly. It's the other way round!'

'The last time you made me sit through that, the machinery jammed and the poor bird got stuck in the wings. What are they like?'

'The Wichmanns? Haven't a clue.'

'What did Gordon have to say about Corinthian?'

'Nothing yet. He wasn't at the meeting. Everyone else was chuffed. I'm due up there now.'

'Don't forget to thank Gordon for the birthday card. I don't suppose he knows anything about it. I expect Margaret sent it. I've put her between you and James, and Gordon next to me and Georgina. I thought . . .'

'I'm sure everything will be wonderful. As usual. I leave it entirely to you. According to my extremely smart chronograph, which can stop the time to an eighth of a second and calculate how many days there are in the month for centuries to come . . .'

'Given to you by your loving wife.'

'Given to me by my loving wife, it is now 9.55 and forty-three seconds. I'd better go.'

'See you then.'

'See you, darling. And don't forget my rain check.'

Jane blew kisses down the telephone. 'When they've all gone home.'

It was 9.59 a.m. when Freddie strode down the fifth-floor corridor between the serried prints of Redouté roses, and ten o'clock precisely, when, having nodded to the security guard, he knocked on the chairman's door. As he entered the room and crossed the pale blue expanse of carpet he was surprised to see Mathew Courtauld, one of the senior directors, already ensconced in one of the Queen Anne armchairs facing the desk.

'Congratulations, Freddie,' Gordon indicated the second chair.

'Thank you,' Freddie said. 'And thanks for your card . . .'

'Card?' Gordon looked blank.

'Birthday card.'

Gordon picked up some paperclipped pages from his desk. 'I meant . . . I have the transaction summary here . . . a note on the key issues of the Corinthian bid.'

Freddie waited for the well-earned praise which had been his life's blood since the time he had come running out of school with an A for his essay, or a ten out of ten for mental arithmetic.

'A quite remarkable outcome, not unexpected, of course, given your track record, but remarkable none the less. *And* a significant contribution. We are now well ahead of budget. A fact not to be sneezed at in these difficult times. Difficult times. Which is really what I wanted to talk to you about, Freddie, why I asked you to come up here.'

Gordon leaned back in his ox-blood-red leather chair which was outlined with antique studs. As always, Freddie remarked the chairman's resemblance to the facsimiles of his father and his grandfather executed in oils, and wondered would it be his own likeness which would one day grace the walls.

'As you are well aware,' Gordon closed his eyes, 'our first-half profits are well down. Together with my opposite numbers in other banks, with whom I have discussed the matter, I am extremely pessimistic about the second half. Extremely pessimistic.'

'I agree that profits aren't up to much,' Freddie said. 'But the way I see it is that we just have to sit tight. The Chancellor is already talking in terms of recovery . . .'

'That is not how it appears to me. All the indications are that we are sliding deeper and deeper into recession. Chancellor or no chancellor, I see no reason to revise my opinion.'

'You're being a bit too pessimistic,' Freddie said. He was beginning to get irritated with Gordon. 'It's not all doom and gloom. I'd give this recession about another six or nine months before it bottoms out.'

'Be that as it may,' Gordon opened his eyes, 'we have already seen a great many job losses in the financial sector. There may have to be some pretty drastic restructuring and rationalisation nearer to home.'

'Restructuring' and 'rationalisation' were euphemisms for reducing staff to cut costs when the number of employees outweighed the amount of work available. Freddie hoped that he was not being asked to carry out any purges within his own department. Despite his tendency to push them, as he pushed himself, extremely hard, his relationship with his team had always been a happy one.

'We are forced to reconsider things within the bank,' Gordon was saying. 'Which is really why I asked you to come up here. What I wanted to discuss with you.'

Leaning forward, with his elbows on the Corinthian dossier, Gordon put the tips of his manicured fingers together and looked directly at Freddie.

'I'm afraid we have to let you go.'

'You have to what!' Freddie almost jumped out of the chair.

'Let you go, Freddie.' The words were clearly enunciated. 'It has been decided. I'm afraid we have to let you go.'

Gordon rearranged the rose he had cut that morning in his buttonhole. 'If you could arrange to collect up your bits and pieces . . . In accordance with usual practice you have two hours to clear your desk.'

Freddie clutched at his worry beads. He thought that he was going to faint. He felt shocked and dizzy. As if he had been personally assaulted. As if he had been mugged. Gordon and the room became distorted, then receded. From a distance, through a filter, he heard the drone of the chairman's voice.

'On a personal level, believe me, Freddie, I am extremely sorry . . .'

Freddie wiped his sweating forehead with his pink silk handkerchief.

'. . . I have always valued your support and friendship – '

Re-entering his own body, the portraits resuming their rightful places on the wall, once more in control of himself, Freddie interrupted him.

'You can cut the crap, Gordon.' His voice was curt. 'What are the financial arrangements?'

Gordon exchanged glances with Mathew Courtauld, the reason for whose presence in the chairman's office had now become apparent.

'I am not *obliged* to give you anything.'

Freddie stood up. The worry beads bruised his fingers. There was a strange tightness in his chest.

'That is a matter of opinion.'

'What I am *prepared* to do is offer you six months' salary plus a small bonus . . .'

'A small bonus!'

As if Freddie had not spoken, Gordon glanced at his memo pad. 'I see that you are taking Hans Wichmann to Covent Garden. The tickets have already been allocated. Saturday night. That will be in order. There aren't too many takers for Wagner.'

'What *about* Hans Wichmann? I'm the only person who knows this client.'

'In the circumstances . . . since you are so far along the road. I don't wish to be . . . I can see no objection . . . You may carry on with Wichmann on a consultancy basis, if you like. Your car and driver will be at your disposal until the end of this week. Your health insurance will run until the end of the year. And don't worry about the press. We'll keep you on the books for the time being. Shall we say no formal announcement for a month? And Freddie . . .'

Freddie waited.

'You will of course have to sign an undertaking not to take away any sensitive documents or client information. Just as a formality. We'll sort out your diary, if you hand it over to the compliance officer.'

Freddie did not remember leaving Gordon Sitwell's office, propelling himself down the back staircase used only for emergencies, and going out into the street. He did not remember leaving the Sitwell Hunt building, walking blindly past the Stock Exchange and the Mansion House, leaving behind him the clearing banks, Lloyds, Barclays, the Midland, the National Westminster, the Royal Bank of Scotland, had no recollection of walking through the City which had been abandoned by the Romans, destroyed by the Great Fire, razed by the Germans, in the 667 acres of which he had spent most of his working life.

Returning fifteen minutes later, he assumed that he must have passed the time of day with Sam, have taken the lift to the second floor. He thought that someone – a member of staff? a tea-lady? – had greeted him in the corridor but he could not be sure. He must, he supposed, have used his key card to enter the corporate finance department and sat down – the psychedelic colours of Rosina's crystal pyramid blurring strangely one into the other before his eyes – he had no idea how long ago, in his office which now seemed strangely unfamiliar.

When his internal phone buzzed he did not answer it. When Susan came in to tell him that Denise, the compliance director, was on her way up to see him, she found him immobile at his desk, a dummy in the window of a men's outfitters. Taking a closer look at him, she was shocked to see that the cheeks of the head of corporate finance were glistening. She wondered if her boss could possibly have been crying.

CHAPTER NINE

Narcissus at his pool, Jane inclined her face towards the mirror. A few fine lines had recently begun to radiate from the corners of her eyes and her mouth was defined by a couple of very definite creases etched, she hoped, by laughter and compassion. At least her face was her own. Some of her friends, heavily into preserving themselves, like long-life food or old furniture, had gone in for cosmetic surgery from which they had emerged terrified to smile, the skin pulled tight over their cheekbones, and the bags beneath their eyes removed. This left them, Jane thought, looking nowhere near as lovely as the women beneath the sycamore tree in her grandmother's village, whose drooping eyelids and well-earned wrinkles bespoke a lifetime of living.

It was 7.55. The groundwork for the dinner party had taken her the best part of the day. In five minutes' time the curtain was due to go up. She wondered what could have happened to Freddie, who usually kept her informed of his movements and called her if he was going to be late. She had telephoned Sitwell Hunt, to be told by the security guard that everyone had gone home, and tried the car number to be answered by the robot: 'The Vodaphone you are calling is not replying, *please* try later. The Vodaphone you are calling . . .'

Jane's preparations did not take her long and her brief session at the dressing-table emphasised rather than transformed her fragile features. She smoothed a translucent foundation over her translucent skin, emphasised her eyes with khol and mascara, glossed her lips orange, and ran her fingers through her spiky, copper hair. She put on a dress she had both designed and made, which had an exceedingly short red skirt and a high-necked black velvet bodice slit to the lumbar vertebrae at the back. She hung heavy enamel discs from her ears, one green, one orange, snapped a matching bracelet onto her wrist (the whole ensemble matching the peppers) and had just taken her narrow black suede shoes from the cupboard when the telephone rang.

Assuming that it was Freddie, she said: 'Where are you?'

'Is that Jane?'

It was Margaret Sitwell.

'I'm frightfully sorry, my dear, I know it's last minute, but I'm afraid we have to let you down . . .'

Damn! If the Sitwells were not coming it was going to throw her table out.

'Gordon's just rung me from the car. He says we're not going to be able to make it. An urgent meeting has cropped up and he won't be home till late. He sends his apologies.'

Standing on one leg as she put on her shoe, Jane thought that if she moved Bingo round to the other side of the table and shoved everybody up one . . .

'I had my hair done specially . . .'

Georgina would have to sit beside her. Two women next to each other.

'. . . And I've got a little something for Freddie.'

'How very kind.'

'I do hope he likes it. I'll give it to Gordon. He

can take it to the bank in the morning. And please
forgive us.'

Poor Margaret, she sounded disappointed.

'Of course.' Jane wriggled her foot into her second
shoe.

'Say happy birthday to Freddie for me.'

'I will. He was looking forward to seeing you. Give
Gordon my love.'

She was looking out of the window for Freddie's car
when the telephone rang again.

'Freddie?' Lilli's voice was plaintive.

'It's Jane.'

'Where's Freddie?'

'That's what I'd like to know.'

'The dinner's getting spoiled.'

'What dinner?'

'He has dinner with me every Tuesday . . .'

'It's Monday, Lilli.'

'Are you sure?'

'Absolutely.'

'If you say so, Jane.'

Hearing the slam of the front door as she put the phone
down on a bewildered Lilli, Jane leaned over the banisters
and, thinking it must be Freddie, waited for the thud of his
briefcases on the parquet, the signal that he was home.

'Darling?'

'It's me, Lavender.'

Beginning to get worried, Jane ran downstairs to await
her guests.

Robert Gould was the first to arrive. In the drawing-
room Jane introduced herself to him and prised the bottle
he was carrying from his chubby hand.

'W-w-w-where's Freddie?'

The young man seemed extremely agitated, presumably
at the idea of being set up with Caroline Hurst, and judging

by the way he kept turning his head over his shoulder, as if Freddie might appear at any moment from behind the curtains, appeared to have a nervous tic.

'Freddie isn't home yet,' Jane said. 'I don't suppose you've seen him?'

'I w-w-w-work in b-b-banking. M-m-m-my office is on a d-d-different floor.'

Jane gave him a drink and complimented him on his tie – which was striped and rather ordinary – to put him at his ease, then sat him down on the sofa. Nodding sympathetically at appropriate moments as he poured out his heart to her about the financial demands which were still being made upon him by his ex-wife, a subject clearly dear to his heart, she listened for the sound of Freddie's key in the door.

Piers Warburton, more taciturn than usual, and the exotic Alex, whose habit of flinging her exceedingly thick mane of wavy brown hair back over her shoulder every few minutes was often unnerving, were the next to arrive. Judging by their faces they had had one of their frequent slanging matches in the car. 'Where's Freddie?' Piers kissed Jane while Alex plonked a magnum of champagne down on the table and moved ostentatiously to the far end of the room.

'That's what I'd like to know.'

Jane mixed a Screwdriver for Alex and poured a tomato juice for Piers as Bingo Ingoldsby, wearing a satin bustier – followed by an adoring Charles carrying a yard of Bendicks Bittermints, Freddie's favourites, and looking as if he had just won first prize in a raffle – ran breathlessly up the stairs.

'Where's the birthday boy, then?' Bingo embraced Jane before, trailing a cloud of Opium, she moved on to the other guests and kissed them – including a blushing Robert Gould – enthusiastically on both cheeks.

Jane had put Charles in charge of the drinks tray by the time James and Dos – the silicone breasts displayed to advantage in gold lurex – arrived with a Harrods box almost as big as themselves and enquired, with some surprise, where Freddie was. Caroline Hurst, tall, even in flat shoes, and not unattractive, sidled in wearing an unflattering haircut and an excess of blusher on her aquiline face. Making no comment about the absence of her host, she singled out her blind date at once and accepting a gin and tonic – which Jane suspected was not her first – from Charles, stayed well away from Robert.

The conversation – precipitated by the appearance of Peter and Georgina from next door – about how those who lived nearest were habitually the least punctual, while guests from a distance were always on time, was interrupted by the noisy arrival of Freddie, who burst into the room with his hair awry, his jacket over his shoulder and his tie dangling from his pocket.

As, apologising for his lateness, he embraced the women and hugged the men, thumping them amicably on the back as he did so, Jane was immediately alerted that something was wrong. When to everyone's amusement – they thought that Freddie was acting – he pulled her into his arms, breathed brandy into her orange mouth, and slid a hand down the back of her dress, she realised that he was drunk. Alarmed, she followed him upstairs and hammered on the locked door of the bathroom. As she called his name, she could not be certain if he really had not heard her or if her voice was drowned by the Credo from *Otello* and the running water of the shower.

With his worry beads working overtime, Freddie was back on his usual form at dinner. Jane dismissed her fears as unfounded and his over-the-top performance as due to a stressful day at the bank, probably followed by a celebration at the City Cellar of his defence of

Corinthian Hotels, and concentrated on the smooth running of her party.

While Tracey, in her Fortnum's uniform, passed the dishes, Freddie attended to the wine. He was an exemplary host. He flirted with a delighted Bingo, laughed at James's stories as if he were hearing them for the first time, and, as he went round the table refilling the glasses, put reassuring arms round Robert and Caroline, who seemed acutely uncomfortable with each other and able to manage very little in the way of conversation.

The appearance of Jane's marinated pepper salad gave a kick-start to the evening which was assisted by Freddie's Minervois. By the time they had finished the *poulets de Bresse* and Tracey had taken away the plates, the talk had turned to the unreasonable behaviour of Robert's ex-wife, which was apparently his sole topic of conversation, at which Freddie and Jane exchanged 'whose idea was it to ask him?' glances. This was topped by Bingo's hilarious account of how *she* had got her own back on her penultimate husband by ordering gargantuan banquets, paid for with his credit card, to be delivered every night to the home he shared with his mistress, which was followed by a discussion about the EMS.

'M&S? What about M&S? That's where I buy my knickers.' Bingo picked up the fag end of the conversation.

'*EMS*, darling. European Monetary System,' Charles said, 'not M&S!'

'In plain English, my sweet,' James said, 'we will soon be swapping our ten-pound notes for ECU coins which can be used as legal tender from the north of Germany to the south of Spain.'

Piers sipped his Perrier water with distaste. 'It doesn't just mean the scrapping of individual currencies. It means loss of control. If the Germans raise their interest rates, the UK must follow. If the European Central Bank puts its rates up by 2 per cent at a time when UK unemployment is high, it's going to affect us far more than a country with plenty of jobs. Am I right, Freddie?'

Freddie was filling the glasses with Beaune in expectation of the cheese. He was, Jane thought, drinking far more than usual, and appeared not to have heard.

'There is a price to pay for everything,' Peter Cottesloe began deliberately, as if he were debating the subject in the Lords. 'Stability of exchange rates may be the overwhelming advantage of joining the ERM, but by keeping our exchange rate stable, we will lose the freedom to move our interest rates according to our domestic economy . . .'

The arrival of the cheeseboard, which was not a board at all but a circular marble platter weighing over three kilos – which Tracey put on the table in front of Robert – distracted Peter from his homily.

Robert, unfamiliar with Jane's monstrous talking point, attempted to pick the cheeseboard up by its handsome brass handle and almost dropped it as he attempted to hold it for Caroline, who took one look at the Brie and shook her head.

'Women who do not like cheese are frigid . . .' James said.

The conversation came to an embarrassed halt.

'. . . That is not to say that all frigid women do not like cheese.'

Everyone avoided looking at the unfortunate Caroline, as James explained that this particular form of reasoning, in which from two given or assumed propositions a third is deduced from which the middle term is absent, was known as a syllogism.

'Because all the women who come from a certain part of Russia have red hair, one is not to assume, for example, that all women with red hair come from Russia . . .'

In an effort to unseat her husband from his hobbyhorse –

James was passionate about the English language, polished off *The Times* crossword before breakfast, and would have gone on all night – Dos interrupted with a toast.

'To the end of this unspeakable recession.'

Georgina, whose wine business was bumping along the bottom, raised her glass. 'You can say that again!'

'I'm very much afraid that the end is nowhere in sight.' Piers, on the receiving end of the cheeseboard, put on his half-glasses to examine the Brie. 'A thousand jobs are going down the drain every day. Half my customers are in some kind of difficulty and the worst is by no means over.' He cut a triangle of cheese. 'Redundancy used to be something that happened to other people. Someone in the north-east, some smart aleck who had priced himself out of the market ...' He speared the piece of Brie on his knife. 'Now it's hitting everyone, in every occupation, in every industry, in every part of the country, at every level. No one is safe. Even *senior* executives are, as they say in France ...' Piers put the knife into his mouth '... being "handed their aprons".'

James, who was in the building industry, had seen the recession coming. By cutting costs, working capital, and capacity, he had managed not only to stay afloat, but to avoid the massive write-downs and spiralling interest charges which had floored so many of his rivals. He refilled his glass from the bottle on the table and leaned back in his leopard-skin chair.

'Have you heard the one about the property tycoon stuck with land which had fallen in value and who was on the verge of bankruptcy? "Things are going from bad to worse," he said to his wife one night in bed. "If only you were a good cook we could manage without the housekeeper." "Sweetie-pie," came the retort, "if only you were a good fuck we could do without the chauffeur!"'

Amid the laughter, Georgina, who was holding on to

her wine business by the skin of her teeth, and who didn't much care for James, said: 'It's no joke, James. People like you don't know what it's like in the real world. My ex-accountant is now a Saturday night shelf-filler, and his wife – she used to have her own estate agency – has started car booting. I had to let one of my own managers go last week. A married man with a whacking great mortgage and four young children, one of them handicapped. It isn't funny to have the door slammed in your face when you're too old to get another job. It was one of the hardest things I've ever had to do. At first he didn't believe me, then he got angry and called me every name in the book. After that he just crumpled up. Slumped in the chair. As if he'd been punched in the gut. And . . . cried!'

There was an awkward silence interrupted by Jane who jumped up to dim the lights. The birthday cake, with its forty pin-points of flickering light, was brought in and set before Freddie. Bingo gave him the serrated knife and put her hand over his, holding it aloft over the candles.

'Make a wish!'

Make a wish, Freddie. Make a wish. Year after year, urged on by Lilli, Freddie had wished that his father would come back, and later for a bicycle with three-speed gears. Despite the fact that he had shut his eyes tightly as instructed by his mother, and kept his promise not to tell a soul, neither dream had come true. Blowing out the candles, he plunged the knife into the soft icing.

'Happy birthday, darling!' Jane said.

'To the future chairman of Sitwell Hunt International.' James raised his glass. 'The smart money's on you, boy!'

'Speech!' Bingo put an arm round Freddie's shoulders.

Freddie stood up and filled his glass with champagne. 'I would like to thank you all for coming, and tell you how much I love you, and value your friendship . . .'

James mimed a maudlin violin to the hummed tune

of an Indian love lyric, 'Pale hands I loved beside the Shalimar'.

'Do shut up, James,' Dos said.

Unsteady on his feet, Freddie looked round at the expectant faces of his friends which refused to focus; Piers with his Perrier, Georgina with her pearls, Charles with his catch, Bingo with her bustier, James with his cigar, Dos with her bosom, Robert with his tic, Caroline with her blusher. At the far end of the table his wife's features danced.

Jane wondered anxiously what he was going to come out with. Freddie caught her eye. They all jumped as, unexpectedly, he hurled his glass into the black marble fireplace.

'Sod the recession!'

Upstairs in the drawing-room Freddie's aberration was not referred to. The conversation drifted back to the economy and the collapse of Canary Wharf.

'Bankrupt property developers have always been the signal for the *end* of any economic cycle.' James took a cigar from his pocket. 'Economic downturns historically follow building booms. Look at William Cobbett and his Great Wen. Look at Belgravia and Bayswater. Look at Kensington Palace Gardens. Look at Notting Hill . . .' He concentrated on lighting his cigar. When it was going nicely he pointed it at Freddie who was helping Jane with the coffee. 'Look at the plans for Regent's Park. John Nash had a hell of a time when the speculators pulled out during the Napoleonic wars. The richer the development the more spectacular the bankruptcy. Freddie sees it every day, Freddie will tell you. It's one of the hazards of living in London.'

Freddie did not answer. He handed Georgina her coffee, complimenting her on the Château Suduiraut she had supplied to accompany the birthday cake. Georgina, as he thought she would, launched into a spiel about *Botrytis cinerea*, commonly known as 'noble rot', which guaranteed wine of exceptional quality and which the Sauternes producers prayed for each year.

While she was holding forth, Piers, watched closely by Freddie, followed Jane to the sofa where he sat at her feet and waxed lyrical about the dinner — Alex's idea of a meal was to grab something on the way home and shove it in the microwave — and told her, for the umpteenth time, how great he thought she was. Alex filled them in on the latest royal gossip, while James, who made no secret of the fact that he fancied women who looked like horses (he thought it was a waste of time introducing Caroline to Robert Gould) pinned her to the wall and asked her euphemistically if she would have lunch with him. Dos treated Charles to stories of sybaritic life on the Côte d'Azure and listened in return to how he was trying to persuade Bingo, who absolutely loathed being pregnant, to give him a child of his own.

At two o'clock, Freddie, who could see that none of them had the slightest intention of moving, put on a CD of *I Pagliacci*. When it came to 'La commedia è finita', he turned off the lights abruptly and sent them all home.

Jane, her hands full of glasses, went down to the kitchen to make sure that Lavender and Tracey had put away all the food. Then, unzipping her dress, removing her shoes, and taking off her earrings as she went, she climbed the two flights of stairs to the bedroom to conduct the usual party post-mortem with Freddie.

She wanted to ask him what Gordon Sitwell had had to say about Corinthian; why he hadn't rung her during the afternoon; why he had arrived so late; why he had come home drunk, and the reason for his unwarranted behaviour. To her surprise, although it was no more than fifteen minutes since they had said goodbye to the last of the guests, she found that the bedroom was in darkness and that Freddie, his worry beads in his hand, was already asleep.

CHAPTER TEN

Opening her eyes at eight o'clock to an eerie and unaccustomed silence, Jane realised that not only was there no opera music to assault her ears but that Freddie was still in bed. She tried to remember the last time he had not woken at six and put on his jogging gear.

'Freddie.' Jane put a hand on his shoulder. 'It's eight o'clock. Time to get up. You've overslept.'

'Leave me alone.'

'Is anything the matter? Are you ill?'

Freddie did not believe in illness. When the children were young and had produced nebulous complaints to keep them home from school, he had packed them off, overruling Jane who was inclined to give them the benefit of the doubt. When Rosina was 11 she had woken with a stomach ache, swearing melodramatically that 'men with swords' and 'great balls of fire' were attacking her entrails. After a battle of wills, Freddie had hauled her out of bed, stood by while she dressed, and delivered her personally into the hands of her teacher. Three hours later, to Freddie's eternal shame, Rosina was in hospital with a ruptured appendix. Jane was already out of bed and struggling into her dressing-gown.

'I'd better wake Rosina.'

When Jane had left the room, Freddie opened his eyes.

He could not move his right hand. Thinking at first that he was in the grip of some paralysis, he realised that instead of leaving his worry beads on the table by the bed as usual, he had fallen asleep clutching them. Painfully, like the sensation which slowly returned to his numbed fingers, the memories of the previous day returned to him.

Denise, the compliance director, had stood patiently by the door of his office as he packed up his personal possessions and handed over his security pass. Sacked employees had been known to appropriate files in the hope of seducing influential clients away from the bank, and the official surveillance was par for the course. There was nothing personal about it. Considering that Susan was part of his management team and had been in his confidence for so many years, Freddie was not surprised when the personnel department sent for her.

She returned, five minutes later, white-faced.

'You too?'

Susan nodded and blew her nose. Unable to speak, she had searched for an old briefcase into which Freddie could put the miscellaneous contents of his drawers – some of it long lost to memory – the oakum of his existence of the past five years. All she had managed to come up with was a couple of Waitrose carrier bags into which he had put his photograph of Jane, his leather desk set, his personal stationery, Rosina's psychedelic pyramid, his birthday cards and presents, while Susan, struggling to hold back the tears, had consigned the flowers she had bought that morning from a barrow, to the waste-paper basket, and packed her pressed-powder compact and her muesli bars and her Fisherman's Friends into empty A4 boxes.

As he unhooked his pictures from the wall, unplugged his desk lamp, rescued his blue-and-orange golf umbrella (which he had brought to the office when Leonard was off sick and it had been raining), Freddie thought that it was as if someone had died. As if Gordon Sitwell had killed him.

Bidding goodbye to the stunned Susan, promising to keep in touch, ignominiously carrying his supermarket carriers, watched with curiosity by Travers, his second in command, he had said goodbye to no one. In no mood to exchange pleasantries with Leonard, he had taken the lift to the underground garage where he had got into the Mercedes and driven up the ramp into the almost deserted street. Too profoundly shocked to notice where he was going, and with no recollection of how he had got there, two hours later he had found himself in Brighton. Turning left at the pier and parking the car by the green railings of the promenade, he had scrunched his way in his city shoes onto the deserted beach where, oblivious to time passing, he sat on the stones, throwing pebbles into the sea. Too numbed, for the moment, to confront the raw wound of his dismissal, he considered his financial situation and, as the stones ricocheted over the dingy waves to sink inexorably into the spume-flecked ocean, made a mental list of his assets.

He had borrowed £600,000 to buy the £850,000 house in Chester Terrace. A few months ago, Porchester Bank – where he maintained a personal overdraft in excess of £100,000 (secured by a second mortgage) – worried by the downturn in the economy, had carried out an informal valuation on his home. Far from his investment having doubled, as five years ago it had been pretty safe to predict, the Nash house was found to be worth no more than the £600,000 which was still outstanding on the first mortgage. Presuming that he was able to find a buyer for it in the almost stagnant market, the proceeds of any sale would be immediately swallowed up by the finance company which had serviced his mortgage. The house was not an asset but a liability and 'negative equity'

– owning a house worth less than it cost – no longer just a bad dream. Five years ago, he was not the only one not to have foreseen the recession, not the only one to have totally misread the signs.

The fact that the Porchester Bank was now uncovered had prompted the manager, Derek Abbott, to write to Freddie at fortnightly intervals suggesting, politely but firmly, that he not only reduce his overdraft, but refrain from writing any more large cheques. Secure in his position at Sitwell Hunt with its substantial salary, supplemented by performance-related bonuses, and with his future chairmanship of the bank on Gordon Sitwell's retirement in two years' time very much in mind, Freddie had ignored the bank manager's letters.

After paying tax at 40 per cent on a portion of his package from Sitwell Hunt, the amount with which he would be left would leave him with insufficient funds even to repay the bank. The situation was extremely serious. His one ray of hope was Universal Concrete with which he hoped to bail himself out.

He was wondering just how he was going to tell Jane what had happened, and getting quite good at the stones, when a slack-bellied, grey-haired woman, wearing a black bathing suit and white swimming cap, making her cautious way alongside the nearby breakwater, reminded him of how as a terrified schoolboy, he had broken the news to Lilli of the loss of his brand new raincoat, which had cost her a week's tuition fees. On his return from an educational day trip to Calais, the outburst with which he had greeted his mother, before she could open her mouth to say a word, had become firmly embedded in the family archive.

'We had breakfast on the boat eggs and beans and sausages and went up on deck and the wind came up gale force eight and the sea got rough and everyone was sick spew spew nothing but spew even the teachers and when we got to Calais we walked round the town the old city and the harbour was destroyed in the war then we went on a coach to Boulogne to see where Julius Caesar set out with 800 boats to conquer the English and Bonaparte tried to invade England with flat-bottomed boats only Nelson saved the day and we had lunch but nobody ate it and I bought you an ashtray with Calais on it I know you don't smoke but it was all I could find and we played cricket on the beach and I lost my raincoat and then we had to get the coach again and nearly missed the boat because we couldn't find Oliver and Mr Holmes was doing his pieces he got on the wrong coach but it wasn't his fault it was the same colour although we had to remember the number . . .'

It was not until the following morning, when he was about to leave for school, that the loss of the raincoat, bought, he remembered, humiliatingly long in the length and in the sleeves for economy's sake, had sunk in. He could hardly employ the same tactics with Jane.

The woman had left her white towel and her flip-flops by the water's edge and was proceeding with infinite slowness towards the horizon in a measured breaststroke. Freddie toyed with the idea of following the swimmer out to sea. Only he would not come back. His discarded clothes would be found by the police. Jane could collect on his life insurance. She would be well-provided for. She could get married again – Piers Warburton had made no secret of his passion for her – there was nothing to worry about on that score.

A pang of hunger reminded him that he had had nothing to eat since breakfast. Stiff from sitting on the damp stones, he returned to the car. In the boot he found the liquor canteen, which Leonard kept topped up for clients, and took a swig from the brandy. Taking the flask with him, he got into the driver's seat and, to the drums and the trumpets of *The Damnation of Faust*, made his way back to London. Conjuring up the disappearance of the cross, the dangling skeletons, the hideous and bestial phantasmagoria of Faust's descent to hell, he considered his own damnation. He did not need Gordon to remind him of the current job losses in the financial sector. Restructuring and rationalisation were terms he had himself used when weeding out junior staff. Convinced of his invincibility, he had had no reason to believe that they would ever be applied to him.

He was not exactly drunk. The brandy was still half full. Or half empty. It depended which way you looked at it. He was doing a steady 70 m.p.h. in the middle lane of the M23 when an audacious red Ferrari overtook him. Leonard kept the Mercedes in good nick. He tinkered with the engine for hours at a time, improving its performance. Freddie took another gulp from the flask, put his foot down, and pulled out into the fast lane. Catching up with the Ferrari he flashed his lights at the driver who took no notice. Freddie flashed again, this time switching the headlights to full beam. The brake lights of the Ferrari flickered for an instant although the car did not reduce speed. It was an old trick. Freddie did not fall for it. Taking a calculated risk, he overtook the Ferrari on the nearside, cutting in ahead of it and assuming the lead. With a glance at Freddie, the driver, who wore leather gloves, accelerated, forcing Freddie to do likewise. At 110 m.p.h., keeping an eye on his rear-view mirror, Freddie drained the last of the brandy. A sense of euphoria overtook him. It was as good a way to go as any. The Ferrari had no intention of letting him get away with it. It came up uncomfortably close behind him. Freddie refused to yield. Taking a leaf out of his book, the driver in the leather gloves overtook on the inside and drew level with him. Neck and neck at 120, 130, 140 m.p.h. . . . Freddie forgot about his dismissal, about Sitwell Hunt. He accelerated hard. The Mercedes swayed.

The Ferrari hooted. Freddie returned the compliment. The sequence of events became blurred. The two drivers kept up the pressure, now overtaking, now steering dangerously close. Imagining it was the Grand Prix, a circuit at Le Mans, Freddie amended and revised his tactics until, to his disappointment, the Ferrari peeled off abruptly at the last junction with what he thought was the indolent wave of a gloved hand.

Reducing speed as he approached the end of the motor-way, Freddie consigned Faust to the flames. He slid a new cassette into the slot and as the overture to *The Marriage of Figaro* – assisted by the brandy – restored his faith in the untrammelled joy of existence, he removed his tie, beat time to the admonition of the basses which was echoed by the violins, and headed for home and his birthday party.

CHAPTER ELEVEN

Freddie's failure to rouse the household with his morning choice of opera had made Rosina late for her rehearsal. When she dashed into the bedroom to say goodbye and ask him for fifty pounds to buy some spandex Gaultier leggings after school, he was still in bed. He was still there when Jane appeared with the present from James and Dos, a life-sized teddy bear, sporting a bow tie and a badge declaring 'I am 40', which she stood in the corner. Freddie was not amused.

Thinking that he must be suffering from the aftereffects of the party – although she had never seen Freddie with a hangover – Jane asked him whether he would like some coffee, and whether, since it was now, incredibly, getting on for 9.30, he would like her to call Susan at the bank. Drawing a negative on both counts, she shrugged and went downstairs.

When she had gone, Freddie returned to the small print of the previous day which, although he had feigned sleep, had kept him awake, like a recurring mantra, into the small hours. His unsuspecting 'La donna è mobile' and his conversation with Conrad Verger, the colours of Rosina's pyramid on his desk, Wichmann with his promise of a new and important deal, the brief meeting with Gordon and its unexpected denouement. He attempted to imbue the events with meaning but none of it was real.

The same detachment, the ability to disassociate himself from painful feelings, had marked the summer's day when he was 6, when in graphic slow motion his father had collapsed within a few yards of his eyes. Although Hugh Lomax had lain spreadeagled on the freshly mown lawn, peculiarly still, the cricket ball still clutched in his hand as if he was about to bowl, Freddie had refused to believe, even after the doctor had arrived and confirmed that he was dead, that he would not get up again. He could not accept that his father would not correct his grip, would not tap the stumps into the ground with the bat, would not fling his arms excitedly into the air, twirling round on his toes, with his excited and triumphant cry of 'Howzat!', the exultant sound of which he could still hear clearly in his head. Thirty-four years had been insufficient to suspend disbelief. Sometimes, even now, when he saw fathers and sons together in the street, by some trick of the imagination he managed to disregard the passage of time and convince himself that *his* father was still alive, not an old man, but exactly as he remembered him. By the same process of denial, he blotted out the sequence of events in Gordon's office and managed to convince himself that any moment now he would get out of bed, take a shower, send for Leonard, and make his way as usual to the bank. The futility of attempting to think otherwise was making him ill.

Jane was putting the remains of Freddie's birthday cake into the freezer – it would do nicely for her next committee meeting – when Gordon Sitwell rang.

'I just wanted to apologise, on behalf of Margaret and myself . . .' Gordon said. 'I hear the dinner party was a great success. I understand Freddie was in good form.'

'Freddie is always in good form.'

'I'm extremely glad to hear he's coping so well.' Gordon sounded surprised.

'He did have something to celebrate,' Jane said.

'Celebrate?'

'Successfully defending Corinthian meant a lot to Freddie. And then of course there was his birthday. I'm afraid Freddie's still in bed. He appears to be taking the day off.'

'Taking the day off!'

'I think he had a little too much to drink . . .'

'I rather think that you had better have a word with Freddie.'

'About what?'

'About . . . Look, Jane. Actually I'm in a meeting. I'm afraid I have to go.'

After Gordon had hung up, Jane went over the conversation carefully – in case she had missed anything – in her head. When Lavender enquired what she should do with the last of the grilled peppers, she did not hear. She was on her way up the stairs.

'That was Gordon on the phone.'

Freddie closed his eyes. Sliding his hand from beneath the covers he located his worry beads.

'He said I should have a word with you.' Jane sat down on the bed. 'Freddie, what's going on?'

He wanted to tell her. He had to tell her.

'Leave me alone, darling.'

'If that's what you want. I'll be downstairs if you need anything.'

'Jane . . .'

How could he tell her that he no longer existed? That the man she saw before her was a facsimile only? That the real Freddie Lomax was dead?

'I'll tell Lavender to hold the hoovering,' Jane said.

Freddie slept on and off all day. Each time he opened his

eyes he met the glassy stare of the teddy bear which seemed deliberately to mock him. He could not bring himself to get up. There was nothing to get up for.

When Jane, who was becoming increasingly worried, came into the bedroom to announce that it was six o'clock, and remind him that it was Tuesday and that he was due at his mother's, Freddie was in the bathroom. His worry beads were on his pillow.

Picking them up, still warm from his grasp, she slid the amber stones through her fingers, their hypnotic click-click taking her back to the poppy-strewn island of Crete where they had spent ten blissful days.

Leaving the baby Tristan with Lilli, they had rented a lamp-lit room in a whitewashed villa set amongst lemon and eucalyptus trees, figs and oleanders which grew untended in the red soil of a sloping garden. While, in the mornings, Jane lay like a lizard on the rocks, her straw hat over her eyes, her delicate skin protected from the sun, listening to the drone of the giant bumblebees, Freddie swam, with his rhythmical crawl, through the tideless waters of the Mediterranean. When he grew restless, which did not take long, Jane took him sightseeing. The Palace of King Minos, the Archaeological Museum – with its ancient 'deads' buried in the embryonic position – where they tried not to laugh at the fractured English of the guide. The afternoons, in the cool of the flagstoned bedroom, with its old Dutch maps and hand-woven rugs, were spent sleeping and making love.

But it was only at night, in the taverna, that Freddie had really come alive. After selecting their meal – *taraba* and pilaf – from saucepans simmering away in the kitchen, they would sit over thimbles of dark sweet coffee while they waited for the sound of the first guitar, the signal for Freddie to lead Jane onto the floor. They both loved dancing. Carried away by the rough Santa Laura, or the

Demestica with which they had washed down their dinner, shoulder to shoulder with the black-booted, moustachioed men of the village – Freddie towering above them – they would dance the night away, until, with the bouzouki music at full, exuberant throttle, cheered on by the noisy Cretans, the striking English couple revolved expertly and alone to the crescendo of the increasingly frenetic tempo in the raucous midst of a stomping and wildly enthusiastic applauding circle.

It was their last carefree holiday. As Freddie struggled to climb the banking ladder, any vacation since had been spent within easy reach not of figs or flame trees, but of English language newspapers and of the telephone, which kept him in touch with the world markets and with his affairs. The odd-numbered *komboloi*, such as was carried by every self-respecting man on the island, which Jane had bought for Freddie on their last day (Freddie had sneaked into the village and bought her a crocheted dress and a gold mask of Agamemnon), had become his *sine qua non*. The worry beads were slid surreptitiously from his pocket in moments of stress, and the reassuring touch of them both helped him to relax and eased the tensions of the day.

Swinging the *komboloi* from her fingers, Jane tapped on the dressing-room door.

'Freddie?'

The door opened. Freddie was in his bathrobe. She thought that he looked pale.

'Jane . . .'

'Freddie, what is the matter with you?'

'Nothing.' Stepping out of the dressing-room he pulled her roughly to him. 'Come to bed.'

'Now?'

'Any reason why not?'

'It's six o'clock, Freddie. Your mother . . .'

'Tell Rosina to go. Tell her to say I'm sick. Tell her to take a taxi. And, Jane . . .'

Jane thought there was desperation in Freddie's voice. She turned at the door.

'. . . don't be long.'

When Jane came back into the bedroom Freddie was standing by the window, twirling the worry beads and staring out across the park.

'It's okay. Rosina's going to Lilli's.'

'I don't want to talk about Rosina. I don't want to talk.'

Slipping out of her clothes, Jane opened Freddie's bathrobe and leaned her white body with its fine alabaster skin against him. When he dropped the bathrobe and took her in his arms, bending to put his open mouth over hers, he held her so tightly, so intensely that she was afraid he would crush the breath out of her. She remembered, as in another country, hearing the slam of the front door as Rosina left the house, then turned her attention to Freddie and the next half-hour which was to become etched like some recurring nightmare on her memory.

Rosina got on well with Lilli and visited her as often as possible. She liked to listen, on her grandmother's more lucid days, to her stories of how she had played the piano for concerts – before Rosina's father was born – and for Old Time Dancing and her description of the dresses, and the movies she had made, and the film stars she had met, and of the time she had accompanied Harry Secombe and Tommy Steele.

Tonight, not in the least bothered that it was Rosina who had appeared on the doorstep rather than Freddie – she rather thought that she had missed Tuesday – Lilli's thoughts were concentrated on her own demise. She liked talking to Rosina. Only with Rosina, who did not discourage her 'when I'm gone' conversations which made Freddie uncomfortable, who did not deny her feelings about death and tell her not to be so silly, did Lilli open up.

They were sharing a large bag of liquorice allsorts which Rosina was unable to resist but which she knew would not only spoil her appetite for the shepherd's pie Mrs Williams was preparing, but would play havoc with her spots.

'It must be nice not to have to worry about spots.'

'It must be nice to be of an age to have to worry.'

'What's it feel like to be old?'

Lilli rummaged in the allsorts bag searching for a round black one with a white middle.

'The same as it feels to be young. Until you look in the mirror.'

'I mean being at the end of your life?'

'I'd like to see Hugh again. I wonder what he looks like. I've been a widow for a very long time.'

'Do you believe in all that?'

'All what?'

'Seeing Grandpa again and all that stuff?'

'Not really.'

'Can you cope with that?'

'You don't have to cope with it. You just have to accept it. Sometimes I think that the world is too complicated. That it can't really exist if there's nothing else. Then I don't know. I shall find out before very long.'

'If you want to know what I think,' Rosina said, 'I think we just fall off the tree. Like leaves. You can't get all worked up over a dead leaf. Do you believe in God?'

'We were not allowed *not* to believe when I was a child. Not any more.'

'Funny.' Rosina helped herself to a pink and white rectangle. She nibbled at the sugar until she was left with a liquorice square. 'One minute you're here, and the next minute you're not. Spooky.'

'One does get extremely tired at my age, Rosina. Sometimes I quite look forward to it. Sometimes I think it will be quite a relief . . .'

Rosina took Lilli's ruby engagement ring from her deformed finger and put it on the fourth finger of her left hand, twisting and turning the facets to catch the light.

'I'd like to see you married before I go.'

'No way! Did you know I have a boyfriend? His name's Henry Dove.'

'Shall you marry him?'

'Marry! People don't get married.'

'A good marriage, Rosina. A good marriage is like a beautiful piece of music. All that carrying-on on television under those vulgar duvets! Settled down then. A nice young man . . .'

'I shan't settle down for yonks.'

'I shall be kicking up the daisies.'

'Probably.'

'I've left you my engagement ring . . .' Lilli's eyes glazed over. 'A shop near Piccadilly. Bond Street. Or Chancery Lane. I remember he had a glass eye. They had a necklace in the window. Something to do with Queen Mary. She wore a toque, you know. Toque. Not a word one comes across these days. I asked the little girl in the Indian shop for doilies. She had no idea what I was talking about. It was the same when Mrs Thingamajig wanted capers. For her mutton. It's not really mutton. We used to have *proper* butchers' shops. Offal. Hugh loved offal. They told her to try household. I don't suppose you've ever seen a lump of coal . . .'

Rosina put the ring back on Lilli's finger.

'Aren't you afraid of dying, Grandma? I wonder what it's like.'

'Much the same as being born, I expect. I dare say one won't even know.'

Freddie lay in the king-sized bed, his eyes fixed on the wall, his back turned to Jane. His inability to make love to her – not even once – for the first time in his life, outdid the ignominy of his dismissal.

'Freddie, it doesn't matter.' Jane tried to comfort him.

'Doesn't matter!' His body no longer belonged to him. Like his life, it was no longer under his control.

'Would you like me to bring you some dinner? You've had nothing to eat all day.'

'I don't want any dinner. There's something we have to discuss.'

'I thought there might be.'

'What's the worst scenario you can imagine . . .?' The worry beads were working overtime.

'You mean like . . . fraud?' Jane was frightened. There had been a recent spate of scandals amongst the higher echelons in the City. The newspapers had been full of it.

'Worse.'

'Insider dealing?'

Freddie wished that it was.

Jane sat up. She took a deep breath. 'Another woman?'

'I am no longer vice chairman of Sitwell Hunt International.'

'Sorry?'

'It's simple enough. I have been "handed my apron". I do not have a job. I am redundant. Unemployed.'

'You mean that Gordon . . .? I don't understand, Freddie. What happened? What went wrong?'

'Nothing went wrong. Put it down to the recession. Gordon didn't give a reason. He doesn't have to give a reason.'

'I can't believe I'm hearing this . . .' Her conversation

with Gordon suddenly became clear to her. She reached for Freddie's hand. Freddie withdrew it. He did not want her to touch him.

'I owe £600,000 on this house, which is now worth only £600,000. I have a £100,000 plus overdraft. I have not paid the school fees – I was waiting for the Corinthian bonus. I presume you're overdrawn as usual on the housekeeping. I have at least £25,000 worth of bills outstanding. We will be completely wiped out.'

'They can't do this to you, Freddie!'

'I'm sorry, Jane. They have.'

CHAPTER TWELVE

Jane's disbelief had given way to a rare anger. It was directed at Gordon.

'What right has he got', she said, over a dinner of leftovers from the party for which she had persuaded Freddie to come down to the kitchen, 'to pull the rug from someone who has not only given five loyal, faithful, committed, years to Sitwell Hunt International, but who has been personally responsible for introducing so many valuable clients to the bank? What right has he got to *use* you,' she removed Freddie's plate and scraped the untouched food into the waste disposal, 'and then have the effrontery to ring up and *speak* to me as if nothing had happened, as if firing you was the most natural thing in the world? I've a good mind to drive out to Tall Trees and rip up his precious roses. Give him a piece of my mind.'

'What good would that do?'

'*Me*. Not Gordon. You'll get another job.'

'Let's hope so.' Freddie's voice was flat.

Although he was still reeling, he had no doubt that within the next few weeks, with a bit of judicious networking amongst senior executives, he would be snapped up by the banking industry or some other suitable organisation eager to benefit from his knowledge and expertise.

They were sitting silently at the table – Freddie's plate

of green fruit salad pushed to one side – when Rosina, returning from Lilli's, slammed the front door. Coming into the kitchen, she looked from Freddie to Jane.

'What's up with you two? It's like a morgue in here.' She put her arms round Freddie's neck. 'You know the Gaultier leggings I was telling you about this morning? Well, there's a shrink-wrap body-hugger that goes with them. Azzedine Alaïa. You get them at Browns. Please, Daddy?'

'Forget it.'

'Daddy . . .'

'I said forget it!' Freddie spoke more forcefully than he had intended.

With his daughter gawping at him in amazement, he went upstairs, leaving Jane to break the news.

He was in his dressing-room, playing, but not listening to, *Stiffelio*, when Rosina knocked on the door.

'Daddy . . .?'

Freddie looked through her. She might have been a stranger. 'About the Azzedine Alaïa . . .' Rosina said.

Freddie held out his arms. He hadn't meant to shout at her.

'. . . don't even think about it.' There were tears in Rosina's eyes as she flung herself against him, presenting Freddie with a mouthful of hair. 'I don't even want a body-hugger, Daddy. I've completely changed my mind.'

Jane's insomnia matched Freddie's. Restless, they turned this way and that all night, unable to comfort each other. When Freddie got out of bed at 6.00 a.m. and put on his jogging gear, Jane knew it was to keep up appearances. She pretended to be asleep.

George, the postman, was waiting outside the house as Freddie, on automatic pilot, completed his circuit.

'Everything all right then, Mr Lomax?' Not waiting for an answer, he handed Freddie his letters.

'Mustn't grumble.'

It was the understatement of the year.

Freddie broke the news to Tristan himself, waiting for ten minutes for his son, who was at breakfast, to come to the school telephone.

'Dad?' Tristan groaned. 'I'm really sorry. I completely forgot. Well, I didn't actually forget because Mummy reminded me. I even bought a card. An angler in waders. I know you don't fish. It was that or mice. Then with all the fuss about Robert's trainer I forgot to post it. Well, actually I didn't have a stamp.'

'That's par for the course.'

'I didn't forget on purpose, Dad.'

'Naturally, Tristan. You never do. In any case I didn't phone about the birthday card.'

'Then it *is* about Robert's trainer. Jeremy promised not to tell.'

Freddie was mystified. Jeremy was the headmaster.

'Tell what?'

'About Robert's trainer,' Tristan said patiently.

'What about Robert's trainer?'

'I shot it with an air gun. It sort of collapsed. It wasn't my fault. It was a dare. They were new this term. Robert's father is doing his number. They cost a hundred nicker –'

'I know nothing whatever about Robert's trainer,' Freddie said. 'I'm not the slightest bit interested in Robert's trainer, Tristan. I rang you because ... I wanted to tell you. I thought you ought to know ... Just in case you happen to hear ... It's about Sitwell Hunt, Tristan. About the bank. I am no longer vice chairman.'

'Oh!' Tristan sounded relieved.

'I have been made redundant.'

'Jesus! Does that mean I have to leave school?' Tristan's voice rose expectantly at the prospect.

'Not at the moment.'

There was a long silence as Freddie's announcement sank in.

'I'm sorry, Dad. I don't know what to say.'

'You don't have to say anything. I didn't want you to hear it on the grapevine.'

'Is that it then? Someone wants to use the phone.'

'I'll be in touch, Tristan.'

'Cheers then, Dad.'

The full truth of what had happened was brought home to Jane by Leonard who stood uncomfortably on the doorstep with Freddie's briefcases, two supermarket carriers, a desk lamp, and his golf umbrella. Taking off his cap, Leonard followed her into the kitchen and put the things down reverently on the table. It was like a wake.

'I found them in the boot.'

Jane stowed Freddie's things in the cleaning cupboard. She thought it the most tactful thing to do.

Under strict instructions not to divulge his predicament to anyone, she told Lavender, who was surprised that Freddie was still at home when she arrived, that he was taking a few days off. When Lavender crept into the drawing-room – where Freddie was glued to the teletext – with her duster, he nodded, but did not address her. There was no light-hearted chorus of 'Lavender's Blue'.

Leonard was polishing the car when Freddie appeared in his City suit and asked to be taken to Eaton Square. From behind his *Financial Times*, as usual, as if he was on the way to the bank, Freddie addressed his driver.

'No doubt the news has got round, Leonard?'

'Yes, sir.'

'It's been a long time.'

'Five years, sir? I couldn't believe it when Mr Travers told me. Neither could Mollie. I'm extremely sorry, sir.' He turned the car into Euston Road. 'I just wish I could repay you for all you've done for us . . .'

'I may have to come to you, Leonard.' Freddie tried to lighten the conversation.

'We'd be in bed-and-breakfast by now if it wasn't for you, Mr Lomax. I've been assigned to Mr Verger. But if there's anything, anything at all I can do, sir . . .'

'There is something, Leonard. I have your services until the end of the week, I believe.'

'That's correct, sir.'

'There's a client coming over from Frankfurt at the weekend. I'm taking him to Covent Garden on Saturday night. If I can borrow Mr Mitchell's Bentley . . .'

Leonard's eye met his own in the mirror. He was grinning broadly.

'It will be my pleasure, sir.'

Freddie found James in the kitchen of his elegant apartment, struggling with *The Times* crossword as he assembled his muesli.

'Ten across: "Customer takes foreign money with hesitation." Six letters.' James grated an apple into the jumbo oats. '*You* should know that.'

'Haven't a clue.' Freddie had other things on his mind.

James counted out half a dozen pumpkin seeds and put them into the bowl. '"Called for someone with skill to reverse adverse economic situation?" Five and three. No?'

From the brightly lit interior of the outsize fridge he took a carton of orange juice.

'Let's try six down and it might help us with the foreign money. "Clerical garb that's sensible clothing abroad." *Sou*tane!' He pencilled in the word. 'That makes ten across *pun*ters. *Punt*. Italian for pound. Foreign money. Coffee?' He drew up a chair for Freddie.

'If you won't help me with the crossword, perhaps you'd tell me what brings you here at this godforsaken hour when all good bankers should be in their counting houses counting out their money. Last time we had a breakfast meeting was when I walked out on Helen. In every relationship there is a flower and a gardener. Unfortunately Helen and I were both gardeners. Nothing wrong with you and Jane?'

'Everything's fine.'

'Out with it then. Or do you want me to play twenty questions?'

'I've been fired.'

James whistled. 'Pull the other one.'

'I wish I could.'

'When did this happen?'

'On Monday.'

'So that was why Gordon wasn't at your party.'

Helping himself to coffee, Freddie recounted the events of his personal Black Monday followed by a brief resumé of the precarious state of his finances.

'My dear chap! I hope you've run screaming to your lawyer?'

'I'm setting everything up. I wanted you to know. You're the only person, apart from Jane and the children, I've told.'

'Keep it like that. It's not the kind of thing one wants to get about. I must admit I have quite a problem taking it in. You were always the rock, Freddie, the serious one. Pillar of the establishment and all that. My friend the vice chairman . . .' He saw Freddie flinch and changed tack.

'Listen, I know the construction business is not exactly your field. To be perfectly honest, it's hardly anybody's field these days . . .'

'Don't worry about it, James. I'll stick to my last.'

'Nobody knows more about banking than you do, that's for sure.'

Freddie was not only a good financier but a mine of information on the history of banking. He had even written a potted history of Sitwell Hunt International, which was routinely handed out to clients. It explained how private banks had been set up in the eighteenth century, when London had become the capital market centre of the Western world, and had served as deposit takers and lenders to the 'specie traders', while the newly formed Bank of England, with no time for goldsmiths, was busy with the government bonds which financed the national debt. Freddie knew everything there was to know about the City from the days when bulls and bears had been traded in Change Alley (later to become the Stock Exchange), and firmly believed that the essence of a good finance house lay not in the range of services offered, but in the manner in which such services were provided. Confidently predicting a future in which the exploration of space and the progress of technology would provide investors with new scope for gain, it had been his personal dream to take Sitwell Hunt International into the twenty-first century.

'There is something I would very much like to do,' James said slowly. 'Remember Cambridge? That day in the Blue when you snitched Jane from under my nose?'

Freddie recalled the summer's day and Jane, in her panama hat, intimately stroking the dog. 'I'm hardly likely to forget it.'

'Tristan is my godson. Not being much of a church-goer I've never really fulfilled my responsibilities in that direction, apart from the odd christening mug, that is, and one or two Cup Final tickets. Things are going amazingly well for me at the moment. Believe it or not I've just sold my new office building in Basingstoke. I hope you won't take this amiss . . .' James got up from the table. 'I'd like you to let me take care of the school fees. For Tristan *and* Rosina.'

'I wouldn't dream of it.'

'Think about it, Freddie. I look upon those kids as my own.' It was James's one regret that he had never had children. 'There'll be plenty of time to pay me back when you've sorted things out.'

Freddie had to admit that it would be a load off his mind. Having to take Tristan and Rosina away from their respective schools at a crucial time in their education was a frightening thought. Swallowing his pride, he accepted James's offer. It was his first experience of charity.

James put an understanding arm round him. '"Lookers on, many times see more than Gamesters; and the Vale best discovereth the Hill." What's the similarity between Mikhail Gorbachev and an Essex girl?'

Freddie had no idea. James didn't wait for an answer.

'Both get screwed by eight men while on holiday! I just wish there was something I could do to help *you*, old cock.'

'Actually there is.'

He asked James if he could borrow his Bentley to take the Wichmanns to the opera.

'If you have to ask, my dear, you don't deserve it,' James reached for a tray and put a large cup and saucer on it. 'Now if you'll excuse me, I must take Madame her coffee. And, Freddie,' tray in his hands, James turned at the door, 'keep your pecker up.'

CHAPTER THIRTEEN

By the time Freddie called at the Porchester Bank, he had got over his initial shock. Before leaving home, he had managed to ring Susan, who had been on his conscience, and left a message on her answering machine to say that he was just calling to enquire how she was, that he would be in touch again, and that perhaps they could meet up for lunch.

Cooling his heels in the bank anteroom, and feeling like a doctor waiting in his own surgery, he wondered what was keeping Derek Abbott.

'My dear boy!'

A pale man, with pale eyes, Derek Abbott, who lived in Purley and rode a bicycle he had had since the age of ten, shook Freddie's hand and led the way into his office.

'Right, Freddie. This is an unexpected pleasure. What's the problem?'

As if he had not been writing to Freddie about it at regular intervals, as if he were looking at it for the first time, Derek Abbott studied the print-out of Freddie's personal balance sheet which lay in organised readiness on his desk.

Freddie opened his mouth in which there was an unfamiliar dryness. It had been bad enough telling Jane and James. Breaking the news to his bank manager, to whom he was heavily in debt, that he was no longer gainfully employed was infinitely worse.

He was tempted to trump up some excuse for his visit and leave. A drink might have helped. A three o'clock meeting had been a mistake.

'What do you want first, Derek, the good news or the bad?'

'Why don't we start with the bad?'

Freddie took a deep breath. 'I am no longer with Sitwell Hunt.'

Derek Abbott looked up sharply. 'What do you mean?'

'Just that. I have left the bank . . .'

'Left?'

'Okay.' The worry beads came out of Freddie's pocket. 'I was *asked* to leave.'

'For what reason?'

'No reason. Reconstruction. Rationalisation. Forced to reconsider things, et cetera, et cetera.'

'You're not playing silly buggers with me, Freddie?'

'I wish I was.'

'After your success with Corinthian! I can't believe it, Freddie. Give me a minute or two.'

'Take your time.'

'There was no indication . . .?'

'None whatsoever. Totally unexpected. My own theory is that that stupid bloody Gordon is looking to his wimp of a son-in-law. No experience. No personality. He thinks he is running a dynasty. He should check out the facts.'

Derek Abbott seemed visibly shaken. 'You were the last person . . .'

Freddie did not want his commiserations. 'I don't want to rush into anything . . .'

'Of course. That would be most unwise.'

'It could be a couple of months before I find something else. The good news is that I have been promised £130,000.

Six months' salary plus a bonus. As soon as I receive it I shall be able to reduce my overdraft by £50,000 . . .'

Derek Abbott smiled.

'. . . I want you to leave the other £50,000 available to me for one year.'

Freddie had been a banker for long enough to know that the gradual eclipse of the smile, the lack of immediate and positive response to his demand, indicated an immediate down-grading of his status and that he had ceased to be a valued client of the Porchester Bank. Derek Abbott seemed to have some difficulty in meeting his eye.

'That *could* be difficult.'

Freddie remained silent. He did not want to presume upon their long-standing friendship.

'I shall certainly have a word with head office . . .'

A discreet attempt to get himself off the hook.

'I suspect that they might agree to six months.' Derek Abbott had no intention of putting his own job on the line.

'There is, of course, Universal Concrete,' Freddie said.

'Quite so. Your put option. I have a note of it. One hundred thousand shares. I trust you know what you're doing?'

Going short on a share was like backing a horse. It called for strong nerves and the absolute conviction that the market would move in the right direction. Freddie's gamble was based on his knowledge of form. He ignored Derek Abbott's comment.

'The shares should net me sixty or seventy thousand by the end of the account. Things might not be as bad as they look.'

'Let's hope not. For your sake,' Derek screwed the top on his fountain pen. 'Why don't you leave it with me, Freddie? Let me see what I can do?'

The meeting was over. Despite Derek Abbott's almost

imperceptible shift in attitude towards him, Freddie felt encouraged. He had cleared the first hurdle, taken some positive action. Given his situation, and the state of the economic climate, he knew full well that the branch manager was in no position to extend his overdraft facilities for as long as a year. With only six months survival, his family and Lilli to support, he had to get his act together fast.

The offices of Mason, Detroit and Fitch were in High Holborn. Pushing open the swing doors with more force than he had intended, Freddie strode up to the reception desk which was manned by two young ladies both of whom were on the telephone.

'Mason, Detroit and Fitch.' 'Mason, Detroit and Fitch.' 'Mason, Detroit and Fitch.' 'Sorry, Mr Fitch is in a meeting. Can someone else help you?' 'Mason, Detroit and Fitch. Will you hold?'

Managing to capture the attention of the younger of the two, whose mug of unidentifiable beverage steamed on the desk before her, Freddie addressed her.

'I have an appointment –'

'Mason, Detroit and Fitch.'

'– with Mr Mason.'

'Sorry to keep you waiting. Mason, Detroit and Fitch. What did you say your name was?'

'I didn't. Lomax.'

'I have a Mr Lomax at reception for you.'

'The appointment was for four o'clock.'

'Take a seat.'

The girl indicated a sofa. Freddie stood his ground.

'It has gone four.'

'Mason, Detroit and Fitch. Mr Detroit is on the other line and there's a call waiting. Mr Mason knows you're here.'

Freddie did not like waiting. His childhood had been spent waiting. For Lilli to finish her interminable piano lessons and earlier – if her advice to Jane after Tristan was born was anything to go by – for his four-hourly feeds.

Glancing pointedly at the clock as troglodytes in motor-cycle gear burst in at two-minute intervals to receive packages or deposit manilla envelopes at reception, and with the refrain 'Mason, Detroit and Fitch' reverberating in his head like the tympany in Ravel's *Bolero*, Freddie sat down on the sofa and picked up the *Independent* from the glass-topped table. 'Gloom over sales and job cuts: Early recovery hopes dashed by double blow. Dwindling hopes of an early economic recovery in Britain were dealt two further blows yesterday with the release of figures showing a decline in retail sales and a sharp drop in confidence among financial service firms . . .' He turned to the City pages. 'Jobs shakeout in the financial services sector still has a considerable way to go.'

'This is ridiculous!' He jumped up from the sofa.

'Sorry to keep you waiting. Mr Mason does know you're here.'

'Try him again!'

'Mr Lomax is still in reception,' the girl said obligingly into the nylon tube attached to her headset, and to Freddie, 'Mr Mason won't keep you long.'

Freddie resumed his seat. Dominic Mason had never before kept him waiting. Not once in the past five years of calling on his legal advisors had he been directed to the sofa. He had not even been aware that there was a sofa.

The *Guardian* was no more cheery than the *Independent*. The fact that banks and building societies were the most pessimistic business category in the financial sector augured badly for the whole economy. Not too bothered by the gloom and doom which, failing any dramatic upturn in the economy which they could get their teeth into, was the bread and butter of City editors, Freddie confronted the switchboard girl once more, demonstrating his chronograph as if he had to get back urgently to his office.

'Kindly tell Mr Mason that I am unable to wait. I shall have to make another appointment.'

'Mr Mason will see you now. Mason, Detroit and Fitch. Will you hold?' And to Freddie. 'Sorry to keep you waiting.'

'So sorry.' Dominic Mason, wearing a pink moiré cut-away waistcoat, was all apologies. Taking off his half-glasses, he came from behind his desk to greet his client. His effusive handshake did little to dispel Freddie's vexation.

'I'm afraid it's been one of those days.' Dominic resumed his seat and replaced his glasses as Freddie took the carved, fruitwood chair. 'How's your game coming along?'

Freddie had been playing golf with Dominic since his family firm, who were the legal advisors to Sitwell Hunt, had also undertaken his personal affairs – at an advantageous rate. He had not come to discuss golf.

'I assume you are *au fait* with recent events?'

'I have spoken to Gordon.'

'Then you'll know why I'm here.'

'I can take a pretty shrewd guess.'

Freddie had the impression that Dominic was not enjoying the interview with him any more than had Derek Abbott.

'I have been employed by Sitwell Hunt International for five years. I have been responsible for £100 million of trading in the past six months alone. I feel that I have been treated extremely badly. Kindly tell me what my legal position is. Do I have any remedies in law?'

'Let me refresh my memory, Freddie. Service agreement. Was there any service agreement?'

Freddie's service agreement (the directors' contract of employment) with Sitwell Hunt International, had expired three months ago.

'You know very well there was a service agreement. I had not got round to renewing it.'

'I understand that Gordon has offered you a certain package ... £130,000, I believe, was the amount discussed?'

'Less tax.'

'Less tax, of course. A not inconsiderable sum. My advice would be to take it, Freddie. Legal costs these days are, as you know ... well, I don't need to tell you about legal costs. You don't qualify for legal aid. If you want my opinion, I see very little point in fighting.'

'Is that *all* you have to say?'

'You know, Freddie . . .' the waistcoat had silver buttons '. . . there could possibly be a conflict of interests here.'

'Am I to understand, Dominic,' Freddie came straight to the point, 'that you do not wish to act for me any more?'

'As far as this particular matter is concerned, I think it might be better all round.' The glasses came off again. 'Why don't I introduce you to a colleague of mine in another firm? I was thinking in particular of Paul Judd. Christopher Hudson, Wingfield, Bancroft and Judd? Paul would look after you extremely nicely.'

'If it's all the same to you,' Freddie stood up, 'I'll find my own lawyer.'

Dominic crossed the room and held open the door. He seemed relieved that the session was over.

'I hope you're not going to let this make any difference to our golf. We must play a round sometime.'

'Good idea, Dominic,' Freddie said. 'Don't bother to call me.' The worry beads were already out of his pocket. 'I'll be in touch.'

Freddie's car was parked on the double yellow line outside the building. Sliding onto the seat, his briefcase beside him, he realised with shock that with his interview with Dominic Mason his day was finished, and it was still only 4.30. There were no more meetings, no urgent appointments, no clients waiting, no plane to catch.

Leonard was waiting politely for instructions.

'I suppose', Freddie said, 'you'd better take me home.'

Opening his front door, he was greeted by a blast of cacophonous sound which filled the house and assaulted his eardrums. Following the racket upstairs to the drawing-room, he found Rosina, dancing in front of the television, like one possessed, to a band of young men in matador shirts brandishing accordians and guitars. Picking up the remote and pointing it at the TV set, Freddie flipped the channel.

'Daddy!' Rosina screamed. 'It's The Pogues . . .'

Two-six-one for the FTSE 100 index/FT 30 index; two-six-two London stocks; two-six-three Dow Jones/Wall St stocks. It was like telling a rosary.

'I've got a date on Saturday night, Daddy. Dancing burns off twenty-five calories an hour . . .'

Indifferent to this fascinating piece of information, Freddie did a quick flip through the Far East and European stocks and the *Forex* report. He was about to hand Rosina back to The Pogues when the words Universal Concrete, in a short paragraph of text, caught his eye: 'Takeover bid for Universal Concrete. Shares jump in response.'

'*Takeover* bid! Takeover bid!'

'Something wrong, Daddy?'

Freddie sat down abruptly.

'Nothing that £11,000 won't put right. I have just lost £11,000, Rosina – money which I don't happen to have – on the certainty that Universal Concrete was about to go *bust*!'

CHAPTER FOURTEEN

Rosina was unable to devote her entire attention to her father's apocalypse. She had other matters on her mind. Sacrificing the Azzedine Alaïa body-hugger and the Gaultier leggings was the least she could do, although it had been her intention to wear them together on Saturday night. In the circumstances she was prepared to make do with a black Agnes B sweater borrowed from her friend Ariadne, whose father was number two at the Greek Embassy, which she had swapped for her scarlet rib-top with the keyhole front, worn with Anglo-American sunglasses and a pair of her mother's fishnet tights.

As she lay in the bath, her face immobilised by a mask of Dead Sea mud, which promised to draw out the dead cells 'like a vacuum cleaner', she reviewed her life. As practically the only remaining virgin in her year – if the boasts of her classmates were to be believed – she had a problem. Sometimes she felt herself to be still a child and wanted nothing more than to lie on her bed with her teddy bear consuming vast quantities of confectionery (dynamite to her skin) whilst she read teenage comics or watched the latest episode of *Neighbours*, and at others she saw herself as a Hollywood icon with a craving to be initiated into the penetrating mysteries of sex.

Jane had, of course, discussed the matter with her.

She had had a long talk with Rosina about safe sex, and unwanted pregnancies, and the risk of HIV, and explained to her that the decision to sleep with a boy was an extremely serious one, which should not be based on the fact that everyone else was doing so, and about the vital importance of the condom.

It was at a gig at the Carwash that Rosina had met Henry Dove who at the age of 18, and waiting to go up to Bristol, was insistent upon 'going out' with her.

There had been boys before Henry. When she was 7 years old, a schoolfriend of Tristan's had lured her to the end of the garden. He had dared her to remove her knickers in return for a glimpse of his own equipment which he seemed to prize highly, but which – from her experience of seeing Tristan in the bath – Rosina thought run-of-the-mill. Her first kiss, which took her by surprise with its moistness, had been received during a game of forfeits on her ninth birthday, since when she had been in love, whether they were aware of it or not, with a succession of boys whose experience had been as limited as her own.

Henry was different. He drank his beer straight from the bottle and was training for his pilot's licence. Familiarity in the cinema, or becoming carried away by soul music while Ariadne's parents were out and Ariadne was occupied with her current boyfriend on their double bed, was not going to satisfy Henry – who had declared himself passionate about Rosina and waited for her every day outside school – for much longer.

'Going out' represented a significant leap into maturity from which there could be no turning back. It was not a question of morality. Times had changed since her mother had been a teenager, and physical relationships between the sexes now started sometimes as early as 12. It was no big deal. What bothered Rosina was whether, if she gave Henry what he wanted, what they both wanted, he would still like her; whether – like her movie heroines who with no fumbling and no flab ripped off their shirts in one sinuous movement – she would do it right. It was not as if she had not mastered the drill. She knew about the importance of foreplay and about male arousal, had boned up on the physiology of orgasm, and, after a few false starts, had managed to produce what she was pretty sure was the phenomenon in herself.

While Henry was taller than she was, and with his blue eyes – made more blue by tinted contact lenses – and his cropped hair, wildly sexy, he was neither as well-built nor as charismatic as Freddie and lacked her father's warmth and sophistication. Her virginity was the last card in a woman's pack. Did she want to squander it on Henry?

She had consulted her stars on the subject. Her horoscope, under Gemini, was unequivocal. 'Never have you been privy to so many secrets (her father's dismissal?) – even people in authority are confiding in you (definitely Freddie). What you discover now will help unravel a mystery that's been puzzling you for some while. You'll have an intimate time too, with that special boy.' No doubt about that. Saturday night was *the* night. Freddie and Jane were going to the opera and she had invited Henry for supper. He had promised to bring a video.

The beep of the timer on the side of the bath reminded Rosina that it was time to remove the 'rich cocktail of potassium, magnesium, bromine, vitamins, minerals and nutrients' from her face, when it would have worked, or it would not. Loosening the mask with a damp sponge according to the directions on the pack, and wondering whether she should perhaps have opted for lemon juice and sour cream and washed her hair in Evian water like Kim Basinger, she reckoned that she still had time to make up her mind.

Freddie's attempt to get the seriousness of his financial situation across to Jane, who had a blind spot as far as arithmetic was concerned, had resulted in his blowing what had, since his dismissal, been an increasingly short fuse. Writing down for her the figures, which landed them in the poverty trap and haunted him like the blind Samson's lament, he tried to get her to understand the anomalous mess in which he found himself.

'It seems perfectly simple to me, darling,' Jane said. 'We don't *need* this big house . . .'

'Even if we could manage to sell the house,' Freddie explained patiently and not for the first time, 'we owe the mortgage company £600,000.'

'. . . We could move to the country . . .'

'It wouldn't help, Jane. Even if we lived in a cottage, I would still have to find the extremely large sums of money which I owe.'

'You must have *some* money, Freddie. We seem to spend an awful lot. And then there's Lilli . . .'

He did not need Jane to remind him of the exorbitant rent of his mother's flat, not to mention the crippling wages demanded by her carers. When Lilli had first shown signs of dementia, he had been to inspect a residential home. In a Suffolk retreat for ex-musicians he had seen rosy-cheeked French horn players and tremulous violinists – put out to grass like aged horses – sitting round the walls of a dilapidated country mansion in varying degrees of inertia while a vacant-eyed ghost played 'Roses of Picardy' on an out-of-tune piano with yellowed keys.

'Why don't *I* go out to work?' Jane was saying brightly.

Bingo had recently bought a disused warehouse in Fulham, into which she had introduced a collection of *fin de séries* garments which she displayed against room settings of antique furniture and sold by word of mouth. With sales flourishing, the alternative economy booming, and her reputation growing, Bingo had been asking Jane to join her in her enterprise for some time.

'That won't be necessary.'

'But I quite like the idea.'

'I said it won't be necessary.'

'I heard you. If I want to go and work for Bingo, I'll go and work for Bingo.'

'I won't let you.'

'Hang on a minute, Freddie. What's going on here? You can't stop me going to work for Bingo. "Bingo's" is going like a bomb. I've always been good at clothes, and the money would come in useful . . .'

'For God's sake shut up, Jane. I'm trying to explain to you, in words of one syllable, what is an extremely serious situation, and all you can do is rabbit on about selling frocks to a lot of idle women with nothing better to do, at bloody Bingo's!'

Retreating into a tight-lipped silence, Jane had left the room. Freddie tore up the figures. They might just as well have been hieroglyphics. For the past couple of days, and just when he needed her most, a wall of glass had come between himself and Jane.

Before they went to sleep, Jane, realising that her offer to go to work might, in the circumstances, have been insensitive, had attempted to put matters right.

'I didn't mean to walk out on you.'

'I didn't mean to shout.'

'I'm not really bothered about working at Bingo's.'

The fact that Jane wanted to go out to work, that she had no problem whatsoever in seeing herself as the breadwinner, exacerbated Freddie's feelings of inadequacy engendered by his continuing inability to make love to her.

'It doesn't really matter one way or the other. We're not going to raise the siege by saving candle ends.'

'Why don't you go and see Didier? You've always said he was a good lawyer.'

'I might just do that.'

'And what about Piers?'

'What about him?' Freddie was on his guard.

'He's a banker. I think you should tell him. There could be something going at NatWest. Would you like me to ring him up for you?' Jane was trying to be helpful.

'Just leave it, will you?'

He knew that Jane was doing her best, but her attitude towards him, as if he were a sick child to be comforted, aroused unbidden feelings of anger and hostility. He did not want her pity. He wanted to be left alone.

Didier was now an equity partner in one of the leading firms of employment lawyers which was itself going through bad times. Over a couple of pints of Sam Smith's in the John Snow, near his office in Broadwick Street, Didier commiserated with his brother-in-law about the reprehensible way in which he had been treated by Gordon Sitwell.

'You want me to come and kick the bastard in the goolies?'

'Just tell me what my rights are. Tell me what redress I have.' Freddie's customary sense of wellbeing, his sanguine view of the world, was slowly giving way to an unfamiliar sense of grievance and gross injustice.

'Based on what you've told me, not very much.'

Didier, who with his pale skin and shock of red hair looked unnervingly like Jane, could not believe that Freddie, who was so meticulous in his concern for the affairs of others – to whom he had always looked for guidance, and to whom he was personally indebted – had shown an almost criminal lack of regard in respect to his own.

'As a matter of interest, how was it you allowed your

service agreement to lapse?' Didier helped himself to a handful of potato crisps.

'I was waiting for the results of Corinthian.' Freddie drained his glass and signalled for a Black Label. 'I took a chance. I thought I'd be able to negotiate better terms.'

Didier whistled. 'It's like going on holiday without paying your insurance premium. Ten to one your house will burn down while you're away.'

'Dominic Mason advised me against entering into litigation with Sitwell Hunt.'

'Dominic Mason is trying to run with the hare and the hounds. Nevertheless, Freddie, in view of what you've told me,' Didier put his hands into the pockets of his trendy cotton trousers, 'I am afraid I have to agree with him.'

Freddie's friendship with Piers Warburton, which had begun at school, had been interrupted when Freddie went up to Cambridge and Piers to the LSE. It had been resumed some years later when they both found themselves in the City. Freddie had lived through Piers's battle with alcohol and the disintegration of his first marriage. He had stood by him – driving down to Winchester every week to visit him at Clouds – through the long process of drying out. After his rehabilitation (he was now actively involved in an alcohol programme and was a part-time counsellor for ALANON) it was through Freddie's influence that Piers had been reinstated in continental banking. He was amazed when Freddie walked in on him in the middle of the day.

'Sitwell Hunt gone into receivership?'

'Not exactly.'

While Piers poured sherry from a decanter for Freddie and orange juice from a carton for himself, Freddie, whose liturgy grew harder rather than easier with repetition, explained the reason for his visit.

'As if I wasn't properly in schtuck, I've just made a balls-up of a put option on Universal Concrete.'

'Universal Concrete?'

'The head office is near us. Was near us! I thought I saw the undertaker go in. I *did* see the undertaker go in, but Tarquin Chapman just happens to be the brother-in-law of the managing director of the company who were, as it turns out, making a friendly *bid*.'

Piers whistled. 'Wheeling and dealing instead of liquidating!'

'I suppose it made a change. Cost me eleven K. I hate to tell you what I stood to gain.'

'I know things are not easy right now, Freddie, but recession or no recession, there's always going to be a shortage of good people.'

It was all right from where Piers was sitting. Freddie did not want platitudes. He wanted a job, with the accompanying financial rewards to which he had become accustomed and which, as far as he was concerned, were the yardstick of success.

Piers, who owed Freddie one, was considerably discomforted. He would have liked nothing better than to be able to be of help.

'There's nothing going – commensurate with your seniority – that I know of at NatWest. I'll ask around, of course . . .'

'Without mentioning any names.'

'Without mentioning any names. I'll let you know the moment I come up with anything in which you might be remotely interested.'

A discreet tap on the door was followed by an apologetic secretary with some papers which she gave to Piers. While he engaged her in sotto voce conversation about asking somebody to wait, and some missing cash flow projections which he had asked for, his intercom buzzed twice and the telephone on his desk rang with an incoming call. Politely refraining from answering either of them, Piers stole a surreptitious glance at his watch. Recognising the feeling, Freddie stood up and polished off his sherry.

He was already in the lobby when Piers, who had followed him, said: 'How's Jane?'

'You saw her at the party.'

'You're so lucky. I envy you, you know. I never seem to get it right. Not even the third time! Look, Freddie . . .' The buzzer, accompanied by the telephone, was still ringing insistently in the office. 'I hardly know how to put this, but if it's a question of a loan?'

Freddie put an appreciative hand on his friend's shoulder. 'You'd better answer your blower. Just keep your eyes peeled for a job.'

Outside the bank, fresh-faced young men in dark suits erupted in hungry streams from stockbroking firms and counting houses into Broadgate Circle. Four years hence, according to the recent estimates, more than 20,000 employees would be concentrated in the recently developed area. Making for the piazza Freddie wondered if he would be among them. With time on his hands, he sat down on a travertine bench overlooking the arena where winter skaters waltzed to Muzak and sandwiches were eaten to the accompaniment of summer bands, and took a letter from his pocket.

Dear Dad,

It's all right about the trainer. Jeremy made me call Robert's father and apologyse it wasn't my fault it was a dare. He sent him a new pair not so expensive Robert doesn't like them. I'm not talking to that geek. I'm not going to India. I'll get a job, hospital porter or something the driving lessons can wait.

Love to Mummy and that ratbag whose name I can't remember. Tristan.

CHAPTER FIFTEEN

Jane did not share Freddie's enthusiasm for opera. She was left cold even by *Don Giovanni* and had managed to sleep her way through an entire performance of *Ariadne auf Naxos*. She was particularly unimpressed by anything by Wagner in which it took half an hour to convey a simple message such as that Siegfried's mother had given birth to him in the woods, musical beginnings never got finished, bent-kneed dwarfs wittered on about rings, grown men pretended they were dragons, and she was expected to differentiate between the motif of the helmet and the motif of the apple.

By the time Saturday night came, Freddie, who was relying on Hans Wichmann's lucrative business to get him out of trouble with the bank, had already sent the Mercedes to the airport on Friday, and having dropped Frau Wichmann at the Connaught, taken the German broker out for lunch.

During both the fish soup (accompanied by an excellent Pouilly Fumé) and the steak and kidney pie (with which they had got through two bottles of Chassagne-Montrachet *rouge*), Freddie had listened patiently while his guest, a serious eater who tucked his napkin beneath his chin and put down his knife and fork for what seemed an age between each mouthful, held forth on the likelihood of a German recession. Having resolved the problems of his own country, Wichmann dealt with the malaise of the British economy, brought about in his opinion, not only by the intellectual paralysis of the British government, but by their refusal to accept that the exchange rate should be left to market forces.

'No ERM currency has ever been revalued upwards against the mark, Freddie. It is therefore quite impossible for you', he jabbed his fork at Freddie, 'to have lower interest rates than Germany.'

'There are plenty of countries, surely, with much lower interest rates.' Unable, out of politeness, to toy with his food any longer, Freddie, an habitually quick eater, put down his knife and fork.

'Outside the ERM, yes! The dollar, the yen, the Swiss franc. "Soft" currencies also.' The fact that Wichmann's steak and kidney pie was congealing on his plate seemed not to deter him. 'If Australia can cut interest rates from 17 to 7.5 per cent, why not Britain? If British interest rates would be only 2 points lower than Germany's . . . then would you have full employment and there would be sustainable development of both your current and your capital accounts.'

Waiting for Wichmann to finish, and wishing that the steak and kidney pie would be despatched with the same alacrity as the Montrachet, Freddie thought privately that if Britain had to suffer a further decade of German-imposed deflation before it could share the benefits of low interest rates and market-determined exchange rates, then the past twelve years of Thatcherism had been in vain.

They were onto the bread and butter pudding, which Wichmann fell upon with relish and beat Freddie to the finish, before the real purpose of their meeting was broached.

'When we spoke again on Wednesday you were mentioning some "interesting developments".' Wichmann leaned back in his chair and wiped his mouth with satisfaction on his starched napkin. 'That was very good. Very good. What are these interesting developments?'

Filling Wichmann's glass, Freddie then poured the last of the Montrachet into his own. Lowering his voice, and leaning confidentially across the table, he said, 'I have agreed to part company with Sitwell Hunt International. I believe that I can do better for you elsewhere.'

'*Ach, so!*'

'As far as your proposals for diversifying are concerned, Hans, I have several contacts keen to do business in the CIS, and they are prepared to give you all the finance you need. I am not only in a strong position to help you, on a personal basis, but at extremely attractive rates.'

Wichmann excused himself from the table. When he returned Freddie opened his briefcase and removed the papers on which he had been working for the past three days. He waited while Wichmann lit his Havana cigar and took an appreciative sip of the special marc Freddie had ordered, then outlined his detailed plan for the setting up of supermarkets, and the guarantees of credit across Eastern Europe.

By the time he had finished talking it was four o'clock and the restaurant almost empty. Calling for the bill, Freddie realised that it would have to be settled not from the generous expense account which he had always taken for granted, but from taxed income from his own pocket.

'The last opera Wiebke and I have seen', Herr Wichmann said, 'was *Der Ferne Klang*. It was in München, *nicht war, Liebchen*?'

This announcement, made in Freddie's drawing-room before they left for Covent Garden, was repeated in German for the benefit of Frau Wichmann, a willowy lady, taller than her husband by an ash-blonde head, whose

English was minimal, and whose subject was herbals, on which she was writing a book. She had arrived in a black wool cloak lined with scarlet, bearing an outsized bottle of *Kölnischwasser*, which Jane, who hated the smell of eau-de-Cologne, mentally priced up for her next bazaar.

'*Der Ferne Klang*', Wichmann went on, 'deals with Art versus Life. The music is divine.' He hummed a few bars from the opera with his mouth full of smoked salmon. 'But in the same moment something of a – how you call it – *eine Mischung*?'

'Mish-mash.' Rosina, who was learning German, came into the room wearing Ariadne's sweater, which reached only to the top of her thighs, her sunglasses, and Jane's fish-net tights.

Her appearance put Wichmann temporarily off his stride. His eyes widened and the canapé to which he had helped himself remained suspended in mid-air some six inches from his mouth.

'My daughter, Rosina.' Freddie put an arm round Rosina and hissed, 'For God's sake, Rosina, where's your skirt?'

Glaring at Freddie, Rosina extended her hand (Audrey Hepburn in *My Fair Lady*) to Wichmann as Jane's eyes went to her best Fogal tights.

'A mish-mash – thank you, my dear – between Strauss, between Debussy, and between the early Schoenberg. Franz Schreker was a composer not popular – for reasons you can imagine – in Nazi Germany. His work starts only now to be revived.'

Unfamiliar with *Der Ferne Klang*, and worried about being late, Freddie glanced at his watch.

'I think we'd better be making a move.'

This remark prompted a torrent of German from Wichmann, followed by a nodding smile of agreement from Frau Wichmann which revealed the lipstick on her front teeth.

'My wife looks forward to your Covent Garden,' Wichmann said, helping her on with her cloak.

Rosina looked out of the window to make sure that her parents were not going to return and that James's Bentley, with Leonard at the wheel, had actually left the terrace. When it had gone she dimmed the lights, polished off the solitary canapé left by Herr Wichmann, washed it down with a shot of vodka, and went up to the bathroom to brush her teeth.

Catching sight of her face in the mirror above the washbasin, she wished for the umpteenth time that she were blonde, or failing that, brunette. She hated her freckles and deplored the fact that her ginger eyelashes were so sparse. She was not all that keen on the lobes of her ears either. They had been pierced, without Jane's permission, at Fenwick's jewellery counter when she was 12. There had been a great to-do about it. To distract interest from them she was wearing drop earrings. Shimmering loops of diamanté. They came from Lilli's box. Lilli had a vast assortment of jewellery, accumulated during her years on the concert platform when it had livened up her black dresses. She kept her collection, gold chains and cabochon rings and interesting brooches of semi-precious stones, in a Burmese casket, the jumbled contents of which had fascinated Rosina since she had been a little girl. Gazing at her reflection, Rosina imagined that she was Henry and pictured his reaction to her image which she hoped was that of a woman in the age of girls. If she half-closed her eyes, ran her tongue over her 'Matte Red' lipstick ('luscious and forties-looking with masses of staying power'), piled her hair on her head exposing her pale neck . . .

Her fantasy was shattered by the double ring of the doorbell. Overtaken by paralysis, she remained rooted to the spot. When the moment had passed, unwilling to entrust her voice to the Entryphone, and feeling the unbidden sweat escape from her armpits onto Ariadne's sweater, she ran down the stairs and pausing on the penultimate step, slunk along the parquet – in a passable imitation of Kim Basinger being auctioned in a North African slave market by Klaus Maria Brandauer – and opened the front door not to her date but to the spotty youth from Pizza Hut.

Not keen to have a rerun of the stilted quartet which had accompanied the Piper Heidsieck served in their box after Act One, Freddie led his party to the Crush Bar for the second interval. So far, so good. René Kollo was an outstanding Lohengrin, Ortrud and Telramund in fine voice, the orchestra on top form, and the Wichmanns apparently enjoying themselves, although the same could not be said for Jane. He was about to congratulate himself on the way the evening was going, when Jane introduced him to Clare Singleton, the treasurer of her charity committee, and her husband, Sir Patrick Singleton, who were sitting on their own in a corner. At Freddie's request, the couple joined them in a second bottle of Piper Heidsieck, and he was delighted when Clare Singleton practised her fluent German on the Wichmanns, leaving him free to discuss the evening's performance with her husband, a fellow opera buff.

The interval warning bell had just sounded, and they were shuffling their way to the top of the stairs, when Sir Patrick, an industrialist, said: 'And what line are you in, Lomax?'

The instinctive response, that he was a banker, was on Freddie's lips when it struck him, like an icy Mongolian wind, that he was not.

'Sorry?' Singleton, deafened by the surrounding chatter, and thinking that Freddie had spoken, cupped his ear.

Wondering just how to answer, unwilling to lie, propelled to the top of the stairs by the jostling throng, Freddie missed his footing. Grabbing the brass rail and assuring Jane, who happened to look round just then, that he had merely stumbled, he regained his balance. Sir Patrick, not bothering to wait for a reply to what had been nothing but a polite enquiry, had meanwhile caught up with his wife and, taking her elbow, helped her down the remainder of the stairs and into the auditorium. The incident, which no one had even noticed, was over, but Freddie could not dismiss it from his mind. He knew that he had been severely hurt by the fact that the bank had seen fit to 'let him go'. The acknowledgement of just how deep the wound had gone blighted his enjoyment of the last act of *Lohengrin* and distracted him from its climax.

Freddie's was not the only big moment which turned out to be a damp squib. By the time Lohengrin had finally disappeared from the stage and Elsa had sunk lifeless to the ground, Rosina's evening had reached its own disappointing finale.

Henry's appearance on the doorstep bearing a video of *Fatal Attraction* and a bunch of spray chrysanthemums had been followed by the consumption of the pizza in the kitchen, which was accompanied by desultory conversation which revolved largely around nervous speculation as to what time her parents were likely to return. Afterwards Rosina thought that they could just as well have eaten the cardboard box.

Sitting primly next to Henry on the sofa in the drawing-room before the gas coal-fire as Michael Douglas bonked Glenn Close on the draining board, she mentally rehearsed what she thought of as her lines, should the evening end in the way she anticipated.

Her knowledge of doing 'it' was based on anecdotal

evidence from her friends at school – who had likened the experience to seeing all the colours of the rainbow – and the couplings she had witnessed on the screen in which the groaning protagonists, shot in grainy close-up, seemed to convey all the torments of hell rather than celestial bliss. She had not yet decided, if (and when) her moment came, whether she would be Harriet Walter in *The Men's Room*, Joan Collins in *The Stud*, Diane Muldaur in *LA Law*, or Uma Thurman being deflowered by John Malkovich in *Dangerous Liaisons*. The decision might have been easier had there been romantic sand dunes (*The Sheltering Sky*) or satin sheets (*Don't Look Now*) on which to dispose of her virginity rather than the prosaic sofa in her mother's drawing-room.

The video was almost over. Although her head was on Henry's shoulder and his arm was firmly around her waist, Rosina was thinking, with some relief, that she must after all have allowed her imagination to run away with her, when Glenn Close – who had apparently been brutally murdered in the bath – suddenly sat up. Rosina screamed. Henry pounced. Taken by surprise by the sheer force of his rugby tackle, Rosina rolled onto the floor followed by her paramour who was devouring her with kisses.

She had wanted to watch the end of the video, but there was no stopping Henry who was making strangled grunting noises as he struggled to relieve her of the Agnes B sweater. Giving up on *Fatal Attraction* – she could catch up on the last few minutes from someone at school – Rosina applied herself to the business in hand. She had seen enough movies to know that now she was down to her new Janet Reger knickers (with which Henry seemed unimpressed) and he was paying homage to her chest, the ball was in her court and she was scheduled to remove her lover's clothes. It was not easy. The tight jeans were like iron cladding and she had trouble, caused by the tumescent state of his anatomy, with the zip.

Rolling on top of one another, now this way, now that, giving and taking, mouths open (Elizabeth Taylor and Richard Burton in *The Comedians*) under Henry's urgent directions, Rosina thought that she had never felt so ecstatic and so close to anybody and that her friends at school were right and this was the ultimate, the don't-ever-want-it-to-end best. She had no idea how long they had been doing battle in a mutual bath of perspiration when Henry, *Fatal Attraction* completely forgotten, dealt summarily with Janet Reger and pulled apart Rosina's thighs. After that there was no more dialogue, no nib-blings and giggles and exhortations not to stop, no tender exchange of endearments borrowed from the big screen. Penetrating her, Henry seemed to enter another planet, one which Rosina did not inhabit and onto which he did not invite her. Like a fly on the wall she watched him retreat and advance, retreat and advance in a crescendo of exertion to the music of some private mantra, then all at once, with a grotesque contortion of his facial muscles, it appeared to be over.

With Henry's ecstatic enquiry as to whether it had been as great for her as it obviously had been for him, Rosina had some problem. If she told Henry the truth – that she had experienced more heart-stopping excitement running for the bus – he might deduce that it was his fault. He would think that she was blaming him for the fact that far from the earth turning somersaults, it had not shifted so much as an inch, and she might not be invited to participate again. She decided to appear cool, and to dissimulate about what had turned out, after so much ballyhoo about losing it and rainbows, to be a decided non-event.

CHAPTER SIXTEEN

It was Lavender who came across the unopened packet of condoms beneath the sofa. She guessed that they must have something to do with Rosina and thought it better not to mention her find to Jane. Going into the kitchen, where Jane was rummaging in the freezer for the unidentifiable remains of Freddie's birthday cake, she slipped the incriminating packet discreetly into her handbag.

Ten minutes earlier, progressing ponderously along Albany Street on her way to Chester Terrace, exhausted after a sleepless night – Tony pestering her for sex, it was all right for him, he had nothing else to do all day; Shaun calling for drinks of water; the new baby kicking unmerciful pockets in her flesh – she had been surprised by the unfamiliar sight of Freddie waiting for a bus.

Although ominous clouds had been gathering earlier as he jogged, it had not occurred to Freddie – on his way to his crucial breakfast meeting with Wichmann – who was accustomed to stepping straight into the Mercedes where Leonard would be waiting for him, that it might be raining. Putting up the collar of his navy-blue pinstriped suit, he had hailed several taxis, some of which were apparently empty and all of which ignored him. Sliding his worry beads out of his pocket and becoming not only wet but irritated, he joined the knot of people – for whom he provided an unwitting diversion with his futile attempts to flag down every passing cab – waiting for the single-decked Hoppa. When the bus came, Freddie stood back courteously to let the other passengers on first. There was room for only three. As the doors sighed closed, he looked anxiously at his watch.

The next bus, fully loaded, sped triumphantly by at speed without stopping at all. Five minutes later the third one was almost as jam-packed as the first. Several women, as shapeless as their capacious shopping bags, got on before Freddie. They flashed their passes at the driver before side-stepping their way down the narrow aisle.

'Piccadilly.' Freddie handed the driver a ten-pence piece.

The youth did not stir.

'Piccadilly,' Freddie said.

The young man, who did not look old enough to be in charge of a bus, explained, as if to an imbecile, that the minimum fare was fifty pence – and had been for some time – and that the C2 only went as far as Oxford Circus.

There were no taxis at Oxford Circus. The rain was now coming down in earnest. Cursing the fact that he had no umbrella, Freddie jumped onto the platform of a Piccadilly bus.

'No standing on my platform!'

Taking the nearest seat, Freddie watched fascinated as a slim Jamaican with shapely legs and straightened hair, plugged into a Walkman, sashayed down the stairs.

'Thank the Lord for music. If there weren't no music I couldn't come to work in the morning.'

Moving her hips and snapping her fingers in time to the beat which presumably emanated from her single earpiece, the conductress took Freddie's fare.

'Love Passion!'

He assumed it was the name of the song to which she was listening.

'You married, darling? Any man I want to share my satellite dish with is *always* married. Fancy my route, do you? Cheers, darling!'

By the time Freddie had run from Piccadilly Circus to Carlos Place, his trousers were soaked and his shoes squelching. As an impeccable Wichmann, from whom wafted the delicate odour of aftershave, put down his newspaper and got up from the table to greet him, the German's hooded eyes briefly registered Freddie's dishevelled appearance as he motioned him to a chair.

Freddie offered no explanation for the fact that he was late. 'Never complain, never explain.' It was part of his credo. Wichmann was at liberty to think what he chose.

Dropping the Wichmanns at the Connaught on Saturday night after *Lohengrin* and a convivial dinner at Scott's, Freddie had judged the evening an unqualified success. Jane had managed to strike up a rapport with Frau Wichmann and, despite the language difficulties, the two women had got on well. While they communicated with each other in a combination of English, German, and French, Wichmann and Freddie had got down to business. Wichmann had promised to spend the whole of Sunday studying Freddie's financial proposals for the supermarkets, and as they climbed out of James's Bentley and said goodbye to each other on the pavement outside the hotel – Wichmann kissing Jane on both cheeks, and Freddie reciprocating with Frau Wichmann – a final meeting was set up for Monday morning.

The broker, who had waited to order until Freddie arrived, asked for grapefruit and porridge, followed by eggs, sausages, bacon, tomato and a round of toast, while Freddie, who had already taken his customary light breakfast at home after his morning exercise, accepted only black coffee. When they had both been served and the waiters had withdrawn, Wichmann dabbed at his mouth with his starched napkin.

'I have read your proposals. The marmalade, if you would be so good, Freddie. Very interesting. Very interesting. If we are able to go ahead with what you suggest, we will be first in the field. We will revolutionise the entire market of the CIS, bring supermarkets to the man on the . . . how you say . . . St Petersburg tram . . . ha, ha, I like that, St Petersburg tram, such as never in his wildest dreams has he imagined . . .'

Wichmann put a piece of sausage into his mouth after studying it carefully, as if it were a laboratory specimen. Freddie sipped his coffee and felt surreptitiously for the beads in his pocket. Scarcely daring to breathe, he waited for Wichmann to continue.

'Wonderful sausages. Have you tried our *Bratwurst*? Unfortunately, Freddie, I am not able to give you an immediate answer. I have first to discuss with one or two of our people in Frankfurt.'

'Take your time.' Freddie's smile was deceptively relaxed. 'I don't think you will find more advantageous terms than I have offered.'

'I am sure you are right.'

Wichmann reached for a toothpick. The meeting appeared to be over.

'Frau Wichmann has asked me to thank you for the Covent Garden and for the dinner. She thinks your wife is quite charming and will send her a copy of her book so soon as it will be published.' He put an arm on Freddie's sleeve before summoning the waiter and pushing back his chair. 'An excellent weekend, Freddie. Excellent. I hope we can do business together. I will come back to you in a few days, yes?'

Outside it had stopped raining. Having nothing better to do, Freddie decided to walk. He went over the past half-hour with Wichmann, searching in his head for clues. He would keep his fingers crossed. If the supermarket deal came off, his worries would be over. At least for a while. One big break was all he needed.

In Bond Street, the desolation of the almost-empty pavements and the boarded-up shop fronts, dotted at regular intervals amongst others in which the prices of the goods had been drastically reduced, epitomised the recession in trade, what was happening in the street. What he saw about him brought home the plummeting line and impersonal figures visible hitherto only on his Topics Screen. Fewer shoppers meant not only less money in the tills, but a slump in profits, as costs – over which desperate retailers, in the death throes of extinction, had no control – continued to rise. Evidence of the excessive rents now being demanded was all around him in the discounts emblazoned in large red letters across the windows: 'Final Reductions', 'Clearance Specials', 'Hurry while stocks last', which threatened to turn the once exclusive thoroughfare into a souk. Shirts 20 per cent off; suits 50 per cent off. Bargains in cashmere and cameras, in luggage and lingerie. Oriental carpets at giveaway prices, in establishments which announced with regret that they were shortly to close down.

The morning's news had offered little encouragement. A further decline in business was anticipated by the CBI, hopes of an early economic recovery had been quashed, companies continued to cut back their investment in new machinery and equipment, more job losses were expected and confidence stood at an all-time low. The export figures were even less promising: 49 per cent of firms reported orders below normal, and 71 per cent were working below capacity.

'Freddie!'

Charles Holdsworth, Bingo's husband, was standing in front of a bow-fronted jeweller's with two brooches: an

Edwardian moonstone heart and an Art-Deco clown with emerald eyes.

'I was hoping I'd bump into someone,' Charles said. 'Bingo will be 38 on Thursday. I'm not very good at presents.'

Freddie refrained from telling Charles of the extravagant gestures with which his wife's last husband had been in the habit of celebrating her birthdays. His final gift to Bingo had been a Ford Mustang, the keys of which had been hidden beneath the top layer in a box of her favourite chocolates.

Passing through the heavy glass door held respectfully open for them, Freddie followed Charles into the Aladdin's Cave of gold and precious stones, wondering if his own days of shopping for Art-nouveau jewellery for Jane were over. Charles fingered the two brooches on the green baize cloth on the glass-topped counter, behind which the salesman held his breath.

'Which do you think?' Charles cocked his head.

Either would set him – or more likely Bingo herself – back a very great deal of money. Worried about the outcome of his meeting with Wichmann, the choice of the heart or the clown seemed immaterial to Freddie. Charles, unable to make up his mind, decided to take both brooches on approval.

Bingo's midnight-blue Daimler, its engine running, was waiting outside the shop.

'I'm on my way to the City,' Charles, whose bank was in Pall Mall, said. 'Need a lift?'

Freddie shook his head. His eye caught the sign Brook Street. 'Meeting . . .' he said. 'Claridge's.'

Charles nodded understandingly. 'I should be finished at Lazard's about three. I'll pop up and see you. Will you be in your office this afternoon?'

Freddie consulted his personal organiser. 'Sorry.'

'Golf on Sunday then? Friend of Bingo's coming in from the States. You owe me a few balls.'

'Fine.' Freddie desperately needed to talk to Charles. Bond Street pavement in mid-morning seemed hardly the place.

'Sunday then . . .' Charles lowered the car window. 'Love to Jane.'

'Love to Bingo.'

The Daimler, driven by Bingo's grey-uniformed chauffeur, pulled smoothly away.

At home, pleasantly tired from his walk, Freddie rushed up the stairs to tell Jane about his morning with Wichmann.

'Jane!'

There was no reply. She had to be in. Her car was outside. The house seemed to be in silence. The doors of the drawing-room were unaccustomedly shut. Freddie threw them open.

'Jane?'

A dozen women, amongst whom he registered the startled faces of Bingo and Caroline Hurst, swivelled round to stare at him.

'Freddie!' Jane, pencil and paper in her hand, rose from the sofa.

Before she reached the doors, Freddie had closed them. He went slowly upstairs to the bedroom which was filled with unfamiliar scent and scattered with strange coats.

In his dressing-room, he turned on Radio 3 to Janet Baker singing 'Che faro', and picked up the Appointments section of *The Times*. The pages were trembling. A half-page advertisement caught his eye. 'Executive Director Corporate Finance. A fast-growing merchant bank invites applications from candidates with extensive experience in corporate banking internationally. Your experience will have given exposure to Money & Capital Markets financing, Mergers & Acquisitions and Multinational Project

Financing. Our compensation package is competitive and negotiable.'

Freddie lowered the radio. It sounded right up his street. He looked at the small print as an outburst of female laughter erupted from the drawing-room below. *Nigeria.* The job was in Nigeria!

Flinging aside the newspaper, he put on his jacket which was still damp, ran down the stairs, picked up the car keys from the hall table and, closing the front door behind him, got into the Japanese hatchback which was Jane's second home. Repositioning the driving seat, he looked with distaste at the crumpled tissues, discarded chocolate wrappers, old parking tickets, random shoes, out-of-date shopping lists, empty cans of de-icer, sundry writing instruments, disjointed umbrellas, scattered coins and boxes of Kleenex, and switching on the ignition headed for the Water Gardens.

There was a smell of cooking, cabbage or apples, in the corridor. Using his key, and ringing the bell by way of alerting Mrs Williams, Freddie opened the door of his mother's flat.

'Mother!'

There was no reply. He called again. Lilli didn't always hear.

'Mother!' He waited. 'Mrs Williams?'

The beds were neatly made. Mrs Williams had been ironing in her bedroom. The iron was still warm. In the kitchen there was evidence of morning coffee and a half-full packet of digestive biscuits, potatoes on the draining board waiting to be peeled. He wondered what had happened, where they could possibly be.

Repeating his tour of the silent flat, he felt a return of the fear he had experienced as a very small boy when, letting go of his mother's hand, he had lost her in a crowded shop, or when she had deliberately pretended to disappear – which brought him out in a cold sweat – hiding behind the sofa from which she would emerge to startle the wits out of him with a triumphant 'Boo!'

As he retraced his hushed steps through the empty rooms his imagination worked overtime. Lilli had been taken ill, although there was nothing wrong with her (except that she couldn't remember the name of the Prime Minister or what she had had for breakfast), the geriatrician had said she had the constitution of a young woman, and Freddie had spoken to her, as he did every morning, only a few hours ago.

He rang the bell of the neighbouring flat. Two dark eyes above a black chador stared at him before slamming the door in his face. With a cavalcade of imagined disasters – Mrs Williams had abducted his mother, Lilli had had a heart attack, had been admitted to hospital with a stroke – chasing each other through his head, he returned to the living-room, pushed aside Mrs Williams' mending, and rotating his worry beads, lay down on the sofa to wait.

CHAPTER SEVENTEEN

The idea of rubbing out Gordon Sitwell in retribution for ruining his life, of eliminating him with a single blow as if he were some errant fly on a windowpane, had been gathering momentum in Freddie's mind. Flies, according to Rosina who had brought the information home from school, had exactly the same life span as human beings. It was just that their hearts beat very much faster. Be that as it may, Gordon Sitwell would have to go. Getting a gun was not easy. Peter and Georgina, who lived next door and had a house in Norfolk to which Freddie and Jane were sometimes invited for the weekend, had guns in their trophy room which they used to dispose of Canada Geese. Freddie did not think that a 12-bore, side-by-side shotgun would be quite right for eviscerating the brains from the chairman of the bank. What he needed was a revolver. With a silencer. Such as was used in all the old Humphrey Bogart movies which he had seen when he was into *film noir*. To his surprise he found a Smith & Wesson in his briefcase. He thought that it must have been Wichmann who had put it there, and wondered if he was a member of the Nazi party and was some sort of *Sturmführer*, but it was Freddie's PA, who smoothed his path and looked after his business and personal life, who was responsible. He asked Susan, who was sucking an outsize Fisherman's Friend, if the gun was loaded. She was clearly upset by the fact that he queried her efficiency, and told him that she had loaded it only that morning with three new-laid bullets bought from a barrow on the way to work. He decided that when he had finished with Gordon Sitwell, he would take Susan to the Hong Kong & Shanghai Bank for lunch. Sam, the Sitwell Hunt commissionaire, was embarrassed when he greeted Freddie. Someone had tipped him off that the vice chairman was *persona non grata*. Freddie enquired as usual after his family but, although Sam answered him, he was unable to hear the reply. It took him an exceedingly long time to cross the entrance hall. It was as if he were floating on marble tiles which stretched away into the distance. By the time he reached the elevator he was exhausted. He pressed the button, but when it came there was no room. Not even for one. The heads of departments, jammed into a solid block of humanity which was revealed by the automatically opening doors, regarded him reproachfully. He waved his bus pass at them but there was not a flicker of response. They did not budge one inch to let him in. He decided to take the stairs. At the top of them, Sidonie Newmark, naked except for high-heeled shoes and outsize spectacles with tortoiseshell frames, was on the telephone to Frankfurt. She tapped her foot impatiently and told Freddie that he had absolutely no right to be on the fifth floor. It took him all day to find Gordon Sitwell. Every office that he entered, despite the fact that it bore Gordon's name inscribed and illuminated by Jane on a place card, contained some startled employee who regarded him with profound distaste. He found the chairman in the dining-room. The mahogany boardroom table was laid for 2,000 people but he presided over it alone. He was surprised to see Freddie, and asked him if he was aware that the bank was in liquidation. Freddie waited politely for him to finish his lunch. Then raised his arm and shot him through the head.

The crack of the bullet, like the violent slamming of a door, woke Freddie from his dream.

'Hugh!'

Freddie opened his eyes to discover that he was in Lilli's flat and that his mother, wearing her outdoor coat and accompanied by Mrs Williams, was looking down at his inert body on her sofa.

'It's not Hugh, it's Mr Lomax,' Mrs Williams said, adding with what he thought was satisfaction for Freddie's benefit, 'We would have been back earlier, but we had a spot of bother with a Cadbury's Flake in Tesco's . . .'

'Don't believe a word she says. I told the man I was going to pay for it,' Lilli said.

'Fortunately the manager was quite charming. He could see mother was a little bit . . .' Mrs Williams tapped her forehead and smiled at Freddie.

Freddie did not return her smile.

'Why aren't you at the bank?' Lilli said suddenly. Sometimes her mind was surprisingly clear, at others the past coalesced for her and she was convinced that the war was on or that her own mother was still alive.

Freddie did not answer. His mouth was dry. He was glad that he had not murdered Gordon, that his homicidal action had taken place only in his dream, and that although his thoughts towards the chairman remained violent, his hands were still clean. He ran his fingers through his hair and straightened his tie.

'Mr Lomax is vice chairman of a bank.' Lilli addressed Mrs Williams. 'Shouldn't you be in the kitchen?'

Taking his mother's hand, when Mrs Williams, muttering to herself, had left the room, Freddie gently read her the riot act about trying to be more polite to Mrs Williams who looked after her so nicely and was only doing her best.

'Her daughter's getting married on Saturday,' Lilli was unperturbed. 'I'd like to give her a hundred pounds.'

Freddie was in charge of Lilli's cheque book. She could no longer be trusted with it. A hundred pounds. A week ago he would not have thought about it twice. He wrote out a cheque and put it in the pocket of Lilli's cardigan where he guessed it was likely to remain.

Freddie had first noticed that something was wrong with Lilli when her personality began to change. From a reasonable, quick-witted, self-sufficient woman, incapacitated only marginally by a measure of arthritis not inappropriate to her age, she had gradually metamorphosed into a despot whose cantankerous behaviour bordered at times upon the offensive. It was not until she showed positive signs of memory impairment that the penny had finally dropped.

At first there were small aberrations. She posted her shopping list in the postbox, filled her basket with cat food (although she no longer had a cat), and although she prided herself upon her languages, could not come up with the French for a frog. When you reminded her of events, no matter how recent, she looked at you blankly, as if they had never taken place. The memory lapses were spasmodic. They came and went with no apparent logic, and for days at a time her mind was crystal clear. The neurologist at the National Hospital for Nervous Diseases, whom Freddie had consulted, had tried to explain the nature of the condition. Freddie got the impression that Alzheimer's disease, of which it appeared Lilli was in the early stages, was not fully understood by the physician himself. He had asked Lilli gently if she knew how old she was, and the time (to the nearest hour), as well as the current year, and the name of the Queen. Lilli had managed to answer all his questions correctly in addition to counting backwards from twenty, and asking whether she should repeat the exercise in German. When she came back from the doctor, she accused Freddie of wasting everybody's time, took off her hat and coat, and put her handbag neatly away in the fridge. Further investigations, including a CAT scan, had confirmed the original diagnosis, which had been made on the strength of the history, as well as revealing a modicum of cerebral atrophy.

Freddie prowled round the room absent-mindedly picking up the photographs of himself which decorated the sideboard; cricket in the long shadows with his father; as Oliver Twist (was that where Rosina got it from?) in the school play; with Lilli at his graduation; on the steps of the Register Office with Jane.

He picked up a photograph of his late father in his army uniform.

'That's my husband.'

Had he been a few years older, a few inches taller, it could have been Freddie. Freddie had the strange impression he was confronting his own ghost. He replaced the photograph next to a sepia portrait of Lilli, with bobbed hair, seated at the piano.

'My first professional engagement,' Lilli said. 'I was only sixteen. They wanted a pianist for a symphony concert at the Philharmonic Hall in Liverpool. Mozart's B-flat major. I was absolutely terrified. My mother made my dress. Black satin. She was an excellent dressmaker. I could have been ... I nearly ... They gave Myra Hess the CBE. Afterwards ... It was too late. I *hated* giving piano lessons. I never thought of them as lessons. They were the first encounter between a child and music. It was no good. I had to grit my teeth. Not one of them really wanted to learn. I think the mothers brought them just to get them out of the house. For something to do. All those grinding scales. All those elementary pieces. My idea of hell is to have to listen to eternity to "Für Elise". It wasn't easy, Freddie. I was so tired at night I used to cry into my pillow ...'

Freddie sat next to her on the sofa and took her hand.

Stuff Gordon Sitwell. There was no way he was going to let Lilli go into a home.

'I wanted so much for you to take up the piano, Freddie. I tried to teach you, but you hadn't the slightest interest . . .'

Lilli seemed to be having one of her lucid periods, to be in touch with reality. It was the moment, Freddie thought, to tell her about his dismissal.

'There's something we have to discuss. Something you ought to know.'

He wondered whether there was any point explaining that there had been exceptional expansion and irresponsibility in the financial markets, that the consequences of that excess and profligacy had to be paid for by someone, that he was no longer head of corporate finance at Sitwell Hunt International, that he had got the sack. But Lilli was staring at him as if he were a stranger, as if she had never seen him before, as her eyes grew visibly empty and her mind wandered off into some past interior accessible only to herself.

'Didn't you play the the saxophone', she said, 'with Harry Roy?'

Freddie gave up.

Mrs Williams insisted that he stay for lunch. It wasn't often, she said, that they had company. She set a place for him at the top of the gate-leg table. He was to be the guest of honour.

Guest of honour. Ten days ago he had been the guest of honour at the annual banquet of the City Livery Club. The invitation had come from the Lord Mayor himself who, as an alderman of the City of London, had been a personal client of Freddie's and had entrusted to him the affairs of the livery companies and the finances of the guilds.

Spawned in the Cambridge Union, Freddie was an accomplished speaker. Any nervousness induced by getting to his feet after dinner was instantly dispelled by a charge of adrenalin as he plunged into a task he was confident he would do well. Speaking without notes, he would picture himself as the hub of a large wheel of which the points he wished to cover – in this case the City, the poll tax, the Peasants' Revolt of 1381, and the Black Death with its resultant shortage of labour – were the spokes. Mentally circumventing the wheel he would eliminate the spokes one by one, until only the tyre remained, at which point he would know that his task was accomplished and his speech was at an end. Dressed in white tie and tails (Rosina's comment was that he looked a right wally), he had taken his place at the top table next to the Lady Mayoress, while Jane in a yellow silk dress from Bingo's – split at the front to reveal her legs as she walked – had chatted up the Secretary of State for Northern Ireland. After Grace recited by the Archbishop of Canterbury, a cavalcade of white-gloved waitresses weaving smartly in and out of the tables to the accompaniment of the 'Skaters' Waltz' and the 'Post Horn Gallop', had served the banquet which was rounded off by the entry of the silver Loving Cup, filled with spiced wine, which in a time-honoured ritual was passed along the tables.

Recalling his well-received address suddenly brought home to Freddie the extent of the fallout from his dismissal, and the fact that from now on there would be no more such prestigious invitations. He tried to convince himself that it didn't matter and that he didn't care; that he had been to too many cocktail parties where the conversation was inaudible, the food unmanagable, and the champagne warm; too many dinners at which he had been forced to listen to interminable orations whilst struggling to be civil to an aurally challenged stranger or entertain somebody's wearisome wife.

His own speech in Guildhall, in which he had compared

Watt Tyler and his revolutionaries with the present day militants, had been greeted with prolonged and enthusiastic clapping which had persisted in undulating waves until well after he had shaken the outstretched hand of the Lord Mayor and caught Jane's approving eye. He could hear the applause now, reverberating in his ears.

'There you go.' Mrs Williams' voice brought him back to earth.

He took his place at the head of the gate-leg table as a plate was put in front of him on which was not the exotic duckling with Anise, as served at the Lord Mayor's banquet, but a dull-eyed poached egg on a watery mound of mashed potato.

CHAPTER EIGHTEEN

Although Freddie was a risk-taker he had never been a gambler. Having walked at a brisk pace up Edgware Road and Park Lane and along Curzon Street from the Water Gardens, he was surprised to find himself standing outside the Vingt-et-Un, a gaming club to which he had been introduced by James, a notorious high-roller, and where he occasionally took clients from abroad. While his guests often took chances, Freddie's speculation was modest. He preferred to play the stock market where the croupiers were the brokers, their commissions the house percentages, and the stocks – despite the advent of technology – behaved with mathematical randomness.

His axiom in business, which he considered fundamental, was that at the top you must sell and at the bottom you must buy. Where most people went wrong was that they were too emotionally involved in their businesses to make the leap between recognising the top and getting out.

As far as the casino was concerned, he acted on the premise that money which you cannot afford to lose produces psychological distress and bad play, while money which means little to you leads to confidence and precision. He always put an upper limit on the amount he was prepared to risk. Having set his initial stake at an acceptable level, he mitigated the possibilities of losing it, either by betting heavily, in the hope of winning a substantial sum fairly quickly (and taking the chance of being rapidly cleaned out), or by dividing his capital into smaller units (so that there was much less likelihood of losing it all) and limiting the amount he stood to gain.

His game was blackjack, for which he used a card-counting system which entailed keeping track of the tens. He had not tried his luck in the middle of the day since he was fourteen years old. Whilst he was growing up there had been few holidays. His excursions with Lilli had largely been limited to 'away days', most of which took them to Chessington or Whipsnade zoos or to stately homes within a few hours' ride of Maida Vale. Freddie's favourite outing was to Brighton, where, while Lilli tried to interest him in the treasures of the Royal Pavilion and extolled the therapeutic values of the sea air, he had counted the minutes until they could go to the amusement arcades. It was here, amongst the heady clatter of the pin-ball and the fruit machines, that he had formulated his belief in his ultimate success and his conviction that persistance would be rewarded, with which he had signed his unwritten contract with fate. While Lilli relaxed in a deckchair, Freddie – who had sprung up in his teens and was exceptionally tall for his age – computed his chances of making his fortune. He counted out his pocket money (supplemented by a variety of after-school jobs), and applied himself to augmenting it. His precocious ability to call a halt to his activities while fortune was still smiling, to get out when he was ahead, not to push his luck, was apparent even then.

In a miasma of fistfuls of warm tokens, calculated manipulation of levers, revolving apples and bananas, the intoxicating rain of pennies from some automated heaven, he was unaware of time passing. When Lilli came to drag him away for lunch, or to tell him that they must hurry to catch the train, her disapproving voice ruptured his fantasies and interrupted his daydreams, that one day, some day, he would be rich.

As he entered the Vingt-et-Un and climbed the impressive staircase, he experienced exactly the same mounting sensation of excitement, harboured the same desires, as he had so many years ago on Brighton Pier.

Although there were few people in the heavily curtained gaming room hung with the stale smoke of cigars, Freddie was unable to get a table to himself. Sitting down at a 'ten pound minimum' table, next to a grossly overweight punter in a crumpled suit and tinted glasses, he took £100 from his wallet. Passing the two fifty-pound notes over to the dealer, an English rose with milk-white skin and soft blonde hair wearing a deceptively simple cornflower blue dress with puff sleeves and a sweetheart neck, he began, as usual, by cautiously placing small bets and keeping track of the 10s. When seventeen of them had been played, he checked that the next round would come from the cards which remained in the shoe and, in accordance with his strategy, increased the size of his bets. After half an hour he had doubled his initial stake. Pleased with his gain, he was about to get up from the table and cash in his chips. The voice of Derek Abbott, with the refrain of his £100,000 overdraft, reverberated in his head. One hundred pounds was a drop in the ocean. He was in need of serious money. Taking out his pen (and his worry beads), and with visions of doubling up his severance pay, he wrote out a cheque for £5,000.

He knew that the odds were against him. 'Good luck' made few millionaires. It was the same in the City. Those who regarded dealing as nothing but a game of chance invariably wound up penniless if not in jail. 'Good luck' was synonymous with good judgement, although it was often quoted, by the man who had lost out, as accounting for the success of his rival. The true gambler, who remembered only his good luck, and forgot his bad, was destined always to lose. It was this fatal optimism that ensured the solvency of gambling houses.

Setting aside all his years in banking, all his experience, all his acquired wisdom, Freddie managed to convince himself that it was some unseen force which had directed him from Lilli's flat to the casino where he was certain to win. What he was playing for was hope.

Moving to a more serious table where there was only one other player, the minimum bet £100 per box, and a more full-blown English rose who dealt the cards with the speed of light, he settled down in earnest to cock a snook at Derek Abbott.

Within five minutes he was dealt two blackjacks. Splitting the 8s, he got a 3 on one, and a 2 on the other. He doubled them both and the bank went bust. Within ten minutes his £5,000 stake had increased to £25,000!

He now had a problem. Twenty thousand pounds was not to be sneezed at. Bearing in mind his financial situation however, it was neither here nor there. The multicoloured piles of chips in front of him represented a chance of getting himself out of trouble. He hesitated only a few seconds. Putting £500 on each of three boxes, he caught the cynical eye of the dealer. It was his day. He could not put a foot wrong. In no time at all his £25,000 became £50,000. He played two boxes, £5,000 on each box. Two 6s on one box and two 7s on the other. The bank had a 4. Splitting the cards, and watched with interest by a young man wearing shades and a ponytail, who stood behind him at the table, he doubled his stakes to the tune of £20,000. On the first 6 he was dealt a 4, and on the second 6 a 3. He doubled again and got a 10 on each split, leaving him with 20 on one, and 19 on the other. His two split 7s got a 10 and a 4, which he promptly doubled and was dealt another 4. His second box had £15,000 running on it. A total of £35,000 on one deal. The anchor man at the end of the table had a £100 chip on his box, on which there was a 2 and 10. Drawing a 6 he stuck at 18. The English rose drew a 10: fourteen! Given a very little luck Freddie stood to make a cool £70,000 from one hand. Rotating his worry beads he willed the dealer to draw another 10. She drew an ace. His palms were damp. Fifteen. The next card *had* to be a 7 an 8 or a 9. It had to be. The bank would go bust, and he would be out of trouble with Derek Abbott. Beneath the gaze of the man with the pony tail, watched anxiously by Freddie, with the tactile certitude of a blind person the tapered fingers of the English rose advanced towards the shoe and withdrew a card. Six! Without a glance in Freddie's direction, she disdainfully swept up his chips and his cards and with them his chance of paying off his overdraft.

Dismissing his reversal simply as an unlucky break, Freddie decided that now his only salvation was to press harder and increase the size of his bets. With the capriciousness of a freak wind, his luck turned. Fourteen hands later, without a single draw and the play running relentlessly against him, he had ploughed back not only all his winnings but his original stake. Five thousand pounds down the tubes!

Considerably shaken, he called for coffee. Leaving his cup on the table, and keeping one eye on the play, he went to the cash desk and wrote another cheque to the tune of £5,000. On his table the bank was now losing. The play seemed once again to have turned. He told the cashier to hurry with his chips but the shift had changed and the girl, whom he hadn't seen before and who did not recognise him, needed authorisation. Flipping his worry beads, Freddie waited for the manager who with the merest inclination of his head signified his approval to the cashier who counted out Freddie's chips, checking and rechecking them with agonising slowness.

By the time he got back to the table, his coffee cup had been moved, his seat had been taken by the man with the pony tail, he had been demoted to a chair at the far end, and he had missed another winning hand. As heedless of time as he had been in the Brighton amusement arcades, he set steadfastly about recouping his losses. He played two boxes. Eighteen on each of them. An 8 for the bank. The anchor man drew a card when he should not have done. A 10. The dealer gave herself an ace, winning at 19 and snapping at Freddie for accidentally touching the cards. As his worry beads worked overtime, his pile of chips swiftly dwindled. He blamed himself. For forgetting his fundamental principle. For not having the good sense to know he was at the top and making the decision to get out.

When he was down to his last £100, he crossed to the roulette table and put the lot on number 2, the second of March, his wedding day. The silver ball, its trajectory closely followed by the croupier and the pit bull seated like some impervious slit-eyed God above him, circled the swiftly revolving wheel, fell, then rose to spin again in agonising circles. Mesmerised by the blob of metal and feeling physically sick, Freddie watched it hover tantalisingly over number 2 before, rattling in its death throes, it insinuated itself into 21 by its side.

He had been in the casino for less than an hour. In forty-five minutes he had thrown away £10,000. Furious with himself, he ran down into the street where he was greeted by torrential rain. The doorman did his best, with whistle and outsize umbrella, to find a taxi. The waterlogged streets of a prematurely dark Mayfair were not the most propitious place. Impatient with the man's abortive, if well-intentioned efforts, Freddie decided, for the second time that day, to walk to Regent's Park.

It was only when he reached Chester Terrace, cold, wet, and extremely angry – he felt quite capable now of carrying out the crime he had only dreamed of committing against Gordon Sitwell – that he realised to his horror that, unaccustomed to driving Jane's car, he had left the Japanese hatchback outside the Water Gardens.

Entering the house quickly and leaving dark pools on the parquet floor, he flung himself up the stairs like a junkie in search of his unfailing panacea.

The performance of *The Magic Flute*, which despite its triteness and banality always managed to elevate his mood, had been announced whilst he was getting ready to meet Wichmann, what seemed light years ago. Before peeling off his clothes, he pressed the button on his music centre which was permanently tuned to Radio 3. Instead of Tamino's flute, Sarastro's invocation to Isis and Osiris, or the coloratura of the Queen of the Night, a bass voice chanted tunelessly to the beat of the bongo drums: 'Peaze Porage in the Pot Nine Days Old. Peaze Porage in the Pot Nine Days Old. Peaze Porage in the Pot Nine Days . . .' Certain that he was in imminent danger of a heart attack, Freddie bellowed for the blood of Rosina who had just come home from school.

'Who told you to touch my radio?'

'Sorry, Daddy . . .'

She was always sorry.

'You know quite well that no one is allowed to touch my radio.'

'I said I'm sorry.'

'That's not good enough, Rosina. You have no respect for other people's property, no respect for anything. This is my house. My dressing-room. And my radio . . .'

Listening to the sound of his own voice as he went on and on about personal space and invasion of privacy and the automatic deference due to parents from their children (which he did not believe) and the fact that he wasn't surprised that Rosina's reports were so poor (not entirely true) when she was constantly watching TV or going out or washing her hair or spending hours on the phone, he was aware in the far reaches of his brain that he was taking out on Rosina his animosity towards Gordon Sitwell and Conrad Verger and Derek Abbott, and Hans Wichmann from whom he hadn't yet heard, but even though he realised it, he was unable to stop himself from reducing her to a state of hysteria (not difficult) and finally to tears which added fuel to the fire of his rage.

'Apart from anything else, Rosina, you know perfectly well that if there's one thing I cannot tolerate it's that racket . . .'

'It is *not* a racket. You don't know the first thing about it . . .'

'And I don't want to.'

'That's your trouble. You're so wrapped up in that terrible caterwauling *you* have on all the time, in your wheeling and dealing, as if everything's down to money . . .'

'I haven't noticed you're averse to spending it.'

'. . . that you're not the slightest bit interested in anything else. You've never bothered to listen to my music. You've never bothered to listen to me. You don't listen to anybody. You only listen to yourself!'

The volcano of Freddie's wrath burned itself out as suddenly as it had erupted. He was ashamed of himself for displacing onto a 15-year-old feelings which belonged elsewhere.

'Tell me about it.'

'About what?'

'This . . . music. What is it about?'

'It's about *black* people.' Rosina helped herself to one of Freddie's handkerchiefs into which she blew her nose. 'It's about decay and death in the slums of New York. About inner city tensions. About project housing. About poetry, about attitude, about style . . .'

'Okay, okay . . .'

'You asked me . . . Daddy what's the matter?'

Freddie had collapsed onto the chair in his sodden suit. His head was in his hands. Kneeling, Rosina put her arms round him.

'I'm sorry, Daddy. I didn't mean to upset you.'

'It's not you, Rosina.' Freddie stroked her hair.

It was the fact that he had just chucked away another £10,000.

CHAPTER NINETEEN

The public humiliation of Sir Gordon Sitwell, followed by his hounding by the press, had nothing to do with Freddie's dismissal but was an indirect result of it.

Gordon was not a bad man, but like the roses in his garden he was a product of his environment. The virtues of uprightness and moral rectitude which he had inherited, via his father, from his grandfather, had been mulched by the belief obtaining when he joined Sitwell Hunt as a very young man, and which he preached to his employees, that security and safety in banking were more important than a potentially large profit.

Since he had fired Freddie, Gordon had not been himself. Margaret had noticed the difference although he had not dicussed the matter with her, and she was unaware of its cause. Gordon was jumpy and nervous. He was more taciturn than usual. When he did speak to her, he was extremely short. He spent more time in the garden, and often went out – without telling her where he was going – at night. Margaret had caught sight of Jane Lomax at the hosiery counter in Harvey Nichols. She had wanted to ask her if she knew if anything untoward was going on at Sitwell Hunt, but as she approached, Jane had turned away, and Margaret could not be sure whether the slight had been deliberate, or whether the vice chairman's wife had not noticed her. Whatever was bugging Gordon, Margaret thought, resigning herself to the situation and turning for her customary solace to the romantic fiction which Gordon decried but which was, in her opinion, no worse than the spaghetti westerns to which he was partial, he was keeping to himself.

Gordon did not regret that he had sacked Freddie. He had taken over Sitwell Hunt from his father in the full flower of its reputation and success, and he had no intention of relinquishing it in anything other than the peak of condition. As with his roses, so with his bank, it was a question of vigilance and protection, of tending and of nurturing, and of cutting out the dead wood.

To this end he had been watching his second in command with increasing alarm for some time. There was no doubt that he owed much to Freddie. In the five years that he had been with Sitwell Hunt he had worked extremely hard and had brought a great deal of new business to the bank, which he had served both with honour and integrity.

In view, however, of the recession, the company's recent losses (in particular the deficit which had resulted from the defection of Bretton Corporation) and Freddie's apparent recklessness – which may well have been a consequence of the sound judgement on which he prided himself, and which had been vindicated by his successful defence of Corinthian Hotels – Gordon had decided, after careful deliberation, to dispense with the highly paid services of his head of corporate finance and promote his son-in-law (which would please his daughter) who would eventually make a more prudent chairman of the bank.

Having made his decision and acted upon it, he was not the only one at Sitwell Hunt unable to get Freddie out of his mind. The news of the vice chairman's enforced departure had caused not only consternation, but a great deal of agitation in the ranks. A few members of Freddie's erstwhile team, as well as some of the senior executives now fearful for their own jobs, had become decidedly jittery. The worried personnel director had been to see Gordon with the suggestion that he take the matter seriously.

'It wouldn't do Sitwell's reputation any good to be known as hire-and-fire merchants,' she said. 'There's the milk round to consider.'

Gordon knew that she meant the annual trawling of potential Oxbridge candidates in the spring.

'. . . We don't want to get a name for dismissing our people, talented or otherwise, at a moment's notice.'

'Point taken,' Gordon said. 'What do you suggest?'

'Basically, I suggest we offer the services of a first-class outplacement firm to Mr Lomax, sir. It might cost you £10,000 but at the end of the day it would be well worth it.'

Gordon was not a man given to spurious friendships. Over the past five years, he had become fonder of his vice chairman than he thought. The pretext of passing on the personnel director's idea, rather than allowing her to do it herself, gave him an opportunity to make contact with Freddie.

Freddie's voice on the phone, not unsurprisingly, was glacial.

'Yes?'

In the background Gordon could hear the dramatic strains of the opera in which the chief of police gets stabbed with a fruit knife.

'I thought I'd just give you a ring, Freddie,' Gordon said, 'To find out how you are getting on . . .'

'I'm getting on perfectly well.'

'And the family?'

'Everybody's fine.'

'I don't suppose you've found anything yet?' Gordon anticipated the silence which followed. 'I have been thinking . . .' he said, as if it the notion were his own. 'I have decided that it would be only fair if we sponsored you for a top outplacement consultancy. At the bank's expense, of course.'

'Not interested.'

'They would work with you. At your level, you would have your own office with full secretarial facilities. They would put you in touch with headhunters until such time as –'

'Not interested,' Freddie said.

'If you take my advice –'

'I've had enough of your advice.'

'I was only trying to help . . .'

'I don't need your help, Gordon. I can look out for myself.'

'You're making a big mistake. Think about it. Get in touch with personnel.'

It was no coincidence that after his rebuff from Freddie, Gordon had instructed his driver to take him to Park Lane and drop him off at the Hilton Hotel for what he liked to think of as his 'happy hour'. Since his run-in with the police, he had forsaken the crepuscular world that abutted King's Cross station, for the more salubrious streets of Shepherd Market, to which he had of late been returning with increasing frequency.

A product of Eton, to which he had been bundled off at the age of eight, and Oxford, where he had managed only a Second, Gordon accepted that sexually he was repressed. He was astonished at the current outspokenness of the cinema, some of the more lurid scenes on late night TV, and the descriptions and permutations of the sexual act about which he read in the gold-embossed airport books he guiltily consigned to hotel waste-paper baskets, which left nothing whatsoever to the imagination. His father, a remote and authoritative figure with a belief in corporal punishment, had been totally uncommunicative as far as either the facts of life or relationships were concerned. His mother had been far too busy socialising to pay any attention to Gordon. His resentment towards her for the fact that all she could manage on occasions when it simply could not be avoided, was the most perfunctory and transient kiss, was expressed in his boyish cruelty to animals – tormenting frogs and cutting up live worms – coupled with a tendency both at home and at school, to show off. Gordon had first become conscious of what he realised only years later was sexual intercourse between his parents, at the age of 4. Woken by some night terror, he had approached the open door of the master bedroom and been stopped in his tracks by sights and sounds which both fascinated and repelled him, and which he was quite unable to understand. At first he had been terrified and prayed that his mother and father would stop whatever it was that they were doing to each other, then he had crept back up the stairs to his own room and lain awake all night feeling left out and resentful. When he was older, on the rare occasions when his mother came into the bathroom to supervise his ablutions, she would greet Gordon's protests at the intrusion, and his hasty efforts to conceal his private parts beneath his flannel, with the dismissive comment that he had 'nothing to look at'. Sometimes, when his mother was getting dressed, he would peek through the crack of the door hoping to catch her without any clothes on. On one occasion she had surprised him, and had turned him over to his father who had given him a sound thrashing.

Gordon had been 20 years old before he had slept – he could not bring himself to utter the current neologism – with a girl, the first one he had managed to lay his hands on since leaving school. The encounter, although aided by her father's Glenfiddich, had been singularly inept. After this initiation there had been one or two similarly empirical skirmishes before his unsatisfactory marriage to Margaret had led to his seeking alternative solace.

There had been a great deal of media fuss and pother recently about the pestering of prostitutes (both male and female), as well as a clamp-down by the police on kerb crawling. Gordon justified his predilection for intercourse with the women who plied their trade in the streets behind the Hilton Hotel, by the fact that he was merely talking to them. He could not see what harm there was in that.

When he was not in the car, Gordon's happy hour invariably followed the same pattern. First the reconnaissance. Stalking the pavements, his head down, his hands in the pockets of his overcoat, he would quantify, as if entering them in some mental ledger, the goods on offer. One was too squat, another was too tall, this one was too scrawny, that one was too fat, one was too up front, one too supercilious, one appeared spaced out, her companion too predatory. Gordon had been cruising the streets for a great many years before he realised that what he was seeking was a remote and patrician-faced brunette, a carbon copy of his mother. Having tracked her down, he was willing to pay generously for her time while he explained, in graphic terms, what he would like to do to her. The prostitutes would regard him with contempt – the more contempt the better – while he catalogued his furtive desires which ranged from watching their performance in the lavatory, to mutual masturbation, and the most profound and prolonged penetration with both his tongue and his penis of every bodily orifice. The catalogue of his innermost fantasies tended towards the sadistic – as they had towards his frogs and his worms – and he frequently dreamed of disfiguring the women and, in his darker moments, of dismembering them, with his father's hunting knife, into a hundred bloody pieces. His fascination with blood had started when as a small, uncomprehending boy, he had accidentally stumbled upon his mother's soiled sanitary protection in the bathroom. It had persisted until the present day when, mesmerised by the bauble oozing slowly from his finger when punctured by a thorn from his roses, he was reluctant to take out his handkerchief and wipe away the fascinating drop of scarlet dew.

On the evening of his abortive conversation with Freddie which left him with a feeling of rejection which echoed those of his childhood, Gordon had dismissed his driver in front of the Hilton and walked briskly through the crowded lobby, out of the back of the hotel, and into the shadowed streets. Tonight he was in search of total absolution. He needed to expiate his sins in the sackcloth and ashes of a comprehensive shrift. Had he not been thinking about Freddie, he might have paid more attention to the police constable with his two-way radio who was lingering in a doorway.

Stopping for a moment, Gordon exchanged a few words with a girl in a scarlet jumper, but despite the tawny breasts, their nipples, like small thumbs, visible through the open lace-stitch, he was repelled by her pitted skin and moved on. An elegant hooker with bare legs, in high heels and a satin suit with diamanté buttons fastened over her naked chest, who would not have looked amiss at a Buckingham Palace garden party, met his eyes but alarmed him with her poise. Turning into Hertford Street, he rejected a fluffy blonde who did not look old enough to be on the game, before spotting an elegant brunette with upswept hair and dangling earrings. It was the dangling earrings which did for him. They recalled his mother's diamond drop earrings, which had seemed to the young Gordon to twinkle above her bare shoulders, in the luminous portrait above the library chimney-piece of the Sitwell home in Scotland. The brunette, identifying a wealthy punter, moved in her slit skirt across the pavement towards him.

'Want the business, dear?'

Gordon noticed that her mouth was painted with a gouache of orange gloss and that on closer acquaintance she did not look the slightest bit like his mother. He was, none the less, about to explain to her that the only service he required was fifteen minutes of her undivided attention for which he was willing to pay the appropriate fee, when he realised that they were not alone.

'Excuse me, sir. May I ask what you are doing?'

Gordon looked at the police constable. He was considerably older than the one who had cautioned him at King's Cross.

'I have been keeping you under observation for the last five minutes, sir, and I have seen you approach several ladies . . .'

'Of course you have.' Gordon was used to dealing with subordinates. 'I am looking for an all-night chemist. I was asking this young lady for directions.'

'Do you live round here, sir?'

'If I did, officer, I would know where the chemists' shops were located. I live in Stanmore. I was on my way home.'

'From . . .?'

'From the City.'

'May I suggest, sir, that Hertford Street is hardly "on the way home" from the City.'

'I'm quite aware of that, officer. My wife is ill . . .' he was sorry to bring Margaret into it, 'and I've had an extremely busy day. Now if you'll excuse me . . .'

'Just one moment if you please, sir.' The constable, who would not have made more than messenger in Gordon's bank, reached for his notebook.

'I should be extremely careful if I were you,' Gordon warned him. 'I think you should know that you are talking to the chairman of a bank and a close friend of the Lord Mayor of the City of London.'

The officer was unimpressed with this pulling of rank. It was his bread and butter.

'Could I have your name and full address, please, sir?'

'I refuse to give you either,' Gordon said. 'There is, as far as I am aware, no pass law in this country.'

'Then I'm afraid I'm going to have to report you, sir.'

'What the hell are you talking about?' Gordon said. 'I've never heard such nonsense in my life.'

'If you refuse to co-operate, sir,' the police constable raised his two-way radio to his lips, 'I have no option but to ask you to come with me to the police station. I am arresting you . . .'

'For what offence?'

'Persistent soliciting . . .'

'You must be out of your mind!'

'. . . Under Section Two of the Sexual Offences Act.'

CHAPTER TWENTY

Freddie had taken over the dining-room. He used it as an office while he read every advertisement he could lay hands on, wrote countless life-and-death letters, spent hours making fruitless telephone calls and following up abortive leads in situations, amongst others, where he had found out that heads of corporate finance had either been made redundant or had died. Looking for work he had discovered – which included continuing his lunch arrangements with his City pals – was a full-time job.

Piers Warburton, with Freddie's interests very much at heart, was doing his best to help. He had tipped Freddie off both about a director of corporate finance vacancy – which had turned out to be a board position for applicants between 45 and 50 years of age – and an opening at Lloyds which had proved to be for a deputy to a head of department considerably Freddie's junior for which he did not bother to apply. There had still been no word from Wichmann. Freddie had called Frankfurt repeatedly. Herr Wichmann was in a meeting. Herr Wichmann was with a client. Herr Wichmann was out of town.

According to the City editors, the mean time taken by executives to find a job was anything up to six months. But it was not the City editors who were being forced into bankruptcy, not the City editors who were being cut back.

At the end of two weeks of unremitting networking which he found exceedingly distasteful, Freddie was not only still in square one as far as his career prospects were concerned, but in the grip of an unfamiliar rage. Sometimes he felt as if his anger, which was triggered by the least provocation, would throttle him. Accustomed to being in charge, not only of others but of himself, he made an heroic effort to overcome it, but his emotions refused to be subordinated. Listening to the sound of his own voice as he attempted to restore what could not be restored, to reconstruct what could not be reconstructed, as if it were a question of will, he took out his pain on his loved ones and afterwards was consumed with self-hatred.

Rosina, who had other things on her mind, was unperturbed by what she considered were her father's unjust and unprovoked attacks on her. His run-ins with Jane were more distressing. Jane had been furious that he had not only borrowed her car without telling her, making her late for her appointment with the dentist, but had added insult to injury by leaving it outside Lilli's flat, and Freddie was annoyed that because of Jane's committee meetings he could not call his home his own.

'I do not want all those women in my house.'

'It's the functions committee, darling, and the Ball's next month.'

'Well, you'll have to hold the meetings elsewhere.'

'Freddie! You are not at the bank . . .'

The problem was not only one of committee meetings. Each time Jane left the house, Freddie asked her where she was going, how long she would be. Sometimes she had no idea, and cheerfully told him so. Used to working to an agenda, to having his day divided into predetermined and clearcut instalments, Freddie did not understand. He expected to be provided with a resumé of her movements. If she was late home he grew fearful that something untoward had happened to her, and asked her to be more precise. If she complained about his vigilance, he said that it was because he loved her, because he worried about her. She told him that paternalism was the worst form of tyranny. He had no idea what she was talking about. Sometimes, during the day, he would ask Jane what she was doing, when she replied that she wasn't doing anything – meaning nothing in particular – he said she must be doing *something*. He told her what *he* was doing: 'I'm just going to the postbox'; 'I'm just going to look at the teletext'; 'I'm just going to listen to *Turandot*'; 'I'm just going to watch the news'. He asked her if she had seen things: his briefcase, his calculator, his memo-recorder, his diary. Sometimes, when he was on the telephone, he would ask her to write down a number for him. He was used to a personal assistant.

With no department to control, he supervised the running of the household with which he had never concerned himself before: 'Where did you get that?' 'Why on earth have we got this?' 'You're not throwing that away?' 'Whose are these?' He interrupted Jane's cooking. Once she lost an egg she was about to crack – she found it later in her bureau where she kept her stationery – when Freddie interrupted her to enquire, as if she kept them in the microwave, if she happened to have a first-class stamp. When he disturbed her in her sewing-room to which, never ever having had too much of Freddie previously, she was now happy to escape, he justified the intrusion by the fact that she was 'only sewing'. When Jane suggested to Freddie – to get him out of the way – that he go for a walk in the park, he replied that she had always protested that he worked too hard, that he would have thought that she would have liked having him around, and that the park was full of people with nothing better to do than talk to the squirrels, and that he did not need anyone to tell him what to do.

It began to dawn on Jane that the fact that she and Freddie

had always got on so well, was perhaps due to the fact that because of Freddie's addiction to work, his need for constant activity, they had, since their marriage, actually spent very little time in each other's company. Even in bed at night, especially in bed at night, it was not like old times. They no longer fell asleep in each other's arms and Jane did not reach out to him. She was afraid to touch him. The king-sized bed had become a no man's land divided down the middle. It was as if, in addition to his livelihood, Gordon Sitwell had robbed Freddie of some vital component, as if he had been switched off at the mains.

Freddie was having breakfast in the kitchen, his stack of newspapers – opened at the Appointments Vacant pages – spread out all over the table which Jane wanted to use, when Lavender arrived for work with her face discoloured and her cheek swollen.

'He went for me,' she said listlessly. 'Lucky for him I didn't have me baby premature.'

'What happened?' Freddie pulled out a chair for her at the newspaper-strewn table, while Jane made some tea.

'He was nicking money for ciggies. He found this packet of Featherlite in me handbag . . .'

Jane and Freddie exchanged glances.

'He thought I'd been out screwing.' Lavender put an eloquent hand to her abdomen distended like a taut football. 'Screwing!'

'What were the condoms *doing* in your handbag?' Jane said practically, putting three lumps of sugar in the tea.

'That's what Tony wanted to know. I told him someone put them there. They weren't nothing to do with me.' She took out a pink tissue. 'He didn't believe me. He went for me!'

Lavender's problem, for which Rosina was unwittingly responsible, released some of the tension, which had been building up over trivialities, between Freddie and Jane.

When Lavender had gone upstairs to do her cleaning, Freddie put his arms round Jane's waist.

'At least I don't beat you up. I don't mean to be angry, Jane. I'm angry with myself. I'm really sorry about the car. And your friends. I blew my top. I wasn't *expecting* them to be here. I didn't think.'

'Don't worry about it. I know how you must feel . . .'

'You have no idea how I feel.'

'If you told me, I might be able to help.'

'I'm okay, darling. I've lost my job. I'm not ill. I am not an invalid. I don't need help.'

Ever since he had been 6 years old and his mother was busy with her pupils, if anything went wrong he had had to cope with it on his own. He would continue to do so. He gathered up the newspapers and looked at his watch.

'I'd better do some work.'

Jane's heart went out to him. 'I'll ask Bingo if she'll have the committee meeting at her house next week.'

Freddie was in the dining-room, listening to *Pelléas et Mélisande* and attempting to make some sense of his accounts, while he waited for the phone to ring, as usual, when Derek Abbott called. By the concern he manifested for Freddie's wellbeing and the exaggerated interest with which he enquired about his prospects, Freddie guessed that the news was not good.

'I have spoken to Head Office . . .' the bank manager began.

Freddie tapped his pencil on the table. He was damned if he was going to make it easy.

'Unfortunately it is as I thought. The bank, being uncovered, would like you to reduce your overdraft immediately you receive your cheque from Sitwell Hunt. They are willing to continue it – in the very short term only – to the tune of £50,000.'

'You do realise that this puts me in an extremely invidious

situation.' Freddie threw the pencil down. 'There is no doubt that I shall find something suitable.' He decided to prevaricate. 'There are already one or two things in the pipeline. As a matter of fact I am waiting for an extremely important call now. But it is going to take a bit of time.'

'The matter is not in my hands, I'm afraid.'

How often had Freddie used that phrase himself?

'I think you could have exerted a little pressure,' he felt his gall rising. 'All I need is a few months.'

'Believe me . . .' Derek Abbott said. This exhortation was invariably followed by a lie '. . . I did my very best.'

The next call was from Hans Wichmann.

'Freddie? I have been trying to send you a fax. I don't have your fax number. How are you keeping? And how is your dear wife?'

Another over-solicitous one.

'I have at last some news . . .'

Perhaps he had been wrong.

'I told you when we met – such a wonderful English breakfast – that I must discuss the matter with one or two of my colleagues. I was worried at the time that there could be problems at this end.'

Freddie did not dare speak.

'We have been over the question of supermarkets with the . . . how you say . . . the fine-tooth comb?'

Wichmann's voice was optimistic.

'At the end of the day, the decision we have made is that, for the moment in the least . . .'

All over bar the shouting.

'. . . We have not got the green light.'

'Thank you for letting me know.' Freddie tried to keep his voice steady. Not to let his disappointment show. 'If anything else should crop up . . .' he said, hating himself for having to crawl to Wichmann.

'My dear boy, I will be immediately on the telephone. *Ja*,

ja . . .' Freddie could hear Wichmann talking impatiently to someone in his office. 'My regards to your beautiful daughter, and to your dear wife.'

He knew that he would not hear from the Frankfurt broker again. Picking up his pencil, he added the £11,000 he had lost on Universal Concrete and the £10,000 he had thrown away at the casino (for which he had still not forgiven himself) to the outstanding bills for the house insurance, and electricity, and gas, and the mortgage interest, and the water rates, and the poll tax, onto his £115,000 overdraft, making the grand total, devoid of any financial cushion, look increasingly alarming. It was like a personal nightmare. If he didn't get some cash together soon he was going to find it impossible to keep afloat, even for a few months, without demolishing the entire structure of his life.

He was gazing grimly at the latest batch of bills, when the telephone on the table rang. To his surprise it was Thomas Glidewell, an ex-Sitwell Hunt client, from whom he hadn't heard for some time.

'Freddie? I rang the bank. They told me you were at home. Not sick are you? I'm in town for a couple of days. How are you fixed for dinner tonight?'

Some years ago, as head of corporate finance, Freddie had been instrumental in bringing Tom Glidewell's small family business, the Derbyshire-based Glidewell Security Grilles onto the market. As a result of his expertise, his efforts to find suitable expansion outlets, and his talent for commercial match-making, the grilles were now in world-wide demand and the Glidewell brothers (no one believed it was their real name) millionaires several times over.

Freddie had remained friendly, on a personal basis, with Tom Glidewell and his young wife, Wendy, and he and Jane had been to stay with them at their farm in Bakewell.

Over dinner at the Savoy Grill, Freddie, who had only toyed with his food but made heavy inroads into the wine, which didn't go unremarked by Tom Glidewell, explained briefly why he was no longer with Sitwell Hunt.

'I shouldn't worry too much if I were you.' Tom tucked into his *mille feuilles*. 'There's no stigma attached to redundancy these days. How are you managing?'

'Fine.'

'Don't bullshit me.' He put down his spoon and fork with satisfaction and ordered coffee.

'Okay, Tom.' Freddie pushed his pudding to one side of the china plate. 'Things are not going as well as I hoped. It's a question of staying afloat. If you really want to know, I'm beginning to get seriously worried.'

'You're not going to like this, Freddie,' Tom signalled for a toothpick, 'but I want you to accept a loan.'

'You're dead right!'

'Listen a minute. And pay close attention. If it wasn't for you and what you did for Glidewell Security Grilles, there'd be no Swiss bank accounts, no offshore funds, no farm in Bakewell. I'd still be living in Badger Cottage, and my brother and me would still be schlepping our grilles from door to door. Have one of these petits fours. I'm going to lend you twenty grand . . .'

As Freddie was about to protest, Tom held up his hand.

'. . . on the strict understanding', he put a chocolate truffle in his mouth, 'that if you can't pay it back, then that's how it will be. Now I'm going to tell you what I'm doing in London.'

'What are you doing in London?'

Tom's face grew grave. 'I've come down to be with Wendy. She's in the Middlesex. She's dying of lymphoma.'

As Tom recounted a poignant chronicle of reprieves, remissions and chemotherapy which had failed to work the hoped-for miracle, Freddie was aware that, while in the grand order of things his own dilemma paled into insignificance, it did not make him feel the slightest bit better.

'I can't tell you how sorry I am.' Freddie noticed that Tom's eyes were suspiciously moist. 'I had no idea about Wendy. I honestly don't know what to say.'

'You don't have to say anything. I didn't mean to dump on you. Sometimes . . . if you aren't going to eat these I'll finish them off . . . it's take the lid off or explode.'

'I wish I could do something.'

'You already have. Sympathy, not solutions. It's what most people want.'

When Freddie got home, taking a taxi from the Strand, Jane was already asleep. Getting into bed quietly, so as not to wake her, he lay on his back, alone in the darkness, going over the evening's conversation and wondering how it was that he was able to share his problems with Tom Glidewell, who meant little to him, and not with his wife. He was no nearer an answer to his own question when his circuitous thoughts, which prevented him from sleeping night after night, were interrupted by the telephone which was on the far side of the bed.

Sitting up, in an automatic response, Jane grabbed the receiver.

'Who? Who?'

Freddie was unable to make out the voice on the other end of the line.

'New York. Some office. Sidonie Newmark? Would you mind telling her it's two o'clock in the morning . . .' Jane said, before wriggling beneath the covers and going promptly back to sleep.

CHAPTER TWENTY-ONE

'BANK CHAIRMAN IN SEX SCANDAL'. Up early for golf with Charles Holdsworth, the headlines in the *News of the World* above a photograph of Gordon Sitwell, caught and transfixed Freddie's incredulous eyes. Although he might in his fantasies have planned to murder Gordon for ruining his career, he had no desire whatsoever to see the old boy discredited.

In all the time that he had known Gordon Sitwell, there had never been the slightest hint of what one reporter referred to as 'City businessman's secret vice'. Whether or not Gordon had been soliciting, whether or not he had been looking for an all-night chemist – and it seemed to Freddie highly unlikely – whatever the verdict of the magistrates, he had already been tried, and his good name destroyed, by the sordid appetite of the press. A nod was as good as a wink from some impecunious police officer, and any tip-off concerning a public figure was always 'appreciated' by the Grub Street hacks.

Shocked as he was by the accounts of Gordon's arrest, Freddie had other things to think about, in particular Sidonie Newmark whom he had neither seen nor heard from in nearly five years. He wondered what had happened to the Italian Count. Sidonie had been unable to say very much on the telephone. Only that she was sorry she had mistaken the time – for which he was to apologise to Jane – and that she was coming to London. She had asked Freddie to fix up an opera, and to meet her for a drink at the Berkeley Hotel where she always stayed.

Although his fling with Sidonie was long over, the sound of her voice on the telephone had disturbed his equilibrium and taken him back to the physical and sexual peak of his mid-thirties. His *coup de foudre* with Sidonie had been a total infatuation with a kindred spirit – the primary erogenous zone being the brain – which, thankfully, had burned itself out. He would not, he thought wryly, be very much use to her now.

On the way to golf in Jane's car (borrowed this time with her permission), Freddie turned on the radio to what appeared to be an omen. Jessye Norman, singing the 'Liebestod', took him back to Venice and the height of their affair when, Sidonie clinging tightly to him, they had crossed a flooded St Mark's Square on planks to get to *Tristan und Isolde* at La Fenice. *Tristan und Isolde* was being performed at Covent Garden on the day Sidonie was due to arrive in London.

Charles was waiting in the clubhouse together with Richard Scott, a psychiatrist, and Irving Weston, president of an American computer company, who were making up the fourball.

'Freddie Lomax . . .' Charles made the introductions. 'Vice chairman and head of corporate finance at Sitwell Hunt International.' Before they reached the eighteenth hole, Freddie resolved to swallow his pride and speak to Charles, who was ten years his junior and on a much lower rung of the banking ladder, about the galling fact that he was in urgent need of a job.

So far, apart from telling Piers Warburton, he had managed to play his cards pretty close to his chest. Peter and Georgina, next door, had found out that he was unemployed

by accident. Georgina left Chester Terrace in the mornings at
the same time as Freddie. Not having seen either Leonard or
the Mercedes outside his house for a few days, she had called
in to enquire if Freddie was all right. Since he had opened
the door to her himself, it had been hard to dissimulate. He
had taken Georgina into his confidence, half-hoping that
there might be some suitable opening in the wine trade
which – having spent a few days in Epernay with Jane
one Christmas – he imagined he knew something about.
Georgina, genuinely distressed by Freddie's revelation, had
said that she was struggling to keep her own head above
water (or rather above wine) and that it was as much as she
could do not to go into receivership herself. She did have a
wide circle of contacts, however, and despite the fact that
many of them were, like her husband, indigent peers of the
realm, promised to keep her eyes open for anything which
might possibly be of interest to Freddie.

The last time Freddie had played golf, his handicap, after
licited arrival later on with a bottle of 1961 Château Latour
(Pauillac) from their personal cellar. Drawn together by adver-
sity, he felt that in the course of a day he had got to know his
rather reserved neighbours better than he had in five years of
inviting each other to dinner.

The last time Freddie had played golf, his handicap, after
winning the weekly medal competition, had been pulled to
five. Charles was playing off nineteen and their opponents
off thirteen. Freddie had to give Scott and Weston six shots,
while Charles received eleven. They agreed to play for five
pounds a head.

The first hole was a long, par four dog-leg, bounded by
trees and bushes, with semi-rough down the right-hand
side. After a couple of practice swings, Freddie, a big hitter,
smacked the ball 230 yards, right down the middle of the
fairway. Feeling his spirits soar for the first time in weeks, he
consigned his problems to a back burner and concentrated

on his game.

Charles's shot, also straight, was 60 yards shorter than Freddie's. Scott hit a long ball but sliced it, and landed up under a bush on the left.

Weston's swing, with his boron-shafted driver, entailed much stance taking, wriggling, foot-shuffling and air-hitting. This virtuoso perfomance, which seemed to go on interminably and was decidedly idiosyncratic, was followed by a distinctly unimpressive drive.

Charles winked at Freddie. 'All gong and no dinner!'

Charles's second shot landed 70 or 80 yards from the green. Scott, chipping out sideways, sliced again, this time badly. He shook his head with disbelief as his ball rolled inexorably towards a bunker.

Weston hooked to the left, well short, and Freddie, using his five wood, arched his ball smoothly onto the green where it pitched tantalisingly by the flag then ran daintily on a few yards past the pin. Neither Scott nor Weston were near enough to one-putt. Giving Freddie and Charles a stroke, the hole was halved.

Walking ahead with Charles, Freddie cleared his throat. To his surprise he heard himself say, 'How did Bingo like the brooches?'

'Delighted.' Charles chuckled. 'I had to buy her both. You know Bingo.'

Freddie cursed himself for blowing his opportunity. He opened his mouth to try again, when the computer king caught up with them.

'What's the buzz amongst you guys on the great depression?'

'Recession,' Freddie corrected him, willing him to go away.

'Recession, depression, what does it matter as long as you love your mother. Our trade went *down* for the first time in twenty-three years. Two point eight billion dollars into the red, $124 million in UK sales alone.'

'*Recession* is quantifiable . . .'

'Dick's the doom and gloom merchant,' Charles said. '"The breakdown of order, the collapse of house prices, the disintegration of capitalism . . ."'

Weston trotted after the long-legged Richard as they approached the second tee. 'Didn't you say you were a *shrink*?'

'Charles . . .' Freddie began.

'He won't get anything cheerful out of Dick,' Charles chuckled. 'He specialises in brewer's droop! A woman goes to the dentist. "I'd rather have a baby than have my teeth filled," she says. "Well, make your mind up, madam," the dentist tells her, "because I have to alter the position of the chair!"'

Freddie played like one possessed. Over the next six holes he and Charles didn't drop a single shot while their opponents vacillated between playing badly and managing to get a par by using their shot.

On the ninth tee, while the others waited impatiently, Weston gave an extended performance before deigning to address the ball. Stopping in mid-swing, he glared at Freddie.

'Do you think you could stop rattling those ruddy beads?'

They were again all square by the time they reached the seventh, a short par three.

'Which reminds me,' Weston said, 'two guys who had played golf all over the world found themselves in central Africa. Guy was about to tee off when he was charged by a water buffalo. His caddy shoots it between the eyes. The other guy finds himself in the bunker, looks up and sees a lion. Caddy takes his rifle and shoots it between the eyes. First guy slices his shot and finds himself on the edge of the water. He's about to hit the ball when a nasty-looking alligator makes for his leg. "For Christ's sake shoot the bloody thing!" he tells the caddy. "Oh no, sir. You don't get a shot on a par three!"'

Freddie, still with the honour, floated his ball onto the green where it landed a couple of yards from the pin. Charles fluffed his drive which flopped 30 yards from the tee.

'My family motto . . .' he replaced his club in his bag '. . . neither up nor in!'

Scott and Weston both made the green, but didn't manage to sink their long putts. This gave Freddie the chance he had been waiting for. Going down on his haunches, he squinted at the hole. Reading the green as having a 2-inch borrow right to left and slightly downhill, he was standing very still and psyching himself up to putt when Scott said: 'Take your time!'

It was an old ploy. Freddie was not fazed. Rolling his ball easily into the hole, to make them one up, he grinned at Charles. They halved the next four holes.

The twelfth was a long par five. Freddie drove his ball again straight down the middle. Charles was 50 yards short of him, and Scott and Weston ahead. Good second shots left Freddie a bit to the left of the green, with Scott and Weston 80 yards short. Freddie hoped that his long distance hitting, which today seemed faultless, might save him an extra shot. Scott pitched his ball high. Hitting the side of the bunker it bounced to the left and rolled gently up to the pin.

'"The more I practise, the luckier I get!"'

Freddie's putt was a give. He was down in four, a birdie, but Weston's shot had left him in a similar position.

'This is where we get that one back!'

Freddie had forgotten that this was a stroke hole. Once again they were all square.

At the sixteenth it was anybody's game. At the approach to the seventeenth, Freddie realised that the round was almost finished, and he still had not managed to speak to Charles.

He took out his worry beads, and catching Weston's eye put them away again. It was now or never.

'Not rushing off anywhere afterwards, are you, Charlie?' Freddie said. 'I'd like to have a bit of a chat with you.'

'As long as it's not about my game.' Charles contemplated the hole which was a very short par four. 'We've *got* to win this one.'

Deciding to take a chance on the section of out-of-bounds ahead, Freddie drove right over it. He was about to congratulate himself, when his ball, which had landed on the fairway in front of the green, hit a mound, bounced off to the right, and rolled straight into a bunker. The others had fairly good drives, but had to play second shots to the green. It was their chance to put the boot in.

Standing in the bunker, Freddie noted that the sand was reasonably soft and dried out. His only hope was to take a full shot about 2 inches behind his ball, which was buried in a heelmark, and attempt to blast it out. Taking his sand iron, he hit the ground with an almighty thwack in which was incorporated all the rage of the past weeks. Followed by three astonished pairs of eyes, the ball rose like a white bird, dropped onto the green, performed an elegant backspin, and settled comfortably 6 inches from the pin.

They had no difficulty in halving the last hole.

In the clubhouse, Weston raised his glass to Freddie. 'Cheers, Lomax! I don't know how you score in banking, but you should be playing off scratch.'

Richard Scott drank to Freddie and Charles, before buttonholing Weston and returning to his hobby-horse. 'What you have to look at is the convergence of five economic cycles . . .'

'You look at it.' Weston sipped his double brandy appreciatively, 'All I need to know is when's it going to bottom out?'

'It isn't going to bottom out. That's the mistake people

make. This so-called recession is the precursor to the end of the world as we know it . . .'

'Sounds like good news for shrinks.'

Scott ignored the comment.

'. . . It happened in Greece. It happened in Rome. Now it's happening here. We show all the symptoms of a civilisation at the end of its tether. A top-heavy bureaucracy, economic and financial crises, dramatic fall in population growth, widespread complacency, decline in traditional values, rise in mysticism, science on the defensive, and a decadent art.'

Leaving Laurel and Hardy at the bar to toll the bell for Western democracy, Freddie drew Charles aside. He wondered if it was his imagination or if it seemed suddenly to have gone quiet. The only way to say it was to say it.

'You may not have heard the news.' Freddie knew perfectly well Charles had not. 'Sitwell Hunt has been "forced to reconsider things . . ."' He used the chairman's idiom.

Charles raised a curious eyebrow.

'I was asked to leave. I am no longer with the bank.'

No matter how many times he repeated it, no matter how elegantly he wrapped it up, the reiteration of his story still made him feel physically sick.

Charles was visibly shaken. Not knowing quite what to say to Freddie, he came up with an anecdote in a clumsy attempt to mask his distress. 'Funnily enough, there's another friend of mine, an accountant actually, quite a senior man . . . He was getting into his Jag. About to go home. The personnel officer stuck his head through the window. "By the way, old chap, we shan't be needing you any more after next week."'

Redundancy was like backache, Freddie thought. Everyone knew someone who had it worse.

'What about your service agreement?'

'There isn't a service agreement.'

Charles almost spilled his drink. 'Come off it! Someone

in your position would not have been so idiotic as to leave himself without a cast-iron – '

'I admit I was negligent.'

'Negligent? Bloody hell! What I would do, Freddie – if I were in your situation – I'd screw Sitwell Hunt for everything they've got.'

'With no service agreement?'

'Bugger the service agreement.' Charles finished his beer and wiped his mouth on the back of his hand. 'Get yourself a damn good lawyer. Knowing Gordon Sitwell and his insistence on keeping a low profile . . .'

Charles obviously hadn't seen the headlines in the *News of the World*.

'. . . he'll be only too pleased to keep such a high-level dismissal out of the courts.' Shaking his head, Charles held out his hand for Freddie's empty glass. 'And I always thought you were such a hot-shot banker!' The words were caustic but the voice was sympathetic. 'On second thoughts, old cock, maybe you should stick to golf.'

On their way to the car park, Charles took Freddie's arm. 'I was having a bit of a think in the locker room. There's this client of mine, Harvey Peters. He wants to buy into the food business. I've got rather a lot on my plate at the moment. Any chance that you could meet him?'

Freddie was damned if he was going to accept charity from an embryo banker. He was used to dealing with senior people.

'Pay only on results, of course.'

'Of course.'

Charles took the keys of Bingo's Daimler out of his pocket. 'There's money involved.'

Freddie swallowed his pride. One good deal was all he needed. He had no option. He could not afford to turn down the offer.

CHAPTER TWENTY-TWO

'I need to use the phone,' Freddie said.

Jane was in the kitchen, her Filofax open on the table, telephoning round to make the final arrangements for her Ball. She put her hand over the receiver.

'You'll have to use your mobile.'

'I can't. I'm expecting a call.'

'I'm talking to Sir John Pawsey . . .'

'Who the hell's Sir John Pawsey?'

'Pawsey and Filtness,' Jane hissed. 'He's sponsoring one of our bands. I'm sorry,' she spoke into the receiver, 'I didn't quite catch that.'

'Are you going to be long?' Freddie consulted his watch.

'I don't know. He's about to leave for Tokyo, on business.' She saw a shadow cross Freddie's face. 'No. I'm sorry, Sir John. I was talking to my husband . . .'

'I have to call Susan.' Freddie mentioned his ex-PA. 'It's important. I need to catch her before she goes out.'

'No, do carry on, Sir John, it's perfectly all right,' Jane said into the telephone.

'Jane, this is very important!'

'I'm expecting the brochure proofs from the printers tomorrow,' Jane said. '"Sponsored by Pawsey and Filtness" will be printed in bold above the name of the band.'

'If Susan goes out that's another day lost!'

'I'm just coming! I think that's about it, Sir John, and the committee is extremely grateful to you. Yes, I will. Thank you. Not at all.'

'Listen, Freddie.' Jane banged the receiver down.

'No, you listen, Jane. Let's get our priorities straight, darling. If I don't get a job pretty quickly there'll be no money coming in. If there's no money coming in, not only will I be unable to pay your household bills . . .'

'*My* household bills!'

'. . . but I will be unable to keep up the mortgage payments on this house. If I cannot pay the mortgage on this house, the bank will foreclose. I will have no choice but to go bankrupt. Bankrupt. Do you realise what that means? Surely my getting work is more important than some damned charity hop –'

'The "damned charity hop", for which I am pitching for all I am worth, is to buy a PET scanner . . .'

'A *what*?'

'A PET scanner. A positron emission tomograph, for research into things like brain tumours, for the Hammersmith Hospital. John Pawsey's daughter *died* from a brain tumour. She was 10 years old Freddie.'

'You're not reading me, Jane.'

'I am charging £250 a ticket for this Ball, for which I have absolutely no ideological anguish, and I have no intention of blowing it. Our £125,000 may make the difference between having a PET scanner and not having a PET scanner.'

'I appreciate that, but *I* have to get a job.'

'Do you think I don't know that?'

'You don't seem to.'

'What's that supposed to mean?'

'You do nothing but put obstacles in my way. How can I make contacts, follow up my leads, if you're always on the telephone?'

'I am not *always* on the telephone.'

'You could have fooled me.'

'It's not easy getting money out of people. The more they have the harder it is to extract it from them. There are skills to it, you know.'

'You seem to be pulling against me . . .'

'Freddie, that's not fair.'

'Well, you're not trying to help me.'

'Didn't I offer to go out to work?'

'Christ, Jane, how many more times? I do not need you to go out to work. I am quite capable of salvaging this situation. Provided I can have access to the means. Provided you do not tie my legs and expect me to dance.'

Jane was in her sewing-room, surrounded by a sea of green velvet, when Bingo, wearing a 1920s cocktail hat, burst in on her.

'Darling, why didn't you *tell* me about Freddie?'

Jane, arranging pleats, had her mouth full of pins, but Bingo didn't wait for an answer. Taking off her hat she stuck it on Jane's dressmaking dummy.

'I couldn't believe Charles when he came home from golf. I thought he was kidding. What did Freddie *do*?'

Jane removed the pins from her mouth. 'He didn't "do" anything. These days it just happens.'

'To *other* people, not to Freddie. Charles is mortified. He looks up to Freddie. You're so clever with your hands. I can't even sew a button on. I don't think green velvet is quite you, darling!

'It's for Rosina. Her *Kiss me Kate* costume.'

'How does Freddie feel about it?'

'*Kiss me Kate*?'

'Being unemployed.'

'I don't know. Freddie talks about his overdraft. He talks about his network. He talks about "drawing up guidelines". He doesn't talk about feelings.'

'What will he do?'

'He's looking for a job,' Jane glanced up from her sewing, 'along with thousands of other people, including hundreds of corporate financiers . . .'

'You should have told me. I know Freddie didn't want you to. They have this *amour propre*. It's no good keeping things to yourself. I never keep anything to myself.'

Jane was glad to confide in Bingo, a loyal and generous friend who had managed – helped recently by a kaleidoscope of pills extracted from an army of doctors – to charm her way not only through several husbands, but through life. She had romped her way through school and RADA, and later through several Robertson Hare farces where dressed in camiknickers she had been chased in and out of bedroom doors.

'Poor Freddie.' Bingo shook her head. 'Poor you! I came to take you to out for lunch.'

'I can't. Freddie's downstairs.'

'I know. You can hear his signature tune a mile away . . .'

'*Tannhäuser*.'

'Oh! I thought someone was being murdered. Surely Freddie can get his own lunch. He knows how to open the fridge. He's quite capable of fending for himself.'

'Of course he can open the fridge, of course he can fend for himself . . .'

'Then what's the problem?'

Jane broke a length of green thread with her teeth. 'Having Freddie around all day has brought home to me the fatal flaw in the feminist argument. What these militant women tend to overlook is the existence of love in a relationship, the existence of goodwill. Sometimes I think it's like going to sea in a sieve.'

'Sorry?'

'Marriage.'

'You and Freddie seem to have made a pretty good

job of it.'

'Until Gordon Sitwell put the boot in.'

'What's that supposed to mean?'

'We fight. We've just had a row.'

'"Tension in a marriage is as necessary as yeast in a loaf of bread." One of my ex-mothers-in-law.'

'This isn't tension. This is dynamite.'

'Don't worry about Freddie. Everybody knows Freddie. Freddie's a high-flyer. He'll be gobbled up.'

Jane tried to explain to Bingo that Freddie's legendary self-confidence covered a pathological fear of being dependent, that while he was able to function in top gear when he felt that he was needed, he had no self-start capacity and was equipped with absolutely no mechanism to cope with failure. Jane could cope, as the oldest of the copperknobs she had had to, but the more she tried to help Freddie bounce back again, the more he withdrew from her. Faced with the brick wall of his intransigence, she realised that the situation which he had to confront, disastrous as it might well turn out to be in financial terms, touched deeper levels. It was not simply an economic problem, but his problem.

'Freddie misses his work.' Jane's eyes filled with tears. 'He misses his boss, he misses his personal assistant, he misses his colleagues. Where Sitwell Hunt used to be there's now a great big hole . . .' The tears overflowed onto the green velvet of Rosina's skirt. 'I've never seen him like this. He's like a stranger. I don't know him any more.'

'Maybe you *never* knew him.'

'He won't *let* me help. I could do a hundred and one jobs. I could work for you. I could be a manager in the voluntary sector – I'm talking serious money – okay, maybe it goes against the grain but I don't see why he has to be so damned obstinate!'

'Freddie's angry.' Bingo handed Jane a drawn-thread handkerchief. 'He's been kicked where it hurts. He wants you at home. He's afraid of losing control. He wants everyone to revolve around him as they did at the bank.'

'I have *never* revolved around him.'

'He doesn't know that, sweetie. He's always been out all day. He doesn't know what you are capable of. He *imagined* you were at home revolving.'

'How come you know so much about it?' Jane returned the handkerchief.

'I've been there, darling. I've got the T-shirt!'

Bingo put her arms round Jane in a warm and compassionate hug before putting on her ridiculous hat and securing it with a pearl hat-pin. 'If you won't do lunch, how about tea? I'm taking the day off.'

'I'm going to see Piers this afternoon. Don't say anything to Freddie!'

'I'm at my wits' end,' Jane said. 'I can't bear to see Freddie like this. I came to see if there's anything constructive I can do.'

'I thought you came to see *me*.'

'Piers, this is serious.'

'I wouldn't be sitting here if it wasn't for Freddie,' Piers said. 'How's that for serious?'

'Now he needs one from you.'

'Do you think I'm not trying, Jane? Merchant banking is in the *merde*. There are no big deals. Clients quibble at the fees. The recession has had a catastrophic effect on the sector. Freddie was one of the lucky ones. He clocked up some extremely useful profits. He was a survivor. That's what I don't understand. Some people in his position have so little work to do that they sit around in their offices all day twiddling their thumbs. He's not panicking, is he? He has friends, people he can trust. He has contacts. He had a first-class network . . .'

'He also has a £600,000 mortgage and a whacking great

overdraft. I thought you might be able to suggest something *I* could do to help.'

'What I would strongly recommend is that Freddie gets in touch with some headhunters. They're always on the look-out for first-class people. Spencer Stewart, Russell Reynolds, or Heidrick and Struggles off the top of my head . . .' He wrote the names on a piece of paper. 'Get hold of a copy of the *Executive Grapevine*, it's the outplacement bible, there must be dozens of specialist firms.'

On her way out, Jane said, 'You won't tell Freddie? He'd kill me.'

'If he did, I'd kill him.'

She knew that Piers was being serious.

'Thanks anyway.'

Piers put his arms round her. 'I only wish there was something I could do.'

When Jane got home Freddie was standing by the door.

'I was worried about you. Where have you been?'

'Out and about.'

He didn't pursue the matter.

'Come upstairs and sit down.'

Pouring Jane a gin and tonic and helping himself to the Black Label, Freddie came to sit next to her.

'I'm sorry about this morning. I didn't mean to shout.'

'It's okay. I know.'

'I know I'm a shit. I can't help it. I thought we might go to the cinema. Forget everything. Like old times.'

'Like old times.' She leaned back in Freddie's arms. 'I ran into this friend,' Jane lied. 'Her husband was made redundant. He went to an outplacement consultancy.' She opened her handbag. 'Spencer Stewart, Russell Reynolds or something; I wrote it down.'

'Those people don't offer anything an intelligent person can't do for himself.'

'You don't *know*.'

'I know.'

'Wouldn't it be worth a telephone call? They'd probably jump at the chance to have an executive from the highest echelons of banking on their books.'

It took Freddie several days to pick up the telephone. As if his name were not known in the City, he was informed that Spencer Stewart, Russell Reynolds were not able even to consider an enquiry unless it was accompanied by a curriculum vitae.

Jane, who felt that Freddie was almost glad to report the headhunters' unenthusiastic response, drew his attention to the 'Computerised Professional CVs' advertisements, printed daily in *The Times*. Thanking her for her trouble, Freddie left the room to listen to *Les Huguenots*. The matter was not referred to again.

CHAPTER TWENTY-THREE

On the squash court, Freddie was engaged in mortal battle with James. They had been slugging it out for forty-three minutes. The score was 11–10 in the deciding game. Wiping his forehead with his wristband, Freddie got himself into position to serve what he was determined would be his winning match point. Noting the decisiveness of his opponent's stance, the grimness of his expression, James guessed that more than the match point was at stake.

With a snap of the wrist, Freddie hit the ball pugnaciously into the front wall. Drawing back to receive it, James countered craftily with a shot which, having hit the wall, dropped deliberately short, forcing Freddie to surrender the T. Hitting with all his strength into the far corner, Freddie leaped back to bump 'accidentally' into James and dislodge him from his stronghold. With a powerful volley against the front wall, right to left, James now forced Freddie to move smartly left. Reaching out for it, Freddie smacked the ball ferociously against the side wall where, just as he had intended, it lost its pace, ricocheted half-heartedly onto the front wall and dribbled to the floor before James, considerably flabbier and marginally less fit, could redeem either it or the match.

'Got your fighting boots on today, boyo!' James held the door of the court open for the next couple in their pristine whites.

'I've got to win at something.'

'Feeling sorry for ourselves?'

'Sorry for Jane. I'm bloody awful to her. I can't help it.'

What bothered him more than anything was that he had been bloody awful to Lilli who had tried his patience more than usual. Although he felt as much like having his Tuesday dinner with Lilli as flying to the moon, he had turned up with his customary champagne and flowers at the Water Gardens the previous night for his weekly rendezvous with his mother. Mrs Williams had 'put a roast in the oven', which was no more, and no less, than the words implied, and had packed her bags.

'What's going on?' Freddie demanded, as he walked into the frigid silence. His mother and Mrs Williams addressed him simultaneously.

'She's a thief,' Lilli said.

'I've never been so insulted in my life,' Mrs Williams sniffed. 'I just waited to hand in my notice.'

Freddie glanced at the suitcases. 'It doesn't look as if you're giving Mrs Lomax any notice.'

'I'll forgo my wages.' Mrs Williams eyed the champagne and the flowers. 'Such as they are.'

'I had it in the bathroom,' Lilli said. 'She knows very well I put it in the soapdish when I wash my hands. She was making the bed. It's for Rosina . . .' Lilli eyed Freddie '. . . when I'm gone,' she said provocatively.

'Mrs Williams,' Freddie's voice was unaccustomedly curt. 'Kindly explain.'

'Your mother has mislaid her ruby ring, Mr Lomax. She has accused me of taking it.'

'It couldn't have been the steward . . .' Lilli said.

'We think we're on a world cruise,' Mrs Williams sighed and rolled her eyes to the ceiling.

'. . . He didn't come into the cabin,' Lilli looked at

Mrs Williams. 'So it must be you.'

'There she goes again!'

'There's no one else here,' Lilli said reasonably. 'If you didn't take it who did, may I ask?'

'You've lost it.'

'We've searched high and low.' Lilli looked at her watch. 'And I'm to dine at the Captain's table. Afterwards I shall play the *Liebesträume* in the Starlight Lounge.'

'I'm worn out with looking,' Mrs Williams said.

Freddie thought that the poor woman did look extremely tired. He turned on the television, which was transmitting a quiz show accompanied by canned laughter, and while Lilli and Mrs Williams stared at the screen in stony animosity as the contestants carried off prizes of washing machines and three-piece suites, he carried out his own search.

He ransacked Lilli's dressing-table with its ivory-handled brushes, and up-ended her many pill bottles, and looked in the sewing basket, and felt round the edges of the carpet which he illuminated with a torch. Brushing the fluff from his trousers he returned to the sitting-room and turned out the tangled contents, the necklaces and bracelets, the jewelled buckles and the paste brooches, that spilled from 'Lilli's Box'.

'Strauss,' Lilli announced, as the quiz master asked a London Electricity Board employee, who had patently never heard of either the composer or the composition, who had written the 'Tritsch-Tratsch Polka', adding for Freddie's benefit, 'You won't find it there.'

Freddie ignored the comment. He gathered up the trinkets, which seemed to comprise every stone but a ruby, and returned them to the box.

While he sat down beside Lilli to establish the last time she had seen the ring, Mrs Williams picked up the vase containing last week's wilting flowers and the budding freesia Freddie had bought, and in the manner of one carrying out a last rite, ostentatiously left the room.

Freddie was listening to Lilli's rambling reconstruction of the events which preceded the loss of the ring, including an account of the weather in the Bay of Biscay, when there was a triumphant shout from the kitchen. Mrs Williams appeared at the door with something in her handkerchief.

'I've found it. It was in the flower vase.'

Lilli sniffed. 'Take no notice. She put it there.'

'You see!' Mrs Williams looked in triumph at Freddie.

'A lot of nonsense,' Lilli said. 'What would my ring be doing in the flower vase? It wasn't in the flower vase this morning.'

'How can you be so certain?'

'I forgot it was Tuesday.'

Freddie was lost.

'I gave them an aspirin. It perks them up.'

It was clear to everyone but Lilli that it was her ruby ring, and not the aspirin, which she had dropped into the flower vase.

Freddie gave Mrs Williams five pounds to take herself to the cinema. When she'd gone, Lilli complained that he had given her far too much. Mrs Williams was a senior citizen. She could get into the cinema for fifty pence. She could have her hair cut too, so long as it was a Monday or a Tuesday.

Freddie had spoken more harshly than he intended. He told his mother that she would positively have to stop making Mrs Williams' life a misery. That if she did not behave herself he would have no alternative but to send her to a home. That he had no intention of replacing Mrs Williams, who had a good heart – he heard Lilli snort – even if he could afford it, which he could not, and that if he did manage to talk Mrs Williams once again into staying, it would be Lilli's last chance.

'I'd rather put an end to it all than sit round the walls with a lot of stuffed dummies,' Lilli said. 'I gave up everything for you, you know, Freddie. I sacrificed my career. And that's all the thanks I get!'

'It's up to you.' Freddie did not rise to the bait.

Lilli went for the jugular. 'You wouldn't like it if I was in a home, Freddie. You wouldn't have a moment's peace.'

'You can't go on like this, upsetting everybody.'

'Me?' Lilli said. 'I haven't done a thing. You don't know what it's like. Anyway I think she's a member of the CIA. What do you mean you can't afford it? I've never kept you short. Does your father know you're the chairman of the bank . . .?'

'I am *not* the chairman of the bank.'

'Who would have thought it? Do you remember those paintings you used to do? Yellow rivers. Grey trees. Blue stones. She sends messages in code.'

'I want you to listen to me,' Freddie said. 'There must be no more nonsense. When Mrs Williams comes back I want you to apologise to her.'

'That'll be the day . . .'

'I don't want to hear any more.' Freddie spoke sharply. 'If you say one more word about Mrs Williams I shall have to go.'

'You can't. It's Tuesday. We haven't had our dinner. Felicity Lott is on Radio 3. I saw it in the paper, *Rosenkavalier*. You like *Rosenkavalier*.'

When Mrs Williams returned from the cinema, Lilli's first words to Freddie were: 'She got in for fifty pence, you know.' And to Mrs Williams: 'Give Mr Lomax the change.'

'Only the first two houses,' Mrs Williams said. She smelled of drink, and it took Freddie almost thirty minutes to persuade her to give the job one more chance.

'You're not a bit kind,' Lilli said as he was leaving. 'Not like Rosina. When I'm gone, Rosina will have my ruby . . .'

She looked at Mrs Williams. 'She's a thief, you know. She stole my engagement ring –'

'That's enough!' Freddie was angry.

'You've no right to shout at me.'

'I don't want to hear any more about the ring, neither does Mrs Williams. People have feelings . . .'

'I suppose I haven't. I gave up everything for you, you know, Freddie . . .'

Without kissing her goodnight, Freddie walked out of the flat. His mother's response to his telephone call this morning had been monosyllabic. Her words, as they were intended, resurrected the painful feelings of rejection which had followed the withdrawal of her love after the misdemeanours of childhood.

'I should not have taken it out on her,' Freddie said to James in the bar over his Black Label.

'She has you by the short and curlies.'

Freddie twirled his worry beads apprehensively. 'For as long as I can remember. Now she can't help it. Growing old and losing your marbles is a punishment for some crime you haven't committed. I don't want to bang her up in one of those *Stalags* before I have to. It would kill her.'

'Kill her, or kill you?'

'I should not have shouted at her. Perhaps *I'm* losing my marbles. Perhaps it's hereditary.'

'Anything on the horizon?' James changed the subject.

'Possible. Not a job exactly. Charles has put something extremely good my way. I'm working on it. It's early days.'

Following his confrontation with Jane about the telephone, Freddie had finally called Susan. When his ex-personal assistant walked into the Café Royal he scarcely recognised her. Without her customary chignon, without her high heels, without the silk scarf at her neck, the life seemed to have gone out of her. She had put on weight and looked miserable. Freddie suspected that she had been drinking.

'I had no idea it would hit me so hard,' she said over lunch for which she had little appetite. 'I've been gainfully employed ever since I left school. I don't know what I'm going to do . . .'

'You should have called me.' Freddie thought that she was strapped for cash.

'. . . with *my*self. No deadlines, no schedules, no meetings. I spent the first week sleeping. Then I washed the curtains. Twice. All my friends are out at work all day. They come round in the evenings to commiserate. I went back to Sitwell Hunt, you know, to sort out my pension. It was horrible. Everyone pretended to be pleased to see me. They were perfectly civil, but I felt like an interloper. I no longer had a function. I was furious with Gordon. I suppose you read about him in the newspaper? I couldn't care less if he goes to prison. What right has he to "waste" conscientious and experienced people like me as if they were numbers on a balance sheet? To deprive me of a position I worked extremely hard to achieve? I've registered with an agency. I've signed on. That took some doing. There's nothing "suitable". Not at my age. I've no intention of being a Girl Friday to some yuppie estate agent. I went to see my doctor. She says that I am going through . . . what was it? . . . "a crisis period of re-evaluation". She gave me some pills. I'm so pleased to see you, Freddie.'

They got through two bottles of wine between them. Over coffee, Freddie mentioned to Susan, casually, that Charles Holdsworth had happened to put him in touch with a client who wanted to buy into the food business. As if Freddie had put a penny in the slot, Susan's mask of despondency was displaced by a spark of her old dynamism, her old managerial flair. Realising straight away that it would be unethical for Freddie to contact a former Sitwell Hunt client directly, in the hope of a prospective deal, she said, almost as if talking to herself, 'I wonder would Bowker & Page be interested? I hear they're still looking for a buyer. I shouldn't be at all surprised if Dennis Bowker didn't get in touch with you one of these days.'

Outside the Café Royal, Susan said, 'By the way, they found out who was responsible for the leak.'

'Leak?'

'Bretton Corporation. Conrad Verger. It's all been covered up, of course.'

As Susan was swallowed up by the crowd which drifted towards Piccadilly, Freddie was shocked to find that the desolate woman who had once oiled the wheels of his life was not only a stranger but an object of pity. Because she had lost her job.

Two days after his lunch with Susan, Dennis Bowker had called Freddie at home to see if, by any chance, he happened to know a buyer for his cake business. Freddie had told him about Harvey Peters, and a meeting between the three of them had already been set up.

'Sounds promising,' James said, as Freddie related his story in the bar of the squash club.

Freddie stood up. 'So did Universal Concrete. So did Hans Wichmann. I don't know what the opposite of the Midas touch is, but I certainly seem to have a large dose of it.'

'Drink?' James reached for Freddie's empty glass.

Freddie looked at his watch and shook his head.

'I've got to dash. Thanks for the game.'

'Where are you rushing off to?'

'The Berkeley. I'm meeting Sidonie.'

CHAPTER TWENTY-FOUR

Freddie approached the concierge's desk, to be brought up short by the fact that he was uncertain whether Sidonie had checked in at the Berkeley as Ms Newmark or Countess Orsini. His problem was resolved by Sidonie, who appeared from the direction of the lifts and shot across the hall like a high-velocity bullet to intercept him.

'Freddie.'

'Sidonie.'

Their hesitation, as each of them assessed the changes wrought in the other by the years, lasted for only the briefest of moments before it was dissipated in a bearlike hug. Sidonie, who was always on a diet – the Cambridge, the Hay, the grapefruit, the Pritikin – was considerably thinner than Freddie had remembered her. The feel of her body in his arms, aided by the olfactory trigger of the scent which she always wore and which she had liberally applied, took him back to Hong Kong and the last time they had seen each other.

It was December. They had been staying at the Regent Hotel where a mammoth Christmas tree had been erected in the atrium made of glass to allow the flow of harmonies to pass through the walls and into the harbour.

On their last Sunday together they had gone to Stanley Market to shop for Christmas presents. As the number 6 bus (three Hong Kong dollars, no change given) recklessly climbed the hairpin bends on the outskirts of the city and rounded the dramatic overhang of Repulse Bay, they were hurled into each other's arms, while from the seat opposite, an elderly Chinese woman carrying three gladioli and a bunch of spring onions, regarded them impassively.

Wandering amongst the booths, draped with hand-embroidered silk blouses, dragon-embossed kimonos, angora sweaters, 'designer' jeans, drawn-thread tablecloths and T-shirts at 'factory' prices, Freddie had bought an embroidered tablecloth for Jane, and a silk kimono for Lilli from a gold-toothed stall holder.

Afterwards, at Chung Hom Kok beach, in the shadow of the steep cliffs, he had made love to Sidonie in the water.

On their last night together (Sidonie was catching the morning plane), Freddie had put on his white dinner jacket and Sidonie a floating dress, and they had ridden the Star Ferry through the bobbing sampans.

Freddie had been back to Hong Kong on more than one occasion since then. Each time he boarded the Star Ferry, wedged in by Chinese, their faces buried in the racing sheets, he thought of Sidonie pulling him by the hand through the turnstile and running, clickety-clack on her high heels, like a small dervish to catch it.

Dinner, at the Mandarin Hotel, had been subdued. They were always loath to part from each other. On this occasion Freddie sensed that Sidonie had something other than her early flight on her mind. As she sat opposite him at the table, sucking at her lobster claws in a manner which never failed to arouse him, he had the strange sensation that she had already gone.

Back in Kowloon, he had bought her a brooch, in the shape of a dragonfly, from a neon-lit shop, and pinned it to the chiffon of her dress before they joined the teeming ribbon of human ants which streamed along the waterfront and, arm in arm, strolled back to their hotel.

Their personal love-drama, an opera with two voices, had been acted out in capital cities across the world. It was a duet of equals. With no emotional baggage to impede them, no constraints on their passion nor on its lower depths, they surrendered themselves, until like Tristan and Isolde they found redemption in each other's arms.

'Freddie, we have to talk.'

'Tomorrow.' Freddie was almost asleep.

'It *is* tomorrow. Freddie I'm getting married . . .'

'Pull the other one.'

'I'm being serious.'

Freddie opened his eyes. Sidonie's naked body, illuminated by the harbour lights, was reflected in the mirror.

'Married?'

'Married.'

'Sidonie, in love?'

'Who said anything about love?'

'Why then?'

'There are other reasons.'

'Not for you, the independent lady, the hot-shot stockbroker who doesn't rate men and wouldn't know a blocked-up sink if she saw one. What's his name?'

'Fabrizio. Orsini. Fabrizio Orsini. Count Fabrizio Orsini.'

'He's after your money.'

'Fabrizio has plenty of his own.'

'What does he do?'

'Nothing.' Switching on the lamp, Sidonie leaned over the side of the bed. Removing a photograph from her handbag she gave it to Freddie.

A tall and extremely handsome young man, with very white teeth, wearing a Nehru jacket and hair down his back, stood next to a Bentley convertible.

'Is he in love with you?'

Putting the photograph away and sitting up against the pillows, Sidonie switched off the lamp.

'That's what the man says.'

'What's in it for Sidonie?'

'I'll be Countess Orsini. I'll have something that every unattached woman in New York would give her right arm for.'

'This is me you're talking to. I know you better than that.'

'Do you, Freddie? Do you know me?'

'Six months? I'd say we've been pretty close.'

'You can live close to someone for the whole of your life and never get to know them. You have no idea why I'm getting married, do you, Freddie?'

'Not a clue.'

'Freddie I'm 38 years old . . .'

'I didn't know there was a sell-by date.'

'You've heard of the biological clock? Well, mine is sure as hell ticking away . . .'

'I don't believe it.'

'What's the problem?'

'Changing nappies? Rushing home from Wall Street to read *Milly-Molly-Mandy*?'

'I want a baby, Freddie. I desperately want a baby. It's been coming on for a long time. I think I was as surprised as you.'

'What's so special about Fabrizio?'

'He makes me laugh.'

'Is this the final curtain?'

Sidonie turned to him, her breasts outlined against the windows. He thought there were tears in her eyes, unless it was the reflection of the lights.

'It's been a great performance.'

At Kai Tak he had held her tightly in his arms.

'Have a good life.' Sidonie's voice was unsteady.

'You too.'

'Call me when they make you chairman of the bank.'

It was the last time he had seen her.

They sat in the lounge of the Berkeley. Sidonie was wearing the dragonfly brooch. It was pinned to the lapel of her suit. Over double Black Labels, Sidonie's straight up like his own, they filled in the intervening years.

'What happened to the biological clock?'

'It ran out.'

'No baby?'

Sidonie shook her head. 'No baby.'

'I'm sorry.'

'That's okay. It passed.'

Freddie held out the bowl of rice crackers.

'And how's the Count?'

Sidonie withdrew her empty fingers from the bowl. 'Fabrizio's dead.'

Freddie was shocked. He had followed the couple's progress through the gossip columns and across the social pages of the glossies whenever he had been in New York. Orsini against the backdrop of his Art-Deco collection. The Count and Countess Orsini bidding for a painting at a Sotheby's benefit night. Countess Orsini receiving the New York award of Business Woman of the Year. Sidonie's face on the front of *Business Week*. One Christmas in Barbados he had seen them on the beach. Orsini had been holding court to a group of topless women. Nearby, Sidonie, Rembrandt's Hendrickje Stoffels (in a G-string), was standing at the edge of the water testing it with a scarlet-tipped toe. As he and Jane approached, his eyes met Sidonie's. The shock of the encounter threw him off balance, and as they passed he was chided by Jane for his overlong glance in her direction.

Since their affair, Sidonie had avoided coming to London.

Taking their seats in the Opera House – for which Freddie,

no longer entitled to the Sitwell Hunt corporate box, had had to dig deep into his own pocket – he recalled other evenings. *Macbeth* in Frankfurt. *Parsifal* in Copenhagen. *The Ring* at Bayreuth. Each night of music followed by its coda of love. Now they sat sedately, side by side like an old married couple, as the conductor took up his baton and the audience, with a final clearing of the throat, grew silent. Freddie wondered why Sidonie had got in touch with him, why she had disinterred what had been long buried, resurrected the ghosts of an affair long over with her telephone call, and how she would react to the news that he was out of Sitwell Hunt.

Listening to the first notes of the Prelude, he wondered if it would be betraying Jane if – for purely technical reasons, to see if he was capable – he went to bed with Sidonie. Glancing at her familiar profile as the curtains between the real and the fantasy world parted, to reveal the medieval ship on which Tristan, within a few hours' sail of Cornwall, bore Isolde to be the wife of his king, Freddie lost himself in the innocence of the song and the loneliness of the singer. Forgetting Sidonie, forgetting his own problems, he gave himself up to the music.

In the intervals, reluctant to break the spell, they spoke mainly of the opera: Tristan who was pushing himself to the musical limit; Isolde who, with a thrilling top to her voice, was turning in an exceptional performance; the magic spell cast by the baton of Sir Georg Solti.

As Tristan's dying 'Isolde!' pierced the silence of the packed auditorium and the final act drew to a close, Freddie put a hand over Sidonie's, feeling beneath his fingers the Count's massive emerald ring. A tear rolled slowly down Sidonie's cheek as Isolde sobbed out her broken heart.

They had dinner at Orso's. As they waited to order, Sidonie leaned across the red-checked tablecloth towards Freddie.

'You're still the best-looking man I know . . .'

Freddie managed his old smile.

'. . . And the nicest.'

'I'm not very nice at the moment.'

'You look great from where I'm sitting.'

'I have something to tell you, Sidonie.'

The gravity of his voice made Sidonie remove the recently acquired reading glasses, with the aid of which she was studying the menu, to fix her magnetic eyes on him.

'Not you and Jane!'

Freddie shook his head.

'It's always been no holds barred with you and me, Freddie.'

'I've been chucked out of the bank.'

'I know.' She put the glasses on again. 'I called the bank. There's no way you would leave Sitwell Hunt unless you were dragged out screaming.'

'Why didn't you say?'

'I didn't want to spoil the evening.'

'I wish it was only the evening that was spoiled. I'm on the scrap heap, Sidonie. Everything I've worked for has gone.' He filled her in on exactly what had happened. He did not bother to prevaricate. He could level with Sidonie as he could not level with Jane.

Practical, business-like Sidonie, no time, no words, wasted in commiseration. 'What will you do?' She reached for his hand.

'Something will turn up.'

'Freddie!' Sidonie took her hand away. 'Things don't "turn up" . . .'

'We happen to be in the middle of a recession.'

'Do we now?'

The waiter stood by the table.

'I'll have the carpaccio.' Sidonie leaned towards Freddie. 'You listen to me, Freddie. You don't get to be head of corporate finance, to be vice chairman of Sitwell Hunt without great skills, great ability . . .'

'I'm beginning to wonder.'

'Since when has hitting the ball into the net once made you a lousy tennis player? You're a success, Freddie.'

'Tell that to Gordon Sitwell.'

'Forget Gordon Sitwell. You've always been a success. You're the most single-minded and determined man I know. That's what I like about you. You've always been in the right place at the right time; like Issigonis with his Mini, like the Beatles. Gordon Sitwell felt threatened by your entrepreneurial spirit, by the fact that you enjoyed challenges, exploited opportunities, made things happen, took risks, by the fact that you wanted every step to be bigger and better than the last one. You scared the pants off him. So the schmuck iced you. It's no big deal. It happens every day. It's how *you* feel that's important. Stop feeling sorry for yourself. Go out there and fuck them.'

Freddie knew that everything that Sidonie said, every word that she uttered was valid. He was no better able to cope with her battle cry than he had been with Jane's sympathy and her tender loving care.

Sidonie immediately had his number. 'Look at it as a challenge, Freddie. Like defending Corinthian Hotels was a challenge.'

Freddie looked surprised.

'I know all about Corinthian Hotels.' She leaned across the table. '"Save thyself, Tristan." Your ship's got white sails, Freddie. Your ship has always had white sails.'

Room 333. The Berkeley Hotel always gave it to Sidonie. Going up in the lift Freddie put his arms round her, wondering whether passion could be rekindled, or if the spark was dead.

At the door of her room Sidonie turned to him. 'I'm hacked

out, Freddie. I wanted to see you more than anything in the world. Now I want you to go home.'

Freddie was puzzled. 'What made you call me?'

Sidonie put the key card in the door. 'I'd like to explain. Darling Freddie, I owe you an explanation. It'll have to wait.'

Putting a hand beneath her chin, he tilted Sidonie's face towards him and bent to put his lips to hers. She turned her head away abruptly.

'Call me tomorrow, Freddie. It's been a spectacular evening. Thanks a whole bunch for the opera . . .' Her voice was distant. Standing on tiptoe, she kissed him on both cheeks. 'Goodnight.'

CHAPTER TWENTY-FIVE

'Let me remind you of the *original* story, that is to say Shakespeare's original story . . .'

Listening to the voice of the drama coach, Mrs Drummond, Rosina, who was to play the lead in the school production of *Kiss me Kate* – which as Mrs Drummond was explaining was based on *The Taming of the Shrew* – put herself on automatic pilot and considered her problem, which although sexual in nature had nothing whatever to do with her stormy courtship by her prospective stage husband, the Hon. Rachel Lloyd (Fred Graham/Petruchio), her real-life arch-enemy, who stood arrogantly beside her on the platform in the Pfeiffer Hall.

Since her first disillusioned foray into the sexual minefield three weeks ago with Henry, Rosina had not only read every article she could get hold of, but had discussed the matter with her peers.

'If you're not enjoying sex,' demanded one magazine, 'is it best to lie back and pretend you're having the time of your life, or to be honest instead?' 'Communication is the key to a happy sex life.' 'Make sure you've got his attention and he's not just getting a "quickie" in before the next football match.' 'Massage is a great tension reliever. Use baby oil to relax and stimulate you both.' 'Don't set intercourse – and orgasm – as your goal, just go with the flow and enjoy each stage as it happens.' 'Having sex with someone is about as intimate as you can get, so it's best to express your true feelings.' 'Many people fantasise about someone – whether it's Tom Cruise or the boy on the bus – and it's nothing to feel guilty about.' 'Good sex requires time, patience, and understanding.' 'Sexual arousal comes in stages. So try to enjoy each step as it happens . . .'

Try telling that to Henry, who had not the least idea what Rosina was talking about. The more she suggested that they set themselves up in a warm, comfortable position (last time it had been in the back of his father's Ford Cortina, which was neither warm nor comfortable), avail themselves of a bottle of baby oil and confine their attention to her nipples, he had looked at her with as much consternation as if she had asked him to take his mind off the action to check the tyre pressures of the car. He thought that she had gone completely mad.

While Henry was working away at the coalface, she imagined that she was Vivien Leigh, being made love to by Clark Gable, or Sharon Stone getting it on with the ubiquitous Michael Douglas, but as much as she thought that Henry was the most amazing thing since Vanilla Ice, and knew that the other girls in her class would give their best winter boots to be in her position (which was ungainly to say the least of it), she could not, in all honesty, say that, when it came to sex, Henry was either patient or understanding, and he certainly never seemed to have a great deal of time.

Since they had been going out together, his mind, which previously had at least affected to have some preoccupations above his belt, seemed to have settled permanently into his boxer shorts. He could not get enough of it. As he pummelled and grabbed her, leaving lovebites like great purple bruises on her shoulders and nuzzling avidly at her thighs, a detached Rosina, whose most mind-blowing sensation was that of cramp in her leg, had difficulty in concentrating on the business in hand. She desired her lover only in his absence, was unable to share his fervour in what she could not help regarding as a grossly overrated act, and wondered if she was lacking in some vital piece of anatomical equipment or whether there was, perhaps, something fundamentally wrong with her. She certainly took issue with the bottom line of all the advice she had read, and which she regarded with the scepticism born of her meagre experience, that 'it' would be worth the wait.

She would have liked to discuss the matter with her mother, but Jane imagined that Rosina was far too young to be in a relationship which was quaintly referred to in Chester Terrace as 'going to bed'. In any case, she and Freddie had other, more important things on their minds at the moment than Rosina's sex life, about which they would probably have had a fit apiece if they knew.

Although at first Rosina had thought of her father's dismissal from Sitwell Hunt in terms of his being unable to take her to school in the car (she now had to walk or make her own way on the Hoppa), his presence in the house, coupled with the fact that her parents no longer seemed to get on so well together, had made her reassess the situation. She did not mention his dismissal to her friends. When Candida D'Arcy's half-brother was made redundant from his job as a rising-star publisher, the conversation, before one maths lesson, had turned to dumpies, an acronym which had superseded yuppies and referred to the new *downwardly* mobile professionals, and Rosina had kept very quiet. When Claudine, of the plum-coloured hair, commented on the morning absence of Leonard and the Mercedes, Rosina hinted that Freddie was engaged on some vital assignment on behalf of the Treasury, the outcome of which could have political repercussions, and that there were more significant things on his agenda than taking her to school. Seeing her father glued to the teletext, making inroads into the whisky bottle, jump each time the telephone rang, work his worry beads overtime, and surreptitiously scan the situations vacant columns in the newspapers under the pretext of immersing himself in the world news, made Rosina uneasy. Her heart went out to him, but she could not talk to him. Not unless she wanted to get her head bitten off. Nobody could. She and Jane, whom anxiety about Freddie had drawn closer together – these days Jane overlooked the state of Rosina's bedroom and even forgot to nag – were hoping that Tristan, who was due home at the weekend, would lighten the atmosphere, but Tristan and Freddie had never seen eye to eye and Rosina doubted very much that he would.

It was not difficult to broach the subject of sex at school. Although the conversation in the cloakroom, over illicit smokes, occasionally became side-tracked to the newest disco or the latest diet, it was rarely about anything else.

'Did you know,' Hannah, who had been on the front cover of *Tatler* and whose mother was a Marchioness, said as she came out of the lavatory cubicle pulling her knickers up, 'the French don't even have a word for it?'

'For what?' Lauren Buckman, who had been taken for an 18-year-old ever since she was 12, and could get away with not doing her homework (if not murder) because her father, Bertrand Buckman, was a well-known film director, asked.

'"It", darling!' The knickers were silk, *café au lait*. 'The nearest you can get is *l'acte d'amour*, which is not the same thing at all.'

There was not much *amour* as far as Rosina's bouts with Henry were concerned. In fact she was sorry now that she had started the whole messy business.

'When did you first find out about it?' Pandora leaned myopically forward and eyed Lauren, who was dissatisfiedly appraising her truly lovely face in the communal mirror.

'I was about 9,' Lauren said. 'From my mother – well she's

not my real mother. She told me about bonking, and about periods, and about contraception, and about babies, and about STD, and about rape. Everything you wanted to know but were too afraid to ask. She doesn't think sex is anything to get steamed up about. She calls a penis a penis.'

'I was at a girls' school in Somerset,' Henrietta who was to play Bianca in *Kiss me Kate*, said. 'They showed a video in assembly when I was 12, but it was a dead waste of time because we'd all known for yonks and afterwards the staff simply refused to discuss it. I think they were all lesbians. I think most teachers are orientationally challenged. I think teaching attracts them.'

'Maybe in Somerset,' Lauren said. 'Monsieur Albert put his hand up my shorts.'

'He's *French*,' Margaret said.

'I think I'm bisexual, as a matter of fact,' Lauren said. 'I think I could well go either way.'

This was a new and brazen departure. It was received in silence.

'You provoked him,' Abimbola, who came from Nigeria said.

Lauren raised her wild, expensively highlighted hair with her fingers and let it fall again about her face. 'Who?'

'Monsieur Albert.'

'You mean about Prince Charles and Princess Di?' Lauren laughed. She jumped up on the bench beneath the coat-hooks and held up a newspaper to her circle of classmates, their faces towards her like upturned flowers.

The front-page picture which poor Monsieur Albert had been foolish enough to show them in class, had been of Princess Di presenting a silver cup to Prince Charles after a polo match, and receiving a perfunctory kiss in return. He had asked Lauren, who had already been reprimanded for looking out of the window instead of paying attention to the fable of 'The Fox and the Crow', to describe, in French, what it was that the royal couple were up to.

'*Ils baisent*,' Lauren said, puckering her lips in demonstration.

Monsieur Albert had blushed from the top of his head to his boots. Patches of crimson stood out on his cheeks like weals.

'*Mais non!*'

'"*Une baise*" is a kiss?' Lauren said.

'*Un baiser*,' Monsieur Albert nodded, obviously regretting that he had started the whole business.

'Well, then . . .' Lauren said.

'Only for children. "*Donne-moi un baiser*." Or in epigrams. "*Dans la vie il y a l'un qui baise et l'autre qui tient la joue*." In life there is always the one who gives the kiss, and the one who gives his cheek to be kissed. *Un baiser. C'est un nom.* A noun!'

'Well if "*un*" *baiser* is "a" kiss, surely *baiser* means "to" kiss,' Lauren said patiently, while the class sat riveted.

Monsieur Albert shook his head. 'In Racine, yes. But you are already three centuries out of date.' He held up the photograph. '*Ils s'embrassent. S'embrasser.* To kiss!'

'Okay. We get the message.' Lauren refused to let him off the hook. 'What does *baiser* mean?'

By that time it was perfectly obvious.

Monsieur Albert folded the newspaper while he collected himself. 'I think you know perfectly well what it means, Lauren.'

Lauren, whose boyfriend was a busker in the underground at Marble Arch, shook her head.

Monsieur Albert, 32 years old, looked at the innocent faces of his class of 15-year-olds, and realised that there was no escape. He was in bondage. They were not going to let him go. He made for the cover of his desk and when he was safely behind it, held on to it with two white-knuckled hands. 'It means . . .' he looked Lauren in the eye '. . . it means "to fock"!'

'It means . . .' Lauren said from the cloakroom bench where she towered above her classmates in their bizarre assortment of garments, largely worn above skin-tight leggings, which passed for clothes. 'It means . . .' she adopted Monsieur Albert's heavy French accent ". . . to fock"!'

'I'm not surprised he put his hand up your shorts,' Hannah said, amidst the howls of laughter, some of it accompanied by hysterical tears at Lauren's performance. 'He'll be putting something else up them next.'

'He would if he got half a chance. All that *baiser* business gave him a hard-on. That's why he had to hide behind the desk. You're very quiet, Ros.' Lauren turned her green eyes on Rosina.

'She's joined the Rosebuds!' Henrietta shrieked, and flung her arms round Rosina. 'Welcome to the fun factory.'

Blushing, like poor, persecuted Monsieur Albert, Rosina admitted that she was now 'going out' with Henry, which qualified her for membership of the club. The girls gathered round her.

'Tell us . . .?'

'Where did you do it?'

'How many times?'

'Did you come?'

'What was it like?'

Rosina imagined them all, Lauren, and Hannah, and Henrietta, and Abimbola, and Christianne from Belgium (who boasted that she was *almost* engaged to be married, as if putting your nose into that male chauvinist noose was something to be proud of) falling into their lovers' arms, their lips parting in deep passionate kisses – as their clothes melted miraculously into thin air and they achieved simultaneous orgasms – and of herself accommodating the engorged member of the eager Henry which worked her inert body like a piston and riddled her like a fire.

She wanted to ask them what it was that was supposed to be so wonderful. Whether she was meant to have some feeling for that great, throbbing, ugly swelling, which seemed to have a life of its own, and of which Henry was so inordinately proud. Whether *their* boyfriends concentrated on their nipples, or massaged them with baby oil. Whether they did not think, in all honesty, in the final analysis, at the end of the day, that the great Nirvana of sex had let them down.

She picked up her Coach bag containing her school books and slung it nonchalantly over her shoulder. Meeting the expectant eyes, the curious faces, awaiting her reply, she put on her enigmatic, heavy-lidded Kim Basinger (*The Color of Sex*) smile.

'It was like . . . seeing . . . and feeling . . . all the colours of the rainbow,' she lied. 'It was great!'

Standing on the stage in the Pfeiffer Hall, donated to the school almost a hundred years ago by Mrs Ida Pfeiffer, and filled with rows of chairs inscribed with the names of past students (an idea filched from Harrow), Rosina listened to Mrs Drummond telling them, as if it was something extraordinary, that they were actually going to have boys – violins, a viola, a cello and a saxophone – in the orchestra, and banging on about the *tempo di valse* of 'Wunderbar' and how, after the introduction, the refrain, 'Wunderbar! Wunderbar!' must be *lively*! – lively Rachel! lively Rosina! – and that they must give it their all.

Rosina was happy at Queen's with its dogma: 'We shall be glad to improve our practice every day, but not to alter our principles'; the fact that there were no marks and no prizes; and that the aim of the liberal education they were given, as laid down by the founder, Frederick Dennison Maurice, was as much to bring out native intelligence as the acquisition of knowledge. Rosina would have liked the opportunity to question Frederick Dennison Maurice on the one matter which was troubling her and about which he had not thought to utter. In his preoccupation with the education of women, in his desire to raise their consciousness, he had quite overlooked the question of sex.

A reason that it failed, according to one bashful journalist (who had referred to the pudenda as 'the secret garden'), was because of worries about home or about school.

CHAPTER TWENTY-SIX

The bad news was that *Tristan und Isolde* assaulted Jane's ears from morning to night causing her to flee from the house on the slightest pretext, and the good news was that Freddie had agreed to come to her Ball.

Selling every available ticket at a time when the downturn on the charity scene mirrored the crisis in the economy at large was no mean achievement. Businessmen were no longer keen to dole out company largesse in support of worthy causes (even in anticipation of a knighthood), and the time had long passed when the glitterati could be persuaded to fork out for any fashionable soirée or film première which happened to be going. The pledged appearance of a show-biz name – or even a royal – at a function made very little difference, and one had to be seen to be extremely careful with other people's money.

In order to entice the 'men in suits', who had tightened their belts and were no longer in a position to give as freely as they had previously done, many of the organisations had had to rethink their appeals.

Jane's idea for raising funds for her PET scanner, from those still in possession of them, was to make her Ball strictly by invitation – an appeal to élitism – and give the invitees the signal honour of taking out a covenant or giving a specified donation to the cause, a privilege which would, she hoped, add to the cachet.

Freddie's promise to accompany her had been extracted on the high of the Bowker & Page transaction, on which, having been made a non-executive director of the company by Dennis Bowker, he had recently been working flat out and on which contracts were about to be signed. His euphoria about the deal, worth £75,000 in fees, had replaced the bout of depression (during which his alcohol intake had increased dramatically), which had followed his rendezvous with Sidonie.

The morning after *Tristan und Isolde*, Freddie had caught the first train to Manchester to spend the day with Charles Holdsworth's client, Harvey Peters, a 35-year-old whizz kid (who sported a gold Rolex and drove an Aston Martin) with a chain of teenage fashion shops, who was now looking to diversify into food. As Susan had intimated that he would over their lunch at the Café Royal, Freddie's old client Dennis Bowker (having been tipped off by her) had contacted him at home. After Freddie had introduced Bowker to Harvey Peters, a meeting which had been followed by further discussions and extensive investigations by his client, Harvey Peters had agreed that Bowker & Page – a monument to private enterprise – was exactly the solid, family business he was looking to buy.

Dennis Bowker had once been a Manchester insurance agent, and his wife, Barbara, a Home Economics teacher at a prep school.

Barbara's sister, Clare, married to Anthony Page, a moderately successful surveyor, taught Maths at the same school. Every June, for the annual Sports Day, Barbara and Clare had been responsible for making the cakes which accompanied the polystyrene cups of tea and which were sold by the slice to the school parents. Barbara's specialities were cheesecake and carrot cake, while Clare's were an orange-flavoured chocolate log, and a white-iced walnut cake reminiscent, to those old enough to remember, of the popular pre-war 'Fullers'.

When the prep school folded, Barbara and Clare were unemployed. Neither of their husbands was doing particularly well, Clare had young children, and they were both keen to make some money. They reviewed their resources and came up with the only asset (apart from their teaching diplomas) which they shared: cake-making. It was Barbara's idea to take her carrot cake to the Arndale Centre and try to sell it to a wine bar.

The manager of the wine bar, who tasted it and pronounced it excellent, said that he couldn't possibly interest his customers in a dessert which had to do with vegetables. Barbara made another carrot cake, covered it with lemon icing, and presented it as 'Lemon Melt'. The manager of the wine bar ordered two. Mainly to get rid of Barbara. The following day he was on the telephone for two more. Barbara and Clare spent a week, during which neither Dennis nor Anthony got any dinner, baking in Barbara's kitchen. They packed Barbara's Lemon Melt and Country Curd Cake (cheesecake), and Clare's Chocolate Orange Delight and Walnut Whisper into Barbara's car, and made the rounds of Manchester restaurants and tea-rooms. By the end of a month they had more orders than they could cope with. Each of them recruited a friend to help, and used her own kitchen, until their cooking bowls were not big enough to cope with the mixing, and they finally had to resort to the bath. They spent the days baking, working not only their own cookers overtime, but borrowing oven space from their friends. They persuaded Dennis and Anthony, who were only too pleased to get away from the ubiquitous smell of baking, to drive into Manchester in the evenings, where they commiserated with each other about their neglect by their wives over a beer, to do the deliveries. After six hectic months, Dennis and Anthony chucked in their jobs.

Dennis came up to London to talk to Freddie, at Sitwell Hunt, about a loan which was to be invested in a derelict factory suitable for small-scale commercial cake-making. While Anthony, making the switch from sand and cement to flour and sugar, assessed and quantified the recipes, Dennis took over the business side of things. Japanese Ginger (there was nothing Japanese about it) and Mother's Madeira were added to Barbara and Clare's repertoire, and 'Bowker & Page', now a household name whose cakes were to be found on the shelves of supermarkets up and down the country, was born. All went well until Anthony Page, by now a wealthy man, fell in love with a newly recruited French-Canadian manageress, left Clare and the children, and pushed off to Quebec where he had started a second family. Clare took the children back to her mother in Dublin and remained there. Left on their own, their future secured by wise financial investments, Dennis and Barbara Bowker decided to get rid of the thriving but demanding business they had built up (which now comprised some 100 lines and which, despite the recession, was booming), and retire to their villa in Spain.

Bowker & Page, which had a £12 million turnover and pre-tax profits of £1.4 million, was now on the market for £4.5 million. If Freddie succeeded in securing it for Harvey Peters, his reward would be more than enough to get him out of trouble with Derek Abbott. It would buy him time to re-establish himself in banking, which was the only world he knew and which he loved.

The meeting in Manchester, at which they were to dot the 'i's and cross the 't's on the contracts, took place at Dennis Bowker's elegant Victorian house in Hale. Lunch was served at a massive refectory table, and by the time Freddie and his client, together with the lawyers, accountants and financial advisors, had finally adjourned for tea (and wedges of Lemon Melt), a day, one month ahead, on which contracts were to be exchanged had been agreed.

An exultant Freddie had returned to London just in time to make his squash game with James and, despite the fact that James tried to put Freddie off his stroke at a crucial moment by telling him the story of the woman who gave birth to a litter of piglets (the police were looking for the swine who was responsible), Freddie won the match. At six o'clock, his towel round his neck, he had gone to phone Sidonie who, starting with breakfast meetings, was always on a tight work schedule, but who he guessed by now would be back at the hotel.

Whistling Don Giovanni's serenade to himself as he put his phonecard in the slot and dialled the number of the Berkeley Hotel, he asked to be put through to Sidonie's room.

When the telephonist came back to him, it was to say that the Countess Orsini had checked out.

Freddie felt himself break out in a cold sweat, which had nothing to do with the squash, and he had the uncomfortable feeling, due to a sudden drop in his blood pressure, that he was going to pass out. There was no way that Sidonie could have left the hotel without leaving word for him.

'Give me the concierge.' The concierge had been there for years and knew Freddie by sight.

'I want to speak to Countess Orsini,' he said when the man was on the line. 'Room 333.'

'The Countess left this morning.'

'That's impossible. There must be some mistake.'

'No, sir, she took the hotel car to the airport.'

'Are you absolutely sure?'

'I saw the Countess into the car myself, sir.'

'This is Freddie Lomax speaking. Did the Countess leave a message for me?'

'I don't have anything here, sir. Let me check with the message desk.'

'I'd be obliged if you would.'

Freddie scrolled mentally through the conversation with Sidonie at Orso's, trying to remember what had actually been said. Was it his imagination or had she in fact withdrawn slightly from him, regarded him with pity, or contempt. Sidonie was a power freak. She was not ashamed to admit it. Her background was not class-conscious Britain, in which success was suspect and excellence unacceptable in anything other than sport or entertainment. Sidonie had been reared in a culture where high-flyers and the wealthy were a source of admiration, rather than envy, and she had never made any secret of the fact that it was from the rich and powerful, both in business and in her personal life, that she got her kicks. Through Sidonie's eyes, Freddie saw himself, like Alice as she went down the rabbit hole, diminish in size. No wonder Sidonie hadn't wanted anything more to do with him, to share her bed with a has-been, an erstwhile banker no longer worthy of her regard.

'Are you there, sir?'

Freddie, holding on with one hand to the receiver and with the other to his worry beads, pre-empted the concierge's words.

'No message?'

'I'm afraid not, sir.'

Returning to the bar, and reporting the blank he had drawn to James, Freddie voiced his suspicions of the reason for Sidonie's hasty departure and downed two double Black Labels in quick succession.

'You may not be head of corporate finance any longer, but you're still the same person,' James tried to console him.

'You don't know Sidonie. That's not the way her mind works.'

'If that's the case,' James said, 'it sounds as if you're well rid of her.'

'I don't *want* her. All that's over. Was over a long time

ago. I only wanted to see if I could come up with the goods.'

'Why Sidonie?'

It was hard for Freddie to explain to James, who deceived his wife with his mistress, and his mistress with his other mistresses, and his other mistresses with his casual encounters, that he was a one-woman man – that woman being Jane – and that it was only his inability to make love to Jane which had led him to pin his hopes on Sidonie.

'Not exactly a success at the moment, am I?'

'It depends how you define success,' James said.

Freddie was now on his fourth Black Label. 'Winning Wimbledon, making money, running an organisation, getting to the top of the professional tree, the Nobel Prize . . . you can't define it. You know damn well what it means.' He signalled to the barman.

'Steady on.' James pushed the potato crisps towards him. Freddie ignored them.

'All my life, ever since I first placed my building blocks one on top of the other, I've needed to make things happen. I've needed to have an idea, to put it into practice, to see it bear fruit. Even if it backfires, even if it turns out to be a damp squib. What I'm doing now is occupational therapy, filling time. You know me, James. When have I ever "filled time"?'

'You underestimate yourself. If somebody said to you, look, I'll offer you a lousy job but you'll get paid £3 million a year, what would you say?'

When Freddie did not answer, James said, 'You'd tell him to stuff it!'

'Three million pounds is a hell of lot of money . . .' Freddie said. He was beginning to slur his consonants.

'Where's my old Freddie? Since when has money been an evaluation of success? Since when has it been a scoreboard, a measurement of how well you're doing? You know as well as

I do, it's the deal that's the fun. It's the shaking of the jigsaw, the fitting of it together.'

'Try selling that jigsaw spiel to Derek Abbott!'

'Your trouble, my friend – for God's sake, Freddie, what are you trying to do to yourself, don't you think you've had enough? – your trouble is that you are unable to cope with unstructured situations.'

Freddie picked up his new drink and through a Black Label mist, thought about what James had said.

'Right! I have to have a strategy. There must be a coherent structure. I am psy . . . psycho . . . psychologically unhappy with random circumstances.'

'One last question,' James said, 'then I'm taking you away from that whisky bottle and we'll have something to eat. Why do you think Gordon Sitwell sacked you?'

'You know perfectly well why he sacked me.'

'You tell me.'

'He sacked me because business failures in Britain are running at 248 every working day. He sacked me because in the past year alone there have been 47,777 liquidations and bankruptcies. He sacked me because small firms have shed almost one million jobs – 15 per cent of their workforce! He sacked me because levels of credit for long-term financial commitments have hit bottom. He sacked me because there are major structural weaknesses in the economy, for which I am not responsible. He sacked me because of Conrad fucking Verger, because he wants to keep Sitwell Hunt in the family, and because he is shit scared.'

'Balls!' James said. 'Gordon Sitwell sacked you because he would be incapable of recognising an opportunity if it got up and hit him in the face. He sacked you for the same reason that he hired you. Because you have an innovative flare which would help Sitwell Hunt to grow. When organisations get to a certain size, Freddie love, they often feel it necessary to get rid of the executive who gave them their much-needed kick up the backside in the first place.'

James stood up. 'You are not useless, old cock, you are not worthless, and you have not been rejected, not even by Sidonie who most probably had quite some other reason for leaving the Berkeley. All you are, my friend – if you will allow me to say so – is pissed!'

Despite what James had said, Freddie's elation over Bowker & Page had been tempered by his disappointment at Sidonie's cavalier treatment of him. He had called her New York apartment at regular intervals to be informed by a machine that she was not available. Her Wall Street office had been instructed to say, on each occasion that he tried to contact her, that Ms Newmark was 'out of town'. As far as Sidonie was concerned, he was yesterday's news.

CHAPTER TWENTY-SEVEN

Gordon Sitwell would not let Margaret leave his side. Whereas Freddie's response to his reversal was to withdraw into himself, to hide his wounds beneath a carapace which excluded everyone, including Jane, to whom he was closest, Gordon's reaction to the ignominy to which he had been subjected by the press, was to cling like a limpet to his wife. He would not go out of the house, except into the garden where he communed with his roses, refused to see visitors, and would not let Margaret out of his sight. The argument, that he had brought his situation upon himself, was not one which he was willing to address. He equated his predicament with penalising a man for eating because he was hungry, and he could not reconcile his apprehension by the police with the truth, as it seemed to him, that he was merely satisfying an appetite, as basic as that for food, which he was incapable of controlling. The fact that he had been charged, and that he was to come before the magistrates, seemed to Gordon grossly unjust. There was so much crime about that was real: thieves who got away with burglary, violators who perpetrated rape, muggers who attacked the old and the innocent, swindlers who cheated, frauds who defrauded, arsonists and wife-batterers, GBH offenders and child-molesters. Gordon Sitwell was not an enemy of society and he did not remotely equate himself with these felons.

All he had done was talk. To a prostitute. He had not even got as far as her room. It would not have made the slightest difference if he had had sex with her. His crime was soliciting. His misdemeanour had been spelled out for him several times. It had been made abundantly clear. That he had both lied to the police officer about looking for an all-night chemist's and categorically refused to furnish his name and address, had, as it turned out, been errors of judgement which had cost him dearly. In a moment of panic, he had taken a calculated risk which, in the event, had misfired.

Whereas Freddie was unable to tolerate what he considered was his unwarranted dismissal from Sitwell Hunt, and dreamed impotently of putting back the clock, Gordon merely wanted to wipe the slate clean of the stigma with which he had been branded. While Freddie's ordeal had resulted in distressing sexual inadequacy with Jane, one of the perks of Gordon's disgrace was, as far as a surprised Margaret was concerned, his renewal of interest in his wife. This nightly distraction deferred the re-run of his arrest by PC Mark Morrell of the Metropolitan Police, which now furnished the ongoing scenario of his dreams.

The three hours – from the time that he had waited unhappily on the Hertford Street pavement next to the young constable, awaiting the arrival of the vehicle into which he would be summarily bundled, to the moment when he appeared on the steps of Savile Row police station to be confronted by the paparazzi – were etched into his memory as indelibly as if they had been seared with a blowtorch. There was no eradicating them, no easy panacea for his shame.

He had mercifully not been handcuffed. He had sat in silence on the back seat of the car next to PC Morrell, his designated minder, until they reached the police station. He had then been escorted to a down-at-heel charge room where he was directed to a plastic chair and ordered to 'keep quiet', an admonition he had accepted from no one since his schooldays.

Glorying, it seemed to Gordon, like a salmon fisherman in the size of his catch, the arresting officer, helmet beneath his arm, had approached the Custody Sergeant, who sat behind a desk which was bolted to the floor.

While he waited, Gordon thought paradoxically of the gilt chair in the ballroom of Buckingham Palace, on which he had waited to receive his knighthood.

Margaret had never quite come to terms with being 'Lady' Sitwell. She did not feel at home in the part. Gordon himself was fiercely proud of the accolade. His photograph outside the Palace – with Margaret in a hat which looked like nothing so much as an upturned soup plate – had pride of place on the chimney-piece at Tall Trees, and he did not mind admitting that the day he had been honoured by Her Majesty was the proudest in his life.

'I nicked this one. Soliciting prostitutes in Hertford Street.'

PC Morell's words brought him back from the brilliance of the Palace ballroom to the charge room which was dismally illuminated by a naked lamp. While the Custody Sergeant did not exactly lick his pencil – his findings were recorded in Biro – the rate at which he wrote in the custody book betrayed a distinct lack of familiarity with the written word.

There was little in the bleak surroundings to delight the eye. There were a great many doors, a large laminated rectangle on which the names of those already apprehended were entered in purple marker-pen, a grim poster, cautioning about HIV and the danger to drug users of sharing needles, and another (carrying a similar AIDS warning) explaining the use of a breathing tube when administering the kiss of life. The only distraction of the slightest interest was a wooden board mounted high on the wall, on which a series of lights flashed repeatedly and which were repeatedly ignored. It reminded him of the panel in the kitchen of his parents' pre-war home, on which numbered tumblers were used to summon the servants. If the inmates of the cells which he had glimpsed were in need of attention, they were certainly not receiving it. The charge room was not, by any stretch of the imagination, a jolly place.

'You!'

The voice of the Custody Sergeant, who must have been close on retirement, was curt to the point of insolence. Gordon realised that he was being addressed, and that the man was indicating a fixed wooden bench in front of his desk.

'Over 'ere.'

Gordon wondered whether he should call Dominic Mason. That it was his prerogative to summon his solicitor, he was well aware. He decided that rather than involve Dominic at this point, he would wait and see what happened. Taking his time — by way of signifying his disapproval — he rose from his chair and traversed the room.

'I 'aven't got all night,' the Custody Sergeant said.

'I beg your pardon?'

'You 'eard. Name?'

Gordon hesitated only briefly. 'Sitwell,' he said. 'Sir Gordon Sitwell.'

The Custody Sergeant exchanged a glance with the salmon fisherman, confirming the importance of his catch. Writing down Gordon's address seemed to take several minutes.

'Pockets.'

'Excuse me?' Gordon said.

'Pockets. What are you, deaf or something? Empty your pockets.'

Gordon had had enough. 'I am quite sure that you are

doing your duty,' he addressed the little Hitler behind the desk. 'Carrying out your job. But there is not the slightest excuse for rudeness. Kindly watch your tongue, Sergeant, or I shall see that your gross discourtesy comes to the ears of your superior officer.'

'Pockets,' the Sergeant said as if Gordon had not spoken, and waited while he went through his overcoat, his jacket, and his trousers, and laid his wallet (with his credit cards which established his identity) and his possessions out on the desk where they were duly logged and, being of an entirely innocent nature, eventually wordlessly returned.

It was the cue for PC Morrell to take out his notebook and read his version of the evening's events as they concerned Gordon. Gordon was tired. He wanted to go home to Margaret. He was only half-listening to the constable's reconstruction of the happenings in Hertford Street but was annoyed by the provocative manner in which he reiterated 'repeated soliciting' to describe Gordon's brief conversation with the girls.

'That is not at all an accurate description,' Gordon said.

The Custody Sergeant glared at him and nodded to PC Morrell to carry on.

'Whereupon the defendant stated that he was "looking for an all-night chemist's . . ."'

'It was not "persistent soliciting" . . .' Gordon objected.

'Why don't you fucking shut up?'

Gordon had never heard such impertinence in his life. There was absolutely no need for it. The man would be sorry. He would see to it personally that he would be sorry.

'Do you want him charged, constable?' the Custody Sergeant asked PC Morrell, when his monologue had come to an end.

Gordon woke up. He hadn't realised that there might be a choice. PC Morrell put away his notebook. It aged one to say that policeman were getting younger and younger.

Gordon thought that this one could surely have been his grandson.

PC Morrell buttoned his pocket. He had had enough of the charge room. He wanted to get out onto the street.

'Down to you, Sarge.'

Gordon groaned inwardly.

'We'd better charge him . . .'

'We do have to protect our young ladies.'

'May I suggest you have a word with the powers that be, before going any further.'

The Custody Sergeant opened a drawer and produced a charge sheet which, Gordon noticed, was in triplicate.

'I'm going to charge you, *Sir* Gordon.'

Gordon invoked his right to silence. He was convinced that the decision was provoked by the Sergeant's envy of his title and position. Having been needled into setting the wheels in motion, he had no choice but to proceed. There was no way, even had he been so disposed, that he could climb down. There was more writing. It was quite ridiculous. It seemed to go on for ever. For the first time Gordon wondered whether they were actually going to lock him up in a cell, from where his plea for attention would go unanswered.

He needed to go to the lavatory. His bladder had been registering full for some time. He conveyed his need to the constable but before his request could be granted the Custody Sergeant turned once again to his ledger.

'What on earth . . .?' Gordon said.

'Nine forty-five, toilet . . .' He nodded to PC Morrell who accompanied Gordon down the corridor.

'Everything has to be logged,' PC Morrell explained as Gordon stood before the urinal. 'In case of complaints.'

Gordon zipped his fly. The younger man was officious but at least he was civil. Better than that pig in the charge room.

'I shall have to have some confirmation of your address . . .' the Custody Sergeant said on his return.

'I have already given you my address,' Gordon snapped. 'You've written it down.'

'. . . an employer . . .'

'An *employer*!' Gordon exploded. 'I am the chairman of a public company. Chairman of a bank.'

'Your wife? A friend?' the Custody Sergeant suggested.

Gordon could not understand why the first person he thought of was Freddie, on whose discretion he knew he could rely. He certainly did not want to involve his daughter, so he did not suggest Conrad Verger. He had just spelled out the name and telephone number of his solicitor, when a mug of steaming tea, brought in by a hefty WPC, the outline of whose structural engineering was clearly visible beneath her white shirt, distracted the Custody Sergeant who looked at Gordon, in his bespoke overcoat, his Garrick tie, and decided to give him the benefit of the doubt.

'Photograph and fingerprints.'

'Fingerprints!' Gordon said, to nobody in particular as he was led away. Fingerprints. For enquiring where there was an all-night chemist's. It was ludicrous. No wonder there were outbreaks of rioting and hooliganism. The country was in danger of becoming a police state.

He was led, like a common criminal, to a podium in front of a fixed camera which took a mug-shot of his face against his name and a number spelled out in magnetic letters. Heads were going to roll for this. He had never been so mortified in his life. He could not imagine why, considering the nature of the charge, it was deemed necessary to fingerprint him, and assumed, correctly, that the Custody Sergeant was extending his powers to the limit. The process, necessitating the despoiling of his carefully tended fingers with black ink, daubed liberally onto a roller, took a painstaking five minutes. Afterwards he was despatched in the direction of a tin of Swarfega with which he was invited to clean himself up.

On his return, the Custody Sergeant, who had taken advantage of Gordon's absence to finish his tea, handed him the blue copy of the charge sheet which requested his presence at Marlborough Street Magistrates' Court two weeks hence. Failure to appear, on the stated day, at the stated time, he was cautioned, constituted a criminal offence.

With his release from the charge room, Gordon had thought that his ordeal, at least until the case was heard (which it would not be if Gordon could help it), was over. The profound shock of walking out of the front door of Savile Row police station to be blinded by the flash guns of waiting press photographers, brought home to him the fact that it had not even begun.

All that Margaret had been concerned about was that Gordon was late for dinner. She had cooked a leg of lamb, to which he was partial, and after four supplementary hours in the oven it was, to say the very least, dried up.

'You might have rung me,' she admonished her husband when, although he had absolutely no recollection of driving himself there, he finally arrived home. 'You know you like it pink.'

'I have been arrested for soliciting, Margaret,' Gordon said. 'You have to know.'

'The mint is from the garden . . . What did you say?'

'Soliciting – prostitutes – according to the police. It will be in the newspapers in the morning.'

'Gordon. What's happened? I don't understand.'

He sat Margaret down in the kitchen and recounted, as if he were addressing a board meeting, exactly what had taken place. He confessed that he had previously been the subject of a caution, and told her, pulling no punches, of his sexual predilection. It was almost the first time he had communicated with her on a personal level since their marriage. The leg of lamb had remained uneaten. When Gordon had finished talking, he had taken the willing Margaret to bed, where he had mentally transposed her pallid flesh into the seductive curves of a street-walker. Imagining that she was a prostitute, he had 'rogered' her in a variety of ways of which she was vaguely aware but which she had never allowed herself to contemplate. It outdid Mills & Boon any day of the week. In the morning she had been despatched down the hill for the newspapers. The newsagent, who came from Bangladesh, hadn't been able to look her in the eye. Assuming an unaccustomed importance in her husband's life, she took the newspapers – their front pages emblazoned with identical photographs of his surprised face – to Gordon in his study, where he had more or less remained incarcerated ever since.

CHAPTER TWENTY-EIGHT

Tristan was nervous about coming home. Firstly because he had no idea what to say to his father – he found the whole subject of Freddie's dismissal acutely embarrassing – and secondly because he had been suspended from school for two weeks for doing drugs. It was hard enough to communicate with Freddie under normal circumstances. Now that he had to be sorry for the old boy, now that he empathised with his father to the extent of being angry on his behalf, dredging up the words was even more difficult. Talking, to anyone, was not Tristan's forte. Talking to Freddie was well-nigh impossible. It always had been. When he did manage to overcome the mental block which prevented him from expressing himself adequately in Freddie's presence, what he did produce in the way of words – if they succeeded in leaving his mouth at all – seemed always inappropriate. He and his father rubbed each other up the wrong way, and the simplest of interchanges, on the most uncontroversial of topics, invariably escalated into paternalistic pyrotechnics on Freddie's part which were met with sullen silences – beneath which mute responses fermented and seethed – from himself.

Talking to Jane was different. Her relaxed attitude, her effortless chatter to which he did not feel compelled to respond, to come up with some worthwhile nugget of information, some informed opinion, some pearl of intellect, some demonstration of aptitude, made such conversation as he was capable of, simple. His mother made no demands upon him. He felt at ease in her company and she allowed him to be himself. He got on well with Jane. When she came down to school for parents' weekends in her colourful outfits, her zany hats, charming his friends, intriguing the headmaster, seducing the staff, conversing knowledgeably with the art department and chattering away to the French teacher in French, he was consumed with pride. When Freddie was away on business, Jane came down alone. It was a relief. When Freddie was around, far from enjoying escorting his mother round the school and showing her off, he was metamorphosed by his father's critical presence into a gibbering idiot, a bag of nerves, and counted the minutes until it was time for his parents to go home.

Freddie was always on his back. Whether he meant to be or not was beside the point. Tristan was aware that, as far as other people were concerned, his father was amiable, generous and well-mannered, that his friendship was valued, that he was highly thought of in business, that he was a considerate employer, a good husband, a good son, and did his utmost to be a good father. He was all of these. Until it came to his relationship with his son when it was an entirely different ball game.

Tristan could not be entirely sure exactly when he had changed from being the legendary apple of his father's eye to the proverbial thorn in his flesh. One of his earliest memories was of Freddie taking him to the playground where, while he dashed happily from swing to roundabout, his father, who was supposed to be looking after him, stood in the middle of the asphalt with his nose in the *Financial Times*. After that it had been a succession of homes from which Freddie was largely absent. When he was around, an event marked by the reverberations of opera music which filled the house, he left Rosina to her mother and spirited Tristan away for man-sized treats to the Natural History or the Science Museums, which he breezed through like a dose of salts.

Sometimes he played cricket with him in the garden. Looking back, Tristan thought that it was the cricket – like the San Andreas Fault – which was responsible for rending the two of them irrevocably asunder. He disliked cricket, as he disliked any form of sport, in which he could see absolutely no point. Cricket was its apotheosis. It was on his sixth birthday that Freddie had bought him his first cricket bat. He remembered it as clearly as if it were yesterday. He had been expecting a drum kit – like that of his friend Matthew – or a train set such as he had pointed out to Freddie on one of their rare visits to Hamleys from which he had had forcibly to be removed. When Tristan had unwrapped the cricket bat and looked up with horror into his father's smiling face as he sat on his bed before leaving for the bank, something in his child's mind told him that he had met his Armageddon. He regarded the dead and heavy bit of wood, with its rubber handle, and was bitterly disappointed. You could not make a noise with it, and you could not set it up on the floor and watch it circumvent the lino whilst peopling it with imaginary figures. Worst of all, if you had to play with it at all, you could not play with it by yourself.

'Saturday,' Freddie said. 'We'll have a game in the garden. Rosina can field.'

And on Saturday Freddie, helped by the 5-year-old Rosina who trotted dutifully after him, had marked out the pitch, set up the stumps and the bails, and polished up the specially light-weight ball on the seams of his trousers. It was all lost on Tristan who would rather have been indoors with a book. In an effort to please his father, he had stood in front of the wicket, taking up his position as instructed, to face Freddie's gentle and accurate bowling. Try as he would, he failed to make contact with the ball. Freddie was patient. Standing behind Tristan he manoeuvred the boy's hands until they were in the correct position, demonstrated the benefits of a straight bat, and while Rosina bowled – not at all badly – showed him how to reach out for the ball. It was no use. Tristan had no eye. Freddie thought he was swiping at the summer air deliberately. His mouth had set into a horizontal line of disappointment (an expression with which Tristan had since become familiar), and he had sent Rosina in to bat.

Tristan had been a disappointment to Freddie ever since. Freddie's buzz words were duty, responsibility, application, and persistence. His morality, as Tristan saw it, was unimpeachable, and work was his ethic. Tristan, lazy, vague, artistic, inspired by nothing so much as a pronounced sense of *laissez faire*, failed his father on all counts. Despite this obvious dichotomy, Freddie had persisted in trying to make over his son in his own image. He took him to the swimming pool and, his powerful shoulders glistening, demonstrated his water polo skills while Tristan, unable to see without his glasses, skinny and pale, not a fine specimen at all, stood shivering on the side of the pool. He ran with him, whenever there was an opportunity, and shouted at Tristan for not keeping up with him. He took the boy out on the golf course, when there was not a competition on, and could not understand why Tristan could not summon up the slightest interest in the whereabouts of the ball. Finally he gave up. He played cricket with Rosina, took her rowing in the park, taught her how to fence, and swam side by side with her on holiday while Tristan mooched off on his own. There was no point of communication between the two of them and when they did come into contact with each other sparks were likely to fly.

One of Freddie's major grievances was that Tristan did not get on with Lilli. Probably because he saw through her.

Tristan recognised in Lilli her need to control, her skilful manipulation of those around her – in particular Freddie – and hated going to see her. Whilst others fetched and carried – her glasses, her pills, her rug, her book – while they willingly looked up telephone numbers and found her slippers and made her cups of tea, Tristan remained, as Lilli told Freddie, as often as she could, 'thoroughly disobliging'. It was not that Tristan was insensitive to the needs of his grandmother, but his awareness of the fact that she was perfectly capable of doing all these chores for herself – as she often did when there was no one around – made him dig in his heels and stick doggedly and silently to his seat when Lilli's demands were made or when she practised her wheedling number on him. He was not her servant and refused to be her slave. It was bad enough that she tyrannised his father, a thraldom which appeared quite out of character in Freddie who became putty in her hands, and which Tristan was quite unable to understand. Sometimes he felt like shaking Lilli, and he was quite convinced that she was not as off the wall as she liked to make out. He felt sorry for her carers, who came and went like migrant birds – there was never the same one in attendance when Tristan came home from school – and was inclined to side with them in their catalogue of complaints. Tristan knew that it was this disaffection which pained his father most of all.

Tristan did not want to upset Freddie, for the simple reason that he adored him. He did not merely love him, as he did Jane, he worshipped the very ground on which his father walked. His deepest desire was to emulate Freddie's quick wit, his easy camaraderie, his business acumen, his sporting prowess, his facile charm, but he was lumbered with an inarticulate tongue, a slow mind, a disregard for physical exertion of any sort, and a sullen demeanour. It was little wonder that he did his best to avoid his father as much as he could and preferred to keep his own company.

The move to Regent's Park had made this easy. He had been allotted a large room on the top floor, next to Jane's sewing-room and well away from his father, over which he was autonomous. This haven which he had created was the next best thing to the geographical distance from Freddie provided by the sixty-odd miles which separated Chester Terrace from school. Paradoxically it was Freddie – albeit indirectly – who had been responsible for his introduction to the jazz music of which Tristan was an aficionado and which now drove them even further apart.

Tristan had had piano lessons with Lilli until the age of 8, when his general intransigence, his refusal to practise, and his dislike of classical music had led her to wash her hands of his musical education. He was 11 years old when, on a visit to the attic in the house in Bedford Park, he had stumbled upon Freddie's collection of 78s, and the wind-up gramophone, inherited by his father from his grandfather Hugh, which was the medium for the discovery that he had jazz in his soul.

While Freddie filled the house with triumphal choruses and bel canto arias, Tristan lay on his bed and lost himself in the gut-wrenching sounds that derived from the tin-roofed lean-tos of the American Negroes, from their desperate bread lines, from their failed cotton crops, from the bleeding hearts of an oppressed people for whom music – dredged from their downtrodden spirits and released from the nets of their suffering – transcended poverty and by-passed politics and touched some abused chord in himself.

It was not Tristan's penchant for jazz to which Freddie objected. How could it be, when his own adolescent passion had been the inspiration for his son's obsession? It was Tristan's total disregard of anything which could not be blown, or twanged to produce a noise, which was not only loud but extremely intrusive, which somehow annoyed Freddie. He saw the bops and stomps, the riffs and raffs which competed with the celestial voices and intricate harmonies of his own compact discs, as a metaphoric call to battle, a deliberate affront.

When Tristan was at home he rarely left his bedroom, other than to sidle out of the house (with a barely audible 'See you' to whoever happened to be around), to slouch, hands in pockets, head bent, not across the road to Regent's Park, but to Parkway, with its pubs and its drop-in centre, in search of vegetable samosas or onion bahjis to be eaten among the layabouts and the winos in the polluted purlieus of Camden Town.

His bedroom was not a tip like Rosina's. Although filled with his music-making paraphernalia, guitars, two synthesisers, and his tenor saxophone, various wooden sculptures – mainly of the male form – which he had brought home from school, books on music and medi-tation, abandoned weights (relics of a desperate attempt to develop muscles like Freddie), Jason Rebello posters, records, headphones, a dozen pairs of sunglasses (behind which he liked to hide), potted plants, plastic carriers and a portable TV, it had an innate order. It was Tristan's asylum and in it, dressed in tracksuit trousers, floppy knitted jacket and decrepit Oxfam slippers (clothes, to Freddie's regret, did not interest his son in the slightest) which he would not allow Jane to dispose of, he felt both happy and safe.

He knew that Freddie worried about him. He worried because Tristan was happy. Because he had absolutely no plans for the future, was not the least bothered about his forthcoming A levels, was concerned only with the moment, and had no interest in girls.

Although he had not mentioned it to Jane, it was this latter which bothered Freddie more than anything. He was worried that Tristan might have gay tendencies. Short of confronting him with it, there was no way that he could find out. Although his anxiety about Tristan had recently been displaced by his own problems, Freddie had it on his agenda to tackle him on the subject.

Jane usually met Tristan at the station. When he leaned out of the window of the carriage and caught sight of Freddie, like Nemesis on the platform, Tristan groaned inwardly.

All the way from Waterloo, Tristan searched the nethermost reaches of his brain for something to say to his father. By the time they had reached the Euston Road, he had come up with nothing. The more he tried, the more tongue-tied he became. Polite observations to do with the influx of tourists, which was in no way remarkable, or with the weather, equally unspectacular, refused to be formulated. Sentences formed themselves brightly inside his head, then shrivelled away into a black hole. It was not that he did not want to talk to his father, who seemed diminished, he thought, by the fact that he was driving Jane's car with its spare pair of tights protruding from the map pocket, but that he could not. Freddie did his best, but the dialogue turned out inevitably to be more interrogation than conversation.

'Glad to be home?'

'Yeah.'

'Robert forgotten about his trainer?'

'Yeah.'

'How's school?'

'Good.'

'Anything new happening?'

'No.'

'How's the work going?'

'Okay.'

'Is that all you've got to say?'

'It's okay. It's going okay.'

Regent's Park was not all that far from Waterloo. Tristan was thankful for small mercies.

After lunch, when Freddie had disappeared into the dining-room to work on his papers, Tristan confessed to Jane about the cannabis. They had been smoking it in the field when they were caught by the Classics master. He left it to his mother to tell Freddie that he had been suspended for two weeks.

Later, he was listening to 'Hill Street Blues' and reading *Playboy*, when Freddie burst into his bedroom. Tristan assumed that the news about the drugs had been passed on, and that his number was up. He had no time to hide the picture of the full-frontal blonde, whose labia were about to be penetrated by her own searching fingers, and whose breasts swung towards the camera like a couple of over-stuffed bolsters. As Freddie looked over his shoulder, he felt the blood rush to his freckled cheeks, his limbs lock in paralysis, and he became totally immobilised. He waited for Freddie to speak, to shout, to read him the riot act about having plenty of time for rubbish but apparently none to spare for his A levels, about wanking – which was what Tristan was about to engage in – or his refusal to have such trash in the house.

In the calm, before what he had every reason to presume would be the storm, Tristan braced himself. The Count Basie stopped. The room was quiet. Into the silence Freddie laughed. It was the first time his laughter had been heard in the house in weeks. The sound of it was infectious. Although he had not the slightest idea what the mirth was about, Tristan was so relieved at Freddie's unexpected reaction that he joined in.

Freddie sat down on the bed. Far from being angry, he flicked through the pages of *Playboy* with what Tristan thought was considerable interest. When he had finished with it, to Tristan's utter amazement, his father put his arms round him and held him close in a strong embrace.

'Mummy told me about the pot.'

Tristan waited for the heavens to fall.

'What the fuck,' Freddie said. 'Get your shoes on, Tristan. Let's go for a drink.'

CHAPTER TWENTY-NINE

Tristan was surprised to hear his father order a double whisky. Freddie had always been an abstemious drinker. He brought his Black Label over to the table with Tristan's lemonade shandy.

'Cheers,' Freddie said.

'Cheers, Dad.'

Tristan raised his glass. He tried frantically to think of something intelligent to say but drew a complete blank. A young couple in black leather, carrying motor-cycle helmets, walked up to the bar. As they waited to be served the guy slipped his hand into the waistband of the girl's jeans.

'How are you getting on at school?'

Tristan groaned inwardly. It was going to be a re-run of the car scenario. The guy's hand had disappeared up to the wrist. He was caressing a chubby buttock. The girl was wriggling with pleasure. He had a girl at school – well, not had. Miranda Harding. Half-French like his mother. She had a white face and punk hair and a terrific figure. He hadn't actually spoken to her yet.

'Reading any decent books for A levels?'

The couple had turned to each other now, mouth to mouth, pelvis to pelvis. He wouldn't half mind doing it with a girl like that. He crossed his legs to hide his discomfiture. He wouldn't half mind doing it with a girl.

'Tristan?'

'George Orwell. *Down and Out in Paris and London.*' Christ! Every time he opened his mouth he put his foot in it. 'I didn't mean . . .'

'Of course you didn't.'

The embarrassed silence was broken by Freddie with a reverberating sneeze which distracted Tristan from his preoccupation and made several people glance round to see who was responsible for the explosion. Unable to locate his handkerchief quickly enough, Freddie found a tissue in his jacket pocket.

'Do you know a sneeze travels at 40 miles an hour,' Tristan said. 'Gale force eight on the Beaufort scale.'

'Is that so?'

'The globules dry out from the friction as they go through the air. If you had a cold – '

'Which I haven't,' Freddie said.

'The viruses would take thirty minutes to reach . . .' Tristan nodded his head in the direction of the inverted bottles '. . . the back of that bar.'

Freddie put the tissue back in his pocket. 'That's if I hadn't stopped the buggers in mid-flight.'

'The globules were through that paper and out 15 inches in front of your nose one second after you sneezed, in a sort of massed bomber attack', Tristan demonstrated with his hands, 'that put the entire room in danger. Remember the conquistadores who landed in South America in the early 1550s?'

Freddie wondered what the conquistadores had to do with his sneeze.

'They destroyed civilisations that had been around for centuries. You know how?'

Freddie couldn't remember the last time he had heard the boy string so many words together. He shook his head.

'Not because they had superior weapons, but because

each time they sneezed they released millions of contaminated micro-darts against which the Aztecs and Mayans, who had never been exposed to them, had absolutely no defences. That's why microbiologists avoid public places. I wouldn't mind being a microbiologist.'

It was the first time Tristan had spoken to Freddie about his future.

'Do you realise that in this room', Tristan went on, 'we could be inhaling oxygen that was in *Paris* a few days ago? Atoms that were breathed out by people smoking . . .' He looked at Freddie. He hadn't meant to bring up the subject of smoking. 'Gauloises,' he ended lamely.

'About the pot . . .' Freddie said.

Tristan cursed himself.

'It's not such a big deal. Just don't do anything worse.'

Tristan finished his shandy. 'I'm not that stupid.'

Freddie nodded.

'I could always leave school before A levels,' he said hopefully.

Freddie knew this was an oblique reference to his current financial situation which Jane must have discussed with him.

'I'd quite like to join a jazz band and do gigs.'

'That won't be necessary,' Freddie said firmly. 'Your godfather is taking care of the fees.'

'Uncle James?' Tristan said. 'That's decent of him. You must be pissed off, Dad.'

Freddie took the glasses over to the bar for refills.

'I am pissed off,' he said when he sat down again. He pushed Tristan's shandy across the table. 'If you really want to know, Tristan, I have never been so pissed off in my life. I've been lucky really. I've always worked hard, but things seemed to have fallen into my lap. The fates are no longer smiling.'

'I'd like to help.'

Looking at Tristan's face on which the pain was evident, Freddie thought that he did not really know this boy. Since his infancy, when Freddie had kissed him goodbye before leaving for the bank in the mornings, and stood over his son's sleeping form in his cot when he came home late, they had been ships that passed in the night.

'I'm a victim of the times,' Freddie said. 'A statistic. Nobody can really help. I've got a few things on the table. A big number in Manchester which should keep the wolf from the door for the time being.'

'Mum's really worried about you. She was crying.'

'She was?' Freddie was surprised.

'She said you don't talk to her about it.'

'I find it extremely hard to talk to anyone about it, Tristan.'

'It's because you blame yourself. You think it's your fault.'

Freddie nodded. 'You're right. I couldn't feel worse if I'd heisted the bloody bank.'

'But you haven't, Dad.'

Tristan's heart went out to Freddie as he went to the bar and came back with another drink.

'Do you have to go back into banking?'

'What's your objection to banking?'

'Dedication to profit is a crass preoccupation,' Tristan said with the lofty sentiment of youth.

'The idea that no good can come from wealth is the most perverse moral judgement in human discourse,' Freddie said. 'Don't forget that the moneybags of today are the charitable foundations of tomorrow. Who do you think builds the concert halls, supports museums, endows universities, funds the arts?'

'Never thought about it.'

'People who flog cars or sell shoes. If it wasn't for the beer barons or the sugar kings, where would the Ford

Foundation, the Whitbread Prize, the Tate Gallery, half the Oxbridge colleges, be? The Western world has always thrived on the injection of new blood and new ideas by the *rich*, whether they be recently ennobled Tudor grandees, the Medicis – sixteenth-century yuppies – or your Clores and Sainsburys. Art follows money. It always has done.'

'I'm not talking about *money*, Dad. I'm talking about grubbing for it.'

'I agree with you that money is not always come by entirely honestly. It's almost impossible to get rich without stepping on somebody's toes. But today's *nouveaux riches*, today's newly created titles, will be seen by your grandchildren, Tristan – just as they were during the Renaissance when the vulgar money came from trade with the New World – not as 'money grubbers' but as philanthropists, the protectors of the nation's heritage, the saviours of its artistic treasures. "*L'argent n'a pas l'odeur.*"'

'I'm doing Spanish,' Tristan said.

'Money has no smell.'

'I'm not saying that money can't be put to good use,' Tristan said. 'But you must admit that there are other currencies in life.'

'There are indeed,' Freddie said. 'Unfortunately they neither feed nor educate your children. Come back in twenty-five years' time and tell me about them. Meanwhile, get me a refill, there's a good lad.'

'Do you think that's entirely wise?'

The impact of the question, with its implicit role reversal, took Freddie by surprise. Tristan, standingly awkwardly with the empty glass in his hand, was the father and he the child.

'Probably not.' Freddie nodded towards the bar. 'But "at this moment in time", as they say, it happens to be what I need.'

And he had come to need it more and more. The whisky,

taken in increasingly large measures, anaesthetised him against the anxieties of his daily life, not least of which was his impotence. In the medical department at Dillons he had surreptitiously flicked through a book on the subject, to discover to his horror that 60 per cent of erectile problems were due to organic causes such as neurological or vascular disease. A personality profile of impotent men revealed that they were anxious (for which he gave himself a tick), depressed (another tick), neurotic (certainly not), suffered from identity problems (Freddie was not sure what was meant), or borderline, which accurately described his mood. Individuals with unresolved Oedipal conflicts, or those with 'repetition compulsion' or 'ambivalent sexual orientation' were also afflicted with what appeared to be a well-researched complaint, the cures for which included intracavernosal injections, which sounded extraordinarily unpleasant, penile implants, which sounded even worse, and a cocktail of drugs such as ceritine, yohimbine, prostaglandin E, papaverine, and phentolamine, which he could not pronounce and had certainly never heard of. When it came to the section on the complications of these drugs as well as reports of fatalities – in men with concurrent coronary artery disease – he decided that he had had enough. As he replaced the book on the shelf, the name on the spine caught his eye. Richard Scott. A glance at the photograph on the back flap above the biographical details confirmed the fact that together with Charles Holdsworth he had played golf with the author. It was not difficult to track him down to Harley Street where he saw his private patients.

'Lomax?' Richard Scott said, shaking Freddie by the hand and indicating a chair in front of his desk. 'Haven't we met?'

Freddie had only to mention golf for Richard Scott to remember the fourball with Charles Holdsworth.

'Having trouble with your swing?' Sitting down at his desk he took out a clean sheet of paper.

'I suppose you could say that.'

After taking a careful history and carrying out a physical examination – Freddie was unable to decide which of these procedures he found more distasteful – Scott made his diagnosis and was able to reassure Freddie that his inability to make love to his wife was psychogenic, rather than organic, in origin.

'You mean it's all in the mind?'

Scott nodded. 'Which is not to say that it is under your direct control. The impotence is a physical manifestation of your loss of self-esteem, which is a direct result of losing your position at Sitwell Hunt.'

'I'm not pretending that it wasn't a blow.' Freddie took out his worry beads, a move registered by the doctor. 'The past few weeks have been decidedly the worst in my life.'

'The psychological effects of redundancy are a problem we unfortunately have to deal with quite often these days,' the psychiatrist said, glancing discreetly at his watch. Freddie assumed that it was time for the next patient.

'I do love my wife.'

'I'm sure you do.' The voice was understanding. 'The problem – as I see it – is that you are having difficulty in loving yourself. Look, Freddie, why don't you make another appointment? Then we can have a talk about how you *feel*. Perhaps I can help you . . .'

'I do not need help.' Freddie stood up. 'Yours or anybody else's. As long as it's nothing serious. That's all I wanted to know.'

'I'd go easy on the whisky if I were you,' Richard Scott said on the way to the door. 'It has a direct suppressant effect on the gonads. It may not be helping.'

Ignoring the comment, Freddie held out his hand.

'You know where I am,' the psychiatrist said.

But Freddie was halfway down the stairs.

He had not taken the psychiatrist's advice on cutting

down on the alcohol, and he certainly didn't want any interference in that direction from Tristan. Alcohol in no way affected his mental performance. If anything, he functioned better after a few drinks.

By the time he and Tristan got back to Chester Terrace, Freddie, assisted by the whisky, was in a decidedly more optimistic mood. They decided to surprise Jane, who was still out, by getting the dinner ready.

Tristan, who washed with as little water as possible, used a non-animal-tested soap, and dressed in unbleached T-shirts in the interests of the environment, suggested making a vegetable 'cobbler' or failing that a tian, while Freddie, who was contemplating the open fridge and wondering why the contents blurred one into the other, opted for the chuck steak in its supermarket packet. Unable to agree, they decided to ditch dinner and make a chocolate cake, which took Freddie back to his childhood experiments in the kitchen while Lilli was giving her piano lessons. While he looked through Jane's books for a suitable recipe, Tristan opened cupboards and drawers in search of eggs, sugar, and cocoa, as well as the *batterie de cuisine*. Having entered into a serious dialogue over the definition of a peak (as in 'beat to stiff peaks'), and the meaning of 'fold' (as in 'fold in the flour'), they put the mixture in to bake while Freddie listened to *Simon Boccanegra* on Radio 3, and Tristan suffered in silence. After the prescribed hour, when they assumed that the raw ingredients would have been transformed, as per the glossy illustration, into a mouth-watering gâteau, they opened the oven expectantly, to find their state unaltered. Losing interest in the whole thing, they slung the mixture down the waste-disposal.

When Jane came home, Freddie and Tristan, their feet up on the table, were debating the vexed question of saving the planet – a subject which, to her knowledge, Freddie had not previously addressed – and the kitchen looked as if it had been stirred with a giant spoon. While Tristan exhorted his father to swap his car (which he no longer had) for public transport, to take positive action against destroying wildlife, exploiting Antarctica, and dumping at sea, a creaking board disclosed Jane's presence and summarily silenced them.

Trying not to laugh, as they related the chocolate cake débâcle, she explained that the oven temperatures were measured in degrees *centigrade*, rather than Fahrenheit, dismissed them both and proceeded to clear up the mess.

As they went up the stairs she heard Tristan say: 'Thanks for the drink.'

'Not at all,' Freddie's words coasted one into the other. 'We've never had much to say to each other. I don't know why.'

Tristan's voice reverted to its customary mumble. 'You never tried, Dad. You never had time.'

CHAPTER THIRTY

Freddie was back on his old form. The Bowker & Page contract and his £75,000 was in the bag, Lilli had come to terms with Mrs Williams who no longer threatened him with her notice each time he set foot in the flat, and the dialogue which he had opened up with Tristan had miraculously been maintained. He had even volunteered to join his father in his morning ritual.

Over dinner, he had glanced up at Freddie and mumbled into his veggie burger: 'You jogging tomorrow?'

Freddie nodded.

'Mind if I come?'

'He's having you on,' Rosina said.

But next morning, Tristan, in his running gear, was waiting in the hall when his father came down the stairs. Freddie had had to shorten his circuit – in deference to Tristan he took the Inner Circle route – and slow his pace considerably, but he was both surprised and impressed by the boy's determination. Tristan tired quickly, was patently out of breath, but struggled doggedly on, wiping the sweat from his forehead and brushing the long hair from his eyes. To Freddie's relief, on this occasion, his son made no attempt to talk, but the thump-thump of their matched stride gladdened his heart. He liked having Tristan beside him. It gave him a sense of continuity and filled him with pride.

In the past two weeks he had got to know the boy. He had even been allowed into his room. When Jane was out, and the two of them were alone in the house, they had listened to jazz which had taken Freddie back to his own youth. He had tried to interest Tristan in opera, but faced with *Così fan tutte*, or even *La Bohème* it was as if he had suddenly become tone-deaf like his mother, which he certainly was not.

Music was not the only subject on which they agreed to differ. Tristan confessed to Freddie the secret fears which led to the hunched shoulders, the shuffling gait, the diffident manner which Freddie had never understood. Tristan, Freddie learned, was afraid. The only time he felt confident, the only time he felt safe, was when he was playing the saxophone. When Freddie, who was afraid of nothing, who did not know what it was to be afraid, tried to extract from him what he was talking about, what there was to be afraid of, Tristan admitted, his pale cheeks turning scarlet, that he was afraid of everything. He was afraid of people, with whom he might be required to communicate; he was afraid of his peer group, in the midst of which he might be called upon to prove himself; he was afraid of social situations in which he might be expected to perform; he was afraid of authority, in the *personae* of his teachers at school; he was afraid of making a fool of himself, afraid of being laughed at, and above all, afraid of failure. The only person with whom he felt entirely at ease was Jane, and to a lesser extent, Rosina.

'You're not afraid of me?' Freddie said.

Tristan did not reply. He could not tell Freddie, for the simple reason that he did not know himself, that in his idolisation of his father – who seemed to him to encompass the sum of all things good, wise, clever, accomplished – lay the root of all his fear.

When his two weeks' suspension was up and it was time for him to go back to school, Freddie, who had nothing better to do, took him to the station. As the train pulled away, Tristan put his head out of the window.

'Talk to Mum.'

The phrase reverberated in Freddie's head all the way home. Talk to Mum. It was not easy. He had got on better with Jane when he had been so busy working that he had hardly seen her. The fact that he was around all day seemed to create friction. He tried to make it easy for her, he even tried to help her round the house.

When Lavender had called to say that she wasn't 'feeling too well' (which meant that Tony had been roughing her up again) and that she wouldn't be coming in, Jane was in the bedroom engaged in a tidying blitz. There was a pile of clothes on the floor.

'Today of all days,' Jane said, putting the phone down on Lavender. 'I have a committee meeting at ten.'

'I'll give you a hand.' Freddie bent to pick up some of the clothes. 'I'll put these back in the cupboard for you.'

'They're not going back,' Jane said. 'It's jumble.'

'Jumble?'

'We've got a charity shop in Fulham. There's this marvellous estate agent, a friend of Caroline's, who gives them to us between lettings.'

Freddie wasn't listening. He had recognised a silk shirt and liberated it from the heap.

'You're not getting rid of this?'

'When did you last wear it?' Jane demanded.

'I like that shirt. I've had it for years.'

'You can't even do it up over your chest.'

'I could give it to Tristan.'

'Tristan wouldn't be seen dead in it.'

'I paid a lot of money for that shirt,' Freddie said. 'Kindly don't throw it away.'

'You're never going to wear it.' Jane began stuffing the rest of the garments into a black dustbin bag.

Catching sight of an empty yellow sleeve, Freddie pulled at it and rescued a shrunken and matted pullover from its fate. He had bought it in California one unseasonable May when he had been playing in a golf tournament. It had the Pebble Beach logo on it.

'It'll do for golf.'

He hated to throw anything away. He had inherited the trait from Lilli who throughout his childhood had had to economise, to practise what she referred to as 'make do and mend'.

'You're always hanging around,' Jane said.

'I was only trying to help.'

Jane tied the top of the dustbin bag in an angry knot. The silk shirt Freddie could not get into, and the pullover he would never wear, were left accusingly on the floor.

'Bingo will be here in five minutes. If you really want to help you can change the bed,' Jane snapped, nodding to a pile of clean linen. As she left the room she delivered her parting shot: 'Take the top pillow slips off.'

Freddie put on *I Puritani* and listened to the love-lorn madness of Elvira's coloratura soprano as he advanced towards the bed from the disorder of which he emerged each morning, to enter it again, neatly made as if by some unseen hand, at night. He studied the used sheets which did not look to him as if they needed changing, and the identical square pillows, a predilection for which Jane had inherited from her mother, and the satin-bound blankets – Jane would not have anything to do with duvets – piled in a haphazard heap.

'How do I know which is the *top* pillow?' Freddie called above the Siberian baritone of Elvira's spurned lover.

'What?' Jane's voice rose from the hall where she had gone with the dustbin bag.

'How do I know which is the *top* pillow?'

'I don't know what you're talking about.'

'You told me to change the *top pillow* slip,' Freddie said

reasonably. 'I can't change the top pillow slip unless I know which is the top pillow.'

'Not the top pillow! The top *pillow slip*.'

It took him some while to persuade the pillows, which seemed to have wills of their own, into the freshly laundered pillow slips which he reckoned Jane must have bought a size too small. When he had finished, they were rhomboid rather than square, and did not look right at all.

'Do I change *both* the sheets?' His voice was almost drowned by the orchestra.

'What?'

'Both sheets?'

'Yes.' Jane was obviously trying to keep her cool.

He stripped the bed down to the mattress thinking what a bloody waste of time and energy it all was.

'I thought you'd be finished by now!' Jane breezed through the bedroom on her way to the bathroom.

'I have finished. What do I do with this woolly thing?' Freddie shouted through the closed door. It was opened again angrily.

'What woolly thing?'

Freddie held it up.

'That's the *under*blanket!'

'How am I supposed to know?'

Jane gesticulated with her foaming toothbrush. 'Freddie, please leave it. I'd rather do it myself.'

When Jane had gone out, Freddie decided to redeem himself by hoovering the drawing-room (to Alfredo Kraus's 'Una furtiva lagrima'). Women made such a song and dance of everything. It wasn't such a big deal. When he inadvertently allowed the duster, which he had taken from Lavender's cleaning cupboard, to be swallowed up by the nozzle of the vacuum cleaner – which began to smell alarmingly of burning – he chucked the whole thing in and went to play squash with James.

The fact that the vacuum cleaner not only had to be repaired, but that it needed an expensive new motor (when Freddie was trying to keep their capital expenditure to the minimum) and would be out of action for the best part of a week, did not improve matters between himself and Jane. Their daily confrontations were symptomatic of the underlying problem which they no longer addressed.

Tristan's words, talk to Mum, reinforced what Freddie already knew. Something must be done before the impasse became irredeemable. On the way home from the station he bought a bouquet of long-stemmed yellow roses, and entered the house determined to make his peace with Jane.

He was met at the door by Rosina who had a finger to her lips.

'Mummy's got a migraine,' she said in a stage whisper. 'And it's the first night of *Kiss me Kate*.'

Freddie put the roses on the table and slipped the worry beads out of his pocket. Rosina was waiting for him to speak.

'I'll see if she wants anything,' Freddie said softly, his foot on the bottom stair.

'What about *Kiss me Kate*?' Rosina said.

'What about it?'

'Will *you* come?'

'Me?'

Freddie took his foot off again and faced Rosina. He had seldom involved himself in sports days, speech days, concerts, prizegivings or PTA meetings. Busy at the bank, he had left that sort of thing to Jane.

'Me?' Freddie repeated.

The concept of sitting in a draughty hall while a bunch of schoolgirls cavorted on the stage in a show of desperately amateur dramatics was totally alien.

Rosina looked in the hall mirror and preened herself. 'I *am* the leading lady.'

'I've some papers to deal with,' Freddie said. 'I'll come another time.'

'It's the *first night*.' Rosina put her arms round his neck. 'You'd really like it.'

'I'd really hate it.'

'Please, Daddy . . .'

Freddie would rather have defended a hundred hostile takeover bids.

'You've nothing else to do.'

It was the story of his life these days. Situations with which previously he had never had to deal, domestic matters with which he had never concerned himself, conspired to fill the void. So it was that he found himself in a packed Pfeiffer Hall, Xeroxed programme in hand, wedged between a power-dressed mother whose scent threatened to anaes-thetise him, and a portly father (he was amazed to see so many men in the audience) whose bulging thigh impinged on his own narrow space, on a straight-backed chair which he presumed was inscribed, as was the one in front of him, with the name of a past student of the college.

He opened his programme. 'Synopsis: The action cen-tres around a small theatrical company directed by Fred Graham, whose ex-wife has been employed to star with him in their production of *The Taming of the Shrew*. The stormy plot of the Shakespeare play is paralleled in the relationships off stage and this − along with the com-edy provided by the 'gangsters' who end up part of the cast − gave Cole Porter the cue for some of his finest music . . .'

Freddie had already appraised the fidgeting and excited members of the orchestra who tuned their instruments at the side of the stage: violins, violas, cello, bass, flute, clarinet, saxophone, horn, trumpet, trombone, harp, piano, percus-sion. He hadn't been expecting anything so comprehensive or so professional in appearance. The cast list, amongst which Freddie recognised the names of some of Rosina's friends, was headed by Rosina Lomax.

As the orchestra struck up, and the lights dimmed, Freddie took out his worry beads to ease his frustration at being hemmed in between the overpowering scent and the intrusive leg, leaned back, as best he could, and prepared himself for 120 minutes of unmitigated boredom.

Two hours later, together with the rest of the audience, he was applauding as loudly and as enthusiastically as he had ever done when the curtain came down after a performance at Covent Garden or at Glyndebourne. From the moment the lights (Lighting: Mr Buckley and Mrs Pycraft) had gone up on Stage of Ford Theatre, Baltimore, to the final scene in Baptista's house and the familiar chorus of 'Wunderbar' (which he was tired of hearing round the house), the evening had been one of pure joy.

As the Musical Director, the Producer, the Choreographer, the Stage Manager, as well as those responsible for make-up, set design, programme and publicity, came diffidently onto the platform to take their bows with the exhausted but radiant cast, Freddie reckoned that they deserved every last bit of their acclaim. There had been the odd hiccup: a backdrop lowered into place upside down; a muffed entrance; forgotten lines; a spontaneous snigger at the 'lovers'' passionate kiss. But the accomplished acting, the professional costumes, the sophisticated production, for which he had not been prepared, made Freddie feel both ashamed of himself and proud. He felt ashamed at what he must have missed over the years, by way of school performances both by Tristan and Rosina, and proud to be the father of the radiant and excited leading lady who had come forward to take her bow. He had not realised she was so talented.

From the front of the stage Rosina bowed long and low, making Freddie wish that he had brought the yellow roses to present to her. Straightening up, she smiled at him, then caught the eye of the viola player, a young man with limpid eyes and shoulder-length black hair. Rosina bowed again, before, to Freddie's horror, subsiding slowly into the green folds of the velvet skirt so lovingly sewn by Jane, she fainted dead away.

CHAPTER THIRTY-ONE

On the morning of her Ball, Jane was woken by Freddie's baritone – '*Figaro si, Figaro la, Figaro si, Figaro la*' – and prayed that the unfamiliar sound signposted the road to his recovery. She was not to know that it was the calm before the storm.

Leaving for Grosvenor House early to put some finishing touches to the arrangements, and knowing what the decision to show his face in public was costing him, Jane tentatively approached Freddie who, dressed in his tuxedo, was already at the drinks tray in the drawing-room. Putting her arms round him, she hugged him understandingly. For the first time in weeks he did not resist.

As he waited for Rosina, who seemed to have spent the entire day washing her hair, he took his Black Label to the armchair and went over the débâcle which had suceeded *Kiss me Kate*.

Ministered to by several members of the audience, a surprising number of whom turned out to be medically qualified, Rosina had quickly recovered from her faint. She was still pale and shaking when Freddie got her home. Downing a couple of whiskies himself while waiting for the kettle to boil, he prepared a hot toddy for Rosina while she got herself into bed.

'Have you got a temperature?' Freddie felt her head. 'Do

you still feel dizzy?' He wished Jane were around. 'Does anything hurt?'

Rosina looked up at him from her pillow. Despite the fact that she still had her stage make-up on, she was cuddling her worn-out teddy bear and looked about 12 years old.

'Shall I call Dr Cardwell?' Freddie asked dubiously. He was unaccustomed to dealing with such crises.

'Daddy . . .' Tears welled up, like green pools, in Rosina's eyes. Freddie waited.

'I think I *may* be pregnant.'

Freddie was speechless. Pregnant! He remembered the day Rosina was born. He had been in Geneva on business when Jane's membranes had ruptured five days early. The moment his meeting was over he had dashed to the airport. It was six o'clock. The last plane to London was at 6.30. The girl at the Swiss Air counter told him firmly that the flight was closed. Bringing all his not inconsiderable charm to bear, he managed to persuade her to allow him through. He had never run so fast in his life. Up the escalator, through immigration, into the departure lounge, through the gate, along the miles of corridor – colliding with startled travellers and apologising in any language which came to his lips – to make the aircraft as the surprised crew were about to close the door. By the time he reached the hospital Jane was in the final stages of labour. To the accompaniment of the silent *Marriage of Figaro* which crashed joyously through his head, he watched the miraculous birth of his daughter who would grow up with all the noble purity with which Mozart had endowed his Countess.

'Rosina?' Freddie whispered, as Jane held the perfectly formed child to her breast.

Jane nodded, smiling her tired smile. And Rosina it had been for the past fifteen years. The fact that she was now old enough to become a mother herself had somehow passed him by.

'Pregnant, Rosina!'

The thought that some scruffy youth had defiled his Countess, filled him with rage. He felt capable of strangling the man with his own hands.

'Are you trying to tell me that you're going to have a baby?'

Rosina nodded.

'Have you been having sex?' Freddie heard himself say.

The massed tears overflowed down Rosina's cheeks in black tributaries of mascara.

'On no, Daddy . . .' she sobbed. 'I *found* it in Lilli's box!'

With Jane still laid low with her migraine, which was always a three-day event, it was Freddie who took Rosina to see Bruce Cardwell, the family practitioner. Waiting outside the consulting room while she was being examined, Freddie rested his head in his hands. He had been awake all night.

'Mr Lomax?' Dr Cardwell's nurse beckoned him into the room where, Rosina, fully dressed, was sitting on the examination couch running her fingers through her hair.

'If it's a question of abortion, Bruce,' Freddie said, taking charge of the situation, 'I'd like her to see the top chap.'

'That won't be necessary.' Bruce Cardwell was smiling. 'I think the lacings were too tight.'

'Excuse me?' Freddie was puzzled.

'On the dress. That, and the excitement – she forgot to have anything to eat – and the heat from the lights . . .'

Freddie realised that he was talking about *Kiss me Kate*.

In the street, Freddie put his arm round Rosina's shoulders and walked happily in step with her along the pavement. He would take her to Jane's Ball.

By some trick of the light, Rosina's appearance at the door of the drawing-room, red hair, white skin, wearing what appeared to be an emerald-green crêpe bandage, woke Freddie from his reverie and made him think for a moment that she was Jane. It happened lately. He'd see some

20-year-old in the street and believe for a moment that it was some contemporary from Cambridge, not stopping to think that any friend of his was now more likely to be a 40-year-old tax exile, a designer-stubbled media mogul, or a middle-aged industrialist.

'Daddy?' Rosina said.

It was not Jane. He looked admiringly at his daughter through an alcoholic haze.

Jane had arranged a table of close friends – Charles and Bingo, James and Dos, Peter and Georgina, Piers and Alex – onto which two more places had been squeezed at the last minute. Henry Dove had been given his marching orders, and Rosina had invited Ferdinand – the viola player of the limpid eyes and shoulder-length black hair – to be her partner at the Ball.

It was like old times. Helped by the Black Label, Freddie climbed out of the pit into which he had been cast by Gordon Sitwell and back into his old skin. It was a long while since he had been at the top of his form.

Observing him, the most impressive, the handsomest man in the room, as he hosted the evening with his old panache, Rosina hoped that if she ever *did* decide to get married, her husband – would it be Ferdinand? – would be as wonderful as her father and that she would be as lucky as Jane.

As if there was no tomorrow, Freddie bought tombola tickets for Rosina (she won Frau Wichmann's *Kölnischwasser* and a pink 'babygrow' the significance of which was lost on all but Jane and Freddie), and an entire book of raffle tickets for an embarrassed Ferdinand – who had put his hand into the pocket of his borrowed dinner jacket and come up with two twenty-pence pieces – and generously tipped the waiters who had marched into the darkened ballroom with their flaming desserts of spun sugar held at shoulder height, and ordered several rounds of brandy and liqueurs for which he refused to let anyone else pay.

After dinner, while the women streamed towards the ladies' room and Ferdinand wandered off to get some air while he waited for Rosina, Freddie, Charles Holdsworth, Piers Warburton, Peter Cottesloe and James remained at the table and closed ranks.

'When's the big day?' Charles addressed Freddie, who knew he was referring to the signing of the Bowker & Page deal.

'Monday.' Forty-eight hours to go.

'Anything else in the offing?'

Freddie signalled for more brandy, a move registered by Piers who was working his way through a bottle of Malvern Water.

'One or two irons in the fire.' It was not strictly true, although tonight, helped by the alcohol he had consumed, Freddie felt it to be.

'Believe me, this is no time to be a banker,' Piers said.

'Or a name!' James, a member of Lloyds, who had lost a considerable amount of money, said ruefully, lighting a cigar.

'There have been some strange goings-on in my own outfit, lately.' Piers screwed the top on the Malvern Water. 'Four market-makers, out of a team of twenty-eight, have just been made redundant. Rumour has it that one of them was responsible for over £1 *million* of trading profit in the past three months. The story is that it's part of a "reorganisation". The powers that be are looking at radical measures and are apparently planning to shed thousands of jobs and hundreds of branches. I shall probably be out on my ear myself very soon.'

'The main problem, as I see it,' Charles kept an eye on the doors for the return of Bingo, 'is assessing lending risks in a competitive market. Bad debts have been accelerating for years; £5.6 billion has been written off this year alone. The clearing banks have been so busy scrambling for the market share that they have failed to recognise – although it's been staring them in the face – that the name of the game has changed . . .'

Listening to them, Freddie felt as if he had a terminal disease. The news that his friends might have it too was, he presumed, intended to make him feel better.

'Freddie's on good form.' In the ladies' room, Georgina, wearing the Cottesloe pearls over a simple black shift, advanced two paces towards the row of cubicles.

'It's the first time I've seen him laugh,' Jane said. She meant since his dismissal.

'We're running an article in the magazine on redundancy . . .' Alex said tactlessly.

Dos glared at her.

'The *emotional* cost . . .' Alex blundered on.

'For God's sake, Alex!'

'It's okay,' Jane said.

'Did you know that Relate', Alex warmed to her theme, 'has reported a 30 per cent increase in marriage breakdown, thought to be brought about by the strain and pressure of redundancy on middle-class, middle-aged relationships . . .'

'Someone in America has invented a gadget for women so that they can pee standing up,' Bingo said loudly as they shuffled towards the head of the queue. 'I'm not sure of the logistics of the thing, but apparently it *looks* like a baseball.'

Having effectively silenced Alex and caused considerable amusement to the other ladies in the queue, Bingo put a comforting arm through Jane's.

By the time they returned to the table, the Latin American band (courtesy of Sir John Pawsey) had struck up, and the dancing was in full swing. Freddie was already on the floor with Rosina, and Piers, seizing the opportunity of getting Jane into his arms, stood up as she approached and invited her to dance.

'She's only *dancing* with him.' Rosina followed Freddie's gaze as he steered her round the floor.

'Let's hope so.'

'Daddy! You're frightfully drunk, you know. I'm practically anaesthetised.'

'Alcohol does not affect me,' Freddie said. His eyes did not leave Jane and Piers. 'It never has.'

Dancing next with Ferdinand, Rosina thought that she had never been so happy. Looking at him, his aquiline nose, his Christ-like face, she knew that having sex with Ferdinand, who was gentle where Henry had been rough, patient where Henry had been impetuous, sensitive where Henry had been like a bull in a china shop, would not be the let-down it had been with Henry – who was now going out with the beastly Rachel Lloyd who deserved him – but that he would treat her with respect, would extract from her body wondrous tunes, as he did from his viola.

As Ferdinand escorted Rosina back to the table whilst firmly retaining her hand in his, a drum roll drew 500 pairs of eyes to the platform, where her mother, whom she thought of more in terms of nagging her to tidy her room or reminding her what time she was to be in at night, was about to make a speech.

Into the expectant silence Jane, who was largely responsible for the success of the evening, said: 'The charity industry, with an annual turnover of £18 billion, represents 4 per cent of gross domestic product . . .'

Freddie sat up. Jane's voice, as she stood at the microphone, was clear and confident. He was unaware that she had even heard of gross domestic product.

'. . . and is larger than the agriculture sector,' Jane went on. 'If the volunteer time was costed, this sector – according to the Charities Aid Foundation – *could* represent 10 per cent. Like most industries, however, the voluntary sector has been hard hit by the recession . . .' She avoided Freddie's eye. 'The main item on the agenda of almost every charity today is funding. Company giving has decreased, individual giving has diminished, and central government has been effectively capping much local authority expenditure . . .'

Speaking fluently, and without notes, Jane held her audience as, standing on the dressing-up hamper as a child, she had captivated the younger copperknobs.

Listening to her, watching her, her white sequins, her red hair, Freddie realised that there were strengths to Jane that he was either unaware of or had ignored. Her final exhortation 'to give generously', to the assembly enslaved both by her words and her appearance which sparkled sveltely beneath the chandeliers of the great ballroom, brought tears to their eyes and charmed the cheque books from their pockets. Leading her proudly onto the dance floor, to the strains of '*La Vie en rose*' which he had asked the band to play, Freddie took her in his arms.

Marching once again to the same drummer, he did not need to remind Jane of the moonlit walks along the Backs, the passionate nights in his Cambridge room. The music did it for him. He had no idea whether it was the remembrance of things past, his pride in Jane, his love for her, or the alcohol he had consumed, but for the first time since his nightmare had begun, he felt capable of making love to her.

'Let's go home,' he whispered, holding her close.

Jane got the car out of the garage. Rosina, her head on Ferdinand's shoulder, sat in the back.

Old habits dying hard – he liked to be first with the City editors' comments on the week's news – Freddie asked Jane to stop for a moment outside Tottenham Court Road station. Getting out of the car, he handed over a note to the man behind the trestle table, who was wearing a woolly hat with a bobble, and helped himself to a stack of Sunday newspapers. By the light of a street lamp he stared unbelievingly at the headline: 'BANKER TAKES OWN LIFE', above a photograph of Gordon Sitwell.

CHAPTER THIRTY-TWO

Margaret Sitwell had not picked up a Mills & Boon for two weeks. She had been too busy looking after Gordon. Since his arrest he had been a changed man. She hoped that after the court hearing he would revert to his old self. The hearing had twice been delayed. On the first occasion Gordon had pleaded lumbago, and on the second, a virus infection, both of which had been obligingly confirmed by the accommodating family practitioner, Malcolm Rowe, a longtime friend. Gordon was indeed ill. But his indisposition was not physical. Since the night he had driven home from Savile Row police station to lay his head in the confessional of Margaret's lap, his very real suffering had been pathetic to behold. He had not shown his face at the bank, had delegated his work to Conrad Verger, and his Rolls Royce had not been out of the garage.

The first indication that Margaret had of the severity of her husband's condition was when he refused to go into the garden. He could not face his roses. It was as if Rosa Rubiginosa, Rosa Xanthina, Virgo and Pascali, and Madame Louise Laperrière, had joined forces to censure him.

Although he had not yet been indicted, Gordon felt that he had been unjustly accused, just as he had when he had spied through the bedroom door on his mother, swearing to his father, so very many years ago, that he had only stopped to fasten his shoe. Somewhere between his apprehension by the police and his decision to take his own life, he had managed to convince both himself and Margaret that he had in fact been looking for an all-night chemist. Margaret thought that it was only a question of time – as soon as he was well enough to appear before the magistrates – before her husband was completely vindicated. She had said as much to her friends in The Pantry where she took her morning coffee. They had nodded their heads in sympathy.

Gordon did not have the support of friends. He would not even let his children into the house. He had no one but Margaret. He relied upon her to find his slippers – he had taken to shuffling round the house in his dressing-gown and refused to get dressed – to accompany him to the morning-room where he sat most of the day doing nothing more demanding than stare unseeingly out of the window, to cook his meals, with which she had all but to feed him, to cradle him in her arms in bed at night, when he would turn to her and act out the fantasies which had led to his downfall. Margaret did not object. She had never had so much attention. She allowed Gordon to ride her, and beat her, to abuse her in ways she would not divulge to anyone, not even under torture, but proudly displayed the black rings beneath her eyes and the huge purple lovebites on her neck, in The Pantry.

Malcolm Rowe, who had long ago retired but continued to look after Margaret and Gordon, said that Gordon was depressed, and told him to snap out of it. Margaret suggested to Malcolm that there were pills for Gordon's condition, she had heard 'Hyacinth from Wood Green' and 'Eroll from Tooting' discuss their efficacy, on the LBC phone-ins. Malcolm Rowe said that pills were for people with *problems*, people who had something to be depressed about, but Gordon had never been depressed in his life, he had just had a nasty shock and that left alone he would get over it.

Margaret, who was not accustomed to thinking for herself – Gordon had always told her what to think – had left it at that. When Gordon appeared to get worse instead of better, she decided that the time had come to consult Sophie, their oldest daughter, married to Conrad Verger.

Leaving Gordon with some lunch on a tray, a flask of tea, and some rockcakes she had bought that morning at The Pantry, she had set off for Rickmansworth, where Sophie and Conrad had a mansion with a swimming pool and a sauna and a fully equipped gymnasium (for Conrad's weight training) and a tennis court for the children. Conrad and Sophie were sympathetic but, busy preparing a barbecue for the neighbours, arranging the chairs on the patio, and wondering whether there would be enough food to go round (Sophie was shouting at the children and wrapping potatoes in tinfoil), were not particularly helpful.

'Of course he'll be acquitted, Mummy.' Sophie seemed more interested in the potatoes than Gordon, whom she took after. 'Jasper stop kicking Miranda and help your father with the chairs. If you can only get him to the Magistrates' Court, all the fuss will die down. The public has a very short memory.'

'Do you think more steaks, or more chops, Sophe?' Conrad said.

'Sophie's quite right . . .' Conrad always agreed with Sophie, it was more than his life was worth not to. 'Yesterday's news is today's fish and chips. The sooner Gordon comes back to the bank, the better.'

'He'll have other things to think about,' Sophie said, and to Conrad: 'We can always make up with sausages.'

Declining the invitation to amuse the children, who were extremely badly behaved, Margaret refused Conrad's offer (made as he looked anxiously at the time) to run her home. Margaret, who had never learned to drive – Gordon said that she was too careless – told Conrad that she wouldn't dream of putting him out, and insisted on making her own way, as she had come, by public transport. By the time she reached Tall Trees, she was almost late for Gordon's supper.

She sensed that something was wrong the moment she opened the front door. It was not merely the fact that she was not greeted with the familiar 'Is that you, Margaret?' – as if it could be anybody else! – but a feeling that the house was too quiet, that it was silently trying to tell her something.

She opened the door of the morning-room quietly, in case Gordon was having a nap. The room was tidy. It was as if no one had been in there. Upstairs the bedroom was empty, there was no evidence that Gordon had been lying on his bed. It was at this point that Margaret began to worry. Possibilities she had no wish to consider were already infiltrating her mind.

'Gordon!' she called, knowing there would be no answer. 'Gordon?' She dragged her heavy legs up to the long corridors, the empty rooms, on the top floor.

There was no question that he was in the garden. It was weeks since he had set foot outside the house. There was one possibility which she had not explored. She had no desire to. Returning to the bedroom she sat on the bed for a long time and enjoyed what was to be her last tranquil moment, her last vestige of hope, then made her way to the garage.

Gordon had never invested in an 'up-and-over' door, and refused to have anything to do with remote controls. He liked the oak doors on his garage. It was the same in the house. Although he must have plenty of money – Margaret knew, it stood to reason, although he never discussed it with her – he was not keen on spending it on what he considered inessentials. The old-fashioned cooker still cooked, the monstrous fridge they had had since their marriage still did what it was designed to do, the massive mahogany wardrobes opened and closed satisfactorily, and he saw absolutely no reason to bow either to built-in obsolescence or new technology. It was the same when it came to redecoration. While Margaret declared the wallpaper shabby, Gordon said it had mellowed, when she suggested modernising the bathroom, Gordon said it served very well. The stair carpet was threadbare but 'serviceable', and the children's rooms had not been touched since their occupants were small. Gordon's only visible extravagance was his car, and even that was not new. It looked as if it was. Ronald, Gordon's driver, tended it like a child. He dusted and polished the Rolls, maintained and repaired it, and, while he waited for Gordon to appear in the mornings, regarded his own distorted image reflected in its maroon bonnet. Margaret knew that she would find Gordon in the garage. She had no idea how she knew. She was not into deduction.

The garage was locked. The large iron key had not been in its place on the brass tray (Gordon had bargained for it in Cairo) on the hall table. The oak doors were locked from the inside. Margaret rattled them abortively, calling Gordon's name. Receiving no reply, she returned indoors to summon the police. Somehow it was not the sight of Gordon as he sat slumped in the driving seat, his cheeks cherry red, his tended hands on the steering wheel, his unseeing eyes staring at Ronald's neatly arranged cleaning materials on the shelf, which disconcerted Margaret, who knew before she knew that Gordon had taken his own life, but the fact that he had bathed and shaved, for the first time since his arrest, and was dressed in the black, pin-striped suit, which he wore for the office, and had fastened a rose in his lapel.

She had tried to ring Freddie. She had let the telephone ring and ring. Only then did she call Sophie. It was half an hour before Sophie and Conrad, leaving their barbecue in full swing, appeared on the scene in their new BMW. In that thirty minutes, the longest in her life, Margaret Sitwell realised just how much she had loved Gordon.

She was not the only one to be devastated by the fact that

Gordon Sitwell (while the balance of his mind was disturbed), had connected a length of hosepipe to the exhaust of his Rolls Royce and switched on the ignition.

The chairman's death had reawakened emotions in Freddie which had lain dormant for thirty-four years. Jane could not understand the effect of the news on him. He could not have reacted more strongly had he killed Gordon himself.

Freddie thought that he had. He thought that because he had dreamed, in Lilli's flat, of assassinating the man who had betrayed him, he was responsible for his death. Notwithstanding the fact that he had been fifteen miles away from the scene of the crime at the time of Gordon's demise, he had killed Gordon Sitwell as surely as he had killed his father in the garden.

Freddie had never told anybody what had happened, thirty-four years ago, by the canal in Maida Vale. He had not repeated it, not even inside his head to himself. With the fresh blood of Gordon's death on his hands, he released the poltergeists from the confines of their dark cupboard.

Freddie's passion, at the age of 6, had been for sweets. He rarely ate them. He collected them up – the jelly babies, and the Smarties, the sherbert dabs and Jamboree Bags, the gob-stoppers and Flying Saucers and liquorice comfits and chocolate buttons – and kept them beneath his socks in a drawer in his bedroom. Sometimes he took them out and counted them, arranging them neatly in rows. They were like money in the bank.

Occasionally, by way of a treat, he indulged himself. Lying on his bed with a comic, he broached one of the sealed bags and delicately extracted a Smartie, or a chocolate button, which he transferred, like a communion wafer, onto his outstretched tongue. He liked to see how long he could make them last. In the case of a Smartie, he took it out of his mouth frequently to watch it change colour. The buttons were assessed for their even, slow melt, until only the puddle of chocolate on his tongue reminded him that they had ever been.

The day that his father had died had been a Saturday. Pocket money day. Freddie had been planning to buy a Walnut Whip. Unlike the other confectionery, the Walnut Whip would not dissolve in his mouth into nothingness, neither would it stay for very long in his drawer. It demanded a quite different approach. This entailed biting off the walnut, which must then be set aside. Into the resulting crater, the tongue, rolled into a neat point, must then be repeatedly inserted to extract the creamy interior. Then, and only then – all this took some time and could not be hurried – could the striated sides of the pyramid be disposed of in small, delicious bites. This left two unexciting walnuts which must be quickly despatched – sometimes they tasted quite bitter – before the acme was reached: the thick, substantial, satisfying chocolate base on which the entire edifice had been built.

Hugh Lomax did not go to his surgery on Saturday mornings. While Lilli prepared lunch, he took Freddie for a walk. On the way he discussed with Freddie what was going on in the world and asked him questions. Which Europeans were the first to sail to North America? How many seeds does a cherry have? What number is represented by the Roman numeral X? How many times a year will a tortoise drink? By the time he was 6, Freddie knew that if you stood on the moon, at a point where you could see the earth, it would always be overhead and never move; which was the widest river; in which sequence the traffic lights changed and how to preserve conkers. The questions he liked best were mental arithmetic. He could already add up quite serious figures in his head, and was equally proficient in taking them away.

On the day of his death, Hugh Lomax had left the breakfast table to talk privately to a patient on the upstairs phone. Whilst he was hanging about, Freddie, who did not much like waiting and was bored, went into the sitting-room where he caught sight of the blue-eyed china cat, which was what Lilli called 'a collector's item', on the mantelpiece. The china cat, Lilli had made abundantly clear, was not a plaything. Freddie was not allowed to touch it. He assessed the risks. His mother was busy in the kitchen and he reckoned that it would be some time before she came to look for him, to see what he was up to. Climbing on the armchair and hanging onto the mantelpiece with one hand, he reached out with the other. Balancing on one foot, he had the cat within his grasp, when Lilli, in a white satin wrapper, her hair wound round jumbo red rollers in preparation for her Saturday night concert, appeared unexpectedly in the doorway. Startled, Freddie lost his balance. He landed, fortunately for him, on the Persian carpet, but was followed, as if in slow motion, by the blue-eyed cat, which dropped like a stone onto the marble hearth and shattered into a hundred irreparable shards.

His pocket money had been withheld and with it went the prospect of the long-awaited Walnut Whip.

Although it was Lilli's cat which had been broken, it was his father who had decreed the punishment. Freddie hated him for it. He seethed, lagging behind him, dragging his feet and refusing to answer a single question for the entire duration of the walk. When they crossed the Maida Vale, dodging the traffic, he had visions of his father being run over, or mown down by a red bus. When they walked, in unaccustomed silence, along the towpath, Freddie had vivid notions of pushing the grey-flannel trousers, as hard as he could, into the rubbish-strewn waters of the canal. Four hours later, amongst the daisies, as if by some divine intervention, Freddie's homicidal wish had been granted. Hugh Lomax, sprawled on the lawn amongst the loose grass clippings in the summer garden, lay dead.

Freddie's thoughts, so long repressed, were sprung from his unconscious by the demise of Gordon Sitwell.

When he had got back into the car outside Tottenham Court Road station on the way home from the Ball, Freddie had been unable to utter a single word. Taking her eyes from the road to glance at the headlines in the newspaper, Jane had almost run the car into the kerb. 'Good God!'

Leaning over Freddie's shoulder, Rosina took the *Sunday Times* from his lap. '"Sir Gordon Sitwell,"' she read aloud, '"chairman of merchant bank Sitwell Hunt International, was found dead in his Rolls Royce in his garage yesterday. Sir Gordon, recently charged with soliciting, was on bail awaiting his trial. Death is thought to be due to carbon monoxide poisoning. According to his wife, Margaret, Sir Gordon has been suffering from depression and he is assumed by the police to have taken his own life . . ." Daddy!'

Turning round, Freddie had removed the newspaper from her hand. He had no desire to hear any more.

CHAPTER THIRTY-THREE

La Traviata, which Freddie had once seen in Milan with Sidonie, and to which he was listening as he drove up the motorway to Manchester for the signing of the Bowker & Page contract, was not a random choice.

There had been no word from Sidonie since he had left her at the door of Room 333 at the Berkeley. Having placed phone calls which were not returned, left messages which were never answered, he had accepted that Sidonie no longer rated him, and that he was erased for all time from her mental agenda. This morning, whilst getting ready for his final meeting with Harvey Peters and Dennis Bowker, when nothing but the deal, and the fact that he would soon be out of trouble with the bank, was on his mind, he had received a letter from her. After reading it, it was only with the help of an early shot of Black Label (out of sight of Jane) that he had managed to get his act together.

Freddie had recognised the letter immediately. He had always teased Sidonie about her handwriting which would have disgraced a child of ten. He had no need to turn over the envelope with its New York postmark to ascertain the name of the sender. Taking the letter into his dressing-room when he came home from his morning jog, he opened it with the aid of his paper knife.

Dear Freddie,
  By the time you read this I will be dead . . .

Dear Freddie, by the time you read this I will be dead. Dear Freddie, by the time you read this I will be dead. Like an old gramophone record with the needle stuck in the groove, the words revolved in his head. It was some time before he was able to proceed.

Dear Freddie,
  By the time you read this I will be dead. You and I always levelled with each other. There is no other way to say it. Not much of an Overture. Not much of an opera. Act One: That last night, at the Berkeley, I told you Fabrizio was dead. That was the moment (I remember I had my fingers in the rice cracker bowl) when I stopped levelling with you. Fabrizio *was* dead. That much was true. He died from AIDS. He was AC/DC. I knew. I'd always known. He suited my purpose. We had a real fun time. There was never any question of love, on my part, as far as Fabrizio was concerned. You know that.
  It was a terrible shock. You can't pick up a paper these days without reading about AIDS. You don't think it's going to knock on your particular door. It was long and slow. Fabrizio was very brave. You don't get a medal. You get dead. Act Two: You're right. You've read this libretto a hundred times before, Freddie. I had the tests. HIV positive. Give it to me straight, I said, when I went for the results, I can take it. Take it! Jesus Christ, Freddie. I was paralytic. I couldn't move. Demons had me by the throat. I thought I was going to die right there in the doctor's office. The truth is. You *can* take it. FOR OTHER PEOPLE. When it comes to yourself it's a whole new ball game. I was only

a kid, a child, a young woman, had my life in front of me, what had I done to deserve it . . . all that bullshit. *They* say you come to terms with your own mortality. With death. You do not, Freddie. You do not. Don't let anyone give you that crap. You live with it twenty-four hours a day. It's called a nightmare. When I came to England, when I called you, I was living it. I'd already been hospitalized with PCP (*Pneumocystis carinii*). I knew I didn't have very long, but I had to see you. I had to see you, Freddie. When I did it nearly blew my mind. Remember *Tristan und Isolde*? The tears were not, on this occasion, for Wagner. They were for Sidonie Newmark, deceased. When we got back to the hotel, I wanted so much to take you to bed, to hold you in my arms for the last time. I knew that there could be no question of anything like that as far as you and I are concerned. I only need to hear your voice on the telephone to . . . It was always like that with us, Freddie. I had to send you away. Act Three: I am back in the hospital. There are purple spots on my skin. I tried to pretend that they were bruises. That I'd banged into something. They go by the name of Kaposi's sarcoma. I have a pain in my chest. I cough persistently, a hard, dry cough. I have been on a ventilator. I am not going to come out again. That much is sure. I have lost a lot of weight. I am very tired. I am very lonely. And shit scared. People are afraid to visit. I talk with the other guys on the ward but we are all dead men. It is hard to write, but I didn't want to go without saying goodbye. I will give this letter to my sister and tell her not to mail it until . . . There's something I have to tell you. I think I have always known. I kidded myself I was not capable of it. I love you. From that moment I met you on the Concorde. Find a little corner in your heart for me, Freddie, and I will rest in peace.

'La commedia è finita.' Sidonie.

From the damp patch on his T-shirt which had seeped through to his chest, Freddie realised that he had been crying. Shit. Shit, shit, shit!

Afraid that he would miss the Manchester train, Jane had come into the dressing-room to see why he hadn't reappeared. She found him, Sidonie's letter in his hand, sitting motionless on the chair.

'Freddie . . .'

He slipped the letter into his pocket.

'. . . what on earth are you up to? You're going to miss your train.'

Jane was right. Going through the motions of showering and shaving, he *had* missed it. The next train would have made him late for his meeting. He had had to borrow Jane's car.

Now he was approaching the Watford Gap as 'Ah! fors'e lui', sung by Montserrat Caballé, heralded the end of the first act of *La Traviata*. Gordon Sitwell. Sidonie. The landscape of his life was changing. One by one, familiar figures were being painted out.

Gordon Sitwell's cremation had been private (no flowers), at his own request. His humiliation had superseded his death. A service of thanksgiving for his life and work had been held at St Clement Danes and, out of courtesy to Margaret, Freddie had attended it with Jane. The Rt Hon. The Lord Mayor of London had read from Henry Scott Holland's 'Death Is Nothing At All', and at noon on a Wednesday morning Freddie had found himself standing amidst a crowd of familiar City figures, many of whom averted their eyes in embarrassment at the sight of him, belting out 'Mine eyes have seen the glory of the coming of the Lord' from 'The Battle Hymn of the Republic'.

As they left the church, he had nodded to Conrad Verger,

standing next to his mother-in-law, and shaken hands with a sad and bewildered Margaret.

'It was good of you to come, Freddie. Gordon thought so much of you . . .'

Freddie looked at her, in her black hat, with amazement.

'He regarded you as a son. He always wanted a son. I don't know why he . . . got rid of you. He never did tell me. Gordon never discussed the bank. I think he thought of it as cutting out a canker from a diseased root. Something which had to be done.'

On the way back from St Clement Danes, Freddie had dropped Jane off at Chester Terrace and gone to see Lilli. Something was troubling him. It had been triggered by Gordon Sitwell's death. He let himself into the flat with his key. Lilli and Mrs Williams were playing whist.

'You're home early,' Lilli said as if Freddie was still at school. 'Wash your hands and have your tea.'

Making a trick, Lilli laid it on the table.

'Freddie,' she said, as if seeing him for the first time. 'What a lovely surprise. Have you brought . . .? Have you brought . . . your wife with you?'

'Jane,' Freddie reminded her. 'No.'

'My housekeeper will make you a cup of tea. You'd like a cup of tea?'

Freddie needed Mrs Williams out of the room. He wanted to talk to Lilli. When she'd gone into the kitchen, Freddie picked up the photograph of himself playing cricket in the garden with his father.

'You remember when . . .' He was not sure how to refer to his father. He hadn't called him anything, except in his head, for thirty-four years. 'When Father died?'

'Of course I remember. There's nothing wrong with my memory. *She* thinks there is. She thinks I don't remember we had a tin of mango slices. She pretended it was hidden behind the self-raising flour. But do you know,' Lilli beckoned

Freddie to come nearer, 'she said she was going to post a letter but she slipped out for another one.'

'That's enough of that Mrs Lomax.' Mrs Williams came in with the tea-tray. 'Mr Lomax has come to have tea with you not to listen to all that nonsense. If you don't mind,' she said to Freddie, 'I'll slip out for a breath of fresh air while you talk to your mother.'

'She's going to meet her boyfriend,' Lilli said.

Mrs Williams sighed. 'If you say so.'

When she'd gone, Freddie poured the tea.

'Three sugars,' Lilli said politely, as if he did not know.

'The day that Father died,' Freddie said. 'Tell me what happened.'

'It was a very long time ago . . .' Lilli said. 'I was due to play at a rehearsal for one of the soloists in *caractacus*. I once taught the piano to a nun at a convent. The mother superior insisted on sitting in on the lessons . . .'

'We were playing cricket in the garden,' Freddie said. 'One minute he was bowling, and the next . . .'

'You were always very keen on cricket,' Lilli said, appearing to concentrate on the circumventions of the spoon. 'I hear Tristan doesn't care for it. Your wife told me.'

'On the death certificate . . .' Freddie said, trying to shock her back into remembering. 'What did it say on father's death certificate?'

'Mrs Williams made those cakes. Used a week's ration of sugar I shouldn't wonder. Unless she got it on the . . .' Lilli's voice dropped to a whisper '. . . black market.'

By the time Mrs Williams came back, Freddie had got no further. Although his mother had told him about a holiday she had spent on the Isle of Man where she claimed to remember that the news had been brought to them that Blériot had flown the channel, and about the time she had met Jean Simmons on the set at Denham Studios, she had come no nearer to answering Freddie's question.

He thanked Mrs Williams for the tea – she said it was a pleasure – and as the two well-matched antagonists settled themselves to resume the game of whist, stood up to take his leave.

'I'll speak to you in the morning.' Freddie kissed Lilli. 'I'll let myself out.'

'Such a gentleman,' Mrs Williams simpered.

Lilli picked up her hand of cards. 'He had trouble with his valve,' she said clearly. 'They didn't spot it when he joined the army. Rheumatic fever as a child.'

Freddie was by the sitting-room door. 'Father had a heart condition?' he said, his own heart pumping.

'Mitral stenosis. Trumps! *And* a cerebral embolism.'

Mitral stenosis. And a cerebral embolism. He had not killed him after all. The diagnosis, as supplied by Lilli, was immaterial. Freddie knew better. He had assassinated Hugh Lomax with the same supernatural powers with which he had conveniently disposed of Gordon Sitwell. He must try to control his fantasies in future, and monitor his thoughts.

Sidonie's death was different. He had not wished her dead. He could not accept that she *was* dead, that the letter had not been some kind of ghoulish joke. Turning it over in his dressing-room, after he had read it for the umpteenth time, he saw that the address on the back was not, after all, familiar. It was not Sidonie's. Neither was the name. He had called her sister, Kathie, who lived in Michigan, waking her up.

There was not much more that Kathie could tell him. Sidonie had often spoken about Freddie to her. She felt as if she knew him. She had been with her little sister when she died. Sidonie had become progressively weaker, then slipped away. The battle was predetermined. The letter to Freddie had been written three weeks before the end. There was nothing more to tell.

'Pray to God,' Kathie said. 'Pray for her soul.'

To Freddie's surprise, he was already approaching Spaghetti Junction, on his way to Manchester, as 'Parigi, O cara', the duet between *La Traviata*'s doomed lovers, came from Violetta's sickroom. The anguish of the closing trio pierced by the mortal shriek – which was echoed by the orchestra – presaged Violetta's death. Verdi's melodrama was a fitting epitaph for the life-loving Sidonie. It would be a long time before he could bring himself to listen to *Tristan und Isolde*.

'End of motorway half a mile.' By the time today was over he hoped to be exiting his own recent motorway of disaster. The breath had been knocked out of him by his dismissal, by the death of Gordon Sitwell, and of Sidonie. The breath but not the fight. *Since when has hitting the ball into the net once made you a lousy tennis player? You're a success, Freddie. It's how you feel that's important. Stop feeling sorry for yourself. Your ship's got white sails, Freddie. Your ship has always had white sails . . .*

There was a half-empty bottle of Black Label on the seat beside him. Opening the window Freddie hurled it out onto the grass verge. He had been a pain in the arse lately. Especially to Jane. He would make it up to her. How he would make it up to her. He flexed his shoulders feeling the power which had been taken from him, like that of the shorn Samson, come flooding back.

Silencing *La Traviata*, with its pale songs and broken hearts, and following the signs to the airport, which led to Hale, he let Cavaradossi's triumphant 'Vittoria!' loose onto the Cheshire air.

CHAPTER THIRTY-FOUR

There were already two cars in the carriage drive when Freddie drew up outside the Victorian mansion. Standing on the red-tiled porch, he had hardly touched the bell when an excited Dennis Bowker, wearing an optimistic red shirt beneath a hand-painted tie, opened the front door.

'Big day, eh?'

'Big day.'

Crossing his fingers, Freddie followed Dennis Bowker into the dining-room where the Bowker camp, Dennis and Barbara Bowker, their solicitor and accountant, was assembled round the refectory table. They were waiting for Harvey Peters.

'Whisky?' At the sideboard, Dennis Bowker held out the bottle of Black Label. He knew Freddie's tastes.

'I'll have some coffee if there is any.' Dennis Bowker was not to know that this was day one of a new era.

Freddie was on his second cup of coffee, and the solicitor, a prematurely bald 45-year-old, and the accountant, a neat row of pens in his top pocket, had run out of small talk concerning their respective gardens – in particular their dahlias – when Barbara Bowker, squinting to look at the jewelled face of her wristwatch, voiced what all of them were thinking.

'It's not like Harvey to be late.'

'There *was* a fair bit of traffic on the M1 . . .' Freddie's worry beads had been out of his pocket for some time. 'Not to mention the usual roadworks and contraflow systems.'

'Our roads are a positive disgrace,' the accountant said.

'Chap's got an Aston Martin!' Dennis Bowker, retirement in Spain within his grasp, bobbed up and down to look out of the window each time he heard a car.

'Why don't you give him a bell?' the solicitor ran a finger round the collar of his shirt.

Dennis Bowker went into the hall, leaving behind him a charged silence broken only by the ticking of the grandfather clock the pendulum of which seemed to swing progressively more slowly as the scratch pads on the table became covered with desultory doodles.

'No reply.' Dennis Bowker came back into the room. 'You're wanted in the kitchen, Barbara. Something about lunch.'

'Do you think he's changed his mind?' The solicitor had drawn a succession of boxes which he was shading in.

'I spoke to him last night.' Dennis Bowker was at the window.

'I'm due in Didsbury at one.'

'And I have to get back to the office.' The accountant looked up at the clock.

'Not here yet?' Barbara Bowker, in her tweed skirt and silk blouse, came back into the room. 'It really is too – '

An imperious ring of the front doorbell accompanied by a rattling of the letterbox, released the tension which had been building up and galvanised everyone into action.

'I'll get it!' Freddie was the first on his feet.

On the polished red step, beneath the porch, stood two police officers.

'Harvey Peters?'

Dennis Bowker was at Freddie's shoulder.

'Bowker,' he said. 'This is my house. Can I help you?'

One of the policemen consulted a paper. 'Sorry to trouble you, sir. There must be some mistake.'

They had turned to go, when Freddie said, 'Hang on a minute. We were *expecting* Harvey Peters.'

'In that case . . .'

'You'd better come in.' Dennis Bowker stood back, and the police officers, removing their flat caps, stepped inside.

Like a man who was drowning, Freddie stood in the oak-panelled hall as the video of his life fast-forwarded before his eyes.

'I'm afraid there's been an accident, sir,' one of the officers said.

'A motor vehicle accident,' his companion added.

'Looks like Mr Peters dropped off on the motorway,' the first officer took up the reprise. 'His car hit the central reservation. It caused an extremely nasty pile-up — '

'Is he . . .?' Freddie said.

'I'm afraid so, sir . . .'

'Dead on arrival.'

'Apparently this address was found on him. The officer thought he *lived* here.'

'Are you absolutely sure it *was* Harvey Peters?' Freddie asked.

'He was identified at the hospital. The other two gentlemen were badly injured.'

'That's it then.'

Freddie was not talking about the death of Harvey Peters — that would come later. He was referring to the demise of the Bowker & Page deal, on which he had been pinning his hopes, and which represented his personal salvation.

'I'm afraid it is, sir.'

Back in the dining-room the accountant and the solicitor gathered up their papers and stowed them away in their briefcases. Despite the fact that he had to drive back to London, Freddie changed his mind about the whisky. In a tangible silence, broken only by the ticking of the clock and the voice of Barbara Bowker babbling over and over about the lobster and champagne she had laid on for lunch, none of them was able to meet the others' eyes.

When the solicitor and accountant had left and Barbara Bowker had gone upstairs to lie down, Freddie sat with Dennis Bowker, who had opened his collar and removed his hand-painted tie, one on either side of the table, making inroads into the whisky bottle. They did not bother with lunch.

When Jane rushed back to Chester Terrace before dinner, eager to hear the good news about Bowker & Page, she found Freddie slumped at the kitchen table next to an empty litre of Black Label.

'Freddie! What's happened?'

He had certainly been hitting the bottle lately, but she had never seen him so drunk.

In a voice that was almost incoherent, Freddie gave her a blow by blow account of his disastrous day in Manchester.

With the deaths of Gordon, of Sidonie, and of Harvey Peters, his life had begun to look like the final act of *Macbeth* in which the stage was littered with bodies. It had taken on the air of *Grand Guignol*. He tried to keep his mind on the widowed Iris Peters, on the three fatherless children, on the baby yet unborn, but as the tears formed in his bloodshot eyes, he despised the fact that he was weeping for himself.

In Charles Holdsworth's office, Freddie stood looking out of the window onto the lines of traffic, like Matchbox cars, in the street below. Charles was with a client. He would not be long. His secretary had asked Freddie to wait.

It was three weeks now since he had returned from Manchester. He had been putting off talking to Charles.

With the collapse of the Bowker & Page deal, and his

package from Sitwell Hunt already swallowed up by out-standing bills, he had – Thomas Glidewell's generous loan notwithstanding – already reached the revised limit of his overdraft. With no prospect of any further money coming in, his financial situation was extremely serious. His new resolve, inspired by Sidonie and reached on the M1, had been short-lived.

Charles Holdsworth, steaming into his office, full of apologies at having kept his friend waiting, stopped short when he saw Freddie. He was in need of a haircut and hadn't bothered to shave.

'Are you all right?'

'As well as can be expected.'

Charles was ill at ease with the older man. He sat down at his desk. Thinking it wiser to steer clear of Freddie's appearance, he broached the subject of Harvey Peters which was what Freddie had come to talk about.

'Poor Harvey. I still can't believe it. Three kids and another one on the way . . .' Rotating his chair, he flicked at the executive toy on his desk. 'Poor bugger!'

Poor bugger indeed. Freddie thought, and not for the first time, that it would have been more appropriate, more convenient for all concerned, if *he* had been the one who had dropped off to sleep, painlessly and conveniently on the motorway.

'In the midst of death we are in life . . .' Charles said, misquoting. 'I'm doing what I can for Iris Peters.' He looked at Freddie speculatively. 'What are we going to do about you?'

What Freddie had come to tell Charles was that he was thinking of pulling the rug on himself, rather than wait for the mortgage company and Derek Abbott to do it. Although socially still unacceptable, the stigma attached to bankruptcy had recently diminished. The number of bankruptcy announcements in the Public and Legal Notices section of the *Evening Standard* was an indication that it was an option being taken by an increasing number of people, who, for one reason or another, and often for no fault of their own, found themselves in a similar position to himself. According to the statistics, more than 25,000 people had declared themselves insolvent in the past year alone. This was due not to a decline in moral responsibility, but to the fact that the 1986 Insolvency Act allowed individuals to go broke without having to go to court. They were now able to retain their personal possessions and could win an automatic discharge at the end of three years. They were still stripped of their plastic however, lost their credit rating, were unable to stay in a hotel without mentioning in advance that they were undischarged bankrupts, and were precluded from having their own bank accounts or becoming directors of companies.

'There's nothing you *can* do for me! If I'd had as many job offers in the past few weeks as I've had lunches . . .' Freddie said bitterly.

Charles had never seen Freddie like this. It made him uncomfortable. He had a sudden thought. Then dismissed it. Then decided that, in the circumstances, it might just be worth mentioning.

'I don't know if this would be of any interest . . . We had a board meeting the other day. My chairman's extremely keen on opening another branch.'

Freddie held his breath.

'The only trouble is, I'm afraid it's in Singapore.'

'Singapore!' Freddie said.

'You know it?'

'Not really. A long time ago. I spent a few days there on my way to the Great Barrier Reef, before I went up to Cambridge.'

It was in Singapore that, as an 18-year-old, Freddie had been relieved of his virginity. It was a long time since he had thought of Amy Low – with her smooth limbs, her persuasive fingers, her butterfly kisses – who had taught him that just as a good cook needs more than a liking for food to put him amongst the *chefs du rang*, any lover worth his salt must start his apprenticeship on the nursery slopes of sex. By the time Amy Low had finished with him, Freddie could put a five-course banquet on the table.

Wearing a brilliant yellow dress, with a purple orchid in her burnished hair, Amy had picked him up as he sat over his Tiger beer in a Scott's Road Bar. Although he had made it quite clear to her that he was on an extremely tight budget (his trip had been financed by a lucky premium bond given to him as his fifth birthday present by his father) and had no money to spare for her services, Amy had taken a fancy to the handsome young Englishman, and he had spent the entire three days of his stay in her company. It was like going to school. From the time Amy had removed her clothes in her little bedroom, decking herself out – to Freddie's surprise – from head to foot in jewellery, to the moment of his departure from Changi airport, when, like a small bright bird, she had flung herself into his arms, sworn undying love for him, and made him promise to return, he had walked another planet.

At first the young Freddie had only to approach Amy's scarlet mouth, appraise her minuscule waist, gaze at her upturned breasts, to light the blue paper, reach the meridian, of his passion. She did not need to touch him. Later, her caresses obliterated by the hanging fronds of her jet-black hair, she showed him, giggling – Amy found sex amusing – how to delay his pleasure in order to augment it. Eschewing the Jurong Bird Park, the Mandai Orchid Gardens and other tourist attractions, he had spent the rest of his time in Singapore playing Sultan and Concubine, Burglar and Maiden, and Wailing Monkey Clasping a Tree, with Amy, who had walked on his back with her tiny feet and massaged his body with the pollen-scented fluid which gushed prematurely from it.

When Freddie declared himself hungry, Amy took him to her favourite restaurants. Sitting opposite him, she selected – with a delicate, red-tipped finger – bamboo baskets, tiny barbecued pork buns, deep-fried taro rolls and parcels of rice steamed in lotus leaves, from the dim sum pushcart, and taught him how to eat 'sweet, sour, bitter and salty' for the sake of his health. Leaning across the table, she fed him with titbits of shrimp and chicken and prawn and squid and Chinese sausage, which she dipped, with dainty chopsticks, into saucers of spicy chilli and black bean sauce, before putting them into his mouth.

One evening she took Freddie home to visit her mother in Bukit Panjang, a faceless tower block on a Housing Development Board Estate. Madam Low, a descendant of the early Chinese settlers who had intermarried with local Malays, had a shrine in her kitchen to the household gods who reported back to the spirit world on the behaviour of the family, and handed out appropriate rewards and punishments. She cooked them *pon tauhu*, clear soup, and *babipong tay*, a beef stew with bamboo shoots and mushrooms, and when Freddie, who could eat no more, left some of the food she pressed upon him, tears welled up into her eyes. Amy explained that her mother was still haunted by the Japanese occupation, during which she had lost four babies as a result of undernourishment, and that food must not be wasted and peace must be treasured, and that she could not bring herself to throw anything away.

Standing in Charles Holdsworth's office, Freddie imagined that he could still hear the sound of Amy's smooth gold bangles, the rings in her ears which tinkled as she moved, but it was the suspended chrome orbs of Charles's executive toy, bumping one into the other.

'. . . It would mean spending at least six months in Singapore,' Charles was saying.

Freddie wondered how life had treated Amy Low.

'Would you be interested?'

'I'd certainly like to give it some thought.'

Setting up a new bank in Singapore, which would no doubt carry a substantial salary, would enable him to postpone the question of voluntary insolvency at least for a while.

'I'm really sorry to see you like this,' Charles said at the door. He meant Freddie's appearance.

'Like what?'

Freddie was touchy lately. Charles had trodden on his toes.

'Nothing.' Charles put an arm round him. 'I'll have a word with the chairman and be in touch.'

Outside, in Pall Mall, Freddie pulled up the collar of his crumpled jacket – he was no longer fastidious about his clothes, there seemed to be no point – and went in search of a drink.

CHAPTER THIRTY-FIVE

Since the collapse of the Bowker & Page deal for which he had worked so hard and on which he had been pinning his hopes, it seemed to Jane that Freddie was intent on destroying himself. In addition to his mental apathy and physical neglect, he had become increasingly suspicious and was convinced that she was having an affair with Piers Warburton.

'You and Piers . . .' he said once, in the small hours.

Jane, unable to sleep herself, was aware that on the far side of the bed, which might just as well have been in another country, Freddie was wide awake. In the old days he had crashed out the moment his head hit the pillow, to wake again, refreshed, six hours later. Now he had trouble sleeping. She had found a bottle of Temazepam (labelled Mrs L. Lomax) in the bathroom. Freddie was not used to drugs. He had never needed to take so much as an aspirin. The pills left him tired and irritable in the mornings, while seeming to do little to improve his night's sleep.

'It was obvious when he came for dinner – I note you sat him next to you – Piers hardly spoke to anyone else.'

'Piers hardly speaks.'

'He sat at your feet afterwards, like some . . . You went to see him at the bank. Someone I know happened to see you.'

'It's no secret.'

'You were dancing with him at the Ball.'

'Of course I danced with Piers. I also danced with James, and Charles, and Peter.'

'It was the *way* you were dancing. You couldn't put a piece of paper between you. I'm not a fool. How long has it been going on?'

'It hasn't been going on.' Jane tried to keep her voice light. 'Freddie darling, please, what's the matter?'

'I've just told you.'

Jane sat up and leaned on her elbow. 'Piers has always been jealous of you, Freddie. You know he fancies me. We laughed about it. It's always been a joke.'

'I don't find it particularly amusing.'

'You used to.'

There were so many things that Freddie used to do. He used to be light-hearted. He used to be caring. He used to be interested in his appearance. He used to go jogging. He used to party. He used to entertain his friends. He used to visit Lilli on Tuesdays, lately he had stopped. He used to go to the opera. He used to make love to her. He used to listen to music. He used to sing. Now he did nothing. Nothing but raid the fridge for anything he could lay his hands on, and put on weight. Nothing but sit in front of the TV in the afternoons with his feet up on the table (like Lavender's Tony), watching old movies (*The Poseidon Adventure* and *Towering Inferno*) the flickering images of which did not, Jane was sure, even get as far as his brain. Nothing but fall asleep in the armchair. Nothing but find fault with herself and with Rosina. Nothing but try to convince them, in his maudlin moments, how useless he was as a husband, as a father, as an employer (although Jane had offered to manage without Lavender, Freddie, with a flash of his old good nature had refused to deprive her, in her present condition, of her weekly wage). Nothing but drink.

It was the amount of alcohol which Freddie was consuming which worried Jane more than anything. She was frightened that he would get cirrhosis of the liver, softening of the brain.

Unable to talk to Freddie, and at her wits' end, she told Freddie she was meeting Bingo, and went to meet Piers for lunch in the City Pipe. Freddie would kill her if he knew.

Shortly after she left, Freddie had a mysterious call from Conrad Verger, who, on some urgent pretext which he was unable to divulge over the telephone, persuaded him to meet him for a drink in the bar of the City Pipe.

Making his way down Albany Street he was surprised to discover that not only was the walk to Great Portland Street taking him longer than usual, but that he was out of breath. Reaching the station, he bought a ticket, fed it nonchalantly into the ticket barrier, walked down the stairs and into an almost empty, graffiti-daubed, train. Sitting beneath a poster 'Discover the Many Faces of Kent', opposite an American tourist wearing white socks and reading *Time Out*, he wondered what Conrad could possibly want. Rumour had it that Verger, catapulted (according to the City pages) into Gordon Sitwell's shoes, wearing his coveted crown – but without his father-in-law's years of corporate experience behind him – had been responsible for some exceedingly unwise decisions, and was getting the bank into a thorough mess. Freddie could not have cared less about Sitwell Hunt International. He had erased it from his mind with the remorselessness of which, since he had been 9 years old, he knew that he was capable.

In the school playground, Timothy Hodson, renowned tormentor of juniors, and the possessor of a new racing bicycle, had snatched Freddie's lunch-box. Freddie, two years younger and half the size of his aggressor – he showed no signs yet of his adult stature – had told him, in front of his open-mouthed claque, that if he did not give the lunch-box back immediately he would not be responsible for the safety of the new bicycle. The older boy had sneered. Bicycles, by common consent, were sacred. He did not return the lunchbox. The sight of Hodson, salivating over the sandwiches made with love by Lilli (who got up early every day to prepare them), had been experienced by Freddie as a personal attack. Borrowing a hammer from the woodwork room, and making for the bicycle shed, he had cold-bloodedly set to work on the red and chrome Raleigh. There had been repercussions. A long session between Lilli and the Headmaster. Freddie had been suitably disciplined and his pocket money withheld for a year to make retribution for the bicycle. While he remained at the school, Freddie was treated with the greatest of respect. Nobody messed with him again.

As the Circle Line train drew level with the Barbican, Freddie stared at the advertisements on the platform for *Manon* and *The Barber of Seville*. Since *Lohengrin* with Wichmann, and *Tristan und Isolde* with Sidonie, he had not been to the opera.

Too early for his rendezvous with Conrad Verger, he dawdled, hands in his pockets, along the concourse at Liverpool Street station gazing unseeingly into the windows of the Body Shop, Boots Pharmacy, and the Knickerbox. A student tried to thrust a leaflet into his hand, 'Diet for Health'. Freddie did not take it.

At a corner table in the restaurant, Jane faced Piers over her salmon salad.

'He doesn't pay his bills – he doesn't even open them – just shoves them in a drawer. All his papers are in a muddle, I daren't say anything. It's the drinking which really freaks me out,' she said. 'He needs help, Piers. I keep telling him to cut down . . .'

Unscrewing his bottle of Perrier water, Piers smiled wryly. 'That's the worst thing you can do.'

'Somebody has to stop him.'

'Only Freddie can do that.'

'Piers, Freddie doesn't think he has a problem.'

'He doesn't *admit* there's a problem.'

'Okay. You're the expert. What do you suggest?'

'The only advice I can give you, darling – and I know it's not easy – is that you don't try to stop him. Criticism in such cases is counterproductive. It will only make matters worse.'

'Sit back and watch Freddie destroy himself? Is there nothing I can *do*?'

Piers took her hand. He hated to see her suffer. 'Detach with love, Jane,' he said. 'Detach with love.'

'He's wittering on about setting up a bank in Singapore. Right now Freddie couldn't set up a game of skittles. I'm frightened, Piers. Is he going to get a job?'

'If he stops trying so hard.'

'What's that supposed to mean?'

'Freddie's still in shock. He's putting out bad vibes. I'd like to do something. You know that. I love that man almost as much as I love you. I've asked around. I keep asking. Things are pretty grim at the moment. You read the newspapers, Jane. A quarter of a million jobs gone in London. Employment due to fall by a further 170,000. Bank lending down. Money supply weak. It will get better. But it will get better slowly. It's a question of hanging on. Freddie's an asset. People will be glad to get their hands on him. In the fullness of time –'

'There *is* no time. Derek Abbott keeps ringing. Freddie doesn't even return his calls.' Jane put down her knife and fork. 'I'm sorry to dump on you –'

'That's what friends are for.'

'I can't talk to Freddie. Everything I say is wrong. We do nothing but fight. I don't know how much more I can take.' Jane pushed her plate away, the salmon salad half eaten. A tear fell onto the polished table. She took out her handkerchief.

'I didn't mean to do this, Piers.'

'Think nothing of it.' He touched her cheek. 'I don't know what that bastard's done to deserve you.'

'Whatever it is,' Jane blew her nose, 'he seems to be doing his best to destroy it.'

At the bar adjacent to the restaurant, Freddie stood next to Conrad Verger, towering above him. He drank his Black Label in silence as Conrad, who had been visibly shaken by Freddie's unkempt appearance, marshalled his thoughts.

'You know, Freddie, things are not going too well at Sitwell Hunt since my . . . since Gordon died,' he said finally.

Freddie took out his worry beads. 'So I've heard.'

'Takeovers are extremely thin on the ground, apart, that is, from a few middle-sized deals.'

Freddie said nothing.

'One doesn't know whether to diversify, whether to risk capital. To be perfectly honest with you, Freddie, we're exceedingly short of fees.'

'What has that got to do with me?'

Concerned for Freddie's empty glass, Conrad signalled for another Black Label.

'All the good bankers and brokers seem to be gravitating towards the big battalions . . .'

Freddie noticed that Conrad was sweating. His top lip was damp. He refused to make it easy for him.

'My father-in-law's death . . . Circumstances alter cases. I'd like to know, Freddie, how you feel about returning to Sitwell Hunt.'

Freddie, holding the late chairman's son-in-law indirectly responsible for the purgatory of the past months, did not answer. He knew that he was addicted as any junkie; that corporate finance was in his bones.

'I can't offer you your old job, of course. Travers is running the department . . .'

Freddie upended his glass and felt the whisky sear into his churning stomach as a burst of masculine laughter from a sombre suited knot of fresh-faced drinkers resounded in his head.

'Suppose we say as a consultant . . .'

Be answerable to Conrad Verger? Not in a million years.

'A non-executive director . . .'

Freddie held out his glass for a refill.

'. . . The board is behind me.'

'What you mean, Conrad,' Freddie swallowed his whisky in a gulp and slammed his glass down on the bar, 'is that you want me to sort out the mess!'

'Hang on a bit, Freddie, that's not fair –'

'Don't even think about it.' Freddie turned on his heel. 'I always thought you were a bit stupid, Conrad. Now I know. I think you've got a bloody nerve!'

As he went through the door into the piazza, something made him turn his head and glance into the dark recesses of the restaurant where the lunchtime tables were packed. In the far corner, leaning across the table, Piers Warburton was kissing Jane.

'Sorry for being such a pain.' Jane put away her handkerchief.

'That's one thing you'll never be, Jane.'

'Freddie thinks we're having an affair.'

'I should be so lucky.' Piers signalled for the bill. 'Things will work out. I'm sure they will.'

'Detach with love.' Jane said. 'I'll try to remember.'

But there was no chance for her to try out Piers's advice. Freddie did not come home for dinner. He did not arrive until ten o'clock. Jane, who was in the kitchen with Rosina, rushed to intercept him, but walking past her, as if she were not there, he went straight upstairs to his dressing-room and turned on *Otello* at full throttle. When Jane knocked on the locked door, he pretended not to hear her. She knocked again, urgently, kept knocking, until the volume was turned down on the Verdi.

'Freddie, I need to talk to you.'

'We have nothing to say to each other, Jane.'

Jane's heart turned over. She was shaken by the icy timbre of his voice.

'I *have* to speak to you! Please, Freddie, it's extremely important. There's something you have to know.'

The key turned. Freddie appeared in the doorway. He smelled of whisky, his hair was dishevelled, his eyes were red-rimmed, he looked for all the world as if he had been crying. He did not speak.

'Freddie . . .' Jane said.

Cold and distant, his eyes focused on something behind her head.

'. . . You're not making this very easy.' She put out her hand to touch him, then, thinking better of it, withdrew it. 'I've been waiting for you. I've been going frantic. I had no idea where you were. I rang James. I thought you might be playing squash. And Charles. He hadn't heard from you. Rosina's been marvellous. We didn't know what to do. I've only just got back. I'm afraid . . . Freddie, please look at me.' Jane took a deep breath. 'About five o'clock this afternoon. Mrs Williams. It's Lilli . . . I'm so sorry, Freddie, darling, there's no other way to say this. Your mother is dead.'

CHAPTER THIRTY-SIX

Freddie, his chin stubbled, wearing a black tie, looked round at the packed pews, at the familiar faces. Although he was as good as bankrupt as far as Derek Abbott – whom he had noticed sitting at the back of the church – was concerned, in terms of friendship he was a millionaire. He derived little comfort from the knowledge.

When Jane had told him that Lilli was dead, he had had some difficulty in taking it in. He had made her repeat the words over and over as he tried to make sense of the fact that he was a 40-year-old orphan, no longer anyone's son. While he had been drinking himself stupid, his mother had disappeared, as she had when she had hidden behind the sofa to frighten him as a child. When he opened his eyes to look for her, she would no longer be there. He would never see her again.

It was Mrs Williams who had found Lilli, lying on the floor in the bathroom, in a pool of her own blood. The preliminary diagnosis, later to be confirmed by a post-mortem, was that Lilli had had a massive haematemesis due to the effects of aspirin on an ulcer which had been lurking silently in her stomach wall. Her death had been sudden and painless.

Jane could not understand why, in his hour of need, Freddie had excluded her. He had shut the door of his dressing-room again and, in an effort to get his act together, listened to *Parsifal*, strengthening himself with the words, fortifying himself with the music, until he felt able to cope with the hysterical Mrs Williams, with his own grief, and with the bureaucracy of death. James and Charles were waiting for him at the Water Gardens. They had embraced Freddie in sympathy then, at his request, left. Despite the brandy James had given her, Mrs Williams was still shaking. She recited the story of the blood and the bathroom over and over, her account reaching a crescendo which broke into fragments each time it approached the climax, as if trying to expunge, by constant reiteration, the horror she had seen. To Freddie's surprise Mrs Williams said that she had grown to love her irrational charge, difficult as she was, and that she was going to miss her. They were in the hushed sitting-room which was redolent of Lilli, echoed with her voice, but was devoid of her presence. He had not yet been into the bedroom.

'I'll not get another job,' Mrs Williams sobbed. 'Not at my age.' Freddie put his arm around the woman's shoulders. She was not a bad sort. 'I know the feeling.'

The bathroom was an abattoir. Mrs Williams had done her best. The carpet would have to come up. Lilli lay in the candle-lit bedroom. Mrs Williams had cleaned her up. Relieved by death of her mortal life, she appeared immune from misery, peaceful and unafraid. It was no consolation to Freddie. He had neglected Lilli recently, as he had neglected everyone, including himself. Her death, before he had a chance to say goodbye to her, was her ultimate reproof. Looking at the calm expression on her alabaster face, he wanted to ask her if she had found the ultimate reality, or if death was the end of the human spirit and the sequel to life was annihilation. He was surprised to discover, as he bent to kiss the cold forehead, that there was a definite tear on her cheek. He spent the night in the armchair, grieving, by her side.

Freddie was flanked in the pew by Tristan and Rosina. Jane, at Freddie's request, was on the far side. Rosina was heartbroken. She had introduced Ferdinand to Lilli, and they had taken to each other straight away. Lilli's death, the first she had encountered, had hit her hard, but it was she who had comforted Freddie.

'Grandma wasn't afraid of dying, Daddy. She said it would be quite a relief. She said it was no worse than being born.'

Freddie had removed Lilli's ruby ring and given it to Rosina. Worn on her right hand, with its bitten fingernails, it glowed in the refracted lights of the church.

Tristan, now home from school, had not known what to do, what to say. On impulse, he had put his arms round Freddie and buried his face in his jacket.

'Dad . . .'

'It's all right, son.'

Standing upright, next to his father, Tristan, who had not cared for Lilli, wondered if his negative feelings had somehow communicated themselves to his grandmother and if they had contributed to her death.

James and Dos. James had been a tower of strength. Charles, and Bingo (in an outrageous black hat) who, appalled by the cold shoulder Freddie was giving Jane had lent her support to her friend. Peter and Georgina (the pearls at the neck of her black suit), Alex, and Piers – whom Freddie refused to acknowledge – none of whom had really known Lilli, all sacrificing their busy schedules to pay their respects to the dead.

Margaret Sitwell, a sad bewildered figure, sat apart, on her own. Jane beckoned her to sit beside her. Since Gordon's death, Margaret had taken up gardening, caring for Gordon's rose bushes. She had refused to disturb his possessions and, despite entreaties from Conrad and from Sophie to move to an apartment on the south coast –

where they had offered to file her conveniently away — she had refused to leave the reverberating house.

Susan, his ex-personal assistant, whom Conrad Verger had lured back to Sitwell Hunt, her chignon once more in place. It was nice of her to come to the funeral. He did not blame her for her perfidy. These days it was *sauve qui peut*. A job was a job.

The vicar ascended the pulpit in his surplice. '"Fear no more the heat o' the sun, Nor the furious winter's rages . . ."' His voice was measured and sombre, although he had not known Lilli who was not a church-goer. '" Fear no more the lightning flash, nor the all-dreaded thunder-stone . . ."'

Freddie tried to connect the Lilli he had loved, but to his shame not always liked, especially of late, with the words from *Cymbeline*, with the coffin lying on its bier, with 'Jerusalem the Golden' with the verses from Blake which had been sung by the choir, as clips from his past flashed fleetingly onto the empty screen of his mind. His mother's unexpected appearance in the doorway when the blue-eyed china cat had met its demise, weaving a necklace from the daisies he had picked for her in the park, snatches of her long-suffering voice from the sitting-room as she coached her pupils at the Broadwood – 'No, no, *third* finger . . .' – her single-minded dedication to him throughout his impressionable years and her unceasing efforts to pour him, like a jelly, into the confines of her mould.

As the organist struck up Berlioz's *Te Deum*, one of Lilli's favourite pieces, he tried to remember his mother as she *had* been, but the memory of a tetchy and dementing Lilli, at war with Mrs Williams, confounded his attempts.

After the service in the church, the service at the graveside. An elm box was lowered into the earth on ropes. It had nothing to do with his mother. The vicar dragged more words, this time to do with ashes and with dust, from the depths of his surplice which moved lightly in the wind. There were flowers. Conrad Verger had sent a wreath. And clods of earth. Faces, of people whom he knew, and of grave-diggers whom he did not. Consoling hands, condolences borne on a black sea. Badly in need of a drink, a depersonalised Freddie watched himself watching the panoply of death.

He did not join the motorcade which set off for Chester Terrace. Charles Holdsworth, lagging behind, was the last of the mourners to leave. He grasped Freddie's hand.

'I'm so sorry, Freddie.'

Freddie acknowledged the sympathy. There are two parties to a death; the one who has died and the one who is bereaved.

'I know this is hardly the time, or place . . . Forgive me. I only heard this morning. I thought I ought to tell you. The chairman feels . . . I'm afraid he's changed his mind about a Far Eastern branch. Singapore has fallen through.'

For all the effect Charles's words had on Freddie, he might just as well have conveyed his message in Chinese.

Charles put a hand beneath his elbow. 'I'll give you a lift home.'

'I'll grab a cab . . .' Freddie indicated the burial site. 'You go ahead.'

Charles nodded understandingly.

When the midnight-blue Daimler had driven off, Freddie returned to the freshly dug grave. He stood motionless, his hands folded in front of him. The tears streamed down his lined face for Lilli, who had tried so hard to make him her golden boy, and for the fact that, in the final analysis, he had failed her.

Outside the cemetery gates he stopped a taxi. He did not give the address of Chester Terrace but asked the driver to take him to the Berkeley Hotel. In the familiar hall, with its tiled floor, its massed flowers – was it a coincidence they were lilies? – its welcoming fire, he checked into Room 333 and instructed reception to have room service send up a bottle of Black Label, and not to put through any calls. By the time he reached the bedroom, the whisky was already there. He took off his black overcoat, throwing it on the armchair, and loosened his black tie. Remembering the Man of Thermopylae, he picked up the coat again, arranged it on a hanger, and hung it in the lobby. He put the 'Please Do Not Disturb' notice outside the door, took a pill bottle out of his jacket pocket, removed his shoes, folded back the quilt, and lay down on the bed, propped up against the freshly laundered pillows. 'Fear no more the heat o' the sun, Nor the furious winter's rages ... Fear no more the lightning flash, Nor the all-dreaded thunderstone ...' Now that Lilli was dead, he no longer had to live up to her ambitions. He was free at last to make his own choices. He opened the pill bottle and tipped the capsules, dark green miniature rugby balls, into the palm of his hand. Cramming them into his mouth, he washed them down with whisky. It was hard going. Some of them got stuck in his oesophagus and burned his throat. He took it more slowly. One capsule at a time. His stomach gurgled. He had had no breakfast. He had been too distressed to eat. It wasn't every day one buried one's mother, confined her to the sod.

Lilli's death left him directly in line for his own mortality. The barrier had been removed. You did not even need a ticket. It was open to everyone. Whatever *it* was. The one certainty: 'In the midst of life we are in death'. The birth of children is the death of parents. As if it were night-time and he was going to bed, he unstrapped the chronograph Jane had bought him for his birthday which stopped the time to an eighth of a second and marked the beginning of the end. Since she had given it to him his life had been measured out in a descending scale of misfortune; the loss of his job, of Universal Concrete, of Gordon Sitwell, of Sidonie, of Bowker & Page, of Jane, of Lilli, of the Singapore commission in which he had not really believed. He wondered how long the drugs would take to work. The chronograph was upside down. He looked at the words engraved on the back of the case. *La Vie en rose*. He had loved Jane. *Tout court*. Had always loved her. They had been an item from the very beginning. Copper and gold. There had never been anyone else. Not even Sidonie. Certainly not Sidonie. Poor, poor Sidonie. Jane was a one-off. He thought that he had been a one-off for her. Jane and Freddie. Freddie and Jane. He had no idea what she saw in Piers Warburton. He abhorred the idea of Piers's hand touching Jane's pale skin, her red hair, hearing her laugh – like a phrase of music – holding her freckled body in his arms. Once, after Tristan was born, Jane had asked Freddie, in an intimate moment, who it was that had given him his lessons in love. He had told her about Amy Low. After Amy, and a spell as a lifeguard on Bondi Beach, he had made his way north. A catamaran, *The Call of the Wild*, piercing the early morning waters with its torpedo-shaped hulls, had borne him out to the garden jungle of black coral trees, delicate staghorns and sea fans, to the underwater oasis of the Great Barrier Reef. Weightless, in wet suit and flippers, scuba bottles on his back, he had slipped through the silent, sunlit waters down to the underground wonderland of calcium carbonate and limestone in which brightly coloured hordes of gyrating predators darted and trembled, employed all manner of offensive behaviour, took every evasive action, in the battle to stay alive. Dodging the sea urchins, and avoiding the coral – coral cuts were notoriously slow to heal – he saw sharks with insatiable appetites home in on distress signals from injured fish (signifying an easy meal), as smaller predators, themselves pursued by larger fish, set upon schools of pilchards and sent them panicking to the surface in synchronised flashes of silver. In the magical landscape, in the relentless struggle for food and space, no holds were barred as the striped trumpet fish used the coral trout as stalking-horse, the hermit crab made skilful use of his venomous spines, and the deadly blue-ringed octopus sneaked stealthily up on his prey. Maestros of disguise, some capable of changing their sex at will, it was kill or be killed, amongst the Venus tusk fish and the whiptails, the blue tangs and the cleaner wrasse, the flutefish and the Moorish idols, the seasnakes and the bivalves who maintained the rhythm of life and preserved the delicate balance of the deep. Freddie wondered should he have availed himself of the outplacement which Gordon Sitwell had suggested, and presented himself, like a novice, for interviews, for psychometric testing, have accepted a work place, in keeping with his seniority, for as long as he needed it. Should he have disregarded his *amour propre* and accepted Conrad Verger's offer. 'All places that the eye of heaven visits/Are to a wise man ports and happy havens./Teach thy necessity to reason thus;/There is no virtue like necessity.' Should he, perhaps, have turned the economic climate to his advantage, employed the same opportunistic flare which had cost him so dearly at Sitwell Hunt, put the recession to good use, made a virtue of necessity? Could he not have set up a consultancy for corporate recovery? Used his expertise to help small, family businesses – makers of plastic pipes or widgets – to keep afloat? The outplacement consultancy would have helped him to identify those companies in need of help. There could be serious money in it. But it was not for Freddie Lomax to whom the fierce battle for acquisitions, the cut and thrust of corporate finance was the breath of life. Behind the Chinese wall, as in the translucent waters of the Great Barrier Reef – where frenzied predators had stripped the flesh from an unsuspecting moray in seconds leaving nothing but the bone – it was hunt or be hunted, kill or be killed. The only way he knew. Somebody had drunk the whisky. The bottle was empty. The pill bottle had rolled on the floor feeling pleasantly drowsy he punched the pillows to make them more comfortable but he was lying on something hard he removed the worry beads the *komboloi* carried by every self-respecting Greek man from his trouser pocket he would not be needing them the ceiling revolved and the flowers on the curtains danced then someone pulled down his eyelids over the past weeks as the voices of the celestial choristers: 'The wine and the bread of the Last Supper, once the Lord of the Grail, through pity's love-power, changed into the blood which he shed, into the body which he offered' and the antiphonal response of the knights: 'Take of the bread; bravely change it anew into strength and power. Faithful unto death, staunch in effort to do the works of the Lord. Take of the blood; change it anew to life's fiery flood. Gladly in communion, faithful as brothers, to fight with blessed courage . . .' filled his head with glorious music and the vicar ascended the pulpit in his surplice fear no more the heat o' the sun nor the furious winter's rages fear no more the lightning flash nor the all-dreaded thunderstone there was a knock on the door housekeeper to turn down the bed sir to turn down the bed sir to turn down the bed sir turn down the bed sir turn down the bed sir she must have seen the notice do not disturb not now or ever and moved on . . .

CHAPTER THIRTY-SEVEN

'Charles? I'm worried about Freddie. He's still not home.'

Bingo stirred in her sleep. 'Who is it?'

'Jane.'

Charles put the light on and squinted at his watch.

'Jane, it's two o'clock!'

'You were the last one to see him. Did he say anything? Did he say where he was going?'

Charles assembled his thoughts. 'Home. I wanted to give him a lift. "You go ahead," he said, "I'll grab a cab."'

'He actually *said* he was going home?'

'Not in so many words. He wanted a quiet moment. He knew everyone was coming back to Chester Terrace . . .'

'I know he's been drinking. He's never not come home. It's not like Freddie. Do you think there could have been an accident?'

Bingo's head was on Charles's shoulder listening to the conversation.

'Tell her to ring the police.'

'Do you think I should?' Jane said.

'It can't hurt. Do you want me to come over?' Charles yawned.

'There wouldn't be much point. I'm sorry to wake you. And Bingo.'

Bingo took the phone. 'Darling? I'm sure Freddie's all

right. He's just upset. He's probably crashed out somewhere.'

'At this time of the morning?'

'At his club . . .?'

'Freddie doesn't have a club. I'll try James. Perhaps
Freddie said something to him. Then I'll ring the police.'

'Keep in touch.' Charles put down the telephone. 'I
don't know what's come over Freddie. I think he's going
off his rocker. He's certainly been acting very strangely.'

'I'm sorry for Jane,' Bingo said. 'He's been giving her a
rough time.'

When neither James, nor Piers, could suggest where
Freddie might be, Jane dialled 999. And waited. She could
have been murdered several times over. Hearing the sound
of her own voice reporting an errant husband, she thought
that the Duty Officer must think her ridiculous. He took her
concern seriously however. He would make some enquiries
and call her back. She was glad when Rosina came to sit
on her bed.

'I'm getting worried.'

Rosina took her hand. 'What do you think has happened?'

'I don't know, Rosina,' Jane was trembling. 'I'm frightened.'

There was no question of going back to sleep. They
waited in the kitchen where Rosina made hot chocolate.

'I heard noises.' Tristan appeared in an old bathrobe of
Freddie's.

Rosina told him what had happened. Picking up the
message pad and a pencil, Tristan took charge of the
situation.

'Let's make a list of places where he might be. Charles?'

'I've called him.'

'James?'

'I've called him.'

'Piers?'

'Daddy isn't exactly on speaking terms with Piers at the moment.'

Tristan looked surprised. 'What's Piers done?'

'That's just the trouble. He hasn't done anything.'

'Have you called the police?'

'I'm waiting for them to ring back. It's 3.30! Did Daddy . . . say anything to you in church?'

Tristan shook his head.

'Think, Tristan.'

'I am thinking.'

The telephone rang. Tristan was first on his feet. 'I'll get it.'

Watching him, gauging from his reactions what was being said, Jane thought how much he resembled Freddie. Even at sixteen.

'There's been no accident reported. They're going to check the hospitals. They said not to worry. People often stay out all night.'

'People,' Jane said. 'Not your father.'

For the past week, ever since she had broken the news about Lilli, Freddie had hardly spoken to her. He avoided being in the same room. He avoided looking at her. His frigid behaviour had had its effect. It had been getting her down.

The day before the funeral she had discussed the matter with Bingo, going over to 'Bingo's' where she had sat before a triple mirror staring unseeingly at herself in a black crushed-velvet hat reminiscent of Napoleon.

'Freddie has got it into his head that just because Piers sat next to me at the dinner party, just because I spoke to him, just because I danced with him, we're getting it on . . .'

Bingo, wearing a leather mini-skirt and platform shoes in a confusion of styles which only she could get away

with, was removing other hats, one more bizarre than the
next, from the drawer of a marquetry commode.

'. . . he refuses to talk to me.'

Bingo pulled out a *chapeau à melon* in cerise felt, and
held it aloft.

'Freddie should go to the doctor.'

'You know Freddie and doctors.'

'He needs therapy.'

'Try suggesting that to Freddie.'

'Not me, Jane. You.'

'You've got to be kidding.'

Bingo held out the *chapeau à melon*.

'Try this one, darling. It will clash gloriously with your
hair.'

She removed the Napoleon number and arranged the
hat on Jane's head. 'You have your ways.'

Jane took off the cerise felt and ran her fingers through
her hair. She was in no mood for hats.

'Not any more.' She met Bingo's eyes in the mirror. 'It's
like sharing a house, sharing a bed, with a stranger. I don't
know how long I can go on like this.'

'Freddie will be all right when he gets a job.'

'There *are* no jobs. Freddie is being totally unrealistic.
He won't even discuss the situation any more. Lilli's death
hasn't helped. I wouldn't say this to anyone else, Bingo,
but there have been times lately when I wish I *was* having
an affair with Piers.'

Jane went back to bed but not to sleep. She dozed fitfully
and waited for the telephone to ring. At five o'clock, in
a state of agitation, she tried the police again. They had
checked the hospitals. Nothing had been reported. She put
her electric blanket on, but she was still cold. It may very
well be that people stayed out all night. Not Freddie. There
was an unfamiliar trepidation, a sense of premonition in
her heart. The last time she had seen Freddie he had

been standing opposite her at the graveside. As the coffin containing Lilli's body was lowered on its ropes into the ground, her heart had gone out to him. His black coat was turned up at the collar. He hadn't bothered, not even for Lilli's funeral, to shave. He had been a good son. He had nothing to reproach himself with. Only that he had not said goodbye to Lilli, had not made his peace. Afterwards she had waited in the funeral car for Freddie to get in beside her. Tristan said that his father was coming later, under his own steam. His absence at Chester Terrace had been commented upon. He had been expected at every moment. When he did not appear, the friends who had come to offer their condolences had drifted away. When they had gone, despite the fact that Jane had Tristan and Rosina for company, the house had seemed desolate. Without him, it was as if Freddie had died.

Getting up and going into the bathroom, Jane opened the cupboard and searched for the pill bottle labelled 'Mrs L. Lomax'. It was not there. Unsure of the significance, she telephoned James. At 6.30, dressed in his tracksuit, he came round. James said Freddie could have finished Lilli's sleeping pills. Could have thrown the bottle away. Jane knew that he had not. She worried away at the fact, which did not help.

It was seven o'clock. Up and dressed, she was making coffee for James in the kitchen.

'I know this sounds ridiculous, James, but do you think Freddie might have gone to stay in an hotel?'

'Why on earth should he?'

'No reason.'

They made a list of hotels. The Ritz, the Connaught, the Churchill, the Portman, Grosvenor House, the Inn on the Park.

Patiently James made the abortive calls.

'I think you're barking up the wrong tree, Jane darling.

Why don't you go back to bed, try to get some sleep? I'm going out to look for Freddie.'

'What about the airports?' Jane said. 'Perhaps he's gone abroad.'

James was shocked at the chaos in Freddie's usually immaculate dressing-room. 'A pile of paperwork is a pile of postponed decisions.' It was Freddie's motto. Papers and bills were stacked on every available surface. The room was in a state of total disarray. They found his passport, amongst the unopened letters in a drawer. Looking at the photograph of Freddie which, despite its size and poor quality, captured his former *joie de vivre*, brought home to Jane how much he had changed.

Going down the stairs she said lightly to James: 'I suppose Freddie hasn't got a girlfriend?'

'Not to my knowledge.'

But something was troubling James. He stopped in the hall.

'You *know* something,' Jane said.

'No, I don't. It was just a thought which occurred to me. The longest of long shots.'

'Please, James!'

'We didn't try the Berkeley.'

'The Berkeley? Why the Berkeley?'

But James was already in the kitchen dialling directory enquiries. The robot gave him the number of the Berkeley Hotel. He did not wait while she repeated it.

'Do you have a Mr Lomax staying with you? A Mr Freddie Lomax?'

'I'll put you through to reception.'

'Please hurry.'

'Reception. Can I help you?'

'Mr Freddie Lomax. Has he checked in?'

'Just one moment.'

'Please hurry.'

'We have a Mr Maxwell, a Mrs Lom. Sorry, sir, no Mr Lomax.'

He replaced the receiver. 'It was just an idea.'

It was an idea which refused to go away. He opened the front door as George, the postman, was delivering the letters. He had been about to ring the bell.

'Recorded delivery.' George handed James a pencil and the red slip.

'Derek Abbott,' Jane said. 'Freddie doesn't even bother to open them.'

'Mr Lomax all right?' George put the pencil back in his pocket.

Jane nodded as James went back again into the kitchen. He picked up the phone.

'Berkeley Hotel, can I help you?'

'Put me through to Room 333.'

'I'm sorry, sir. Room 333 isn't taking any calls.'

'Could you tell me who's staying there?'

'Hold a moment. I'll put you through to reception.'

'I called you a few minutes ago,' James said. 'I was looking for a Mr Lomax. A Mr Freddie Lomax. It's possible he checked in under another name. Could you tell me who's staying in Room 333?'

'I'll have a look for you.'

James waited.

'A Mr Smith.'

Freddie never did have much imagination.

'I'd like to speak to Mr Smith.'

'I'm sorry, sir . . .'

'Okay, okay. What time did Mr Smith check in?'

'I'm sorry, sir. I'd need to ask my colleague. I've only just come on duty . . .'

'Forget it,' James said. Putting down the receiver, he took Jane's hand. 'Come on,' he said. 'I think we've found him.'

Time extended itself in tenuous threads as James, at the wheel of his Bentley, drove like a madman through the early morning park. The dedicated joggers reminded Jane of Freddie. In Wilton Place, ignoring the doorman, who said he could not leave his car in front of the hotel, James ran up the steps with Jane.

The concierge, who tried to make sense of his story, had no reason to suppose that Mr Smith, who had checked in the previous day while he was on his break, was anybody other than Mr Smith. And even if he was, it was not the business of the hotel. It was 7.30 in the morning. It was not their policy to disturb a guest.

'Call the police,' Jane said.

James held out a banknote.

The concierge wanted to get rid of them. They were cluttering up his hall. Putting the money into his pocket, he picked up the house phone.

'I'll get Mr Fourbouys. He's the manager.'

'Please hurry,' Jane said.

'It could be a wild-goose chase,' James said, while they were waiting.

Jane did not reply. She wondered what she was doing standing in the lobby of the Berkeley Hotel at 7.30 in the morning. In addition to Freddie being missing, she felt that perhaps James had gone mad.

Mr Fourbouys, in his black jacket and striped trousers, took them into his office. He had just come on duty and as well as looking very young, looked very clean. He listened sympathetically to them and, although he had been trained not to show it, thought privately that James and Jane were grabbing at straws. Making a series of calls, which seemed to Jane to take for ever, he established that Mr Smith wore a black overcoat, that he carried no luggage, that he had had a bottle of Black Label sent to his room, and that he had asked not to be disturbed.

'That's Freddie,' James said, and not waiting for the lift, ran up the stairs to the third floor.

Outside Room 333, hung with the green plastic trapezoid 'Do Not Disturb', Mr Fourbouys elbowed James aside.

'Just one moment, if you please.'

He tapped gently on the door.

'What the fuck . . .?' James said.

'Allow me to deal with this, please, sir.' He knocked more loudly. 'There are procedures which must be followed.'

Motioning James and Jane to remain in the corridor, he slid his master key card into the door and, coughing discreetly, tiptoed into the darkened room.

'Mr Smith. Excuse me, sir, Mr Smith.'

But in the light from the corridor Jane had recognised Douggie Hayward's handwriting in the overcoat in the lobby. She pushed past Mr Fourbouys and made her way to the bed.

'Freddie,' she said, shaking the inert form. 'Freddie! Oh my God . . .'

'Take it easy, Jane.' James picked up the empty pill bottle from the floor.

'Freddie!' Jane was screaming.

James eyed the empty whisky bottle.

'Freddie, wake up!' Jane put her face to the stubbled cheek. 'Please wake up.'

Mr Fourbouys picked up the telephone. 'Fourbouys here. Get an ambulance. Quickly. The *back* door. Then call the police.'

CHAPTER THIRTY-EIGHT

Rosina and Tristan were at the hospital. James had phoned them from the car. They sat on either side of Jane in the visitors' room, but she had never felt so desperately alone. Someone, somewhere – it was not easy to find out from the overworked staff exactly what was going on – was washing out Freddie's stomach. Getting rid of the poisons. No one had bothered to inform her whether or not he was expected to live. Taking them out, very carefully, one at a time as if they were precious, Jane examined her thoughts. Rolling back the years, like a carpet, she went back to the beginning when she had first set eyes on Freddie in the snug of the Cambridge Blue.

On holiday from the Union Centrale des Arts Décoratifs, she was staying with her aunt, Marie-Hélène – like Jane's mother she had married an Englishman, a history don at Magdalene – when James, mesmerised by the red hair beneath a hat with yellow ribbons, had followed her round Heffers and picked her up in the French Literature department. A few days later, enervated by the heat, it seemed in those days always to be summer, after walking Marie-Hélène's wire-haired terrier in the Botanic Garden, they had landed up at the pub in Prospect Row. James, whom Jane found extremely attractive, was giving her a rundown on the cricket at Lords (the West Indians had just won the first World Cup) whilst she wondered whether or not she was going to go to bed with him, when, her mind far removed from the defeated Australians, she happened to glance idly into the next room. Coming through the low doorway, inclining his golden head, was Freddie, and she knew immediately that she was not going to go to bed with James. She was not surprised when Freddie made his way to their table. She had always believed in fate.

'Jane, this is Freddie, Freddie Lomax. Freddie, Jane Morley.'

It was as if not only James, but everyone else in the room had ceased to exist. As she held Marie-Hélène's dog with one hand and held out the other to Freddie, an attachment was forged which was to last for seventeen years.

The precise sequence of events which followed had, with the passage of time, become blurred. The three of them, if she remembered correctly, had made their way down Silver Street to the Mill Pool, then strolled back to Marie-Hélène's, where they had taken tea on the lawn.

'Jane and I were thinking of going to the cinema.' James handed the fruit cake to Freddie. 'Care to join us?'

'What's on?'

'*Jules et Jim*. You like Truffaut.'

'You know very well I've seen it.' Freddie didn't take his eyes off Jane.

'Actually I have a bit of a headache . . .' Jane brushed away the midges.

'Look . . .' Freddie addressed Jane.

'Have a bit of fruit cake.' James held the plate out to Jane.

'She doesn't want any fruit cake, James.'

'How do you know she doesn't want any fruit cake?'

'As I was about to say,' Freddie eyeballed James. 'Why don't you go to *Jules et Jim* and Jane can come back with me . . .'

'Hang on a minute!'

'. . . I've got a new recording of *The Barber of Seville*. You do like opera?'

Jane looked from James to Freddie and pulled down the brim of her hat. The sun, over the high stone wall, was in her eyes. 'I adore opera.' It a stupendous lie.

For Freddie's sake, sitting over a glass of white wine in his armchair, while Freddie paced the room, conducting in time to the music and explaining the finer points of the plot, she had tried to differentiate between the voices of Dr Bartolo and Count Almaviva, to get worked up over the toings and the froings and the billets-doux, to give credence to the sotto voce intrigues of the lovers.

'Listen to this,' Freddie begged her excitedly, singing, with the cavatina, '"Una voce poco fa"!'

She did her very best to show enthusiasm, to concentrate on the music master and the soldiers (by whose pranks Freddie appeared unaccountably amused), but by the time Rosina and Almaviva had signed the marriage contract and Banolo been outwitted, she was bored out of her mind. She forced herself to stick it out because of Freddie. She did not know then how many times she was destined to do so over the years.

When the last record was finished, when the opera was over and the room, thankfully, was quiet, like opposite poles of a magnet, they found themselves, as if it was the most normal, the most natural thing, drawn into each other's arms. It was the prelude to a night which coursed like a flowing river, in which there were no decisions to be made. Jane did not remember either of them removing their clothes, only standing in the moonlight while Freddie worshipped at the shrine of her dappled body, turning and turning it again. She remembered the golden hairs which covered his slim torso, glinting in the same moon, and how, like a young god, he had led her to his narrow bed. If they slept at all she did not remember it, only recalled hearing the dawn clock strike, and from the haven of her lover's arms, understanding, for the first time, the importance of physical happiness between a man and a woman, and the bond it creates.

After that night, during which she had the distinct impression that Tristan was conceived, neither she nor Freddie had eyes for anyone else. They were Abelard and Heloise, Aucassin and Nicolette, Paul and Virginie, their names uttered in a single breath both in Cambridge and in Paris, where Jane was finishing her course.

Jane's affair with Freddie had followed the biblical progression. She had known him, then she had loved him. There was so much to love. Freddie did not play games: what you saw was what you got. He was generous and considerate, he was clever and he was funny (he and James did a double act in the Footlights), he was dependable, and he was gentle which was what women needed most of all.

After their marriage, the birth of Tristan, and Freddie's first job — with which he was orbited into the perpetual motion of his career — like halves of an equation, the two of them had led separate lives but were always in close touch. When they came together, the aggregate never failed. She and Freddie had done their growing up together, and the chemistry which had drawn them together in Cambridge had blossomed rather than withered, waxed rather than waned. They had had their ups and downs. Their rows, both major and minor, had sometimes descended into slanging matches in which words were uttered which were later regretted and possessions had been known to fly through the air. They did not allow the arguments to fester however and had never let the sun go down on their wrath. Until Freddie lost his job, and another Freddie, a Freddie she did not know, aimed the arrows of his unaccustomed anger unerringly in her direction to inflict the round-the-clock pain of their wounds.

She had tried, on more than one occasion recently, to explain to him that it was Freddie Lomax whom she had married, Freddie Lomax that she loved, that she had always loved, and not the vice chairman of Sitwell Hunt, the head of corporate finance. But Freddie did not want to know. It was as if he had worn an invisible label, 'successful executive', and without it had ceased to exist.

His suspicions about herself and Piers Warburton had been not only unfounded but ridiculous. It was as if the house she and Freddie had built together, on firm foundations of loyalty and love, was built of cards, and Freddie was deliberately trying to pull it down. There had been several occasions, over the years, when she *had* been drawn to men and propositioned by them. Times, mostly when Freddie was away, when she had dallied with the idea of an affair – although Piers Warburton had never been on the agenda. The temptations had served only to reinforce her belief in her marriage vows and the relevance of fidelity, and she had remained faithful to Freddie.

Now Freddie had turned away from her, had shut her out of his life which he no longer appeared to value himself. If Freddie died – putting an end to it all seemed such an un-Freddie thing to do – she stood to lose her husband, the father of her children, her best friend, and her lover. She prayed that he might live, and for courage to weather the storm until their relationship – which had endured for so long and acquired new dimensions of knowledge and respect – was back on the familiar rails. She thought of Grandmaman and the maxim which had enabled the baker's wife to surmount the vicissitudes of a life which had survived the hardships of war, marriage to Grandpapa, who had a definite eye for the village girls, and the premature death of a child: *la vie pardonne*. Jane prayed that Freddie would recover, and give life a chance to forgive.

In the seat next to her, Rosina, holding, but not reading, a tired magazine, the mascara she had worn for Lilli's funeral still conspicuous on her cheeks, was praying too. She was not religious, not in the accepted sense, she had not been brought up to be. But while she waited for her father's stomach to be washed out, for him to be restored to life, she made all sorts of pacts with God. If Freddie lived she would put her heart and soul into her school work, would do her very best to make him proud of her, would strive for nothing but excellence in her GCSEs. If Freddie lived she would never again lie about her whereabouts, never fiddle with the tuning on his radio, never use his music centre, never make snide remarks about his operas, never play her ghetto blaster loudly, never outstay her curfew, never tattoo her arms. Yesterday, witness to the grisly rite of passage with which she had difficulty in coming to terms, she had comforted her father by Lilli's graveside; now she slid her fingers, the nails bitten to the quick, into Jane's icy hand.

'There's a machine outside,' Rosina whispered. 'Shall I get you some coffee?'

Jane shook her head. She was very pale. Rosina could see that she was near to tears and concentrating on her prayers for Freddie. Since the business with Henry Dove, Rosina had got on better with her mother. Freddie's relief at the news that Rosina was not pregnant had been succeeded by a dose of the heavy father in which he declared his intention of inflicting all manner of punishment upon her seducer, until Jane reminded him that this was the 1990s and that Rosina was not Tess of the d'Urbervilles. When the two of them were alone, Jane had told Rosina exactly what she thought of her squandering her 15-year-old virginity upon Henry Dove, cautioned her in no uncertain terms about the dangers of promiscuity, and, to Rosina's relief, ceased treating her like a child.

'I don't even like sex,' Rosina had confessed in one of their heart to hearts when she was sprawled on Jane's bed. 'I can't see what all the fuss is about.'

'Give it time,' Jane had said. 'You will when you're older, when you are emotionally prepared, when you find the right man.'

And Rosina had. Ferdinand. Who seemed in no great hurry to have it off with her, unlike the precipitate Henry Dove, but enjoyed her company and her conversation and getting to know her as a person.

'They're taking an awfully long time.' Jane addressed Tristan, but her anxious voice broke into Rosina's thoughts. 'Do you think they've forgotten about us?'

While Tristan fidgeted nervously with the lock of red hair which flopped over his forehead, pushed his Armani glasses back up his nose, and tried to summon up courage to confront one of the harassed, white-coated doctors who were rushing around, Rosina stood up.

'I'll go and ask.'

Through the glass door Jane watched her approach a passing nurse. She could not hear what was said.

'He's still in resusc.' Rosina resumed her seat.

Tristan, his palm damp, squeezed Jane's hand reassuringly.

'Dead. . .' He stopped, appalled. He had meant to say Dad. 'Dad will be okay.'

He wished he believed it. He wished he was not shit scared. He wished he wasn't such a wanker. He wished he didn't have sex on the brain. He wished he was not awkward and clumsy. He wished he didn't blush at his fantasies or at the drop of a hat. He wished he had the courage to tell Miranda Harding that he was in love with her. He wished he was decisive like Rosina, could stand up to authority and didn't mind making a nuisance of himself. He wished he was not rotten at games. He wished he was not timid inside. He wished he did not feel left out. He wished that Freddie would not leave him, just when he had found him. He wished that he believed in immortality, rather than the brevity of existence. He wished that he had been able to cry at Lilli's funeral. He wished that the world would go on for ever, and that there were no black holes. He wished that he did not think, privately, that all was vanity, that we have but an hour to strut upon the stage, that the days of wine and roses vanish swiftly, and that we must die. He wished Freddie to make an effort. To fight back with all the forces at his disposal, all his larger-than-life strength, to respond to whatever it was the medical team was doing for him. He was only 16. He did not want to be abandoned. He wanted to keep his options open. He did not want to have to think about mortgages and life insurance. He did not even want to tie his own shoelaces. He did not want to grow up.

James, who had been down to the canteen, came into the visitors' room. He looked worried.

'I bumped into the staff nurse . . .'

He helped Jane to her feet and put his arms round her, drawing her to him.

'Freddie . . .?' Jane's voice was strung tight with anxiety.

'Freddie's fine. I've just seen him. He's pretty incoherent. He keeps banging on about this guy in Thermopylae.'

'"Who couldn't do anything properly."'

Not even take his own life.

'He's going to be all right,' James said.

'Where is he?' Jane, uncertain whether to laugh or cry, was halfway out of the room. 'Show me where he is.'

'Hang on a minute!'

'There's nothing wrong?' There was fear in Jane's voice as irrational thoughts of possible complications crossed her mind.

'Freddie's fine,' James reassured her. 'He's sleeping it off. The thing is . . .'

Jane stood by the door.

'He doesn't want to see you. He absolutely *refuses* to see you.'

'What are you talking about?'

James shrugged. 'I don't know, darling. I'm just the messenger. I haven't a clue what's going on.'

CHAPTER THIRTY-NINE

Freddie had been in the Chesterfield, a private psychiatric clinic and crisis intervention centre to which Bruce Cardwell – who had taken an extremely serious view of the fact that he had made an attempt on his own life – had referred him, for two weeks. He had not thought that he would stay in the rambling, run-down place, which comprised three large houses in a street off the Fulham Road, for two days.

He had been a difficult and uncooperative patient. He did not like his room, which was small and cramped, hated being kept waiting – for the routine blood tests, for his meals – found the food inedible, was hostile to the nurses (he never seemed to see the same one twice), impatient with the grossly inefficient domestic staff, had nothing in common with the other patients with whom he was expected to socialise, disliked the consultant, Martin Wells, who was looking after him, and wanted nothing whatever to do with his team of multi-disciplinary experts who offered everything from yoga and massage to relaxation classes and seminars, which he expected Freddie to attend.

There was nothing the matter with him, and he was unable to see why the fact that in a bad moment he had swallowed a few pills, washed down by a litre of whisky, made him a suitable case for treatment, a candidate for the funny farm.

He had already asked for his account which – thanks to Gordon Sitwell – would be taken care of by the insurance company, and was ready to walk out of the place, when

Dr Kay Chapman, who was standing in for Dr Wells, who had left for a psychiatric conference in Rio, had knocked on the door of his room.

'Have you got my bill?' Freddie was getting his overcoat out of the cupboard.

'That's not my department.'

Kay Chapman was small and had grey eyes. She had curly blonde hair and wore a mini-skirt.

'If it's more blood you're after, forget it. I'm discharging myself.'

'I'm Dr Chapman. Dr Wells has asked me to look after you, Mr Lomax.'

'I can look after myself, thanks.'

Dr Chapman looked at the notes she was carrying. 'You don't seem to have been making a very good job of it. Why don't you sit down, Freddie? I'd like to have a chat.'

'You carry on.' He pulled the chair out from the table for her. 'I prefer to stand.'

'I gather you're not happy at the Chesterfield.'

Freddie collected the newspapers from the bed, arranging them into a neat pile. He took his mobile phone from the locker and slipped it into his coat pocket.

'If you really want to know, I think it's a load of bullshit. I don't want to mix with a bunch of neurotics, I can have a massage at my squash club, and I have no intention of going to a group and playing stupid games.'

'Okay. That's what you don't want to do. What *do* you want to do?'

'Go home. Get on with my life.'

'Your *life*?'

The words hung on the air.

'Your wife has been enquiring about you. She's worried. I understand you don't wish to see her.'

'She's been fooling around with one of my friends.'

'How does that make you feel?'

'Terrific.'

'I'm sorry about your mother. You must be feeling sad.'

Freddie wished that he was. There had been murmurings at the funeral as condolences had been offered by the congregation: 'Such a brave lady.' 'Such a wonderful person.' He had tried to make the sentiments ring true, but much as he had loved Lilli – and he had loved her – he was consumed with guilt by the fact that the only thing he felt was relief. Not only was he absolved of financial liability for Lilli, a considerable drain on his empty pocket, but he was no longer required to live up to her expectations of him.

'I believe you've lost your job . . .'

'You know very well I have.'

'Dr Wells tells me that you were an extremely successful banker.'

Freddie was not going to blow his own trumpet, about being a damned good head of corporate finance, to Dr Chapman.

'When did things start to go wrong?'

Freddie put on his overcoat. In an effort to be civil – the poor girl was only doing her job – he had started to tell her about the inexorable change in his fortunes over the past few months, the £11,000 he had lost on Universal Concrete, the £10,000 he had thrown away at the casino, the fiasco of the Bowker & Page contract, his feelings of failure and worthlessness, when a woman in a navy-blue suit barged in with his bill.

'Not now, Jean.'

'Sorry, Dr Chapman.'

'That's typical of this place,' Freddie took the worry beads out of his pocket.

'It *is* very irritating. Mr Hartley, he's the hospital administrator . . . well, let's say there are some administrative problems.'

'You can say that again.' The worry beads were working overtime.

'Would you do something for me, Freddie?'

The grey eyes. She reminded him of Sidonie.

'I'd like you to give the Chesterfield a few days.' Dr Chapman referred to her notes. 'Dismissal. Not much luck with a new job. You seem to have been getting off at the wrong stations lately? Sometimes it's because you're on the wrong train. I think you need a break, and some medication to make you less agitated . . .'

Freddie slid the worry beads back into his pocket. 'I'm not the slightest bit agitated.'

'Until the end of the week, say. No visitors,' the grey eyes went to the bed, 'no newspapers, no phone calls. Then we can have a look at what appear to be your negative thought processes . . .'

Freddie had no idea what she was on about, but he had been feeling like a zombie, his head like a balloon, since he had taken the whisky and the pills. He was still extremely tired. Had it been Martin Wells he would have told him to stuff it. He could not get over Dr Chapman's resemblance to Sidonie. She was still talking.

'. . . Suppose we say Friday?'

'Then you'll let me go?'

'It isn't a prison.'

The RMO, who came from Sri Lanka, had written him up for medication. When it finally arrived, Freddie slept on and off for three days. On the fourth day, tired of waiting for his breakfast tray, which when it did arrive was as likely as not to belong to someone else, he went down to the dining-room where the bacon was cold and the toast hard. He sat next to an emaciated girl wearing black leggings. She was toying with half a grapefruit.

'Just arrived?'

Freddie had come down for his breakfast, not to talk.

'No.'

'Becky. That's my name. Anorexia.' She eyed Freddie's plate with disgust. 'What's your problem?'

'The bacon is cold. Is the food always cold?'

'I don't eat it. That's *my* problem. I only weigh 41 kilos. I was in an adolescent unit when I was 13. They locked me up. My thyroid and pituitary glands are down. I like it in this place. They don't fill you up with a lot of philosophical shit. Have you got a name?'

'Freddie.'

'Where d'you live?

'In Regent's Park.'

'Can't you afford a house? I live in Clapham. I'm a hairdresser. I'd like to go to college and get a diploma. You could do with your ends trimming. I've got two kids. My mum's looking after them. It turns my boyfriend off when I'm thin. What do you do?'

'Nothing.'

'Nothing!'

'I *was* a banker. I've been made redundant.'

'Gave you plenty of dosh, did they?'

'A hundred and thirty thousand . . .'

'A hundred and thirty grand!'

'I owe my bank manager more than that.'

'It's not exactly a Greek tragedy.'

'I didn't say it was.'

'You put me in mind of my father . . .'

Freddie looked again at the girl. She was young enough to be his daughter.

'. . . He was a big fella, like you. The perfect daddy.'

'I'm flattered.'

Becky put the spoon down on her uneaten grapefruit and got up from the table.

'No need to be, mate. He abused me until I was 15.'

Freddie had intended to go home, but he was too tired to

make the effort. He lay on his bed listening to *Der Freischütz* on the radio but heard no more than the ubiquitous overture before falling into a deep sleep. In the evening he was visited again by Dr Chapman.

'Can we talk?'

'If you like.'

'How are you feeling now?'

'Fine. I don't know what I'm doing here. I hate these places. I'm perfectly all right.'

'You did try to take your own life.'

'What makes you so sure?'

'Come on now, Freddie. You checked into a hotel, you didn't tell anyone where you were going, you took more than thirty 10 milligram Temazepam capsules, you drank an entire bottle of whisky. What did you imagine would be the outcome?'

'I didn't think about it.'

It was true. Standing by Lilli's graveside, surrounded by his family and friends, he had tried hard to endow the tableau with some meaning, to relate it to himself. The vicar *is* the vicar. A man of God, whoever 'God' was. Freddie knew that the man was an impostor, a minor actor from central casting, reading his lines, made up for the part. The extras, in their sombre clothes, facsimiles of James and Dos, Piers and Alex, Charles and Bingo, Peter and Georgina, with some of whom he had shared the most intimate moments of his life, had been carefully selected for their roles. The 'chrysalis son'. The 'adolescent daughter'. The 'faithless wife'. The 'grieving carer' (nice of Mrs Williams to come) had been suitably positioned, a little apart, at the back of the gathering. The trees and the sky had been painted on, the grave-diggers came straight out of *Hamlet*. The design department had had a ball with the gravestones. Lurching this way and that, some of them were quite old, the inscriptions illegible. The more recent ones, like double beds, left spaces for their partners.

The vicar in his surplice, Lilli in her box. So the undertakers said. It was probably weighted with stones although they all *thought* that it was Lilli. You could see by their faces, suitably downcast. But they were trained thespians, schooled for the part.

Freddie knew better. Lilli, her face alight, her hair bobbing, her shoulders swaying, was seated at the Broadwood playing Chopin's Polonaise, her hands pursuing each other deftly up and down the keyboard after the last of the pupils had gone, and the teacher, in a moment of release, was free to play what she wished, for the boy standing at the door waiting for help with his homework and—caught up in the moment—for herself. You did not put people in boxes. Did not commit them to the earth.

The mourners dispersed. He remembered grasping hands which had held his in the grip of emotion, theirs not his, as the knot around the graveside disintegrated. There remained a man, Charles, and a message, something about Singapore, then he too was gone. Freddie had said goodbye. To the box. He knew it was expected of him. The rest was silence. No semblance of reality. Least real of all was himself. At Sitwell Hunt he had been the vice chairman. He had had a place to go to, colleagues to connect with, work to confirm his competence and a salary to put a value on it. There was no longer any point in pretending that he was Freddie Lomax. Sidonie had been right. The comedy was over. It was time to end the charade.

'You told Dr Wells a great deal about your mother, Freddie.' Dr Wells had made copious notes. 'House in Maida Vale . . . Brought you up single-handed. Gave piano lessons. That must have been a big responsibility . . .?'

'It was. She worked extremely hard.'

Dr Chapman looked at him. 'For you, not her.'

She flipped over the lined pages covered with neat handwriting.

'I don't see anything about your father?'

'He died. Thirty-four years ago.'

'Would you like to tell me about him?'

'I was 6 years old. He was playing cricket with me in the garden.' Freddie took out his worry beads. 'There's nothing to tell.'

'He died suddenly then?'

Freddie nodded.

'How did that make you feel?'

'Upset, of course.'

'That's how you feel *now*,' Dr Chapman said. 'How did the 6-year-old Freddie feel?'

Freddie was 40 years old. It was a stupid question. The extended silence which succeeded it, and which he had no intention of breaking, was punctuated by the clicking of the beads. How was he supposed to know?

To his surprise, Dr Chapman closed her folder. Standing up, she said: 'I understand you talked to Becky at breakfast.'

'Becky?'

'Becky Bostock. Black leggings? She's been here for quite a while. You're the first person she's opened up to. She needs someone to listen to her.'

Becky Bostock. Making up his mind to leave the Chesterfield next morning, he had sat next to her at dinner. Just looking at the meat and vegetables on Freddie's plate had paralysed her with fear.

'My Dad used to force-feed me.' She put her fork down on the minute quantity of mashed potato she had taken. 'I've got chronic constipation . . .'

Freddie was looking with horror at her arm. She had pushed up the sleeve of her sweatshirt and a network of scars, like pink tramlines, traversed the skin.

'I self-injure,' Becky said. 'Glass. I used to do it at school with the compasses. Sometimes I pour boiling water over myself. I'm in a transitional relearning phase. I suppose you think I need a good kick up the bum. You got any kids?'

'A son, and a daughter of 15.'

'What d'you call her?'

'Rosina.'

'Rosina! Bet she's not like me. Bet she goes to a posh school and got a cupboard full of clothes. Bet she's a daddy's girl. I flipped when I was fifteen. Drinking. Clubbing. One-night stands. People like you make me sick, you know, Freddie. Bloody bankers. With their bloody chauffeurs, and their bloody briefcases. I see them in the salon. Sloane Street. If ever I met my father you know what I'd do to him?'

'What would you do?'

'I'd chop up his willie and stuff it in his mouth.'

She pushed her plate away and got up from the table.

The next morning at breakfast, she moved away when Freddie sat down next to her, refused to say a word.

'Don't take it personally.' The educated voice came from a man of about 30. He sat opposite Freddie and looked familiar. 'Becky's not exactly all sweetness and light. Bill...' He held out his hand. 'Alcohol dependency.'

Freddie remembered the face. His name was not Bill and he had seen him on TV reading the news.

'How long have you been in here?' Freddie said.

'Three weeks. Saved my life. I'm dry as a bone.'

'Full of heminevrin!' Becky was going past the table on the way to the door.

'Better than being full of vodka, my love. I got through two bottles a day and two wives.' He crossed his fingers. 'I'm doing it for Emma. She's my new partner. We're getting married when she gets her divorce. That's Sebastian.' He pointed to another table. 'Executive burn-out. Electronics business. Crashed his jet. The big guy in the T-shirt is Eddy. Some nerd threw himself in front of his HGV on the M1 two years ago. He hasn't been able to work since. The pretty one's Paul, good family, degree in Russian, diploma in business management, made redundant, unemployed, doing drugs – still smuggles them in – a direct result of the recession . . .'

'I know all about that.'

It was a revelation to Freddie to find that the Chesterfield, which he had imagined would be full of nutcases (not that it was full, he had noticed that half the beds were empty), was full of ordinary people like himself.

He had had a massage, and found himself telling the masseur, a trained counsellor, about Jane and Piers, the sight of whom at the corner table in the City Pipe he had been unable to get out of his mind. He had attended a cognitive thinking seminar with Bill, and although he had always associated it with weirdos in sandals and with brown rice, had been so relaxed by the voice of the yoga instructor – *telling* him what to do, so that there was for once no need to think – that he had fallen asleep on the floor. In the Jacuzzi he had beefed to Sefton, an American businessman who spoke the same language, about the gross mismanagement of the Chesterfield, and he had been to a problem solving group where, while others had freely explored their feelings and discussed issues, he had not opened his mouth. He had changed his mind about going home. There was nothing to go home for.

CHAPTER FORTY

'You're angry,' Kay Chapman said. 'Why are you angry?'

Freddie paced up and down his room twirling his worry beads. 'This place makes me angry. I'm angry about Bill.'

In the past two weeks he had struck up a friendship with Bill, who had been doing very well on his detox programme until a colleague had informed him that Emma – who had chickened out of telling him herself – had been persuaded to go back to her husband and had moved out of his flat. Bill had disappeared from the Chesterfield and had been found by Paddy, the staff nurse, in the pub opposite, roaring drunk.

'He should never have been allowed to leave,' Freddie said.

'He slipped out while Mike was on his tea-break.'

'That's not good enough. In a place like this, that desk should be manned at all times, the street door locked, and a log kept of everyone who comes in or goes out.'

'You care about Bill?'

'I care about running a department properly, Kay.'

'We don't seem to have made all that much progress in the Freddie Lomax department.' Dr Chapman consulted her notes. 'I understand you're down for the psychodrama group today?'

'I promised Kylie.'

Kylie was his New Zealand nurse.

'You still don't have much faith in our programme.'

'I don't *need* a programme, Kay. I don't *need* aerobics . . .'

'The exercises get you up in the morning, get you moti-
vated.'

'. . . I need a job.'

'So do three million other people in this country. They
don't all feel they're shits because nobody wants them,
because they miss out on a few deals; they don't all fall
apart because they're no longer the life and soul of the party.
They don't all try to kill themselves.'

'Maybe it's different when you're a bricklayer, a shop-
floor worker . . .'

'Maybe it's different when you're Freddie Lomax, when
everything has to be black or white, when you *have* to be
successful or you're nothing, when everything *has* to be
perfect. Maybe you're making negative assumptions, that
you can only be an adequate human being if other people
approve of you? If they show their approval by giving you a
job? Maybe we need to challenge your assumptions, to turn
them into hypotheses instead of facts. Maybe you should
start by putting a disk into your personal computer, Freddie.
Maybe it's time to scroll through "erstwhile vice chairman",
and "Universal Concrete", and "Bowker & Page", and open
up the file marked "loss".'

The psychodrama group, a humanistic action group for
patients at every stage of therapy, was held in a room in the
basement. Kylie had explained to Freddie that psychodrama
was an extension of the Living Theatre, pioneered by Jacob
Moreno of the Moreno Institute in the USA, in which
audience participation was encouraged. She thought that
Freddie, who still could not see that he had a problem, in
the sense that Bill had a problem, or Becky had a problem,
or Eddy had a problem, would benefit from taking part.
Freddie had agreed. To pass the time. Anything was better
than going home to his real dilemma and having to face Derek
Abbott, to cope with his inevitable bankruptcy, to confront
his unpaid bills.

A dozen chairs, most of them already occupied by patients – amongst them the news reader, the lorry driver, the hairdresser and the banker – homogeneous in their leisure wear, had been arranged in a circle in the otherwise bare room. Julian, the therapist, a bearded Scotsman wearing a polo-necked sweater, was removing his shoes, an exercise which revealed a hole in his sock. The rest of the group followed suit. Freddie kept his shoes on.

'This is the warm up,' Julian explained to Freddie, who sat next to him, before turning to the group. 'What I'd like you all to do is to wriggle your toes. When you feel yourselves nice and free, why don't you give each other a bit of relaxing massage.'

Freddie folded his arms across his chest while Becky rubbed at Eddy's T-shirt, her thin hands, at the end of fragile wrists, seeming to make little impression on the muscular back. He recognised Lavinia, who had come down from Oxford where she had been abusing heroin, and Pamela, a Cheam housewife whose mouth drooped permanently downwards and who was seriously depressed, and thought how damned stupid they all looked wriggling their outstretched toes and rubbing away at each other's backs. When they had finished wriggling and rubbing – they seemed to enjoy it – Julian placed a spare chair in the middle of the circle.

'I'm going to go round and ask each of you in turn', he said, 'who would you most like to talk to in your imagination. Who is it you would like to see sitting in that chair. Freddie?'

'Pass,' Freddie said. 'I don't talk to empty chairs.'

'No problem. Becky?'

'Three guesses! My father.'

'Lavinia?'

'My boyfriend.'

'Pamela?'

'My mother.'

'Eddy?'

'The cunt who threw himself in front of my lorry.'

'He's dead,' Becky said.

Julian dismissed the objection. 'That doesn't matter.'

At the end of the round he came back to Freddie. 'If you *were* to play the game, Freddie, who would you most like to see in the chair?'

Freddie was taken off guard. 'My father.'

'Okay.' He looked round the group. 'You'd like to see your boyfriend, Lavinia; Pamela would like to see her mother. Wouldn't it be great if we could find out more about some of these people? Let's nominate one of them to put in the chair.'

'I'd like to know more about Freddie's father,' Bill said.

'Has anyone an objection?' Julian looked round the group.

'Okay, Freddie, what I want you to do now is to sit in that chair and pretend to *be* your father. What was his name?'

'Hugh.'

Feeling like an idiot, wondering what he had let himself in for, Freddie got up reluctantly and took the chair in the centre of the room.

'You'd be more comfortable if you took off your shoes.'

Freddie unlaced his trainers and kicked them beneath the chair.

'Okay,' Julian said, 'I want you to adopt your father's posture. I want you to sit exactly the way he would sit.'

'I haven't seen my father since I was 6!'

'It doesn't matter. You're Hugh now. You've become Hugh. None of us here has had the pleasure of meeting you. Tell us about yourself, Hugh, introduce yourself. What clothes are you wearing, what are you thinking about, what's going on in your head?'

Freddie looked at Julian. He looked round the circle at the members of the group. He made himself smaller, straightened his back, pulled back his shoulders, and sat upright in the chair as if he had served in the army.

'My name is Hugh Lomax, Dr Hugh Lomax. I am 43 years old . . .'

It was stifling in the basement (Freddie had complained to the office about the old-fashioned radiators which blasted away and which you could not control), like the heat of a hot summer's day. He pushed up the sleeves of his sweater, rolled them up like the sleeves of the white cotton shirt – which was tucked into his grey flannel trousers – over the dark hairs on his arms.

'What year is it, Hugh?' The voice was Julian's.

'The year is 1958.'

'Could you describe what you look like?'

'I am five foot nine tall, I am clean-shaven, I have brown hair brushed back with Brylcreem – I keep the jar in the bathroom.'

In the medicine cupboard above the washbasin, next to the tin of Germolene and the Andrew's Liver Salts.

'Where are you just *now*, Hugh?'

Freddie was taken by surprise. 'I'm dead.'

'Okay, but where *are* you?'

'I'm dead. I'm not anywhere.'

'Don't you exist as a spirit?'

'No.'

'If you were to exist as a spirit, Hugh, where would you be?'

Freddie thought about it.

'Out there . . .' He waved his hand vaguely towards the fluorescent lights in the ceiling. 'I suppose.'

'Would you be at peace?'

'No.'

'What would you be doing?'

'Watching.'

'Who would you be watching?'

'Freddie.'

'But you left Freddie?'

'Yes.'

'Did you want to leave Freddie?'

'No.'

'Why did you leave him?'

'To punish him. He wanted me run over by a bus, he wanted to push me into the canal, he wanted me to drown.'

'Evil thoughts are not evil deeds, Hugh. If you were to hear about Freddie's success as a banker, about his family, about the way he has cared for his mother, about what he has achieved, what would you think of him?'

'I . . . suppose I'd be proud.'

'Would you like to meet Freddie?'

'I'd like that more than anything in the world.'

'If you were able to meet him, what would you say to him?'

'Why . . .?' There was a break in Freddie's voice. 'Why did you let me down?'

'But Freddie didn't let you down, Hugh.'

'He got the sack.'

'Due to the economic climate.'

'He lost his job. He always loses things. He shoots himself in the foot. He broke the china cat.'

'Small boys lose things, they break things. Did you say goodbye to Freddie?'

'There was no time.'

'Would you like to say goodbye to him?'

Freddie nodded.

'Okay, Hugh, you can say goodbye to Freddie. What would you tell him?'

Freddie opened his mouth. His throat had seized up from the heat, the dry air in the room. He was unable to answer.

Julian threw the question open. 'What about the rest of you? Has anyone else any ideas?'

Becky raised her hand.

'Hugh's run into difficulties, Becky,' Julian said. 'Would you like to come and double for him?'

Becky got up from her chair and stood behind Freddie. She put a hand on his shoulder.

'If you were to say goodbye to Freddie, Hugh,' Julian looked at Becky and repeated the question, 'what would you tell him?'

The group waited expectantly.

'I love you, Freddie,' Becky said.

'For Christ's sake . . .!' Freddie put his head in his hands.

'Okay, I want *you* to sit in the chair now, Becky,' Julian said. 'You play Hugh, and Freddie can come back here and play himself.'

Taking out his handkerchief, Freddie blew his nose and resumed his seat.

'Talk to your father, Freddie.'

Freddie put away his handkerchief. 'Hi, Dad.'

'Hallo, Freddie,' Becky said. 'Nice to see you again. How are you feeling?'

'Pissed off.'

'Why's that?'

'Why do you think? I've lost my job. I can't get a job. Let's face it, there are no prospects of getting a job. A proper job. You only get one bite at the cherry. One chance. I've blown mine. There are no deals around. I've lost my touch . . . My wife has turned her back on me. My children don't need me. My mother. You must know what happened to Lilli . . .'

'Is there anything you want to say to *me*?'

'You're a bastard,' Freddie's voice rose. 'A rotten bastard! Why did you leave me, Dad? Why did you go away?'

'I'm here, Freddie, I'm still around. I'd like to see you again. It's been a long time. I haven't seen you since my funeral . . .'

'I didn't *come* to your funeral! Mummy wouldn't let me come to your funeral.'

'Oh!' Becky said. 'You know where I'm buried . . .?'

Freddie shook his head.

'If I tell you where I'm buried, will you come and see me? Will you visit my grave?'

'I'd really like that.'

'Will you bring me something?'

'What shall I bring?'

'What would you like to bring?'

'Flowers . . .?'

'Not flowers. Something special. Something dear to you. Something you love very much, Freddie. Something you'd like to show me.'

'Jane.'

'Jane?'

'My wife, Dad. Dad?'

'Yes, Freddie?'

'I wish I *could* see you again.'

'What would you do if you saw me, Freddie?'

Freddie was back in the summer garden. He stood rooted to the spot unable to move his feet in their Startrite sandals as his father, still clutching the cricket ball, lay motionless on the lawn.

'What I'd like to do, what I'd really like to do . . .'

'Yes?'

'I'd like to give you a big hug, Dad.'

Watched by the group, Freddie got up from his chair, crossed the silence that filled the room, and the brown lino, and, kneeling at Becky's feet, buried his head in her lap. She put her skinny arms round his shoulders and held him close. From her strangled sobs, Freddie knew that Becky was weeping. Through her black leggings Becky could feel Freddie's warm tears.

'What was there in that for you, Becky?' Julian asked later, when they were into the 'sharing' part of the session. 'Tell us what it felt like, being Freddie's dad?'

'Amazing! I only wish *I* could have given my dad a hug like that.'

'Why couldn't you?' Eddy said.

'I wouldn't dare. He would have started touching me up, the dirty bugger.'

'You got pretty close to Freddie.'

'That was okay. I was safe with Freddie. I was his father. I wasn't a woman . . . I was a man.'

CHAPTER FORTY-ONE

Freddie was flexing his biceps and expanding his pectorals in front of the open window. A late developer, he had been nicknamed 'sparrow chest' at school and had been exercising – press-ups and weights – since the age of 14. He grinned when Kay came into the room.

'You've got a great smile, Freddie, I didn't know you could smile.'

'Got to get back in condition. Believe it or not I was a rowing blue. My muscles have gone to pot.'

'What did you think of the psychodrama?'

'Load of bullshit. I think Becky got something out of it. Poor kid, she wants desperately to be hugged.'

'I understand you've been hugging her. And introducing her to music. Art heals. It helps us to get in touch with ourselves. You're doing a great job. Kylie tells me that you're discharging yourself. Do you think that's wise?'

'All this rest and relaxation has made me feel better. I must admit you were right. I was in pretty poor shape when I came in here. I didn't realise. Now it's time I went home.'

'Back to the Black Label?'

Freddie shook his head. 'I told you, I feel good. A couple of jogs round the park and I'll be back on form.'

'What about your therapy?'

'With all due respect, Kay, I don't need therapy. I've been talking to Sefton.'

He had taken to meeting the American in the Jacuzzi

before dinner. Sefton had never divulged to Freddie what his problem was, and Freddie had not asked. Some of the patients at the Chesterfield preferred to keep their troubles to themselves. All that Freddie had managed to get out of Sefton was that he was in business in Colorado, and was as irritated as Freddie at the way the Chesterfield was run. Freddie looked forward to the daily discussions in which they put not only the world, but the hospital, to rights.

'It's a question of gross mismanagement, administrative bungling, and a criminal lack of organisation,' Freddie had said a couple of nights ago as, with arms stretched along the sides of the tub, they faced each other through the steam. 'That Hartley couldn't organise a piss-up in a brewery.'

'Hartley's not a businessman. He came to the Chesterfield from alternative medicine. He had some kind of practice in Bournemouth.'

'It wouldn't surprise me one bit if he was lining his own pockets, taking a bit off the top.'

'Someone is knocking off the food, that's for sure,' Sefton said. 'One of the dining-room staff told me.'

'In that case they must be gluttons for punishment! The food's inedible. The chef needs to be shot. The whole place is over-manned, the staff turnover is phenomenal, and morale is non-existent. What I would do . . .' Freddie dunked his shoulders beneath the water '. . . is get rid of Hartley, put in a hands-on administrator who knows how to liaise with the nursing administration and the domestic administration, tighten up the the whole operation – man the front entrance, make sure telephone messages were passed on, and patients were not kept waiting – have a blitz on internal communication and time-keeping, jack up the therapeutic input – half the bloody beds are empty – refurbish the place from top to bottom, fill the common parts with some decent furniture and contract flower arrangements, put some pleasant pictures on the walls, and market the place properly.'

'You think you could make a better job of it?'

'I think a retarded child could make a better job of it.'

'How would you like to try?'

'Try what?'

'Taking over the administration of the Chesterfield?'

'What are you talking about?'

'I'll come clean, Freddie. My company, Colorado Clinics Inc., owns the Chesterfield. It's been dying a slow death. I was sent over to check it out.'

'I'm a *banker* . . .!' Freddie said.

Sefton nodded. 'I've been checking you out.'

Freddie smiled, a man after his own heart.

'I'm perfectly aware it's not your field, but I thought that while you were looking for something more suitable, you might just consider getting the Chesterfield on its feet.'

'I'd need to think about it,' Freddie said. But the microchips were back in the motherboard, and in the split second that had elapsed since Sefton's question and his own reply, he had made up his mind.

The Chesterfield was not a corporate finance department, neither was it a merchant bank. But in the two weeks that he had been a patient, Freddie had remarked – much to his surprise – that the clinic, far from being a haven for neurotics, was both doing valuable work and fulfilling a definite need. The salary commensurate with being a hospital administrator would enable him to repay Tom Glidewell and be sufficient to persuade the Porchester Bank to look more favourably upon the amount of his overdraft. Tristan, he thought, wryly, would be more than pleased.

Yesterday morning he had been in his room listening to the final moments of *Idomeneo* – Idomeneo calling to the Gods of love and marriage to instil their spirit of peace – when Sefton, dressed in his street clothes, came in search of him. Putting his Burberry and his briefcase on the bed, as Freddie switched off the radio, the American outlined his proposal.

'I don't mean to pressurise you, Freddie, but I had a call last night. I'm booked on the Pan Am flight. Am I to tell CCI that I've found an administrator who's willing to turn the Chesterfield around?'

Hospital Administrator. It was not what he was used to. He wondered what Lilli would say, then realised that it no longer mattered, that he no longer had to live up to her expectations of him, he was no longer accountable to her for his actions. Lilli was dead.

'It's certainly a challenge.'

'My impression is that you like challenges, Lomax.'

'When you're going under for the third time, and a lifebelt is chucked into the water,' Freddie said, 'what choice do you have? When do I start?'

As Freddie finished telling Dr Chapman about the outcome of his exchanges with Sefton in the Jacuzzi, there was a knock on the door. Not waiting for an answer, the cleaner came in with her mop.

'Not now, Maria,' Dr Chapman sighed.

'That kind of interruption will be a thing of the past,' Freddie said as the door closed behind the girl. 'You're not getting rid of me, Kay. From next month on you'll be seeing me around.'

He had had no idea how hard it would be to leave the Chesterfield. He could not believe how close he had grown, in two short weeks, to a bunch of strangers who had become his friends. It was like saying goodbye to his family. He had had a long session with Eddy in the dining-room over lunch, and had exchanged cards with Bill with whom he had developed a close rapport and who needed all the support he could get. But it was leaving Becky which had really creased him up. Becky, who had been swimming with Freddie (the first exercise she had taken in years), showed a new interest in life, and had actually started to eat again, had been distraught.

'Don't leave me, Freddie. You're the best thing that's ever happened to me.'

'I'm not leaving you, Becky. I'm going to take you to the opera, remember? We're going to keep in touch.'

They were sitting on the sofa in the Day Room.

'I know you'll think this is stupid, Freddie, but I want to ask you a favour. Will you do something for me?'

Freddie wondered what was coming. He wondered why he felt choked at leaving this undernourished, untidy waif.

'I'd like to have a picture of you, Freddie. Will you send me a photo of yourself?'

It was Becky who came to the door with him. Becky who saw him off. He had never clung to Rosina as he had clung, choked with unfamiliar emotions, on the steps of the clinic, to Becky. She was his loving child.

Whistling down the King's Road, inhaling the bouquet of the diesel fumes as if they were vintage wine, catching sight of his reflection in a window, Freddie returned his own smile.

His main reason for discharging himself from the Chesterfield was that he wanted to see Jane. He wanted to apologise, to make it up to her for the way in which he had treated her over the past few months. Passing a florist's, he retraced his steps. Yellow roses. Jane's passion. 'La Vie en Rose.' Sorting the long stems into an arrangement, the Cellophane stapled and garlanded with ribbons, which she scraped with her scissors until they trailed seductively off the table in long green tendrils, the girl in the checked overall wondered what Freddie was smiling about as he tendered the plastic he had been so near to losing.

In Chester Terrace, George, the postman, was delivering the midday mail.

'Good holiday, Mr Lomax?'

Freddie looked at his bag and his flowers 'Yes, thanks.'

'Been somewhere warm?'

Freddie thought of the radiators blasting away at the Chesterfield. 'Very warm.'

'We can do with a bit of sunshine. Cheers then.'

'Cheers then, George.'

Freddie, his heart thumping, put his key in the door.

'Jane?'

The house was silent. There was a wilting plant on the table amongst the piled-up mail in the hall.

'Jane!'

Somewhere he thought he heard a baby cry.

'Jane? Darling?'

Lavender appeared at the top of the stairs. In her arms was a bundle wrapped in a shawl.

'It's me. Lavender.'

'Where's Jane?'

'Not here.'

'Where is she?'

'I don't know.'

'What time will she be back?'

Freddie dumped the flowers on the kitchen table. There was a baby's bottle in the sink.

Lavender did not answer. She followed him into the kitchen.

'She's gone away.'

'Who has?'

'Jane.'

'What are you talking about?'

'There's only me and Prosperchine.'

'Prosperchine?'

Lavender advanced the bundle.

'I've left Tony. They've taken the other two into care. I'm stopping with Rosina. Do you like it? I read it in a magazine.'

Freddie sat down. He felt all the new strength in his muscles leech from his legs.

'Do you know where she's gone?'

Lavender shook her head and pulled back the baby's shawl. 'Think she takes after me?'

'Lavender, I need to know where my wife is.'

'Don't you like babies?'

'I do like babies. She's very pretty. Did she take any luggage?'

'Couple of cases.'

'Where's Rosina?'

'At school. Want a cup of tea?'

Freddie looked into the uninhabited drawing-room and the silent bedroom. The house was neglected, as if it had been abandoned and was up for sale. Calling to Lavender that he was going out again, he ran through the mews into Albany Street, hailed a passing taxi and gave the address of the National Westminster Bank.

Piers Warburton was taken by surprise.

'Where's Jane?' Freddie demanded, marching into his office.

'Jane? How the hell do I know?'

'Come off it, Piers. She's not at home. I saw you together in the City Pipe.'

'That was weeks ago . . .'

'You don't deny it.'

'Why should I deny it?'

'You were kissing her.'

'I was?'

'You know very well you were.'

'I might have done. Jane was upset.'

'About what?'

'About you.'

'I was the one who was upset. I thought . . . You don't know where she is then?'

'Haven't a clue.'

'I'm sorry, Piers. I think I'm going a bit mad.'

'Drink?' Piers reached for the sherry decanter.

'I won't, if you don't mind. Sorry to butt in like this. I've got to find Jane.'

Pacing up and down as he waited outside Queen's College for Rosina, Freddie worked his worry beads overtime.

His homecoming, which he had anticipated would be greeted with the blast of trumpets and the crash of cymbals, had fallen decidedly flat. Finding his way amongst the numbers in Jane's idiosyncratic address book – in which 'Bingo's' was under W (for warehouse) and Hurst under C (committee) – he had telephoned Bingo, who had no idea of Jane's whereabouts, and had drawn the same blank both from Dos and from Caroline. He had the impression that the women were closing ranks, that they were ganging up on him.

Rosina, amazed to see him, left the posse of girls in whose midst she had come out of school, and flung herself into Freddie's arms.

'Daddy!'

Holding her close, all 140 pounds of her, he thought of the skeletal frame of Becky Bostock, and how much he loved his daughter and how very little he really knew her.

They walked, Rosina clinging tightly to his arm, up Harley Street.

'I'm so pleased to see you,' Rosina said.

Freddie hoped he could make the words sound casual, as if he were not torn apart with grief. 'Where's Mummy?'

'Oh. You've been home then?'

Freddie nodded. 'Where's she gone?'

Rosina let go of his arm. 'You weren't very kind to Mummy . . .'

'I don't need a lecture, Rosina.'

'She's fed up with you.'

Coming to a halt on the pavement, Freddie felt himself grow cold.

'Has Mummy . . .? Is she coming back?'

Rosina did not answer.

'Rosina, where is she? Please! I've got to know.'

'I promised I wouldn't tell.'

'Don't be ridiculous.'

Facing him, Rosina looked up at her father's anguished face. He had suffered enough.

'Mummy's in France,' she said. 'With Grandmaman.'

CHAPTER FORTY-TWO

'Welcome to Air France flight 3533 to Nice. Our flying time will be one hour and forty minutes and we will be cruising at an altitude of 33,000 feet . . .'

Freddie sat in economy class, his legs wedged awkwardly against the seat in front of him, sipping the mineral water which had replaced the Black Label, and facing but not sampling his plastic tray of food.

When Rosina had told him that Jane was in France, he had wanted to get on a plane immediately, but Rosina was late out of school and by the time she had told him of Jane's whereabouts he had missed the last flights both to Nice and Marseilles. He had wanted to talk to Rosina, to pump her about what had happened, to find out if Jane had said anything, and exactly what she had said, before she left. But he no longer had his daughter's attention. Halfway up Harley Street she had caught sight of Ferdinand. Walking, with Rosina on his arm, towards the black-clad young man with his flowing hair, his viola case, Freddie had the bizarre impression that he was leading her not across Weymouth Street, but up the aisle, and delivering her into the arms of her bridegroom. Standing a little apart as the two of them embraced, he felt momentarily marginalised as he had been marginalised by Gordon Sitwell, as if Rosina no longer needed him and his task, *qua* father, was over.

Rosina and Ferdinand were off to a concert at the Barbican. Having no desire to stay in Chester Terrace with

Lavender and her crying baby, Freddie had taken a taxi to Lilli's flat before spending the evening with James. The porter at the Water Gardens had greeted him respectfully, offered his condolences, and in the same breath, the glint of a commission in his eye, enquired – because a gentleman from Saudi Arabia, whose brother lived in the block, had been putting out feelers – when Mrs Lomax's apartment would be free. Notions of guilt – that he had deliberately annihilated Lilli in order to pay off his debts – had overwhelmed him. Taking a deliberate moment, he forced himself to take an alternative view before jumping to irrational conclusions. Challenging his thoughts for accuracy, as he had learned to do, he modified his beliefs. Of course Lilli's monthly rent, not to mention the money he would be saving from her carers, would be extremely useful in pacifying Derek Abbott, but the fact that he would benefit directly from it had nothing whatsoever to do with the reality of her death.

The unsolicited mail had piled up on Lilli's mat, making it difficult to open the front door. In the minuscule kitchen an opened packet of digestive biscuits lay reminiscently on the sink. Walking slowly round the flat, laying the ghosts, he thought of Lilli in her heyday, on the concert platform in her satin dress, and wondered if amongst the hopes and aspirations of her life's overture the thwarted seeds of the finale had already been sown. Her musical career had been truncated, and her golden boy had failed . . . Hang on. Not *her*. Himself. There *had* been successes, since he had picked the daisies for her daisy chain, since he had counted the windows in Buckingham Palace. School. The scholarship to Cambridge. His subsequent career. Not even Gordon Sitwell could rob him of that.

Returning to the musty sitting-room, the muted roar of nearby traffic penetrating the hermetically sealed windows, he braced his shoulders and assumed the self-respect which, in addition to life itself, he had come close to losing. There were things which must be done and only he to do them.

He picked up the photograph of Hugh Lomax taken shortly before his death and struggled to make some sense of the fact that the two people responsible for his existence were no longer extant. He tried to think of his parents as astral bodies – composed of higher matter, with some sort of senses (Lilli's in full working order) or organs, finally reunited with each other – and of the place to which they had repaired as spatial, with properties analogous to the shape size and location of the universe they had departed. But where was this other world? Was it somewhere high above the Edgware Road in the night sky which he could see through Lilli's curtains, or buried deep beneath the underground car park in the nether reaches of the earth? Could it be reached, by rocket, or by digging a tunnel? Did he really concede that physical space was the only space, or was there, perhaps, a New Jerusalem somewhere on the other side?

In the presence of his mother's ghost, Freddie was unwilling to believe that there was no purpose to life, and that it made no sense to enquire about the point of it. Replacing the photograph, in its silver frame, on the dust-bloomed sideboard, he wondered if the real reason for existence was not to provide memories which could be drawn upon, from which an image world could be constructed after we were dead.

Taking out his jotter and pencil he made a note of tasks to be carried out and, feet astride on the faded and familiar Persian carpet which had been transported from the house in Maida Vale, was aware as he did so of a sudden sense of power and of freedom, as if a great weight had been lifted from his shoulders.

James had taken Freddie to dinner at the Ivy in celebration of his recovery. When Freddie had explained to him, somewhat diffidently, about the job he had been offered at

the Chesterfield and about the work of the clinic, especially
in the field of stress management, James had become quite
excited.

'It's not exactly head of corporate finance,' Freddie said
over his fishcakes.

'Fuck corporate finance, it sounds like a brilliant idea.'

'What does?'

'The Chesterfield.'

'Hospital Administrator! Come off it, James. I can't see
what's so brilliant about it.'

'You've worked long enough in the City, Freddie, you've
seen enough people hit the wall. It's a bloody marathon out
there and not everyone can cope with the pressures. How
many times have you seen an executive lose his cool, find
himself unable to think clearly because things are coming
at him from all sides, fail to prioritise his work load, become
prone to a suspicious number of accidents, turn in poor job
performance, fall by the wayside, find himself incapable of
staying the course? It's always been tough at the top. Now
it's tougher. Those who *have* the jobs have to fight to hold
on to them, they have to run that little bit faster in order to
stay where they are. Centres like the Chesterfield will become
a growth field . . .'

'I'm only an administrator!'

'Freddie, what's happened to your entrepreneurial spirit,
the ability to see over the parapet which enabled you to defend
Corinthian Holdings, which scared the shit out of Gordon
Sitwell?'

'Entrepreneurs need money.' Freddie put down his knife
and fork. 'All *I* have is negative equity.'

'We'll go into partnership. You learn the ropes, and
once you've got the hang of it I'll *buy* the Chesterfield.
We'll open up a chain of hospitals. We don't have to
stop at London, we'll set them up the length and breadth
of England, expand into Europe . . . Who wants to be a

banker!' He picked up the menu. '"Ivy" Clinics. How does it grab you?'

'It's not exactly what I'm used to.'

James raised his glass. '"There is a tide in the affairs of men . . ." Freddie what's the matter?'

'I'm sorry I can't be more enthusiastic, I'm worried about Jane.'

At the mention of Jane, James had clammed up. Like Dos and Bingo and Caroline Hurst, he had refused to be drawn.

It was not until after the coffee that he said: 'You pushed Jane to the edge, you know, Freddie,' before changing the subject and deciding that it was time they got the bill.

'*Terminé*?'

The stewardess, in her Air France uniform, addressed him. Meeting her eyes which lingered a fraction of a second too long on his, before she removed his tray of untouched food, confirmed the return of Freddie Lomax to the land of the living.

What a fool he had been. To think that Jane, his wilful Jane, whom he had treated so cursorily, would be sitting at her sewing machine, like Penelope at her loom, patiently waiting for him.

He had pushed her to the edge. So James had said. He hardly remembered. Only that he had somehow displaced his own fears and anxieties onto her, and now on his return – not from his Odyssey but from some private hell – he had to win her back.

As he packed his bag in the echoing bedroom to *The Barber of Seville*, to which he had first wooed Jane, he had realised just how much Jane meant to him, how much she had always meant to him, and how paradoxical it was, after so many years, to have not only rediscovered your children but to be falling in love with your wife. He had been appalled at the piles of neglected paperwork and unopened letters which confronted him accusingly in his dressing-room as he searched for his passport. He could hardly believe that, once obsessionally tidy and expecting similar standards from others, he was responsible for the mayhem.

Finding a spare photograph of himself amongst the debris, he wrote on the back 'Life is fantastic!' before putting it into an envelope and addressing it to Becky Bostock. He would post it at the airport.

Lavender's baby was on the kitchen table when he left. Glancing into the Moses basket, to find the kitten eyes blinking speculatively at him, he had a sudden desire – before it was too late for Jane – to have another child.

First things first. He had to find Jane, to persuade her to come home. His plan was to hire a car at Nice and drive west, as he had done so many times in the past, along the motorway until the concrete landscape with its pall of diesel, gave gradual way to umbrella pines and the sweet smells of Provence. Leaving the race-track at Le Muy, he would cut a winding swathe through the groves of grey-green olives. Thirty minutes later, inhaling the smoke of woodfires through the open window, he would arrive at the double row of plane trees, flanked by the ordered vineyards, which lined the entrance to Grandmaman's somnolent village.

The changing tone of the engine signified that the Airbus had started its descent. Abandoning *Newsweek*, with its gloomy predictions of increased unemployment, Freddie was surprised to discover that picturing Jane in Grandmaman's kitchen, in the *appartement* above the *Boulangerie*, his heart was beating at an increased rate. He guessed that the two women would be cooking – a goose stuffed with prunes soaked in Armagnac, a *gibelotte* – and, jumping the gun, wondered if Jane would consider coming into business with him and taking over the kitchens of the Chesterfield.

He had been thinking about James's idea for a chain of hospitals, and mentally considering the pros and cons. The market for treating stress-related illness, the symptoms of which – absenteeism, inefficiency, bad relationships at work, poor performance – undoubtedly cost employers considerable sums of money, was by and large untapped. If a manufacturing company with say, 2,000 employees, had ten days of absence per employee through health problems per year, the total number of days for sick leave would be 20,000. If the average daily wage per employee were £43, the total annual cost to the company would be a staggering £860,000. At a rough guess, at least 30 per cent of that cost was likely to be from sickness and absenteeism due to mental or emotional disturbance. If it was possible to reduce the sum by offering the necessary advice and treatment, paid for by the insurance companies, for those employees with problems, it would give business and industrial employers the chance to recognise the warning signs, such as changes in behaviour and/or performance, and prevent the situation developing into something more serious. The time and concern which would be invested, would be repaid many times over both in financial benefits to the company, and in the general wellbeing of the employees.

Working out the benefits, both of in-patient, and out-patient care, Freddie felt a surge of the excitement he had formerly associated with the challenge of acquisitions and the fierce battle for takeover deals.

In cutting his new teeth as hospital administrator at the Chesterfield before throwing in his lot with James, he would, in addition to providing services for business and industry, be helping people such as Bill and Becky – who had, through no fault of their own, fallen by the wayside – to dust themselves down and resume their useful lives. Perhaps Gordon Sitwell had done him a favour. Perhaps he was well out of corporate finance where, behind the Chinese wall, just as in the hostile waters of the Great Barrier Reef, it was a question of hunt or be hunted, kill or be killed.

He had been so busy thinking about the future, assessing the feasibility of James's proposal, contemplating restoring some balance to his life (not that he was going to be less committed, he would simply organise things differently) that he was unaware that in the last few moments they had swooped low over the Mediterranean and were already taxiing along the runway at Nice. Stowing the *Newsweek* in his briefcase, and ignoring the statutory injunction to wait until the aircraft had come to a complete halt, he stood up, tucked his shirt firmly into the waistband of his trousers, and retrieved his jacket and his bag from the overhead locker.

As he shuffled his way impatiently through the club class section, he recognised the camel-coated back of his opposite number from a City bank currently under investigation from the DTI, and reckoned, in a flash of clarity, that it was better to be an economy class hospital administrator than have a club class seat and down-market morals. Running down the steps he made the waiting bus, managing to squeeze his large frame inside the doors as they sighed pneumatically shut. The journey was only one of a few hundred yards. Nearer to Jane. He could hardly wait. In the terminal building, his passport, a small red one – he was a new European – was waved through dismissively. He had no baggage to reclaim. Walking purposefully through the archway of scrawled placards held aloft by expectant hands, he made straight for the Hertz desk.

'Freddie! Freddie!'

The passengers in front of him turned their heads to see who was being addressed, as a slim red-headed figure ran uninhibitedly up the luggage ramp waving a flowing white scarf.

'Freddie! Freddie!'

Allowing himself to be overtaken, Freddie was momentarily overcome with emotions so powerful that he was unable to move. Then, arms outstretched, Rodolfo returning to Mimi, Bacchus finding Ariadne, Nemorino united with Adina, certain that loving, and being loved, were the only things that mattered, he walked slowly towards Jane.